PAUL JONES;

BY

THE AUTHOR OF "ROBIN HOOD" AND "WAT TYLER."

VOL. II.

I have a tale to tell—'tis of the sea,
Filled with wild wonders, blood, and mystery.

CHAPTER I.

"Fierce, bounding forward, sprung the ship,
Like a greyhound starting from the slip
To seize his flying prey."

LORD OF THE ISLES.

"Onward it came; and lo! a second follow'd—
Now seen—now hid—where ocean's vale was hollow'd;
And near, and nearer

* * * * *

Away! away!
They clear the breakers, dart along the bay,
And towards a group of islets, such as bear
The sea bird's nest and seal's surf-hollowed lair,
They skim the blue tops of the billows; fast
They flew, and fast their fierce pursuers chased.
They gain upon them, now they lose again,
Again make way, and menace o'er the main.

* * * * *

And now the refuge and the foe are nigh—
Yet, yet a moment! Fly, thou light ark, fly!"

THE ISLAND.

When the interview between John Andrew and his mother had taken place, and when many not-to-be-deferred little love passages had been performed by the sailor and his mistress, they turned their attention to the best mode of communicating with Eustace Prior, endeavouring to devise the speediest, as well as the most effectual means; a matter rather fraught with difficulty. In the first place, Prior's address was unknown to them; secondly, if it had been, Andrew had forgotten whether he had ever learned to write; and Martha confessed that she had seen Miss Florence do it, but had never tried her hand at it. They were loath to apply to Squire Chough or his lady, because Martha knew that the name of Prior was forbidden even to be mentioned in their presence. In the height of their quandary a friend unexpectedly appeared, whose assistance was most desirable and readily proffered, and thus it was that it was obtained. Martha still continued her servitude at the Hall, and managed to find an "unaccountable" number of excuses for visiting that portion of the village where resided her John. During one of these transits she was accosted by a tall, well-looking, bluff man, who, after passing several flattering encomiums upon her features, which she thought very much "like his imperdence," he asked her if she was not the waiting woman of Miss Florence Ranklyn, and she tossed her head half angrily as she asked if "he wouldn't like to know?" He replied that he should most particularly; and added that it would be to her benefit if she told him. She dropped a little of her haughtiness, and requested him to keep his hands to himself as he patted her playfully upon the shoulders; while requesting an answer to his previous inquiry, she gave him the information he required, by stating that she had been Miss Florence's maid, but that since Miss Florence had been smuggled away, she had shared the duties of the housemaid; and then followed a long history of her young lady's extraordinary and inexplicable absence, with all the surmises, suspicions, speculations, and reflections thereon—the means employed to reach her in the shape of rewards, of descriptions of her person, age, manners, and dress, and parties of young men who had scoured the country through without avail—all was without success, every effort had failed, and Martha concluded by a strong desire to know if her young mistress had not been carried off by a ghost, who else it was, that was all."

"Why, Jasper Chough," said the stranger, with a smile.

"That's what my John says, and sticks to," exclaimed Martha, earnestly.

"And who is your John, my pretty lass?" demanded he.

To have seen the colour which rushed up into her face and spread over it and her neck, would have gladdened the eyes of a lover of roses. After much embarrassment, she confessed to her John being a sort of a friend whom she had known a long while, and whom she rather liked; that led to a description of Andrew's interview with Jasper; what followed it, and the determination which they had both come to that Florence's own true lover ought to know all that had transpired, and would, but that they were at a loss how to convey their intended communication. The answer which she received gave her considerable delight.

"My godfathers and godmothers," said her interrogater, "gave me the name of Lucky, with the hope that it would name my future fate. My father gave me the name of George because he couldn't help it—it was his surname; had been his father's, grandfather's, and great grandfather's before him, and so you see I was called and am called Lucky George, and lucky I have been. My father was always poorer than I have ever been. One of my slices of luck was to get into the service of Mr. Eustace Prior's family; I have been near him since he was a child, until within these three or four years, and then I had another slice of luck. I got, through the interest of my master, the father of young Eustace, a place under Government in the Customs—what is called an exciseman, lassy, but of a better description than the common run. My duty is to discover the nest of smugglers, so that the swindling knaves, with their ill-gotten stores, may be brought to justice. Some information I received brought me into this neighbourhood after the same Jasper Chough of whom we have been speaking. He has cheated the king—"

"Lor!" exclaimed Martha, with extended mouth and eyes.

"Aye, lassy," rejoined Lucky George, "and a slice of luck brought me up with my gentleman just as he was about to play some rascally tricks with your young mistress, but I spoilt his sport for him. I trussed him as you would a fowl, and led Miss Florence back to the Hall—"

"Yes," exclaimed Martha, with breathless interest.

"Now you must know, my lass," continued Lucky, "that I have a knack of what my master use to call, drawing conclusions; which means putting this and that together, when any strange affair comes before you; and many's the time, since I have been in my present service, has it been useful to me. Well, I heard that ill-conditioned scoundrel, Jasper, call the young lady Florence several times. Florence is an uncommon name, lassy; I know that my young master that had been was in love with a young lady named Florence, that she was hidden away from him somewhere in the country, and as the young maiden I rescued was evidently of good birth, it struck me that she might be the verry identical sweetheart young Mr. Prior had lost sight of. I hinted a little, by way of speculation, to her, as we stood at the door of the Hall, and the start she gave convinced me I had suspected correctly. I therefore resolved, if she would consent, to carry her to some friends in London, where she might await the arrival of Mr. Prior, who was expected shortly in England. But all my intentions were put a stop to by a sudden order which compelled me to go to St. Bee's Head, in the next county, just at the time, too, when I intended to have made Jasper Chough my prisoner. I left him a day and a half in a place up in the mountain yonder, by way of disciplining him a little for his behaviour to the young lady, and when I received my summons, I made my way to the cave where I had left him bound; unfortunately I chose a different route to the usual one; and, as a foolish youth, set him free while I was on my way there, he escaped me; I had just time to have a shot at him, but missed him; I had no time to follow him, but went to Cumberland. I have been kept there ever since, and now I'm back again, determined if I can to catch Mr. Jasper, and one or two others whose names are down on my list. So, now you see, my lass, that whatever information you can give me respecting the lady and the gentleman, wlll be for her good, and not exactly, perhaps for his, but that's no matter. I can see your tongue has been waiting impatiently for a run, therefore let it slip at once, and I'll listen as well, I am sure, as you can talk."

Martha, thus exhorted, complied with the request, and set her tongue to work in good earnest, and chattered away with all her might, repeating a great deal of what she had previously said, stating considerably more, and could hardly believe she had said all, when she found she had nothing left to tell. Lucky George heard her to an end with most exemplary patience, and then told her he would instantly communicate with Mr. Prior, and the first step he should advise him to take was to come down to Grasmere, hear all, and let him proceed as he thought proper. With this decision Martha fully agreed, and then they parted. Martha, loaded with intelligence, went with speed to the cottage to take John Andrew and his mother by storm with her news, and Lucky George to fulfil his promise.

On the close of the fourth day from this meeting, a post-chaise with reeking and tired horses entered the village, bearing Mr. Prior and John Paul in the interior, and Gasket on the exterior, all tired with their long, and what was at that period considered, rapid journey. Mr. Prior could scarcely be prevented from having an interview with Martha, until he was told the lateness of the hour precluded her absence from the Hall; he was, therefore, compelled to retire to rest without satisfying the longing he possessed to hear everything connected with his beloved Florence. The morning sun was out of his chamber but a short time before him, and with excessive impatience he waited the arrival of Martha, who was no sooner given to understand that the "real and only original" lover had come, than she was as much agog to see him as he to see her. Their meeting was not long delayed, and then, after the first bashfulness, assisted by the first impression of Mr. Prior's being such a nice young man, had been got over, there followed such a burst of eloquence it was quite charming to hear, save that the incidents related were of a painful nature, and wound Prior up to a state of intense excitement. He would scarcely hear the narrative to a conclusion, when he requested John Andrew to set off at once with him and his companions, and point out the spot where Jasper had parted with him, and then it was his intention, he said, to track the villain, Jasper, step by step, until he discovered him, and compel him either to give up Florence or point out the place of her concealment. John Andrew readily consented, and Martha made no objection to "her John's" going, for its object was to restore her dear mistress to her. Lucky George, who had made his appearance and lent his aid in the narration, was also made a partner in the proposed expedition, and it was expected that his knowledge of the locality would render his assistance valuable. They were not long in preparing for their departure, and when equipped with arms and ammunition, they started up the mountain, Lucky George and Andrew leading the way, though from the eagerness displayed by the others, it was difficult to say which was first, the leaders or the led. They wound up the steep ascents with enterprising spirit, carefully noting every object, in the hope of discovering something which might prove a clue to the discovery of Jasper; but they found nothing. They searched the cave from which Lucky George had rescued Florence; everything remained as he had left it, but would not much longer, it being George's intention to convert the whole of its contents to the storehouses of his majesty as soon as he had an opportunity. They quitted it immediately they ascertained she was not in the place, and wended their way towards the cottage of Trusty Tom, expecting, if they did not fall in with Jasper, to be able to extract some intelligence respecting him from that worthy individual. Evening was drawing on apace before they reached his abode, and when they reached the door they knocked for admittance, but not receiving an answer they raised

the latch, and the door being without other fastening opened readily, and they entered the room. It looked dismal, everything was in confusion, no fire blazed on the hearth, no person was in sight to receive and welcome them. Andrew shouted Tom's name, and a groan echoed his call. They all hastily approached the spot from which the sound originated, and quickly found themselves in a small back room, which contained a wretched bed in one corner, and upon it rested Trusty Tom in a state approximating dissolution. He uttered a succession of feeble groans, which were mingled with oaths; he half raised himself on the bed upon their entrance, demanded what they wanted, and before they could answer, he bade them go about their business and leave him to himself. But that was not their purpose, and Eustace Prior, whose anxiety to obtain news respecting Florence superseded every other feeling, at once stated the object of his visit, offering a reward for an open confession, and promising punishment for any obstinate refusal to comply with his request. Tom listened to him at first impatiently, but as he proceeded he paid great attention to him, and when he finished he regarded him earnestly for a minute, and then said, eagerly—

"And if you nab the man who's carried off the girl, will you twist him or send him across the herring-pond for life?"

"One or the other shall assuredly be his fate," returned Eustace, warmly.

"And you will pay me well if I split?" he rejoined.

"You shall be rewarded handsomely, if I find you have spoken the truth," exclaimed Eustace.

"Well, then you shall know all," said Tom, with a rancour in his tone that gave his voice a vehemence scarcely to be expected from one so weak. "You are on the wrong scent. Churleigh is the man who's got the girl."

"Churleigh," cried Lucky George. "What, Jack-in-the-Hole, of Grasmere?"

"That's him," answered Tom; "he's the man that's got her, not Jasper Chough. I knows nobody of the name of Chough."

"That's a lie, friend," exclaimed George: "you do; or, at all events, you know one Geoffrey Smith, and he and Jasper are one and the same."

"Well, it does not signify; Jack Churleigh has got the girl," said Tom, doggedly; "he took her from this cottage."

"From here! When? at what time? Speak, man," eagerly cried Eustace.

"Yesterday," returned Tom; "he brought her here the night afore, and took her away to the Isle of Man. If you look sharp you may overtake him. There's a creek this side of St. Bee's Head; he will take water there and run for Ramsey. A couple of good horses, kept at a gallop, and you may come up with him."

"Is this truth?" inquired Eustace, doubtingly.

"I haven't much faith in it," said Lucky George, shaking his head; "Chough is the man who has carried her off, and it is not very likely that he would entrust her to an old reprobate like Churleigh."

"Well, don't believe me," said Tom; "only if you've made up your minds that I shall tell you nothing but lies, why have you asked me any thing at all? I have told you the truth. Smith did have the girl, but he and old Jack quarrelled about the old man's daughter, who Geoffrey has made too free with, and so the old one in revenge has carried off your girl to the Island, where he intends to sell her to one of the captains of a smuggling craft, or murder her to make up for what his own girl has suffered."

"God of heaven! man, are you speaking truth?" cried Eustace, with frantic earnestness.

"I am!" returned Tom, with emphasis. "I interfered to prevent her going, and this is what I've got for my trouble."

As he concluded, he drew aside the bed clothes, and displayed his wounded side.

"Which path did the old scoundrel take?" cried Eustace, unheeding the ghastly sight. "Quick, man, I'll be on his heels ere I am a minute older."

"Across the hills to Cumberland. Take the right hand path that leads from here, and at the end of a short five miles there's a house where you may get horses, and then don't let the grass grow beneath your feet."

"Follow me," cried Eustace to his companions; "we will not lose an instant. A moment wasted may bring her death, and me everlasting despair."

"I will be your guide," exclaimed Lucky George; "I know every inch of the ground."

"Lead on," exclaimed Eustace, impatiently; "and my first act, on meeting the old villain, shall be to send a bullet through his accursed head."

He rushed out of the cottage as he concluded, and his companion followed him. Tom watched them depart with a grin of exultation, and then he muttered—

"Now, old Jack, if I ain't revenged on you for the dig in the ribs you've given me, it ain't my fault."

He turned upon his side, and the exertion caused the bandages to slip from their places. He was unable to replace them; he bled profusely, and in a few hours he became a corpse—a frightful object for the next comer to discover in that lone house.

Lucky George proved his knowledge of the route they were to pursue by leading them through some bye paths, which enabled them to reach the house Tom had pointed out to them speedily. Here they fortunately obtained a vehicle and three horses, two of which were attached to the chaise, and one which George rode, and scarce waiting to take refreshment, they set forward again in pursuit. Eustace urged on the driver, promising him a handsome gratuity if he succeeded in overtaking the persons of whom he was in pursuit, and the man did his best to earn it. Relays of horses were obtained at the end of the two first stages, but then delay ensued. Once more Fortune smiled upon them to again withdraw her favour, though neither expense or exertion was spared to obtain the desired object; but it was not until the next evening that they arrived at the point for embarkation, without even having met with a trace of the fugitives. They had made inquiries in every shape at every place, even at the expense of a little time, but in vain; and being unable to describe the manner in which Churleigh and Florence had progressed, it was impossible to ascertain any information concerning them. All they learned by repeated inquiries was, that the night previous a boat, containing a few persons, one a female closely muffled up, had left the creek and gone in the direction of Ramsey. Eustace inquired for a boat, but there was nothing but a passage-boat, and that did not leave St. Bee's Head until the next day. The distance to Ramsey was thirty-four miles; a row-boat, therefore, would not do, but there was a fine galley belonging to a pilot lying idle. There were no hands, however their informant said, to work it, or it was his belief the pilot, for a consideration, would lend her to them. They ascertained the pilot's direction, and had an interview with him, which ended by his granting them the use of his boat. Their nautical knowledge now stood them in good stead; they stepped two masts and bent a suit of sails belonging to her, which were made lugger-fashion. It was blowing half a gale of wind, but this they cared not for. They obtained the assistance of two men, and gallantly put out to sea in their frail vessel. It was a fine clear evening, though it blew freshly, and they trimmed their sails fore and aft, carrying on until they were half blown out of water. They had quitted St. Bee's Head about two hours, and in that time had run nearly fifteen miles, when Paul observed a revenue cutter, which was at a considerable distance, making signals to them. He communicated it to Mr. Prior.

"They are signalising us to lie-to, are they not?" exclaimed the lieutenant.

"Ay, ay! sir," replied one of their new hands, with a laugh, "that's their talk; they want to overhaul the stowage. As light a craft as this, sir, has made a clean run with a cargo of tubs, and, for that matter, who knows but this has also. Perhaps they knows as much, and wants to see whether she carries more than she shows."

"What is to be done?" exclaimed Eustace, earnestly, to Paul.

A bright flash, followed by the heavy report of a gun, succeeded his question, and at the same moment they saw a ball come skipping towards them, glancing along the surface of the waters like a wild sea bird. They watched its bounds and leaps in silence, until its force was expended, and then threw up the spray; with a sudden dash it sunk, at no great distance from its mark.

"She throws her mettle prettily," exclaimed Paul, admiringly, and then added, quickly, "there goes her gaff-topsail, and flying-jib too; she means to come up with us hand over hand."

"What course shall we steer, Paul?" urgently inquired Eustace; "we ought to lie-to for them, for we know the rules of the service, and have no excuse for standing on if they should overhaul us; but if we bring up, we shall lose an hour simply to gratify an absurd delusion of theirs, and in that hour God knows what may happen to Florence."

"Let us stand on," answered Paul, readily, his eye kindling as he spoke. "It is blowing fresh, and will blow harder yet," he said, observing the sky as he spoke: "the commander of yon saucy cruiser, proud as he is, will have to douse his gaff-topsail and flaunting jib, if he would not carry his top-mast by the board. This is as tight a boat as any I ever sat in, and will carry all she now bears through a heavier wind and sea than this; she flies like a gull, and it strikes me forcibly, the king's cutter, with a brailed mainsail and close-reefed jib, will have a hard chase ere she runs alongside of us. My advice is, sir, that we crack on as now, with everything set that will draw, and let him catch us if he can. What say you, Gasket?"

"I never know'd you say anything that didn't turn out as right and true as eight bells make four half struck," was Gasket's reply; but be that as it may, I am for crowding all sail for the young lady, lord love her sweet face! a stern chase is a long chase—the king's cutter LOOKS a clipper, but I think this boat is one, and as no catchee is no havee, I'm for giving them work to catch us afore they haves us."

"That's what I call talking sense," cried Andrew, rubbing his hands, "it isn't a spanking jib and a whacking spanker that makes a Baltimore clipper; the cruiser shows plenty of duck, but she's not obliged to be a flyer for all that."

"Ah!" exclaimed one of their supernumeraries, "but that cruiser is a flyer. Have you never heard of the Curlew? You have seen blue water I knows, and have the cut of men-o'-war's-men—have you never heard of the flying Curlew?"

"No!" was the general reply.

A second flash, more vivid than the first, accompanied by a louder report, burst upon them, and they saw the blue wreathing smoke of the gun, they watched the coming of the speeding ball. This time it was nearer its mark, and dashed the salt water over them as it sunk within a foot or two of them.

"There," continued the man who had previously spoken, "you see they draw on us, and they have a long Tom that will follow us faster than we can fly; it's my opinion you had better heave-to, and show your credentials—you will only get a hearty curse or so for running them out of their course—and then they will set us free."

"I'm rayther inclined to doubt it, Bill," observed his companion; "there are those aboard of the Curlew who knows this galley has carried more tubs than pilots; they won't be so ready to take our word for honesty and good meaning. For my part, my jib is as well known to them as their own figure-head, and they knows, too, that I have run more tubs than I've caught fish, though I've hung out nets at the door of my cot as a sign, like a ship shows her colours at the peak to tell her nation. I'm for standing on: I don't like the company of those who sail under a pennant, when their duty is cruising for smugglers; it ain't by no means agreeable, the more 'specially when I recollects they've a spite agin me, and wants to stow me under hatches, in their prison house. My advice, gentlemen, is, that we crack on; I know what this craft can do, and I know what the people on board the cutter will do if they catch us."

"But isn't it better to be caught, even if you are clapped into prison," retorted the man, warmly, "then be sent to Davy Jones by a piece of their metal? the next shot may take us between wind and water—where shall we be then? I can't swim."

"You're a miserable croaker," exclaimed Paul, with contempt; "we will take our chance, Mr. Prior—the safety of the maiden is worth a greater hazard than this."

"Paul, you have a noble heart," returned Prior, energetically: "I'll carry on until I run this craft under water, before I'll give up my chance of making Ramsey, and if you will only stand by me, the cutter may treat us with a great many messages from her long Tom before she makes us bring up under her lee."

"We will stand by you to the last," cried Paul, warmly, "so hurrah! for a trial of speed. I think, if the gear is strong enough to enable us to hold on at this rate, we may defy them yet. Take a pull at the sheets, my lads," he continued, addressing Gasket and Andrew, "and see that they are tautly belayed. Let me take the tiller, Mr. Prior," he added, "I think I am stronger in the arm than you; besides, I know the coast well; I have not run from Kirkcudbright to Whitehaven so often but that I know the bearings hereaway well."

"With all my heart, Paul," said the lieutenant, immediately resigning the tiller to his care, adding, "I place every reliance on your judgment."

"I will not wrong your dependence," said Paul, "perhaps, too, I know a thought or so about the Island of Man. I have been a trip or two there, and am acquainted with sufficient to help us much if we are lucky enough to make it. The wind freshens fast," he added, surveying the clouds which were rising fast above the horizon, and hurrying across the heavens; "there will be a heavy gale, which your eye is practised enough to see as well as mine, and in this channel such a gale is not a thing to smile at; we might be farther from death were we any where than in this boat when the fury of the storm bursts upon us; but a long face in the hour of danger never belonged to a heart ready to meet it; there is time for us yet to escape. Ah! by heaven, the people of the Curlew can read the weather with a skill equal to our own—they are preparing to send down their gaff-topsails; we shall have some of their metal quickly,"

The words had scarcely quitted his lips when again the white smoke of gunpowder rose up from the bow of the cutter, and a loud report followed it; a hard sheer of the boat up in the wind, by the strong arm of Paul, alone saved them from having the ball crashing amongst them—as it was, it passed close to their stern and went beyond them, burying itself in the curling foam of the swelling sea.

"It was neatly done, Paul," exclaimed Prior, who had anxiously watched the messenger of death and the prompt act to avoid it.

"Keep her a little closer to the wind, eat into it more, sir," exclaimed the supernumerary who had advocated holding their career, addressing Paul; "she'll bear it, and there's nobody here to care for a wet jacket."

"Will the gear hold?" he asked, anxiously.

"It will bear any strain you can put on it," was the ready reply.

"Then I'll lay her closer to old Boreas than they can yon rapid cutter, pretty craft as she is. Ah! here comes another of their pills."

The cutter's long gun discharged its contents as he spoke, and the same means were employed to keep the galley clear of the shot as before; with greater skill and readiness was it accomplished, but barely were they saved from its terrible effects; it just grazed the stern post as it flew with tremendous speed and force by them, and they all drew a long breath at their narrow escape.

"The fellow that points that gun deserves a pension," exclaimed Paul; "I never met with greater precision in such a rolling sea; two inches nearer to us would have left us without a rudder, completly at their mercy. What spar is that?" he asked of one of the men, pointing to one that lay at the bottom of the boat.

"It's a spare spar, to be rigged as a jury mast in case of accident to either of the others," the man replied.

"Can you rig it as a top-mast?" asked Paul quickly.

"Ay, ay," he returned; "here s caps, and in the fore locker there's a square top sail; it's made to rig on to the foremast here, in fine weather."

"We'll set it," exclaimed Paul, decisively; "you know the trim of it—up with it."

"What! in this weather," inquired the man, with astonishment.

"We shall have the next shot through us if we don't quicken our speed; the cutter's only begun her fun: unless we change our distance we shall end before they do. Gasket and Andrew, lend them a hand, and bear a fist, we shall not be able to carry it long."

"Ay, ay," was instantly returned, and with alacrity the two seamen set to work to assist in adding this accession to their small suit of rigging.

Another blaze from the bows of the cutter put Paul on the alert: he saw that it was directed across the fore-foot of the galley, and by the time he reached the line it was taking it would come in contact directly with the centre of his fragile craft, or, as it is nautically termed, amidships; if he fell off before the wind it might catch him in the bows—if he brought his vessel up in the wind he might carry away one of his masts, a loss more hazardous than running the chance of the damage the shot might do. With an eagle's glance, he saw that, as on the leaping waves it glanced, its direction was slightly changed, and perhaps by lying his vessel more in the trough of the sea, he might avoid it. He resolved upon it, and did it—the thought and act were but the work of an instant. No sooner was it done than they were made aware of the arrival of the shot: fortunately the boat sunk rapidly into the trough, and the shot caught only its gunwale, which it tore away, carrying with it the sheet of the after main-sail, and in an instant the sail was flapping violently in the heavy wind. Paul shouted to his followers to brail it up until they drove another sheet in its place; his order was obeyed with the readiness and dexterity which is only to be met with in men-of-war's men, and once more it was extended to its position, and the speed of the galley, which had by this incident been considerably lessened, much increased, and then they returned to their previous object, urged by Paul, who saw in their loss of distance and the increasing rapidity with which the cutter discharged her long gun at them, as well as the greater precision of every fire, great cause for apprehension. He knew nothing could save them but great dexterity, perseverance, and greater swiftness than they at present possessed, and therefore all his powers must be directed to that one point. His energies were equal to it, and he knew it; he resolved to call them forth, and even resigned the tiller to Mr. Prior's hands to assist in hoisting the fresh mast and sail, which, considering the weather, notwithstanding their desperate situation, seemed little less than an act of madness. He, however, had calculated the chances, and was determined upon abiding by the consequences; his friends were accustomed to the old sea rule, "obey orders if you break owners," and therefore they did what they were ordered without considering whether it would end in their destruction or not. They knew the tremendous strain there would be upon every line, and with the skill of thorough seamen they looked at every point which was calculated to fail, and secured it. At length, and, considering the circumstances, it was but a short time, the mast was raised, the topsail added, and filled with a velocity which, but for the skin of Paul, would have capsized them; at first, the vessel shook about restively, like a young horse at the whip, as if impatient at the additional means of enforcing speed, and then shot forward like an arrow from a bow. She threw up the spray from her bows in showers, and leaped from wave to wave with a rapidity that made Paul's heart glow to witness.

Now came the trial; the people on-board the cutter observed their movements and made fresh efforts to come up with them; gun after gun she fired, but unsuccessfully—the heavy roll of the sea, and the great speed at which they were flying through the water, prevented the accuracy of aim for which the gunner had long been famed. They even mounted a topsail, too, but their topmast, already bending like a piece of whalebone, would not bear it. The two vessels flew along at a tremendous pace over a sea which threatened each instant to overwhelm the smaller boat, and play with the larger as though it had a feather tossing about—every sail was extended to its furthest extremity, every line tautened, the wind as fresh as they dare wish it, their vessels lying as close to the wind as it was possible for them to be put, and with all their efforts, the distance seemed still to be the same; the galley might be drawing a little upon the cutter, but it was scarcely enough to be named in their favour. The sky was growing more gloomy, a scud was driving across the heavens, the wind each moment increased, and each watched the other with intense interest. The people in the cutter, accustomed as they were to witness deeds of daring in their intercourse with smugglers, were astonished at the apparent recklessness which Paul and his companions appeared to display in thus holding their course in defiance of foe and of elements, and were filled with as much eagerness to know if they would escape a watery grave as they were to discover if they could overhaul and capture them. On the other hand, the crew of the galley, desperate as was their position, were less anxious about the conduct of their boat in resisting the elements than they were respecting the intentions of the cutter's crew. Both running so close to the wind there was but little change in their movements, still every change which the cutter made was anticipated by Paul, who had resumed his station at the helm, and provided for accordingly. Presently he cried, in a short, stern voice—

"Now they feel the gale. By heaven! there goes their topmast, gaff-topsail, and upper riggings by the board; the spar has snapped like a piece of thread. Stand by, boys, to let the sheets fly: quick, boys, stand by to in all sails."

There was a slight bustle, hands moved rapidly, and then the voice of Gasket, in a brief professional tone, was heard to cry—

"All ready with the sheets!"

Paul watched with breathless anxiety the motions of the cutter which was

to be his guide, and saw her laying down before the fury of the blast, as though she were on her beam ends, beyond a possibility of righting again. The rags of her top-sail and flying jib, which with obstinate and imprudent perseverance they had carried until torn from their respective stations, were flying wildly in the air, and everything about her denoted imminent danger and irremediable confusion; one moment she appeared engulphed in the world of waters—the next, she appeared ploughing her way furiously through them: but soon, with a speed which denoted the most practised hands, she was clear of the wreck of her upper rigging, and with her mainsail reefed and trussed up, and her jib close reefed, she continued the pursuit as hitherto. The galley, in the meanwhile, held on her speed, dashing through foam and spray, cresting the huge waves, and anon sinking into their deep furrows with a velocity which appeared to threaten dissolution. The countenances of the men, though stamped with the usual indifference which mark seasoned seamen during the conflict of the elements, wore yet an air of anxiety respecting the issue of their proceedings. Each moment, as they saw the bellying canvas strain the cordage almost to breaking, and bend the slim masts almost to snapping, they expected to see them carried away, and the boat swamped, but still they obeyed orders and held on at the sheets, though their death had been involved in their obedience. Paul stood erect in the boat, his hand firmly grasping the tiller, his eye ranging along the turbulent sea in the direction of the cutter, and occasionally taking a glance at the angry sky; his teeth were compressed, his aspect stern, but yet there was an air of coolness which augured well of his judgment, and gave confidence to his companions. There was a dead silence reigned among them; no one spoke, each almost holding his breath waiting the next order, which they knew must be given, and prepared to perform it in as short a space as possible. The roar of the wind, the dashing of the waves, as they leaped madly round them, was undisturbed by human voice, until, the boat surmounting the crest of a huge wave, the clear voice of Paul exclaimed—

"Stand by!"

"All ready," was the brief reply.

He waited until, having descended the trough of a sea, he rose again, and had once more a view of the turbulent waste around him, and then, with a voice which startled his companions, he shouted—

"Let go the sheets, brail up, brail up for your lives. Mr. Prior, supply my place at the helm; take a turn round the tiller with the end of that sheet, you'll not else be able to keep it steady."

As he spoke—rapidly he uttered his words—Eustace grasped the tiller, and he sprung to the aid of the busy seamen, who, with a rapidity quite surprising, laid all bare to the masts, and as the frail bark reached the crown of the next wave she did not show a rag of canvas. The sea had greatly increased, and the wind, in the shape of a complete hurricane, was roaring like a wild beast in the wilderness, as it rushed towards them, threatening each moment to engulph them in the angry waves it created. Their danger was imminent; nothing but the extreme bouyancy and admirable construction of their little vessel could save them from instant destruction. One minute they were raised upon the pinnacle of a wave, having an extensive view around them; the next, the boat darted almost perpendicularly down the hollow of an immense wave, as though she must inevitably bury herself in the yawning gulph, and then would rise again unscathed, breasting the lofty surges like a bird. Now that they had no canvas to help them they were exposed to a new danger. The fury of the wind had compelled Paul to steer a little out of his course and run before it, and with all the sail set which he had recently carried, he flew along with extraordinary velocity distancing the leaping waves as they followed in the same direction; but now that the spars and cordage were alone exposed to the blast, the speed of their little bark was materially decreased, and it became rather more than probable that a rapid wave would overtake them and bury them beneath it. To add to the anxiety which a knowledge of this alarming possibility created, was the fact, too evident to be mistaken, of the cruiser gaining fast upon them. It is true that the latter had been compelled to change from a trussed main-sail to one brailed close up, and to substitute for its immense jib a considerable smaller one, denominated a storm-jib, measuring scarcely one half the size of the other, still there was enough left, in addition to the rigging, to hold a great deal of wind, and drive their always swift vessel with great velocity before it, and should the relative speed of the two vessels continue, there was little or no doubt that half an hour would place John Paul and his companions in the power of their pursuers.

Not one iota of the danger, and the frail chances existing of escape, eluded the vigilant mind of our hero. Death was staring him in the face, and he returned the gaze with an aspect of calm, cool defiance. The raging waters, dashing furiously around, presented even to the practised eyes there an awful appearance, coud not make his spirit quail. There was a fire in his eye, and a perceptible heaving of the chest, as he returned to his post at the helm, but it was simply the expression of a spirit rising superior to the evils by which he was surrounded, and from no fear of the probable doom that awaited him. It is the nature of men in danger to look to each other for counsel, and it is extraordinary what consolation they will derive—what fond hopes of safety they will entertain—if there is one among them cool, collected, and confident in his demeanour. The worst part of their fears vanish; the prospect of impending death decrease; the evils lose their magnitude, and it is not until destruction absolutely ensues that they can believe the courage of him who had been their stay had no real foundation for its existence. There was not, perhaps, one in the boat possessing less courage, or feared death more than John Paul; but the bravest men are alive to a sense of danger, and though they meet their fate bravely, they may still want sufficient coolness to invent means to extricate them from their peril. Such would probably have been the case with Gasket, Andrew, the two auxiliaries, and even Paul himself, had they been placed in a situation, the imminence of whose danger called suddenly upon their energies, and the calm exercise of solid judgment to avert. Paul, however, possessed the attributes which lift a brave man into a great man. However extreme the peril, he could look it in the face, grapple with it, and, in the compass of human means, conquer it. He was young, but reflection and some hard service, added to native firmness of character, placed him upon a level with those older and more experienced than himself. He was not rash or impetuous in his deeds, so as to make their reasonableness questionable, but he was sufficient enthusiastic in what he did undertake to obtain that character from those unthinking minds who looked upon such conduct rather than its results; but even these shallow people, had they seen him in this hour of peril, guiding the frail vessel with cool decision and steady judgment, would have acknowledged that the hasty, precipitate youth possessed the qualities of the calmest brave.

In the present instance he had intuitively assumed the part of leader—it was ceded to him unconsciously by all accompanying him. They never questioned his right to the position, or for a moment felt that he was unequal to it: he was the master mind among them; the star in their dark hour of danger; their hope; their guide. They looked up to him for release from death, as children to their parents in moments of strait and difficulty, and were not less trustful or confident that his energies and superior capabilities would bring them safely through. It was done without pre-though, without counsel, without deliberation. It was the spontaneous act of spirits singling out one of their number who possessed powers of action sustained by sound judgment, higher than their own, and he as much self-elected as by their unanimously, though it had no voice, committing themselves to his care, undertook the office as a right of mind, strongly impressed, though without egotism, with the bare fact, that if he could not succeed in saving them, no one there could, and they must perish. In this perilous position, he seemed to have grown from the subordinate into the superior at one step. Prior, so recently his officer, seemed to have changed places with him, and though a talented and highly-couraged young man, equal to many a trying situation, to acknowledge his present superiority, and take the duties of an inferior with a manner which displayed no sense of degradation of rank or station, but rather a graceful concession of exalted merit in our hero.

The position was something to Paul as a probationary exercise of his powers— a kind of test to prove to what extent his qualifications and energies would fit him for the high part shadowed forth in his bright hopes of the future. The face and form of Alice shone upon him during the storm like a tutelary angel. Her sweet countenance and glittering eyes played around him as a halo of light, and he felt, amidst the howling of the winds and the dashing of the battling waves, an emotion of soft joy blending with his stern thoughts, which made the horrors of the scene fall upon him, shorn of their grim forebodings. His heart was nerved to his task, his courage was equal to all his judgment, and the hazards of his situation might counsel; and having held his way thus far, in defiance of the elements and the enraged pursuer, he determined to run every risk to keep his course rather than give up in despair, either to the devouring ocean or to the fast approaching cruiser. He stood with his feet planted firmly on the stern-sheets, grasping the tiller with the grip of a vice, surveying the wild scene before him; while his companions were seated with eager eyes fixed upon him, entirely resigned to his judgment, and ready to fulfil any order the instant it was uttered. No one spoke; the anxiety was too intense to be interfered with by an exclamation, even of hope, and they remained in their respective situations with thoughts of home mingled with a wonder of what would be the end of this adventure.

The clouds, which had increased with the wind, now swept across the sky in deep masses, threatening each moment to burst over their heads. Daylight fast decreased, and as it departed the wind seemed to strengthen, and the sea to rise higher, giving fresh cause of uneasiness. Their progress before the blast was very rapid, but nothing to what it had been, and all on board perceived, as they mounted the caps of the waves, how alarmingly nearer each minute brought the Curlew. Paul was not less keenly alive to this fact than any there, but although his eyes were fixed sternly upon the cutter, broken by an occasional and apparently nervous glance—though that was more seeming than real—at the progress of the galley, and at the sky, he had taken no means to alter the state of things. However, his quick eye detected an enormous wave coming after them at a greater speed than that at which they were advancing, promising to bury them as it broke, and it was with difficulty, allied to rapidity of action, that he contrived to remove the boat from the danger threatening it. Immediately he had succeeded, he cried aloud to Gasket and Andrew—

"We must carry a little headsail at every hazard; set that square topsail, and see that the barrel and the lifts and braces are well secured. We can spare nothing to part now: bear a hand, or the next wave that strikes our stern will swamp us."

After the brief exclamation of "Ay, ay!" the seamen proceeded to obey his order with alacrity, and being well assured the gear would hold, they set their small sail. At first the strain was tremendous, every one expected to see the cords part like threads, and, indeed, the topmast itself carried away, but they stood the pressure bravely, and after the first shake, remained in their places steadily. The effect upon the galley was great, she leaped through the waters where she had only comparatively crawled, and if she would but live in this heavy sea, Paul had no doubt that he should yet baffle the efforts of the cruiser to capture them.

The Island of Man was in sight; they saw the bay stretching out its arms to receive them, as a mother would fondly proffer shelter to its offspring in danger; but the wind was contrary for them to make it. Their only chance of keeping afloat was to run directly before the wind, and that blew obliquely to the object of their desires. Paul, however, as much as he dared, consistently with their actual safety, eat into the shore, and found to his satisfaction that, although they might be compelled to run past Ramsey, he had still the chance of running the boat among the shoals beyond it, where the Curlew dare not come, unless her commander desired her to go to pieces. It seemed as though the captain of the cutter had some shrewd suspicion of his intentions, and determined to overhaul him before he could accomplish his purpose, for he hoisted his spanking jib again, and though he still kept his mainsail—the boom of which was directly athwart the backstays—brailed, yet it was sheeted out to the boom-end, as far as even imprudence could dictate. Once again the Curlew, therefore, had the advantage of the galley, and again she drew nearer to her, rendering the hope of escape less and less. Paul was, however, nothing daunted; he saw deliverance where others could only see despair, and nothing but being actually run down by the cutter would make him surrender. He watched the speed of the two vessels, it is true, with anxiety, and occupied his mind with schemes to increase his own velocity, or by some other contrivance to render abortive the efforts of their pursuers, who were now closer upon them than they had ever been. The distance to the shore was still considerable, the sea was running mountains high, the cruiser was bearing down upon them with the speed of a racehorse, and it seemed certain that if they survived the almost inevitable prospect of being swamped, nothing could save them from the power of their pursuers.

Still had they all reliance upon our hero, and still did he grasp the tiller and direct the flying vessel as calmly as though he was sailing on a summer's eve " upon a silent sea," unmoved by the near approach of the enemy. At length their proximity grew sufficient for them to distinguish the people on board the Curlew quite plain, and once more a gun was discharged at them, but, with such a tremendous sea, it flew far wide of its mark. The report was followed by another, having a somewhat different sound and less startling effect. All eyes were directed to the cutter, from whence the sound proceeded, and it was with no little pleasure they perceived the jib was rent asunder by the wind, and the fragments were flying about in the wildest confusion. An accident had also taken place with the gaff, and the Curlew was now placed in a more critical situation than the galley. Paul saw the occurrence, and seized upon the advantage it gave him with avidity; he ordered the seamen to look well to the stays, braces, and lines upon which there was any strain, and set a fore-sail, to keep the head of the boat steadier, and enable him also to eat closer into the shore. He was obeyed, and they quickly had the satisfaction of seeing they were drawing a-head of the Curlew and nearing the shore rapidly. The people on board the cutter all this time were not idle. Once more the small jib was set, the accident to the gaff was repaired, and again she stood on after the little craft which had so long and successfully baffled them. Night was fast closing in, the gloominess of the clouds added to the approaching darkness, and bronght a fresh anxiety to bring this adventure to a close. The shore was now the object for which Paul exerted his energies to the utmost, and which the cutter's crew strained every effort to prevent his attaining. The superiority of the Curlew, in point of sailing, was, if possible, more manifest than before, and Paul noting it, said—

" She makes two feet to our one; but if fortune does not desert us, we shall yet run among the breakers before she can put us under her lee."

" Do you know the passage among the shoals hereaway ?" asked one of the auxiliaries of our hero.

" I do," he replied, laconically.

" I'm glad of that," replied the man; for if you didn't, I'd rather trust to the open sea than be running among those desperate channels."

" Do you grow faint-hearted?" inquired Paul, sternly.

" Not I," replied the man, with a short laugh. " I think there's little difference whichever way you steer. If we keep to sea we shall be taken by the cruiser, and perhaps with a short turn round one's gullet with a yard tackle, be run up aloft; or if we are not overhauled by the cutter, we shall be sent to Davy Jones' stern first with a heavy sea, and if we get among the breakers, not even your knowledge, with such a beating sea as this, will keep us from bumping upon the bight of a shoal or a reef, and knocking a hole in the bottom of the galley before you can count two. It's my belief that half-an-hour will be more than we shall want to send us over the standing part of the main sheet, and I must confess, if we do haul our wind, I'd rather it wouldn't be where we shall be bumped and banged fore and aft agin a reef of breakers: it ain't a pleasant way of slipping your cable to my thinking."

"Nor to mine," replied Paul, when he concluded; "but I am not like you, as full of fears and expectations of being run down by death as a young fishwife, who sees in every catspaw that ruffles the ocean a brewing gale."

"Well, if you wouldn't have a man overhaul his log for a bit about a berth in the next world in such weather, and in such a cockleshell as this, why I've no more to say," observed the auxiliary, rather sententiously; "I've only to tell you that I am ready for the long voyage, and feel as if I was under weigh and my anchor stoppered already, that's all."

"Your life-lines will unreeve before their time," said Paul, shortly; "you love living too well. However, look to your duty, I've nailed my colours to the mast, and death must tear them down when he wants me to strike. Now silence, fore and aft, the time has come for reading the riddle—the answer will be, life or death."

By this time the near approach of the boat to land sufficiently explained the earnestness with which he uttered the last words, and most anxiously did the little crew watch their progress to the shore which was to rescue them from a disastrous fate or consummate it. They could see the surf beating to a terrific height, rendering it impracticable for a small boat like the one in which they sat to land without instantly being beat to pieces, and to those who had no knowledge of the locality, it appeared to be the only means left of endeavouring to escape a watery grave, and even then was loaded with prospects of meeting with a last resting-place on the beach—a miserable alternative, truly. The galley was about a mile from the shore, yet seemed closer. Paul still kept her directed full towards it, though the aspect was frightful, and the cutter stood on in pursuit, striving her utmost to overtake them ere they could gain a channel through which it was dangerous for a craft of her calibre to venture. The minutes seemed dreadfully long and the wind still raged with violent fury, and drove the vessels before it with extreme rapidity; yet, to the crew of each, they appeared to crawl along, for neither kept pace with their wishes. The cutter, which had almost recovered her lost ground, still drew fast on the galley; but the commander saw with most nervous anxiety the chance still left for "the contrabandist," as he believed them, to escape his clutches; and though warned by the master, who knew the dangerous nature of the coast, that he risked the safety of the vessel in drawing so close inland in such tremendous weather, he listened impatiently, waved his hand impetuously, and still stood on. The dashing of the sea upon the breakers now added its terrible sound to the roaring conflict, and appeared to utter a foreboding voice to those who came within their precincts. Still the galley kept a-head of the cutter and drew closer into the land, until even the enraged commander of the Curlew himself saw it was madness to follow them further without desiring to embed himself in the shoals which abounded here, and venture his own destruction, as well as his vessel and crew; he, therefore, reluctantly determined to give up the contest, but not until he had given the people a taste of his kindness: he gave the order to the men to discharge a number of small arms at them, while the gunner was once more to try his powers with the "long Tom." But few discharges were made, and those under an impossibility to take an aim, then they were ordered hastily to be thrown aside by the shout of the men in the bow, crying—"breakers a-head," and others, "breakers on the lee-bow," and the destruction of others was forgotten in effort for self-preservation.

The coast of the Island of Man, especially at the part which they approached, was rocky and precipitous, abounding in immense masses of rock, denominated breakers, rising in every direction, through which channels exist deep enough even to navigate a vessel of some size, if the bearings are accurately known by the "attentive timoneer," but the smallest deviation is sure to involve the destruction of his bark—few were acquainted with them, and those few would have hesitated to take a vessel through them with any hope of threading them with safety. Paul was thoroughly acquainted with every inch of way, and steered boldly among the rude rocks. It was a perilous sight for those deficient in nerve. At every turn rose up huge rocks, like monsters threatening death, and the sea broke over them with a fury which rendered them still more appalling. Now the small vessel appeared rushing on its destruction, as a tall breaker started up in its path, and as a vigourous sweep of the helm would make it fall off before it, there would be another upon which it appeared directly to sheer, only to be avoided by the readiness and skill of the steersman. Like the mazes of a labyrinth were the positions of these rocks, and equally bewildering, save to the experienced eye of one who had often, for sport, found a safe way among them. Paul, though he had thus far eluded the Curlew and her crew, did not lose sight of her, even though he had plenty of work for his eyes in steering clear of the obstacles in his path, and presently found that he did well still to watch her motions. She had approached as near to the shore as she dared, and had taken in everything, had tossed out her anchors, and was evidently preparing to toss out her jolly-boat also, and filling it with men, to start in pursuit of them. The policy of such an act, with such a sea running, to say the least was questionable, and the probability of their success still more so; but the "captain's order must be obeyed," and the men ordered into the boat, doubting, as well they might, the possibility of their return, complied with the command as coolly and as cheerfully as if the weather had been fine and the sport agreeable. The captain took his post at the helm, gave the word cast off, and in an instant they were swept from the vessel's side by a tremendous wave. Through the interposition of Providence alone, they were saved from being swamped, and had barely recovered the heavy lurch ere the captain ordered the men to give way; he followed the path Paul had taken, and steering as he steered, still hoped to make the galley and its crew prisoners. Paul, once acquainted with their purpose and movements, appeared no longer to regard them: he directed all his attention to his own progress, giving his orders to Andrew and Gasket, who tended the foresail and topsail, with precision and coolness, while he steered the boat skilfully through the dangerous passage. Hitherto their progress had been swift, and though frequently rendered hazardous by the suddenness by which the

masses of rock appeared to start up before them, apparently too close to be avoided, and to augur certain death to come in contact with them; still, by the address and dexterity of the steersman, no evil had yet attended it, and their success hitherto led them to entertain hopes that it would still continue: but the breakers appeared suddenly to multiply and magnify, the wind to grow more violent, and the sea heavier still; the roaring of the dashing waves and fierce blast was almost deafening, while the strain upon the slight cordage and slighter sails, seemed greater than it was possible for them to bear; they cracked, they stretched, and creaked with warning voice, at the same time, by their means the boat was urged over the sweeping waves, and among the jutting rocks, with a velocity which appeared frightful. It was nearly dark; one of the men was stationed in the bows to shout notice of every breaker he saw, and the constant exercise of his voice alone told the terrible nature of their situation. As yet there had been a broad lurid streak of light along the horizon, the last look of the sun ere he quitted this quarter of the globe, but now it diminished rapidly, apparently as if the daylight was being gradually shut out by an immense pall of heavy dense clouds. It had been Paul's object to gain a certain distance before night completely set in, and thus, seemingly against all prudence, he had carried as much sail as he could, as long as it would hold; but now that it had become so dark, objects could scarcely be distinguished a hundred yards a-head: he gave the order to strike the top-sail and stand-by with the sweeps, if the near approach of the cutter's boat rendered their use necessary. The pursuit, notwithstanding its dangerous concomitants, was still kept up with great spirit: occasionally they could see the jolly-boat, crowded with men, dashing after them, and then the next instant it would be lost to sight as if swallowed up by the remorseless waves, to again appear persevering dauntlessly in its object.

On they flew, each minute appearing to rush into the jaws of destruction to escape when death seemed inevitable; yet the difficulties increased, and still fortune preserved them. For a considerable time none had spoken, save Paul to give his orders, or the look-out to hail the presence of breakers; but now Eustace Prior exclaimed, in a low but earnest tone—

"In what is this to end, Paul?"

"Success, I hope," he replied, calmly.

"Breakers a-head!" shouted the look-out, and Paul steered accordingly.

"To land with such a surf and on such a shore is impossible," continued Eustace; "and if by threading this channel you can gain the open sea, I doubt whether this boat, after all the straining she has had, would live. What is your purpose? speak freely! If escape is hopeless, let us know, that we may be ready to meet death as becomes men. If there is still a prospect of weathering the danger, inform us by what means it is to be accomplished, that we may exert our energies with renewed vigour to enable you to carry out your designs."

"Breakers on the lee bow!" shouted the look-out; "breakers broad on the weather-beam! breakers a-head!" he cried, rapidly, and at the top of his voice. The quickness with which each warning followed the other was a fearful evidence of their critical position; but Paul seemed equal to the task he had undertaken. The bows of the boat fell off before each mass of rock as though she intuitively knew her danger and shunned it. A larger space than usual appearing, he took the opportunity of replying to Eustace Prior.

"Mr. Prior," he said, in warm, energetic tones, "whatever the emergency in which I might be placed, though at the very last extremity which the most sanguine could find a straw to catch at, I would still hope, and exert myself to the utmost to realize it. As we are now placed, I could draw hopes of safety from twenty different sources. I *never despair.* If I had to land here, no other means left to save us, I would attempt, and strive to the last to accomplish it with safety. If I was compelled to seek the open sea as the only chance for life remaining, I would run for it, and not give up my exertion, though the boat sunk beneath me, and I was left to battle the waves with nothing but a spar and a good heart to support me. But, sir, we are not to trust to either; it is my intention to escape the elements' rage, and the claws of our pursuers. I hope to baffle both. Not far from hence is an inlet where the water is as smooth as a lady's skin, in the heaviest weather. Let us gain that, and we are free from the dangers which now surround us, and must meet whatever hazards may then present themselves with different measures."

"There is danger, then, even in the prospect of escape from our present situation," said Prior.

"Of a certain description," returned Paul; "we shall take refuge among men who never admit strangers to their secret haunt without making use of them in their fashion, or shortening their lives, if they prove refractory."

"You mean smugglers," exclaimed Prior.

"They call themselves free traders," answered Paul, "and carry on their business on a large scale. They have schooners and privateers of magnificent build, which are well manned. They bring choice merchandise from foreign ports, and contrive to send it into England without contributing a single coin to his Majesty's revenue. They have done this to such an extent that the drowsy eyes of a weak, though venal, government have been pulled open. A sharp look-out is now kept, and a revision of the laws of smuggling has been the consequence—higher penalties and severer punishments being now inflicted than ever; the consequence of which will be, it is believed, a serious loss to this island. They are, therefore, bitter against all who wear his Majesty's costume, or are in his service."

"You know these people—you have had some intercourse with them?" said Eustace, inquiringly.

"Some years since I had," replied Paul, evasively. "My present information is derived from one I met lately in London. If we make the inlet safely, our greatest difficulty will be to prevent being taken for spies. If once they become convinced of such a suspicion, our lives will not be worth a half-sheave. Seeking their haunt is a disagreeable alternative; but of two evils, we must choose the least."

"Breakers a-head! Luff, sir, luff! or we shall be dead on to them!" almost shrieked the look-out.

Paul obeyed the warning, and the head of the boat cleared them only time enough to prevent being hurled upon them by the next wave that broke over it. It was now light; all sight of the pursuing jolly boat was lost; and, indeed, in the frightfully hazardous situation in which they were placed, it was almost forgotten they were surrounded on every side by rocks against which the sea beat furiously, throwing the surf high up into the air, like sheets of froth, and the body of water itself eddying and boiling as it swept in long volumes through the narrow channels between the breakers appeared as though it was over the crater of a volcano. The boat was tossed madly to and fro; the foresail, which was all that dared be shown, could not steady it, and shivered every now and then, as it was necessary to alter the direction of the vessel to avoid the rocks, as if it would burst into shreds; spray flew over them in all directions, half filling the boat with water; they were evidently in the most critical and dangerous situation they had yet been. Instant death stared every one in the face, save Paul, and he still stood calm and collected, directing the vessel with untiring vigilance and firm hand, as it leaped forward on its hazardous career. The place of the look-out was supplied by Gasket, the man being incapacitated by nervous alarm from keeping his post, although he declared it to be caused by the showers of spray which covered and blinded him. Gasket, a tougher sea-bird, accustomed to rough weather and hard labour, leaped into the bow of the boat at a word from Paul, and stood there impervious to wind or weather, giving the necessary warnings with a readier tongue, guided by a steadier eye than his predecessor. At best it was but a sort of blind steerage, but he gave to Paul a short description of the shape of the masses that rose up before him, and though they were no sooner in sight than they were passed, yet it enabled our hero, from his knowledge of the bearings, to know in what direction to keep the head of the boat. At length the roar and dash of the sea became tremendous—there was a hollow drumming sound, almost like a peal of thunder; there was the howl of the blast like the wail of a hundred spectres, and then Gasket shouted, with a voice which startled himself as well as the others—

"A cliff dead a-head!"

At the same moment he prepared to doff his jacket and swim for it, for safety in the boat now seemed impossible; he was, however, checked by hearing Paul thunder forth—

"Let go the foresail! cast off the sheet! down with it, lads, down with it; bear a hand, our lives depend upon it!"

Gasket waited not to cast it off the cleet or belaying pin, but out with his knife, and cut it away at once; the boat's head fell off the leeward, she was jerked on for a short distance, and then she was suddenly riding in smooth water. The change was so extraordinary that it appeared the effect of magic; no one seemed to know by what agency they had thus wonderfully been transported from a raging sea to a calm lake, and Eustace Prior, who was the first to find his tongue, exclaimed aloud—

"We are saved!"

"From wind, water, and breakers, certainly," responded Paul, "but whether from death remains to be proved. We must be cautious: the boat has lost her headway—there's no steerage way upon her. Stand by to toss out the sweeps before we put them in use; however, we must know a little more about our companions here; whatever we do, we must not have any enemies to stab us in the back. Now, my men, you who accompanied us from St. Bee's Head, do you know where you are?—No equivocations, out with the truth."

"If I was to say I did not," said one who bore the cognomen of Harry Hardstaff, "I should be telling a straightfor'ard lie. I does know the place, for many's the time I've been here; and I must say this, that I never seed a boat attempt to make the place in such weather as this, and I didn't believe there was the man living that would try to do it; hows'ever you are he, and if ever a boat could be prettier handled than you've done it to-night, I'll consent to drink bilge water for grog."

"Are you one of the crew of any of the craft belonging to the people here, or are you in their service at all?" asked Paul.

"That's not exactly the question to answer to one whose rig tells him to be in his Majesty's service," replied Harry Hardstaff.

"Whatever my dress, I am not in his Majesty's service," replied Paul, hastily; "and though I have been, and that recently, you forget that you acknowledged to me, on our passage hither, that you had run more tubs than you have caught fish. If I wished to take advantage of you in any way, that would be sufficient; but I simply want to know what connection you have with the men who make this place their haunt, for mine and my companions' good, but from no harm to you. You see *I* know the place well, and if I sought to do you or the people ill, I could as easily have brought the cutter's crew here as ourselves."

"Why to be sure, that's true," returned the man, a little less suspiciously; "and to say the truth, it's my belief that the Curlew never had the weather-gage so completely taken of her before. Well, I don't see why I shouldn't answer your question plainly. If you means foul play, why perhaps two can play at it; but if you means fair, as I think you do, it wouldn't be doing the handsome thing to pitch you a lot of lies or clap a stopper upon my tongue."

"I mean you fair," said Paul, emphatically.

"Then I am one of the crew of the Scud, Geoffrey Smith, commander," replied Harry Hardstaff; "and if you wants a good turn done, I thinks I can do it you."

"Thanks for your kindness," responded Paul, "we may accept it."

"Geoffrey Smith!" echoed Eustace Prior. "It must be the same. Do you know whether your commander bears another name besides Smith?"

"I have heerd say he comes of good family, either in Cumberland or Westmoreland, but I knows nothing about that. I only knows he's a devil to fight," returned Harry Hardstaff.

"You know one Churleigh, perhaps?" asked Paul, fixing his eyes upon him, although the darkness was too great to detect any change of features. The man's voice, which might serve as a tolerable guide was, however, frank and unconstrained.

"What, old tiger Jack?" he said, with a laugh; "yes, I should rather think I did. There's few in any service in the island who doesn't know old Jack Churleigh, and know, too, it's better to leap from a crag into the sea than quarrel with him."

"Is he in the island now?" asked Eustace, his voice trembling as he spoke.

"He is," returned the man; "he left the gap last night, and brought a young damsel with him here."

"Here!" cried Eustace, in a loud voice, betraying his emotion.

"For what I know," answered the man; "you seem to know him. What do you want with him?"

"Nothing particular; only to get a little information from him, as well as to give him a little," instantly answered Paul, fearing Eustace would say something which might place them in an awkward predicament with the smugglers when they went among them.

"Oh, I dare say I can find him if you want him," observed Harry, coolly.

"If you will," cried Eustace, eagerly, "I will—" he paused, for Paul squeezed his arm with vigour.

"What?" inquired the man, finding him hesitate.

"Return the service to the best of my ability," he replied, and became silent.

"And what of your mate, whom you call Bill?" asked Paul. "Is he of your crew?"

"He is," returned Harry. "Bill Grissoll is his name, but we calls him Bill Grizzle, because, though he likes smuggling better than living by the law, he's always expecting to be put under hatches by the Philistines, and says 'die' before we get within hail of Davy Jones."

"Better that than be foolhardy," observed Bill, quietly.

"I am satisfied," said Paul: "now listen to me. I know the cave; I know the laws of the people; I know that when a man enters the cave they make him swear to join them or never suffer him to leave it alive. We are compelled to enter the cave, but we do not intend to join them. We do not seek to betray them in any way, I pledge my honour; we are simply the victims of necessity; we require their hospitality, and that is all. We shall, therefore, lead them to believe we have already joined them, through some of their agents in London, of whose existence and place of meeting I am cognisant. All I require of you is to join in our story, see that no evil is done us, that no faith is broken with us ere we depart, and you shall neither of you have cause to complain of our gratitude. I know our position will be dangerous and suspicious, our dress betokening that we are in the service of the king—a fact which is not calculated to make friends with those whose sole occupation is breaking his laws, and the chances are, we shall be taken for spies. I ask you, therefore, to stand by us in our denial of it, for that we are not so I am ready to take oath, and when we leave the haunt scot-free, you have only to name your reward and have it. If you refuse, we are five to two, we will put you over the side: enter alone, and trust to fate; but if you consent and break your faith with us, understand that we are well armed, and the first who falls in the affray, if one ensues, shall be you, for treachery. We have seen some service, and will not perish without selling our lives dearly."

"I can't say who you are, or what you are," began Harry Hardstaff in reply, "'cept that you are a riddle. You say you don't belong to us, and don't mean to join us, nor betray us, and yet you know how to fetch this cove as well, if not better, than the best of our people. You are men-o'-war's men, you serve the king, and yet don't come as spies among those who cheat his gracious majesty. Overhaul it which way I will, it won't coil away smoothly. Hows'ever, there's something about you fair and above board. You ain't acted, as I've seen, in a mean skulking fashion. I don't believe you've hoisted false colours, and so I'll stand by you—won't you, Bill, eh?"

"Yes! and wouldn't have made half the palaver you have in saying so," he exclaimed; "only I expect we shall be found out, and if we are, we might just as well have sat astride a barrel of powder, and tapped the bung with a red-hot poker."

"That's Bill Grizzle!" observed Hardstaff with a laugh.

"If you have such doubts of your safety, why do you consent so readily?" asked Paul, sternly.

"Oh!" replied Bill, "you've promised to put me over the side if I don't, therefore I take the best chance for my life."

"You will not betray us when we are with your comrades?" said Paul, in a tone which carried with it an implication that he had better not.

"No," he returned: "I lose two ways if I do—those who introduce strangers among us who may turn out to be spies, are the first to suffer our vengeance, and so if I split I lose life and your reward for being true—that's enough to content you, I hope."

"As far as I see fit," said Paul; "however, I'll trust you both. Now out with the oars, and put way on the boat."

The men obeyed him, and once more they were progressing forward. The inlet which they had gained was formed by a narrow passage through what might be termed an immense wall of rock, which extended a considerable distance obliquely into the sea, and then, after running almost horizontally for about five-hundred yards, it branched inwards again, divided from the main land only by the narrow opening or gut through which Paul had steered to save himself and companions from their pursuers, and a watery grave. It thus formed a complete harbour, protected entirely from winds and waves by the high masses of rock which formed the wall spoken of, and rendering, even in the wildest weather, a place of shelter and refuge for those who knew how to steer for and make it. On the outer side, the sea, even in calm weather, beat with violence upon the rocks, which were extremely numerous, uprising in all directions, and rendered the place altogether, to those unacquainted with the channels, of most dangerous access, if not inaccessible. The inner side was the reverse, calm and smooth at all periods, and possessing a cavern of great extent, which formed an abode for spirits as wild as the winds and waves without. For this cavern Paul steered. A few lusty strokes of the rowers brought the boat beneath its shadow, which was adding blackness to darkness, and sent it gliding swiftly up its wide entrance; but little more exertion was sufficient to send it grating upon the land. Harry Hardstaff gave a shrill whistle, which was instantly responded to, and the next instant two or three torches came flashing through the gloom, borne by men, who, as soon as they could be distinguished, betrayed an aspect in which ruffianism was legibly written. They greeted the new comers with manifest surprise, and one of them exclaimed—

"What's afloat now, eh, Harry? This is not the weather for you to handle a boat, and bring her safely through the devil's teeth and witch's gill. What's in the wind, and who are these Jews?" he added, surveying Paul and his companions from head to foot.

"The Jews are no Philistines," retorted Paul, quickly, "and can play at long bowls with fists or pistols when a convict hulk hoists signals of clapping on too saucy jawing tackle. The boat was brought here by one who knows a jewel block from a thick scull, and how to make a wide berth when a monkey boat wants to fall foul of him. Now, my fine whisker-jib, you may belay your questions, and—"

"Why, damn your saucy lip," roared the fellow; "I'll clap my fin on your figure-head, and squeeze you as flat as a scollop—"

"Silence!" shouted Paul, in a fierce tone; "know whose presence you are in before you grow mutinous, or you may find yourself brought up with a round turn double-bitted."

"Who are you?" inquired the man, in a wavering tone.

"One to whom you may have to doff your cap for pardon for your insolence," he replied. "Now lead me to Captain Grayson, if he's in the haunt."

"He is here, sir," exclaimed, rather respectfully, a companion of the man Paul was addressing, suspecting our hero to be some influential man among their community of whom at present he knew nothing. He offered to lead the way, and Paul accepted of his guidance, followed by Eustace and his companions, the rough spoken-smuggler bringing up the rear—muttering and swearing at what he esteemed an unpardonable attack upon his consequence. The cave was capacious, containing several winding passages, through which they passed ere they reached the chamber in which the mass of lawless companions congregated. They soon were made aware of their contiguity to it by the rude sounds of boisterous mirth which issued forth, and on entering were struck by the size of the apartment, as well as by the number of persons assembled. The chamber was of vast size, and evidently owed its space and conveniences more to human labour than to nature. It presented an extraordinary mass of confusion—here and there, in corners and in open places, were piled bales, barrels, crates, implements of war of every shape, make, and description—masts, cordage, sails, even boats, all apparently in indiscriminate confusion; in various parts were slung hammocks, each containing its due proportion of bedding and blankets. Along the centre of the chamber ran a long table, supported on rude but massy trestles; around it, on benches, tubs, three-legged stools, and seats of all fashions, were seated a large number of rude ruffians rather than men; some shouting, some singing, many laughing, and all drinking. At the top of the board, reclining lazily upon a high backed chair, whose frame was of oak richly and beautifully carved, perhaps by "Anthony of Trent," was the acknowledged commander, leader, lord and master of this motley group; his dress was picturesque, much of the lawless apparent in it, though it aimed at better things—as the naval coat with massive epaulettes, the richly gold-embroidered waistcoat with long lappets, the high boots made of soft leather, would testify, but the red face and black moustachios, the blue and red striped cap which half hid his long curly black hair, and fell gracefully upon his left shoulder; his broad belt with a pair of handsomely chased pistols,

and his reckless carelessness, bespoke the pirate rather than the naval officer—the rude companion of rough fellows rather than the gentleman. The entry of our hero and his companions excited little or no attention among the revellers, and although the captain was aware of their entrance, he did not cast his eyes towards them until they stood before him, and then he threw his eyes indifferently upon them; but in an instant his whole aspect changed, his eye flashed, his brow knitted. He bent on them a penetrating look, and exclaimed with unconcealed surprise—

"Strangers!"

"Strangers!" echoed Paul, with an easy, careless tone, which surprised Eustace, being so different to that he usually wore; "aye, Captain Grayson—strangers we are, it's true, but friends also."

The captain sunk into apathy again, rather affected than real. He threw his leg over the arm of his chair, and leaning back, said—

"I am to suppose so by seeing you here; foes so weak as you are would hardly presume to come hither thus. It is blowing a hurricane, I am told—by what means did you fetch the cave?"

"In Peter Tiller's galley," said Harry Hardstaff.

"In what;" he cried, elevating his eye-brows.

"In Tiller's galley," repeated Harry.

"Why, where did you start from?" asked the captain, with surprise.

"From the creek," he returned, readily; "we were chased by the Curlew all the way."

"Ha! how did you elude her?" cried the captain, once more throwing off his air of indifference, and looking eagerly at Hardstaff.

"It is the work of this——" Harry was at a loss for a word: he hesitated for a moment, and then pointing to Paul, he continued, "he took the helm, dodged the Curlew, navigated all the channels and narrows hereaway, and though the Curlew run us up to the reef, and then sent out her jolly-boat after us, we gave her the slip, and here we are. Now I've made a clean log, captain: if you wants more, you must speak to him," he concluded, pointing to Paul.

"What has become of the Curlew's jolly-boat?" inquired the captain, eagerly.

"Swamped long ago, I'll wager," said Bill Grissoll, shaking his head; "I didn't expect to get here, I can tell you; if the Curlew's crew ain't gone to Davy Jones, natur' is more mysterious than I believed her to be."

"You are always a damned croaking raven," cried the captain, with disgust. "Ho! there, Jigger."

"Here sar," replied a mulatto, instantly approaching.

"Bear a hand and jump into the skiff that lies in the mouth of the cave—pull to the Gut, and see if you can discover anything of a jolly-boat with a crew of Philistines aboard of it."

"Iss, sar," replied the mulatto, and immediately disappeared.

"You must be a skilful steersman," said the captain to Paul, eyeing him attentively; "in the best weather it is blind steering to make this port. I have known many a boat find a hole in her bottom before she reached here, and no more wind astir than would blow a lady's curl from her cheek: perhaps Harry Hardstaff conned——"

"Not I, sir," interrupted Harry; "I don't want to sail under false colours, or get to windward with another man's merit; it's all his own doing—he run clean through the Gut when the spray was flying over us as thick as sleet in a snow storm, and had only one of his own mates at the time for a look-out."

"You know the points and bearings to this place well," said the captain, fixing his eyes scrutinizingly and sternly upon Paul, who neither bent beneath his gaze nor appeared at all embarrassed by it, but returned, coolly—

"Moderately well."

"I should say VERY well." uttered the captain, quickly; "I have been to and fro for several years in fair weather and foul, in daylight and in dark, but do not consider myself quite master of the points to bring a boat hither safely on such a night as this. You have served with us when younger—not recently, or I should have known your face? You do not answer," he added, as Paul preserved a silence when he put the last question to him.

"I am tired and hungry; I do not like answering questions upon an empty stomach," replied Paul, evasively.

"You shall be well fed," answered the captain, tartly, "or you shall be made food for fishes. When we have visitors who have the broad R on their rigging, it is our custom to know to what we are indebted for the favour of their presence. It is not my intention to depart from the usage in the present instance; you will perhaps pay out a little of your line, to save us from giving you a clean run into the other world."

"If I was an enemy, captain, could I have known the channels and soundings of this wild coast to this cave better than your own people, and even, by your own confession, better than yourself?" replied Paul, bluntly. Should I have given the Curlew a long chase in a cock-boat, in weather it was not safe to be anywhere but in a good offing or a snug bay—should I have come, with only four friends, among a hundred?"

"Spies take many ways to gain their ends," drily answered the captain.

"Possibly!" retorted Paul; "but they don't come among smugglers singly, rigged in his Majesty's slops, that every one may see who they are and what they come for. If I were a foe, it would have been as easy for me to have brought a dozen boats' crews as the scanty one I have steered here, instead of hazarding my own life and the lives of those accompanying me to give his Majesty's cruiser the slip."

The captain listened to him quietly, but gazed with his bright black eyes upon him, as if he would read him through. He paused a few minutes after Paul had ceased ere he spoke, and then he said, in measured terms—

"It is easier to trust and be deceived than to find in trusting the confidence has been well placed. I have been deceived by men as specious and plausible as yourself. I will know that you are a friend before I trust you as one: you came hither, if friendly, to join us, and therefore cannot object to take the oath which binds us to each other through life unto death."

"What if we have taken the oath?" said Paul.

"Then there can be no hesitation on your part to take it again, to rob me of my suspicions," returned the captain.

"I can satisfy you without the trouble," said Paul. "You shall have sign and countersign; and, if more, you shall have the message of Grantham Grierson, given with his own lips to me."

"When, and to whom?" interrupted the captain, eagerly.

"When your doubts subside, I shall not feel an objection to tell you," said Paul, coldly.

"I can compel you to tell me even before you have my word for safety," angrily cried the captain.

"How?" inquired Paul, coolly.

"How!" iterated the captain. "How! why by torturing you by means to which the rack is a miserably foolish engine. How! why I'd extract it from you as I would your wretched life, piecemeal."

"Neither threats or torture will make me speak if I do not choose," observed Paul, still preserving his air of cool indifference; "and look you, captain, I am something prepared for resistance, if foul play is shown me." He drew a small pair of exquisitely finished pistols from his belt as he spoke. "A single word or look from you to one of your fellows, for the purpose of doing me harm, would be sufficient to ensure your destruction. I have a quick eye and a ready hand; I have a heart, too, to stand by me in need. To move a limb or finger threateningly at me, or those with me, would cause me instantly to dispatch a bullet at thee with an aim which has never failed. I can answer for the bore of these weapons being true. I have tried them; and, mark me, I should think little of being cut down by your fellows when I had had my revenge of you—and have it I would, before they could lay a cutlass upon me. Now, Captain Grayson, the message I have for you is important to your interests; give me your promise for our safety, and Grantham Grierson's words shall be yours; withhold it, and you shall not have a letter of them, but he will know of their non-delivery, why they were withheld, and will revenge me amply."

During Paul's speech, the countenance of the captain assumed many hues; it waxed red and pale by turns, purple and brick-brown, and when he finished it was hard to say which colour had the mastery. He did not immediately reply to Paul's words, but kept staring at him with a ferocity of expression which would have made a weak heart tremble. By degrees, however, it faded away, and with a change of expression, as if some new light had struck him, he exclaimed—

"You and I have met before—I am sure of it; I knew not your face until that curl of the lip you gave but now brought to my recollection a deed of other days. We served boys together in the brig Kircoobree,* Mr. Younger, owner, bound from Kircoobree to Whitehaven: you went then by the name of Johnny Paul."

"It is my name now," replied Paul; "you are right. I have, however, no remembrance of your face."

"Likely enough!" he cried, with a laugh; "a new name, an African sun, and a pair of mustachios, is enough to alter a handsomer face than Sandy Sanderson's."

"And are you he?" exclaimed Paul, with astonishment.

"The very man, sins and all," he replied; "nothing better than when you knew me, and, I much fear, considerably worse. I was always a racketty rascal when we were together, but never criminal; I wish I could say as much now—but moralizing is of little use. Sit you down, you and your friends—you are safe with me. Ho, there, Guttle! let us have some eatables here! We'll soon have a good landfall for you, and plenty of the best spirits in the universe to wash it down with—some of the real "lackremy crisste," as your

* Kirkcudbright.

foreigners call it. Now, Guttle, bear a fist, you scoundrel, and let us be raked fore and aft with the best in the grubbery stowage. Now, Jigger, what cheer?" he added, addressing the mulatto he had despatched to see what had become of the jolly-boat of the Curlew, as he saw him making his way towards him; "now, you dark-skinned luff, what have you made out, eh?"

"Noting, sar; he make out noting but spray, sar, like shower ob hail, rain, an' snow, sar; him pull a skiff into de surf, but him soon half full a water, sar, and so him pull back agen."

"You cowardly scoundrel, you should have pulled out into the grip—you could see nothing, you know, you black vagabond, on this side the Gut," roared the captain.

"Den he mus' do him wid a boat bottom up ards, sar," returned the mulatto: "no craf' lib in such wedder but a devil's, ho sure a' dat."

"I'm sure that you shall have a rope's-ending if you don't start at once, pull out beyond Hell's Grip, and see whether the jolly-boat has landed, whether she's swamped, or whether she has returned to the cutter."

"I'm tink her swamped, sar," said the mulatto, in reply to the order.

"Why so?" demanded the captain.

"Cos, sar, a sea make right ober a cliff, sar, and a vessel now on a rock and a firing signal of distress," replied the mulatto.

"What the devil's all this—a vessel on the rocks—what is she?" cried the captain, eagerly.

'Me no make her out, sar—spray tick as a mainsail of a seventy-four, sar—no see troo 'em 'less a eye make ole troo a stone wall."

"It must be the Curlew," cried Paul: "I expected her captain would run her too close into the land; he must have a good sea-boat to claw off such a lee shore as this on such a night."

The report of a gun now reached the ears of all, and the howl of the blast followed it, filling the cavern with its mournful sigh. After a moment's pause, when even the rude mirth of the boisterous half-drunken men around ceased, the captain said—

"It is an awful night, it must be: I have been in here, Paul, when there has been some of the heaviest gales blowing, but never heard I the wind so high up this cavern before."

'What do you mean to do?" exclaimed Paul, rising from a seat he had taken near the captain.

"What! why sit here and drink, to be sure," he replied, laughing.

"And know there are some fellow-creatures at hand, perishing, without moving to assist them?" he cried.

"Why you wouldn't have me hazard my life to save the fellows who would hang me if they caught me," exclaimed the captain, as if he thought it a stretch of humanity rather beyond his accomplishing.

"The moment of danger and death, such as this, is superior to every other consideration," ejaculated Paul, earnestly. "Grayson, by the recollection of the one deed you have alluded to in our boyhood, I conjure you to lend a hand to save these poor fellows. Would you not bless the hand of an enemy if it rescued you from a dreadful death? Come, you have plenty of hands at your command to aid us; be noble, pipe them to the service."

"You know the fable, Paul, of the man who carried home the dying viper," exclaimed the captain; "I do not desire to be stung by those I save from death."

"Nor can you, if you exercise common prudence: a bandage may prevent eyes from being too curious respecting the approaches, and the good deed may stand your friend when you may well need it. Will you follow me, or shall I go alone?"

"Heave a-head with you!" cried the captain—"I'll do your bidding. Ho, there! sea-horses, away, there!" he shouted. "Idlers and roisterers, away, there!"

A large party of men sprung from their seats at this call, and hastened towards the mouth of the cave. A heavy sea-boat was speedily put into requisition, and manned with twelve stout rowers, the captain taking his place in the stern-sheets: a second was also brought from a nook, of which Paul took the command, accompanied by Eustace, Gasket, Andrew, and half-a-dozen stout fellows. Scarcely knowing the service upon which they were bound, the men gave way at the urgent command of their captain, and the space between the mouth of the cave and the narrow opening which led direct to the dangerous channels was speedily passed over; then they found themselves battling with the wind and waves in fierce contention, and so much themselves the sport of the furious elements, that, although they were well supplied with torches, they were unable to see a yard beyond the bow of the boat. The flaming brands were gradually extinguished by the falling showers of water, and the terrific blasts of wind which succeeded each other in rapid succession. It was in vain they endeavoured to discover traces of the jolly-boat. The vessel in distress, too, had ceased firing, and, save themselves, there seemed no appearance of living thing near that wild spot; they, however, still stood on some distance with much perseverance and considerable personal risk, but it was evident that they must either return or meet with the same fate which, they concluded, had befallen the crew of the jolly-boat. Paul had been the first to advance, and his little vessel led the way. Gasket was stationed in the bow of the boat as a look-out, and just as Paul, convinced of the futility of his errand, with such fearful odds to contend with, was about to give it up, Gasket shouted—

"Boat bottom up'ards, dead a-head!"

Another stroke of the oars brought them in contact with it. A man was clinging to the keel, all but insensible; he was grasped by Gasket and hauled into the boat, utterly exhausted. To put questions to him was useless; Paul, therefore, in the hope of picking up others, kept on still; but even his dauntless heart was convinced that certain destruction would ensue further progress, and listening to the oft repeated shouts of Captain Grayson for him to return, he replied to it assentingly, and turned the boat's head in the direction of the cavern; a quarter of an hour found them once more in the place from whence they started.

The man whom they had rescued was carried carefully into the cavern, and placed before a wood fire which blazed upon the ground in one corner of the rude apartment, and when the light, which the fire threw around, fell upon his face, several of the men by whom he was surrounded at once declared him to be Geoffrey Smith, or, as the reader better knows him, Jasper Chough.

The surprise of Paul, when he heard the name, was equalled by the anxiety of Eustace, who looked with feelings almost of torture upon the villain who had subjected the maiden he loved to outrages, he feared, of the worst description; he felt almost mad: the sympathy excited in his breast for the half-drowned man as a stranger gave place to a wolfish desire of revenge, to a fear that death would rob him of all chance of retaliating the injuries his beloved had endured from this scoundrel. To have him thus in his grasp, and be denied the power of extorting a confession of his guilt and punishing him for it, worked him almost to a pitch of frenzy; exclamations escaped his lips, which Paul easily perceived would excite suspicions in the bystanders that might prove inimical to their safety, and he endeavoured to draw Eustace from the spot; but he was not to be diverted from the object of his hate and vengeance, and with a lack of prudence, the offspring of the bitterest animosity, he kept close to him, breathing muttered vows of the deadliest determination to avenge Florence. Several of his exclamations caught the ears of those who were endeavouring to restore Jasper, and they fixed their dark eyes scowlingly upon him; his garb and words augured him little of a friend, and there were plenty of knives ready to find a sheath in his breast if they discovered him to be the foe they rather suspected him to be. It was in vain that Paul gripped his arm, even whispered to him to keep a bridle on his tongue and actions, if he would not lose every chance of accomplishing his wishes, as well as life itself; he seemed lost to everything but a sense of the presence of him who had carried away Florence; he could barely restrain himself from springing on him, and consummating what the elements had but half done. His eyes, like balls of fire, were fixed upon him immoveably; his brows were buried over them until they seemed to touch his cheek bones; his teeth were set, his hands clenched, and his whole frame exhibiting the sharpest rancour to the prostrate being before him. While urging him by secret endeavours to retire, Paul felt a hand laid upon his shoulder; he turned, it was that of the captain of the greater part of the rude beings around him.

"Your companion knows the commander of the Scud?" he whispered in a low tone.

"Why should you think so?" inquired Paul, hesitatingly.

"A man does not need the sun for a binnacle light to read as much," he returned, rather satirically. "Smith has done him some ill turn, it is plain, and you have all come here with him to pay off the score—I see it all. Paul, you are no fool—you never was when you were but a young luff; but did you ever know a man, who owed a tiger a spite, to clap all sail on, and run into a den to pay it, where there were a hundred others? You saved my life twice; I owe you a good turn, and will venture something to do it. Now, take my advice, get your mates and yourself out of this as fast as you can; there is a passage from here up into the island, which Jigger shall show you. I shall risk something in letting you depart thus, but that is my affair: be prepared, when I give you the signal, to slip your cables, and waste not an instant in shoving off."

"What if my friend refuses to come?" asked Paul, who saw little use in disguising the truth which the captain had thus readily jumped at.

"Gag him, bind him, and carry him off by force; the fool will be knocked on the head in a few minutes as it is, if he continues his present display," returned the captain: "my signal will be, to tell you that Jigger will show you where you can turn in for the night. Farewell! God bless you; when next we meet, may it be under better circumstances."

Paul returned his pressure of the hand, and the next minute the captain hastened to another part of the cavern, while Paul essayed once more to draw Eustace from the spot.

"You will ruin all our hopes, by thus obstinately remaining," he said, in a low energetic voice. "You can do nothing as he now lies, surrounded by his friends. Wait patiently until you can be sure of ascertaining what has become of the maiden, then we shall know how to act. Be ruled, sir—come away!"

It was with much reluctance that he would suffer himself to be moved, and he had scarcely retired three steps ere a sudden buzz announced the restoration of Jasper to life. Paul would have dragged Eustace on, but he stopped instantly, and seemed rooted to the spot, fascinated by what he beheld. Jasper was on his knees, his face as white as ashes, his eyes rolling wildly to and fro, and his head moving from side to side as if following some dreaded object, but apparently quite oblivious of all that surrounded him; he unclosed his parched lips, and exclaimed in a hoarse, guttural tone—

"Legions of hell haunt me! I knew Nehemie was hanged; I heard his screams; I saw his ghastly face grin distortedly until it became black and livid; I heard his last shivering shriek, and yet he sat on the bow of the boat and gibbered and mocked at me like a fiend; and she stood by his side howling at me—she pointed to heaven and to hell! Was she dead too? Can the living link with the dead to drag me to perdition! She stood on the breaker that swamped us; she seized me by the hair of my head, and held me up, screaming in my ears that my doom was not yet fulfilled; she sat on the boat's keel, and taunted me; she rode like a witch of Norway on the crest of every leaping wave, and cursed me! Where is she now—where—where?"

He looked shudderingly round him, covered his trembling hands over his eyes, and groaned aloud.

"His brain wanders," exclaimed one of the men supporting him; "give me some moonshine, and I'll pour it down his throat."

A comrade, as requested, gave him some brandy, and he held it to Jasper's mouth; he drank with avidity, leaving off but to take breath, and then drank again.

"He likes it," observed one of the bystanders, with a laugh.

"It's few as don't," responded another, with a shake of the head, signifying

that he was uttering an incontestible truth; "brandy's seducing drink, and that's the truth."

"Yes," returned the other, grinning, "the spirit will mix with the salt water in his lower hold and make uncommon good grog."

Jasper, after a few wild glances, seemed to understand where he was, which Eustace observing, made an advance, as if to approach him; but Paul, grasping him firmly by the collar, held him back, saying in an under tone--

"You trusted your life with me to-night, Mr. Prior—trust your honour to my keeping now. I promise you, you shall have fair chance of being revenged on yon wretch, but do not madly throw away all chance of life and succour to your lady."

"Do as you will, Paul, now," replied Prior, "I am too excited I know to act with judgment: but whatever the consequence to myself, though a dreadful death a thousand times awaited me, I will be revenged on that execrable scoundrel. God of heaven! if he should have brought her in the boat with him and she has perished!"

"Have no such fear, Mr. Prior, be more calm," exclaimed Paul, as Eustace, roused almost to madness by his thoughts, made towards Jasper again, as if he would rush upon him; "she is safe, Churleigh is the man who has carried her away—this fellow knows no more where she is than you do. We will find out what has become of Churleigh, and then take measures to be revenged on both. We are observed; for your own sake, and for the maiden's, be cautious. Follow me."

Eustace, with much unwillingness, suffered himself to be persuaded, and retired to another part of the cavern, where Andrew and Gasket were sitting, discussing the meal from which they had been unceremoniously summoned to attend the Curlew's people. As soon as Andrew could get private speech with Eustace—for, with so many curious eyes, and open ears directed towards them, it was no easy matter to accomplish—he ceased the nods and winkings which he had rather largely been dealing in, and said with much earnestness—

"That ugly, long-mugged, white-gill'd varmint we hauled from Davy Jones' grappling irons, is the very howdacious vagabone that convoyed me out of my path to Grasmere; the very man as I was telling you on. He that Matty says laid his damned piratical hands on Miss Florence, made prize of her, and—"

"We know all," interrupted Paul, cautioning him silence. "Say no more for the present, but look to your weapons, and see they are ready to use when you want them, though the need may come as sudden as a flash of lightning. We may find it harder work to get away from here than we did to come; I know how to read the looks of these rascals; we have had too many of their glances, and there has been too much whispering together, to let us depart from here easily."

"They be d——d," ejaculated Gasket, "there doesn't seem one of 'em that would stand a lee-lurch; I wouldn't be afeard to fight my way through 'em all, black muzzled as many of 'em are. If they comes any of their palaver with us and wants to run athwart our fore-foot, why I'll side out with a bend, and if I falls foul of any one, let 'em keep a sharp look out a-head: one of us may be run down—I don't mean it should be myself."

"No one doubts your courage, Gasket," observed Paul; "let us see whether you have as much prudence. A bullet may do sad work, though a scoundrel or a coward discharge it; it may be brave and daring in a sloop to fight a seventy-four, but it cannot be productive of success. See nothing, hear nothing, likely to disturb your comfort, until I bid you out pistol and then make the best use of your time and bravery."

"It's for you to give the word, Paul," exclaimed Gasket, "we are ready to do your bidding."

"It is well," returned Paul, "await my return here, yonder is Captain Grayson—I will exchange a word with him respecting our berths here, and then return. Mr. Prior, be prudent; upon your caution rest our hopes of success."

"I shall remember," said Eustace, thoughtfully, and sunk into a seat by the side of Gasket; while Paul hastened to the captain. On reaching him he took him on one side, and uttered in a low tone—

"Sanderson, you partly guessed our errand, but have mistaken the person. Old Jack Churleigh has carried off the betrothed of the young lieutenant who accompanies me: his purpose in doing so, I can hardly guess at, unless it is to make money by her ransom. Know you aught of him? can you put us upon his track?"

"Paul, you ought to know more of our rules than to ask me such a boon; are we not sworn not to disclose the retreat of a brother to any one who would seek it for his destruction?" returned the captain.

"You can tell me if he has been in the cavern since yesternight, and if he has, whether he had the young female with him;" said Paul urgently.

"So much I may answer," replied Sanderson, "he has not been here, but there are those in the cave who accompanied him, and to whom he made known his route. He will not go out of the island for some little time; it is not very large—a strict search might unkennel a more cunning fox than he is, especially if he has halted midway between Ramsey and Douglas," he added with a significant smile.

"I understand you," returned Paul. "I thank you—I shall know how to make use of it. One thing more, I have observed your people watch us, since the arrival of Smith, with suspicious glances; there have been some communings and some threatening looks, foreboding little friendship to us. Are we likely to be intercepted in our departure?"

"Your friend the lieutenant is not the man to be trusted where a rigid face and a cold indifference is wanted; he wants a little intercourse with the Indians, to teach him how to affect a calmness he does not feel. He has betrayed himself—he must take the consequences!" returned the captain.

"We who accompany him will stand or fall by him," observed Paul, laconically.

"Which I call little better than downright madness," said the captain, "a waste of life for nothing; but you were always obstinate—it is of no use arguing with you. I will see what can be done; my power does not extend very far, but as far as it goes it is yours. Be careful, for your own sake; remember you are over a mine, a spark will explode it. If the fellows have marked you down as spies, they will be very hard of belief in thinking you aught else; and as in their opinion a knife or a bullet is the best mode of settling any doubt, to suspect foul play from you is to whip a blade into your ribs. Now back to your friends, they want as cool a head as yours to keep them safe. Stay, what said Grantham Grierson to you—a message he gave you important to my interests to know, you said; let me have it."

"His words were these," exclaimed Paul quickly. "That eyes and hands were sharp in Cumberland and Westmoreland, that tongues wagged as freely there as they did in the cavern, telling tales which were never meant for the ears they were poured into. That all the Philistines were not in his Majesty's service, and a quick wit and searching eye might find the truth of this without going further than the rendezvous."

"Was that all?" said the captain, as our hero paused.

"Is it not enough?" demanded Paul.

"Quite," he returned. "I merely asked to know if there was aught else to follow—any order."

"None at present, said Paul; "his orders will be despatched to you shortly by other means; this message was a warning to you."

"Why did he entrust you with it?" inquired the captain.

"We met by accident in the port of London," responded Paul; "he inquired my destination, I told him home; he knew that I could take the island on my way home; he needed a trusty person to deliver his message; he was satisfied he could place faith in me; he tried me as a boy, or he would never have taught me so truly the navigation of this blind place; and thus he asked me the favour which I consented to perform. It was my intention to have come hither alone. The chase which the Curlew gave us (for if we had brought-to for them, we should have been much delayed, and therefore we run away from them), compelled us to put in here for safety; you will see, therefore, we came not as spies, and being suffered to depart unmolested, shall not remember whate'er we have seen or heard."

"I am satisfied," said the captain, "I hope the people will be. Away to your place, let us not be seen too long conferring together; even that may tell against you."

Paul took him at his word, and departed to his companions, with whom he remained until a late hour; at last Sanderson gave the signal agreed upon, and the mulatto stood ready to show them through the intricacies of the cavern to the secret opening above. They obeyed it. Paul had to seize Eustace firmly, and almost drag him with him, for his eyes had found out Jasper, and darted the fiercest looks of hate upon him. It happened, unfortunately, that in their progress they had to pass close to a group of men who had marked them most suspiciously; they were surrounding Jasper. Paul had noted them, and 'twas his wish to pass them without exciting their notice, but Eustace hung heavily upon him, seeking some pretence, however small, to attack Jasper; and as they arrived close to the men the opportunity was granted to him. The smugglers extended their circle until they nearly inclosed the small party. Dark looks were immediately fastened upon them, and the fellows stood firm, evidently determining to bar their further progress. Among them was the man who had accosted Paul on his landing with such rude language, and no sooner had he and his companions approached him than he exclaimed, with a bitter laugh—

"These are the Jews I told you on, mayhaps the Philistines; who knows but they are Philistines," he added fiercely; "and if they are, why shouldn't we give 'em the benefit of the law?"

"Who do you call Philistines? you half-cobbed whole swab," exclaimed Andrew, wrathfully; "whose a Jew? you sneaking lubber's loblolly boy. Dam'me, if you call me a Jew agen, I'll spoil the shape of your figure-head, ugly as it is, you see calf, I will!"

Andrew looked as if he would, and as if he could keep his word. He advanced close to the fellow, and his broad chest and brawny limbs not looking like playthings, the man gave a little ground—more disposed to retort with his tongue than with his fists; ere, however, he could reply, one of the men fixing his eye upon Lucky George, said loudly—

"If you ain't Philistines, here is one that is."

"Do you mean to say I'm a Philistine?" roared Gasket, stepping before George, and nearly running the fellow down by pushing against him.

"You all are," shouted two or three voices together; "Down with the Philistines! down with 'em! Out with knives, and clear the decks of Philistines!"

There was an instant glitter of blades in the air, and a rush made to the little party. Both Gasket and Andrew flung their two opponents to the ground, and the latter got possession of a cutlass, which was brandished in the hand of one near him, by twisting it with amazing dexterity from his grasp. Eustace sprung at Jasper, and Paul drew a brace of pistols for instant use, when a voice cried loudly—

"Hold! hold! down there, you sea dogs! down, I say. By the devil's blazing hearth, I'll send a bullet through the skull of him who strikes another blow. Down, I say! Who is commander here? Am I? or have each knave of ye a will of your own to do as ye list, in defiance of my command?"

With some grumbling the men held their hands, and Sanderson stepped authoritatively into the centre of the group; he looked around him with a frowning brow, and then said sternly—

"What means this sudden brawl? Have ye lost your tongues, ye that were but now howling like wolves," he added, as no one spoke.

"They call us Philistines," exclaimed Andrew, indignantly, "the pirat—"

"Your men suspect us to be spies," interrupted Paul, as the honest tar was about to favour them with his opinion of the nature of their occupation; "you can undeceive them, captain."

"They wants to get the weathergage of you, captain," roared one of the men. "Here, Rough-and-ready Bill says he knows one of 'em to be a regular built Philistine, always cruising under a pennant; and ain't all on 'em cutter-rigged with the broad R on 'em? They're spies as clear as Snafield on a fine day. Our laws says, death to all spies, and I says down with the Philistines! Hurrah, lads! down with them! down with—"

A tremendous blow from the but-end of a pistol, dealt by Sanderson, alighting on his forehead, precipitated the brawling ruffian to the ground, and stopped his noisy clamour.

"That's my law, when my orders are disobeyed," exclaimed the captain; "you may thank the devil or any other saint that you did not have a bullet instead of the butt-end. It is time enough when I give the word to out knife, but not before. Step forward, Rough-and-ready Bill, and let me hear what you have to say."

A fellow with an aspect which presented a singular compound of brutishness and cunning, with features composed of the peculiarities of several nations, issued from the body of his companions, and said, in a gruff voice, as he pointed to Lucky George—

"That ere long land bird is a Philistine, I knows, 'cos he grabbed me once; he's the werry one we calls the 'nabbing skirk.' He's made prizes of more of our people and more tubs than any Philistine in the service, and his death's been sworn on every pint o' coast hereaway."

"Are you sure of this?" said the captain.

"I'll take my oath——"

"No!" returned the captain, sternly; "we know you as lying Bill quite as well as by Rough-and-ready. You must give me proof."

"He's got a scar on his left arm, where I cut him with a knife when he took me," said Bill.

"Let me see your left arm," said the captain to Lucky George.

He turned up the sleeve of his coat and laid his arm bare. There was no mark.

"It is on his right, then," said Bill, on finding his mistake; "shew your right arm."

"Not I," replied George, coolly; "you should have named the right first. I'll not show my arms again to satisfy any of you. If I am the man you assert me to be, why are you the only one that knows me?"

"I know you," exclaimed Jasper, suddenly advancing and fixing his eyes eagerly upon him.

"And I know you," cried Andrew, as instantly confronting him. Jasper started back with surprise and dismay; he had not recognised Andrew before, and the sudden sight of him raised remembrances by no means pleasant. He was, however, surrounded by friends—men who would support him, but who would not view with eyes of satisfaction and display of apprehension, not to say cowardice, on the part of one they believed to be a daring spirit. This speculation flashed through his mind like lightning, and restored his self-possession: he bent a hardy gaze upon the sailor, and said—

"Where have you known me? By what do you know me?"

"I know'd you first afore I went my last voyage," said Andrew, speaking rapidly; "I know'd you next when I was homeward bound. I trusted to your conning, and you run me right out of my latitude, playing me foul like the thieving Malays in a captain's cabin; and I'd a known more of you if you hadn't have parted company with me like a jib blown from the bolt-ropes in a gale, when that old likeness of father Neptune, a grizzle-jawed, tow-wigged, old anchent hove in sight, and carried all sail in chase of you. I knows you now by the long-leached, chany junk cut of your jib; but with all I knows of you, there's no good coiled away along with it."

"You know me by our meeting upon the mountain, when you had stolen the maiden from beneath your father's roof, having murdered your brother," said Lucky George, in a quick voice; "I bound you hand and foot, and left you in the cavern you had used for other purposes, unconnected with the interests of this community."

"Yes, and its well for you you haven't the young lady now," exclaimed Andrew, ere George had ceased, "or you would have gone below before this, like the lead in a hundred fathom water; but we knows where she is, and who's got her, and it won't be long afore we have her agen, provided we get clear of you, which we means to do if we can."

Jasper looked at him with a glance of lightning—a sudden thought flashed through his mind ; he hesitated for a minute, and then turning to the assembled men, who had now gathered round, to a number exceeding a hundred, he exclaimed, in a voice he tried to render loud, but he was not sufficiently recovered to accomplish—

"Are the crew of the Scud here?"

"Ay, ay!" was repeated from mouth to mouth.

"And ready to obey my orders?"

A reply in the affirmative was unanimously given, and then he said, to the unequivocal surprise of all present—

"It is my belief they are not spies, and I command those belonging to my vessel to suffer them to pass unmolested."

"I agree with you, Captain Smith," cried Sanderson, eagerly, and then turning a fierce gaze around him, he said—"Let him who says nay stand forward."

A complete silence followed his words, which, observing no one break, he took Paul by the hand, and shaking it, said—

"Farewell! no words; you are safe. Away at once. I know we may trust *you*."

"And I will answer for my companions," responded Paul.

"It is enough," exclaimed Sanderson. "Jigger," he cried to the mulatto, who still stood holding the torch, "heave a-head with the light!" He then waved his hand to our hero and his friends, who all turned to depart, save Eustace, and he walked up to Jasper and said, in a voice which was heard by nearly all there—

"Jasper Chough, look on me. I am Eustace Prior: if you are not a coward as well as scoundrel, we shall meet again."

Jasper's eyes opened to an unusual width as he heard his words: he gazed at him as an object of extreme wonder: he scanned him slowly from head to foot, and his whole frame seemed to swell and dilate, as he, with a smile of mingled scorn, triumph, and hate, replied—

"We shall."

He turned his back on him as he spoke, and Eustace, with a proud bearing, though burning for instant revenge, followed his companions.

The mulatto led the way through various winding passages and up flights of steps until he reached a small chamber cut in the rock, and then turning to the party he was leading, he said—

"We stop here."

"Why?" asked Paul.

"Cos 'em hab 'em eyes blind, sar,"

A shrill whistle brought two men in masks, armed with cutlasses and pistols, and one of them told the little party they must, from motives of safety to the band, submit to be blindfolded ere they left the entrance to the cavern. Perceiving that prudence rendered the precaution necessary, they all assented, and when the operation was completed, each to his surprise felt his arms suddenly seized, a rope in an instant passed round them and made fast. In anticipation of foul play resistance was offered, but upon the strong assurance of the men who bound them that no ill was intended them they bore their bonds quietly, and once more, under the direction of fresh guides, set forward. Not a word transpired from any of the party, save when their conductors directed them how to proceed when an inclination or depression in their path required an alteration in their mode of progress. After much serpentine perambulation, they felt the cool air of heaven blow upon their faces; they were not, however, suffered to stop, but were hurried forward at an accelerated pace, the guides urging them on by complaining that the time allotted for directing them had expired, and there still remained some distance to traverse. The little party obeyed their request, moving on rapidly, until the rugged nature of the ground compelled them to exercise more caution than before. Then Paul made an observation to one of the guides, but not receiving an answer he repeated it, until he discovered that they had either decamped or pertinaciously refused to answer him: he struggled with his bonds, and found they were loose; he was not long, therefore, in removing the bandage from his eyes, and found that the guides had vanished. He released his friends immediately, and though they strained their eyes in every direction, they could perceive no trace of their conductors. They were in a gloomy spot on a considerable elevation. The wind had lessened its fury, but still howled and whistled as it flew boisterously past them. A solitary star might be seen here and there looking brighter from the gloom which surrounded it, and the brightness with which it displayed its twinkling light. The thundering dash of the surf, as it broke upon the beach, and against the "beetling cliffs," like distant reports of heavy artillery, told them they were still near the mighty sea. The consideration now to be discussed, was how to proceed. The slight clue which Paul had obtained from Sanderson respecting Churleigh was all they had to guide them, and he hesitated whether in the darkness, with but a faint knowledge of the locality, it was advisable to continue the pursuit of Chnrleigh, or make for Ramsey, rest a few hours, gather whatever information it was possible to obtain, which could be of service to them, and then start on fresh. But Eustace would listen to no counsel which proposed desisting from his purpose, even for a few hours, to take the necessary repose required by nature. He had upon him the desire to save his beloved, like a death thirst—and would know no rest, no slumber, no cessation of exertion, until he had rescued her.

"I know," he said, in answer to Paul's proposition, "that ye have not the same incentive to exertion that I have; I know the feeling which lifts me above fatigue or exhaustion dwells not in your breast, and I would not be so selfish as to wish ye to labour beyond what nature can endure, for me. I will therefore go on alone; you can return to Ramsey, and follow me when you are rested and refreshed.."

There was not one of them would agree to this; and the conference ended by their coming to the determination to keep with him, and at once go in pursuit of Churleigh.

A ridge of mountains, composed chiefly of rocks of mica, slate, and clay slate, crosses the Island of Man from north-east to south-west. Many of them are of considerable height, and congregate mostly in the centre of the Island. It was in one of the passes of these mountains, near where the high road from Douglas to Peel is intersected by the one from Castletown to Ramsey, in the vicinity of the tumulus at Tinwald, that Paul hoped to fall in with Churleigh; such at least were the hopes raised by what had fallen from Sanderson, but despite his information, he had some misgiving that he had taken his station nearer the coast. There was no time, however, to waste in hesitation, and he promptly decided upon proceeding in the direction the captain had named. He led the way and the rest followed, endeavouring to forget their fatigue in expectation of success, and in discussing the scene they had recently been actors in, striving to find some solution for the extraordinary behaviour of one whom they had expected to find most resentful; but their speculations, though conducted with much ingenuity, did not bring them to the true cause.

Jasper's first intention, on discovering them in the cavern, and ascertaining their object, was, if he possessed still any influence over the band, to cause their immediate destruction; and it is doubtful whether he would not, if he had persevered in his ruthless purpose, have succeeded, despite Captain Grayson's efforts in their behalf. Security being naturally the most important consideration of the band, they were likely to throw off allegiance to any leader whose acts were calculated to compromise their safety; and although Grayson, not an older man than Jasper, possessed the greatest power, he would in all probability have been in a minority in extending protection to our hero and his companions, if Jasper had not so suddenly coincided with him, and gave his assent to their departure. His reason for thus strangely altering his first determination was his unexpected discovery of their being aware that Churleigh had possession of Florence, and were in pursuit of him when they took refuge in the cave. In an instant a plan flashed through his mind for securing the maiden, and inflicting summary vengeance upon all the rest. He concluded that by setting Prior, Paul, and their companions, on Churleigh, they would hunt him down, rescue Florence from him, probably at the expense of the old man's life; for he knew his resolute and vindictive nature would not permit him to yield up the maiden without a deadly struggle to retain her. He would then be at hand with a party of the most desperate of his followers to tear her from the hands of Prior, and murder him, Paul, and all the rest—make the best of his way on board the Scud with his prize, and sail to some island in the Mediterranean. Churleigh was too great a favourite with the band, and possessed too much of their confidence, for him to even propose to the lawless ruffians companioning him that they should lend him their assistance to slay the "old tiger;" they would have bid him, if they had a quarrel, fight it out—and would not have interfered, or laid a hand upon one whom they knew had for years served their interests well and faithfully; otherwise Jasper would have urged them to slay Eustace and his companions, and backed by a party each more ruthless than himself, have sought out Churleigh, and subjected him to a most terrible fate. Prevented, however, from doing the latter from the cause ascribed, he hit upon the contrivance which, if carried out as he expected and as appeared probable, would successfully accomplish his base designs.

Paul, who conducted the party, was in the act of striking into a by-path which would bring him and his friends by a near route to the spot where he hoped to encounter Churleigh, when he heard a loud hail in the rear. He turned his head quickly, as did the rest of his companions, and discovered a man running swiftly towards them. They paused and waited until he came up, and when he arrived, found him to be Bill Grissoll; he was out of breath and spoke in broken sentences.

"You have made good way," he said; "I gave chase to you almost as soon as you left us, and bore down hard after you, but you had gathered such headway, I began to think I should never run you under my lee; however, I have—"

"And what is your object in doing so?" interrupted Paul, hastily.

"Why, to ask a question or so," returned Bill, readily; "first, you see, you said if I and Harry Hardstaff stood by you, you would do something in the shape of reward. Now you knows it was the turn of a vane that you wasn't made Mother Carey's chickens on, which wasn't from anything I or Harry let slip, as you—"

"All this we are aware of," interrupted Prior, impatiently; "you shall not go unrewarded. What else have you to communicate?"

"Why this ere," said Bill, a little vexed at the shortness with which he was taken up; "I heerd you say you wanted to know where old Jack Churleigh had coiled himself away."

"I do—can you tell me?" cried Prior, eagerly.

"Why, then, I think I can," replied Grissoll, without evincing any of the eagerness to unfold his intelligence which he had at first displayed.

"Then out with it quickly," exclaimed Paul.

"Why that's another thing," he replied, with a jeering laugh.

"How about the 'speche?' There was a reward promised for bringing you to bear on old Jack's anchorage."

"Name it, and you shall have it," cried Prior.

"What down in my fist!" ejaculated Bill Grissoll, "without any standing off and on—no box-hauling?"

"Now, this instant," replied Eustace, drawing his purse from his pocket.

"Well, then," he said, eyeing the purse with a most covetous expression, "a brace of real golden shiners, one for I and one for Harry, would be about putting the helm amidships."

"Here they are," returned Eustace, producing a couple of guineas, and placing them in his hands. "Now unfold his hiding place."

"Well, you see," he exclaimed, pocketing the gold, and buttoning his pocket up carefully after placing it in its recesses, "while Jigger was convoying you from 'the rondavoo,' I gets along side a messmate, one Jem Junker—a real good fellow Jim is: you don't know Jem? He had a Brummagem father and a chaney mother—he was born on the line, and so—"

"We want to hear none of the history of your messmate—tell us what he has to do with Churleigh," cried Paul, sternly.

"Well, it's what Jem Junker said to me that I am going to heave out," said Grissoll. "He was talking about you and your mates, and was a wondering, as we all were, why Captain Smith should let you sheer off without firing a shot, when he ups and says, 'Aha!' says he, 'if old Jack Churleigh was here,' says he, 'he wouldn't ha' let 'em,' says he, 'clear out,' says he, 'without scuttling, or keelhauling, or cobbing 'em,' says he, 'or something of that 'ere sort,' says he. 'Ah,' says I, 'you have it clear of kinks there,' says I; 'but where *is* old Jack?' says I—'cos, don't you see, I wanted to overhaul his berth for you;" he accompanied the last remark by giving Eustace a dig with his thumb in the side, and winking his eye most knowingly at him. Eustace, however, was not disposed to receive this familiarity with complaisance, and, therefore, requested him not to repeat his pleasantry, but continue his story, abbreviating as much as possible, that no time might be lost in arriving at the point most important to be disclosed. Grissoll professed a disgust at any one being given to palavering, and proceeded to show that he was not, until Paul, in a rage, cried out for him instantly to disclose the lurking place of the old man, or refund the money, and take himself away, without delaying them longer.

The talk of returning the gold had the effect of quickening Grissoll's tongue, and he said directly—

"Well, Jem Junker says to me, says he, 'Why I made the trip from the creek to Ramsey along with the old man; he'd got a young lass with him,' says he, 'small and trim,' says he, 'like the spars of the Scud,' says he. 'Well, this young gal was as unhappy as a ship in irons. Heave and Paul,' says he; 'how she did pipe her eye; her lee scuppers run salt water,' says he, like them of a schooner in a gale that's shipped a heavy sea. Hows'ever, nobody said nothing to her, 'cos Churleigh's business was nobody else's, as they'd ha' found if any one had a signalled him about her, and so you see,' says he, 'we axed no questions, but put 'em both ashore at Ramsey, and run for the cave. But afore we shov'd off,' says he, Churleigh says to me, 'if Captain Smith should ax about me and a young lady,' says he, 'tell him if he looks he'll find us at Spanish Head.'"

"At Spanish Head!" cried Paul and Eustace together.

"Ay, ay," replied Grissoll, "that's the place. I made Jem repeat it, that I mightn't shoal when I was fetching the point in my story; and when I found he had veered out of his line till the glass had run out, and he cried 'stop,' I parted company with him and made sail a'ter you."

"It is as I suspected," exclaimed Paul; "Churleigh has hugged the coast. Come, Mr. Prior, we will bear away at once for Spanish Head. I know its situation well."

"Anywhere, Paul—anywhere where we are likely to overtake the villain," cried Eustace, with intense excitement. "Let me but meet with him—let me but overhaul him—I'll have his heart's blood, or perish in the attempt."

"We shall run athwart him, never fear," said Paul, soothingly, observing how powerfully the young lieutenant was wrought upon by his feelings; and then suddenly addressing Andrew and Gasket, he said—

"Clap on to Mr. Grissoll; we will take him along with us. There may be foul play intended; if there is, we will not be the only persons who suffer."

It was without effect that Mr. Grissoll protested he meant them fair—swore by his honour, and his religion, that he had no such stuff in his thoughts as intending them evil. "Safe bind, safe find" was their motto, and deaf to his appeals, they made assurance doubly sure by compelling him to accompany them.

Once more they hastened on in pursuit, but ere they had gained any degree of distance, Eustace, overcome by overwrought emotion, superadded to his fatigue, became suddenly dizzy—the scenery appeared to turn round him, and reeling forward, he fell insensible upon the earth.

CHAPTER II.

"There stood an old man—his hairs were white,
But his veteran arm was full of might.

* * * *

Though aged he was, so iron of limb,
Few of our youth could cope with him."

BYRON.

"To this point I stand—
That both the worlds I give to negligence,
Let come what comes; only I'll be revenged
Most thoroughly."

SHAKESPERE.

"Round he spun and down he fell;
A flash like fire within his eyes
Blazed, as he bent no more to rise,
And then eternal darkness sunk
Through all the palpitating trunk;
Nought of life left, save a quivering,
Where his limbs were slightly shivering."

BYRON.

"God tempers the wind to the shorn lamb," is an old and beautiful proverb; one that applied to the situation of Florence, too, in an eminent degree. It might be imagined that one so fragile and delicate as she was would have sunk under the trials she had to undergo—that the agony of mind she suffered, in addition to the bodily exertion she was compelled to exercise, would have reduced her to the verge of the grave; but no, she had hope—

"The miserable have no other medicine,
But only hope."

and that supported her. Her exigencies had been many and great, still had she relief and succour when despair was eating its way into her soul; and even now, though she discovered Churleigh to have forfeited his promise, and was conveying her to some wild place, to her unknown, and with a purpose equally obscure to her apprehension, she still confided in God's mercy, and hoped for the help which seemed impossible to reach her. It was a consolation, though a meagre one, to know she was not in Jasper's power; and the few words respecting him which had fallen from the old man's lips, which were of the most acriminate and bitter description, convinced her that she was not in the hands of one who was his friend. It was impossible for her to understand why Churleigh had made her prisoner; but from the respect he displayed towards her, and his constant reiteration of assurances, when he found her weeping bitterly, that she had no cause for fear—that beyond being subjected to temporary inconvenience she should not incur any ill—she augured more favourable of the future than, perhaps, might have been expected from one in her situation; and thus when her heart sunk despairingly she would raise it by conjuring up fond speculations of speedy deliverance, of restoration to her friends, and happiness with him without whom life would be a cheerless blank.

Bill Grissoll's tale, stated by him to have been given by Jem Junker, was, as far as it went, correct. Jem Junker had accompanied the old man and his fair prisoner from St. Bee's head to Ramsey, and to him had been given the message to Smith; but Churleigh, instead of proceeding direct to Spanish Head, stopped at a house in the outskirts of Ramsey, for the sake of refreshing Florence and giving Jasper time to overtake him. The inmates of the dwelling at which he halted were persons who were in connection with the band, and never asked questions. They listened to all that was told them, but took no notice of anything strange they saw, unless their attention was specially directed towards it; they, therefore, testified no surprise at the introduction of Florence—received the intimation to hear, see, and say nothing, as a matter of course; and although the unhappy girl made several appeals to a woman who waited upon her, she received no sympathy in return. She had arrived with Churleigh at Ramsey in the forenoon of the day subsequent to her departure from Cumberland, and remained in the house to which she was taken the whole of that day and the next; but the following morning, refreshed in body, though her mind was still in a state of considerable anxiety, she was conducted from it by the old man, with the purpose of proceeding to Spanish Head. It was useless to attempt resistance; she perceived she could not gain by it, and there was little doubt that if she tried it she would be the only sufferer; she, therefore, made no opposition to Churleigh's request for her to attire herself in her cloak and hat and accompany him. A horse was provided for her, which carried her the greater part of the journey, and was dismissed when they were a short distance from the place in charge of boy who accompanied them, and then she and the old man went on alone.

The ground was rugged and of steep ascent. Masses of slate peculiar to the island lay in rude confusion here and there; rocks, all formed of the same material, rose up on each side of them, and each step they took in advance the scenery grew wilder still. The day was fine, and the view extensive; the sea, so lately agitated by boisterous winds, now lay like a huge lake, calm and placid—studded here and there with vessels of various sizes, like gems upon a sea-green robe, they reached the summit of the cliff and stood three hundred feet above the level of the sea. They gazed with interest on the scene. They could hear the roar of the mighty waters as they laved in restless motion the base of the promontory, and Florence felt giddy as she gazed at the fearful depth beneath her. The coast at Spanish Head is wild and picturesque. It is formed of jutting crags, of headland, and precipices, varying from two to three hundred feet in height. They are stationed in irregular positions, but have all communication with each other on the top, although in some places a path lies between them; in others it winds along the summit. There were thousands of acquatic birds wheeling and screaming in all directions, disturbing the otherwise serenity of the place by their ceaseless cries, and peregrinations, with flapping wings to and fro.

Churleigh wandered about, leading Florence by the hand, without any apparent object. He spoke kindly to her, pointed out the different objects in sight. Snafield, the highest mountain, more than two thousand feet above the level of the sea, and North Barrule, the next in importance, above eighteen hundred feet in height; and pointed out the opposite coasts, explaining that upon a clear day England, Ireland, Scotland and Wales, may be seen from the summit of these mountains. The tone of his voice was softened as he spoke, and his manner most respectful. He was well versed in the history of the island, and gave her a brief history of the celebrated defence of Castle Rushen by the heroic wife of the Earl of Derby, when it was attacked in consequence of that noble's adherence to Charles the First. His language, though rude, was impressive, and she could not but feel interested in his story, although it was related at such a season. During his narrative they seated themselves upon a clump of grey rock, and when he had concluded he rose, and bidding her follow him, he wandered among the passages which lay between those rocks whose summits rose boldly up above them. There was a strong wind blowing on these high places, coming from the sea, and conveying the sound of the incessant "wash of waters," as well as the chattering and screaming of the birds, with great distinctness, rendering every other noise, save its own soughing, inaudible; it was, therefore, with an unexpected suddeness, which made Florence scream with terror, and almost faint, that a young man sprung from behind a rock, and presenting a brace of pistols at Churleigh's head, bade him in a loud voice desist from advancing another step, on peril of having a bullet sent through his brain. Churleigh, who held Florence by the wrist with one hand, and his gun in the other, was a little in advance of the new comer; he, like Florence, was startled by the sudden appearance of the stranger, but was differently affected. He shifted his musket instantly, that his hand might rest upon the lock, and with flashing eyes glanced towards his detainer, in the expectation of seeing Jasper, but to his astonishment it was a man of even youthful appearance in the garb of a sailor. He was the more surprised, as he could not at the moment find a reason for being stopped in this fashion by such a person, and therefore obeyed the command, while Florence, who in an instant saw deliverance in store for her, placed her disengaged hand upon Churleigh's which held her wrist, and strove to wrest it from his grasp. As well might she have attempted to have drawn from a vice.

"Now, youngster," he exclaimed, addressing the young man; "what is your will, which you seek to enforce by holding a brace of pistols to my head?"

"Your instant resignation of that young lady to my care," he replied, in resolute tones.

Churleigh laughed scornfully.

"By whose authority?" he demanded.

"My own," was the reply.

"Thine?—pah! Boy, thou'rt mad," cried Churleigh, in harsh tones.

"My madness may prove fatal to you if you do not instantly resign your infamously obtained prisoner, and give yourself into my custody."

Again Churleigh laughed in bitter derision.

"Who and what are you?" he asked, contemptuously.

"My name is John Paul," was the cool reply. "I am that young maiden's friend and your foe; and mark me, old man, if you attempt to detain her or resist, nothing shall stay me from sending you to your Maker, with a fearful account of crimes to answer for. I have a hair trigger and a true eye—do not compel me to make use of them to your detriment."

"I have boarded a ship on the quarter when her cannon have belched fire and shot, without a nerve quivering; do you think your brace of puny weapons could move me from fear to do what you desire?" exclaimed Churleigh, with scorn.

"A vain boast," cried Paul; "death is death, come in what shape it may. A cannon-ball may scatter you to pieces, but a bullet, small as it is, can make a hole large enough to let out life. Resign the maiden without further parley, or take the consequences."

A smile of sinister aspect lurked upon the iron features of the old man; he rested his gun with its breech upon the earth.

"You call yourself a friend to the maiden?" he said.

"I do, and I am so. I have tracked you hither to rescue her from your accursed hands, and I depart not without her," replied Paul.

"Is she willing to believe you?" he said, turning to Florence.

"I have but to mention the name of Eustace, and she will, I know, gladly trust herself with me," exclaimed Paul, eagerly.

"Oh, yes," replied Florence, quickly; "I will go with you; you look honest; you do not look treacherous—I will trust you." She struggled as she spoke to get her hand at liberty, but Churleigh still held it.

"You require me for your willing—or, as it may be, unwilling—prisoner also, do you not?" he said, fixing a glittering eye upon our hero.

"You sneer," exclaimed Paul; "still will I have the young lady, and you shall be my prisoner. I command but what I can compel. The smallest attempt on your part to shift your gun towards me, or a longer continuance of opposition to my demand, shall seal your fate, I swear by all that is sacred."

"I am in your power, I suppose, and must do your bidding," exclaimed Churleigh, and let his gun fall heavily upon the ground. "I here resign the maiden." He released her as he spoke, and she ran towards Paul, and "you must take me—if you can," he shouted, and before Paul could have anticipated his intention he sprung upon him, knocked the pistols up with a sudden dash, and attempted to seize him by the throat; this, however, Paul avoided, and he only caught him by the collar. One of the pistols fell to the ground through the violence of the blow Churleigh gave it, and our hero threw the other from him in order to have both hands at liberty, and made a grip at Churleigh's throat, which proved more successful than the old man's attempt upon him. Florence shrieked with affright; she had no power to fly, and stood watching the combatants with a horror which rendered her scarcely able to support herself.

"Now, dog! now boy!" roared Churleigh; "you shall be *my* prisoner,

and shall be sent headlong to the devil from the summit of this cliff for your saucy bragging."

"You have yet to accomplish it," was Paul's short reply.

Churleigh found, too, that he spoke truth; the old smuggler was possessed of great strength; it had been immense, but age had reduced its power, though among his companions he had the credit of still retaining it. Paul was excessively strong too; a strength was his which he had hitherto untried—of whose possession he was ignorant, until in the present struggle it was called forth. Churleigh, with a rage almost amounting to frenzy, found that he had one to oppose who equalled him in power, that with straining every muscle to its furthest limits he could not fling to the earth. He discovered, too, that he had the grip of a lion pressing his throat, and producing the effect of strangulation upon him; it was in vain that he strove to dispossess Paul's hand of its hold—it clung there as though it grew to his neck and would not be shaken off, strive what he would. They twisted, and struggled, and twined, dragging each other to and fro, no words escaping their lips, save a solitary oath or so from Churleigh. The struggle was fierce, and well sustained; the efforts of each to fling the other were tremendous, and various were the temporary successes which each obtained that promised victory, as they gained them only to meet with some instant foil. Once Churleigh essayed to draw a knife from his belt; but Paul defeated his purpose. The attempt was fatal to the old man's success, for the next instant he was flung heavily, and Paul, with his hand still grasping his throat, kneeled upon his chest.

"Do you yield?" he cried sternly.

"Never!" returned the old man, hoarsely, "never! do your worst."

He struggled hard to rise from his abject position; but Paul held him firmly, and cried out to Florence—

"Maiden, cease your fears, you are safe—upon the ground lies a pistol, bring it me quick. Old man, do you yield?" he cried again to the prostrate smuggler.

"Never!" exclaimed the old man; "to such a boy as thee, never!"

"Your blood be upon your own head, then," cried Paul, fiercely.

"Be it so, I am ready; better death than crying craven," uttered Churleigh, making a last and terrific struggle to rise.

"Paul, however, kept his hold, and his triumphant position, although he had to exercise his utmost strength to retain it, still he was successful, he again urgently requested Florence to bring him one of the pistols. Before, however, she could obey him, a figure flitted past her, and the next instant both pistols were seized and presented at the head of Paul, by Joan Churleigh.

"Let go your hold," she cried, in strong tones; "let go your hold, man, or I send you to eternity without a moment's grace for a single prayer."

Paul fixed his clear eye upon her, and never wavered an inch; he quitted not his hold, but seemed rather to take a firmer grip. Churleigh, however, as soon as he caught sight of her and perceived her act, cried loudly—

"That's my own Joan, my bonny child—send the bullet through his head girl; wait not to ASK him to let go his hold, fire—fire—blow his damned brains out."

"Oh, spare him! have mercy—have mercy!" cried Florence, suddenly flinging herself upon her knees before Joan. "Spare him; he is a friend to me, the only friend I have near me. Do not destroy him, or I am lost for ever."

"Heed her not, girl," roared Churleigh; "pull the trigger; 'tis but the movement of a finger, Joan, and you set your father free. I am choking—fire, or I am strangled."

"You will not," shrieked Florence; "you will not—you may know what it is to need a friend in the hour of hopeless desolation, and think of your despair at having that friend struck dead before you. You are a woman; you cannot coolly commit murder; you will not destroy one who never harmed you, and plunge me, heart broken, into hopeless misery."

It is life for life" cried Joan, sternly; "my father is perishing beneath his grasp. I am hopelessly miserable; why should I spare him and you."

She held the pistols still more directly at Paul's head as she spoke, but, though there was a flush on his cheek and his eye gleamed like a star on a moonless night, he still continued his powerful possession of Churleigh's throat, even though he expected each moment to see a blaze of fire leavethe mouth of the pistol levelled at him. He did not speak a word, nor did he exhibit the smallest intention of relinquishing the advantage he had obtained over the old man. Florence, however, stung into eloquence by her desperate situation, still appealed urgently to Joan to withhold her deadly purpose.

"He will set your father at liberty — I will pray him to do it," she exclaimed, in earnest tones; "he will not destroy him if you spare his life; do not discharge those terrible weapons—do not!" and the tears flowed down her cheeks in torrents. Joan seemed moved by her anguish, and altering the tone of her voice, which had been harsh and excited, she said to Paul—

"Remove your hands from his throat. Release him, and I will not fire."

"I know too well with whom I have to deal to comply," replied Paul; "his first act, upon gaining his liberty, would be to do what you hesitate in doing."

"Fool!" cried Churleigh to Joan, making at the same time a desperate struggle. "Fool, am I to expire while you are parleying? Fire! Waste no words—fire! and scatter his brains like spray before the wind."

Despite Churleigh's violent struggles he was unable to alter his position, and once more he was compelled to remain where he was, Joan still, without heeding his command, said to Paul—

"If I guarantee your safety, will you promise me not to lay hands on him again, or in any way seek to injure him?"

"No," he replied, instantly.

"Oh yes, he will do so," cried Florence. "You will, for my sake," she added quickly, turning to Paul; "set the old man free, and let us away from this dreadful place."

"Will you agree to my terms?" said Joan, sternly. "If not, your blood be upon your own head."

"I will take my chance," returned Paul, cooly. "I will first know the extent of the outrage inflicted upon this maiden ere I make any such promise."

"He has done me no wrong, save to bring me from Westmorland here," exclaimed Florence, energetically; "save one forfeiture of his promise he has been all kindness to me, I swear by my hopes of heaven."

"You hear!" said Joan, emphatically, to our hero.

"Oh, release him, I implore you; release him for my sake, [illegible] own," urged Florence to him. "I have suffered but little from him: pray take your hands hfrom i , andlead me away from here," and she laid her hand upon his shoulder in the urgency of her appeal.

"It is the prayer only of this maiden that induces me to consent," said Paul to Joan. "Now what is your guarantee for my safety?"

"I will place these weapons in your hands," she returned, "and will whisper a few words in my father's ears which shall turn the whole of his wrath from you to another; in return, you will give me your oath to observe your part of the agreement."

"I consent," said Paul; "propose your oath—yet stay, I make one reservation; should this old man break the treaty, I shall hold myself irresponsible of my oath."

"I am willing that it should be so," returned Joan. She tendered a simple oath to our hero, which he took, and then pr offered the pistols to him; he sprung to his feet, took them, and before Churleigh could rise he got possession of his gun. The old man, when he rose to his feet, raged like a tiger, and coolly acknowledged that had not Paul exhibited the forethought to have seized his gun, he would have shot him with it the moment he regained possession of it. He uttered a thousand invectives against Joan, which she bore quietly and patiently, and when he had exhausted his vocabulary, she placed her hands upon his shoulder, and whispered a few words to him; the effect upon him was marvellous, he started, and then became as docile to her as a child, listening with the greatest intentness to all that she had to communicate. Their conference was conducted in too low a tone for either Paul or Florence to catch a word, but they could tell they were alluded to, by occasional glances directed towards them, and once by Joan's pointing to Florence in a moment of excitement, and speaking with considerable emphasis. They were not long ere they finished, and then Churleigh advanced towards Paul, and said—

"You have gained your object—take the maiden and depart; but as you quit here take the left-hand passages, keep as wide a circuit as you can, that when you emerge into the open country, you may have a good start of whatever pursuers may appear in chase of you."

"I have friends at hand," observed Paul; "I fear no pursuers."

"Be not fool-hardy," exclaimed Churleigh, grinding his teeth, "you may plume yourself, young man, upon your victory over me—you are the first I ever fell before; you may be proud, but let not that make a fool of you, and with vain boastful feelings cause you to lose the chance you have obtained. There are twenty men prowling in search of you and this maiden; keep a wide berth, and away while the opportunity is yet yours."

"Oh, let us depart," said Florence, "each moment I remain is a day of terror to me."

Paul hesitated, and Churleigh muttered an oath of impatience at his tardiness.

"I confess," said our hero, "I am rather doubtful about the policy of following your advice: it is singular that you, having suffered defeat from me, with much cause for the indulgence of revenge, should advise me of the best manner of escaping from a threatening danger."

"Look not at its seeming," exclaimed Joan, urgently; "I pledge my soul of its truth. Away with you, if you would not be again in the power of those from whom you have recently escaped; they are close at hand, led by one ruthless and iron-hearted, one whose only desire is to get yon maiden in his accursed power.'

"I understand you now," said Paul, hastily, as Florence shuddered, "that villain is marked; he shall not escape though he is surrounded by fifty followers."

"You are right," cried Joan, "he is marked—his doom is fixed; he shall not escape though he had thrice three hundred followers. But be you advised; tarry no longer."

"Restore my gun, ere you depart," said Churleigh to him; and observing him hesitate, he added, "you need not fear, the charge is reserved for another."

"Place it in my keeping—you may trust me," exclaimed Joan.

"I will trust you," said Paul, frankly; "take it, and God judge you as you prove false or true."

"Amen!" she returned, and received the gun into her possession. Paul at the same time took Florence by the hand, and led her from the spot, in the direction Churleigh pointed out as the safest to pursue. They had proceeded but a few paces, when they heard a rapid footstep following them; they each turned instantly, and their astonishment was great to see Joan Churleigh clutching at the robe of Florence, and when she reached her fell upon her knees at her feet and give way to a passionate burst of grief. It was uncontrollable, and they were compelled to let it proceed, even though Churleigh came up and essayed to move her from her humble position. She wept in a frenzied manner, and resisted every effort to raise her; at length, when she was able to articulate, she sobbed forth—

"Do not move me, father; do not touch me until I have spoken with this maiden."

"Are you mad, Joan?" he asked.

"Perhaps I may be. God knows I have had that which would make me so," she replied, bitterly. "Do not speak to me yet," she added, waving her hand impatiently, "I must utter a few words to this maiden, and then I will do your bidding. Sweet young lady," she cried, addressing Florence, after a short pause, caused by her thickly thronging tears, "twice we have met before—this is the third and last time. I feel that my time in this wretched world is short—we shall never meet again. I promised you when last I saw you, that should we meet I would explain to you the mystery of having unconsciously caused my misery; it is told in a few brief words. Oh, heaven! in how small a compass may long years of the bitterest anguish be contained! Jasper Chough, the villain who has persecuted you remorselessly, once loved me—no, not loved; oh no, he never knew what it was to love. He professed to love me—he cunningly acted in such a manner as to make me believe him. I did believe him—too credulously, to fondly—I loved him in return; my whole soul, undivided by thought, by mortal, was his—he knew it, and—made me the wreck I am."

"For which, were he thrice a giant, I would tear him limb from limb," growled Churleigh through his teeth, with rancorous hate in his tone.

"Until he saw you," continued Joan to Florence, rapidly, "he was kind and fond as of old; but when his eye had fallen on you it never returned to me. I saw the change—I knew it. Oh, how quickly the woman who loves as I loved can detect the smallest change in the object of her affection! I taxed him with it—he denied it, and tried to convince me of its falsity, and though his attempts were weak and paltry, so poor and shallow that I could see through them, yet so credulous was I, so much did I wish to be deceived in my suspicions, that I would have believed him, might still have loved him, but for one act—one monstrous, diabolical, fiendish deed which tore my love for him from my heart for ever, and substituted the deadliest hatred in its place. As a punishment for my weakness, God sent me a little child; it was an evidence of my shame, an irrefragable proof of the blot which blasted my purity. But though to gaze upon it was to remind me of the sin I had committed, I loved it, I adored it, maiden, though the offspring of guilt and shame. It was something to weep over, to cherish; something which might be made to love me; it was an object which shared my lonely hours, and complained not of my tears, of my dreary, miserable thoughts, of my sadness, but would smile, and, infant that it was, testified its affection for me in numberless ways. In an evil hour I consented to part with it TO HIM, that it might be treated better than I had an opportunity of doing—that it might not, in a fit of my father's anger with me, fall a victim to his passion. I parted with it, maiden, as I would one of my heart-strings, as I would a limb, as I then would have yielded the better part of my life. I suffered it to go, and he who took it—ITS FATHER! maiden, consigned it to a watery grave—the little sinless innocent, all I had to love, he destroyed. From the moment I knew that accursed act I changed; my heart became fire. I cursed him with the bitterest curse my anguish could invent; the curse has clung to him—he feels it each instant he breathes, and it shall curse his destruction eternally. The love he conceived for you has made him sacrifice me—has made him look upon me with an eye of loathing; but you are not to blame, though my happiness through you is wrecked. You are pure, maiden; your soul is spotless, though you have been sorely tried. I feel that I should die easier if I had your blessing; I feel that the Almighty might look with an eye of mercy upon my errors, and suffer my spirit to rejoin my little babe's—that the misery I have endured here may be lost in bliss hereafter—if you would raise your hands to heaven and pray for the redemption of Joan Churleigh."

"You shall have my prayers and blessings," replied Florence, deeply moved by the brief but miserable history the wretched woman had related. "I will pray for you night and morning," she added; "may the Almighty pardon the past, and hereafter bless you for ever," she concluded solemnly.

"And if God will here the voice of one sinful as myself," cried Joan, fervently, "may he grant my earnest prayer, that you may enjoy every happiness he can bestow. Farewell; your benediction has lightened my heart, which has been heavy with woe for a long period. I will no longer detain you; let speed govern your footsteps—your danger, while you remain here, is great. No more words—away."

She wrung Florence's hand as she uttered her last words, and, accompanied by her father, hastily retreated until they were both lost behind a jutting crag. While Paul, supporting Florence, departed in the direction he was advised to pursue, finding a difficulty to answer the questions which the maiden poured upon him.

Jasper Chough witnessed the departure of Eustace Prior and his friends from the cavern with a chuckle of delight. The opportunity for revenge upon all, even the dainty maiden, seemed within his grasp, and with sanguinary determination he resolved upon seizing it. He was too feeble and exhausted by that night's adventure to proceed instantly to mature his projects; he, therefore, sought in slumber the means of regaining the strength he had lost in battling with the wild sea—a situation he was placed in through the following cause, which he explained in a conversation with Captain Grayson, who questioned him respecting the plight in which he had been discovered. When Nehemie met with his terrible fate, he fled from the spot at the top of his speed, and it was not until his limbs and breath were exhausted that he paused to reflect upon what had taken place, and what course to pursue. The miserable end of Nehemie filled him sick apprehensions of his own fate, and his first thoughts were to make, by bye-roads, to London—ship himself on board a vessel bound to America, or the East Indies, or any remote clime, and thus rid himself of the dreadful chain which fettered him. Then again, as though there was a secret influence dragging him to destruction, as the burning flame lures the moth to its death, he resolved upon following Churleigh, whatever the consequence. With this stern intention he made the best of his way to St. Bee's Head, which he reached at noon, as Paul and his companions arrived in the evening, and sailed, in the passage boat, for Ramsey, which he gained early in the evening. He encountered accidentally one of the crew of the Scud, and questioned him respecting the truth of Joan's words, regarding their opinion of him in reference to the murder of his brother and Joan's child. He found they knew nothing of the matter, and held the same opinion of him as of old; he, therefore, resolved to trust himself among them while he devised means of crushing Churleigh, and, accordingly, accompanied by the man he had met, he entered a small boat and pulled towards the haunt. The gale sprung up, but they persevered, the more particularly as they witnessed the chase of the galley by the Curlew, and wondered at its meaning, as well as at what its termination would be. The increase of the storm, however, prevented their observing the result, and they ran foul, before they were scarcely aware of their proximity, of the crew of the Curlew's jolly boat, then pursuing the galley. They were instantly captured, and the pursuit continued, but the frightful increase of the gale, and the dangers of the channel they had to navigate, checked their progress, and eventually the boat was swamped and all perished save Jasper. The beautiful cutter, the pride of all the people connected with her, then shared the same fate: she went to pieces on the rocks, and in the morning nothing but her shattered hull and fragments of her rigging floating around remained of her to be seen.

"Jasper's first care in the morning was to discover Churleigh's locality, and this he ascertained by receiving the message Jem Junker had been commissioned to deliver; he believed at the same time, without asking himself why he should entertain the thought, that Eustace and Paul also knew where he had stationed himself, and would lose little time in pursuing him; he allotted them a certain time to accomplish the rescue of Florence, and picking a large number of his followers from the rest of the band, the most reckless and evil-disposed he could light upon, he communicated to them that he had a piece of service to perform, and commanded them to attend him, which they did freely enough. He set forth at their head, fully expecting to encounter Eustace with Florence in his possession, and determined to make a short murderous strife, place the maiden in his power, and consummate his revenge: he, however, arrived close upon Spanish Head without meeting with the desired event. He thought it as well to reconnoitre before he proceeded further; it struck him that Churleigh might have given Junker the message to elude him, and he possibly had come thus far in a wrong direction: at all events, there could be no harm in a close investigation of the spot, to see whether the old man still lurked with his fair prisoner there, in consequence of Eustace not having discovered him, or whether the young lieutenant had gained possession of his beloved, and had succeeded in getting safely away with her. As his own interest in the discovery of all this was concerned in the greatest degree, he resolved upon a personal inspection. He therefore stationed his men in secret recesses among the rocks, bidding them not move until they heard his whistle, and then they were to spring forward and do his instant bidding. The spot where he delivered this command to them was among a mass of rocks, which rose high above him on every side, and the men easily found hiding-places to lie in until the moment of action arrived. As soon as none were to be seen he cautiously crept forward, unconscious that his words had been overheard by one he deemed far away; he walked cautiously along for some distance, skirting the brink of the tall cliffs, and looking impatiently around him for some sign of those whom he sought; but flights of birds, wheeling with restless motion to and fro, were the only living things that met his eye. He wandered on until he left his men beyond the sound of his voice: he went on cursing, for he believed the spite fortune had lately shown him was still clinging to him, as he looked in vain to discover either Churleigh and the maiden, or Eustace and his companions. He had gained the summit of a tall cliff, which was nearly isolated; he approached its brink and looked over; it was three hundred feet to the sea, which foamed at and lashed the base; he shuddered at the dreadful depth, and turned to depart, but started back almost to the very edge on discovering that Joan stood before him. Her face was pale to extreme whiteness; her features were wan and ghastly, but rigid, as if fixed in death; her demeanour was calm and cool, and her voice, though hollow, was firm and stern.

"Jasper," she exclaimed, emphatically, "we have met again, we have met for the last time on earth; thy hour is come! The hand of God alone can avert thy doom, and THAT will never be stretched forth to aid thee; but, ere thou'rt sent howling to perdition, tell me the name of him who, at thy bid-

ding, took my child and cast it into the deep. Let me know who, with a ruthlessness little inferior to thine own, damned his soul eternally for thy base gold."

At first Jasper cowered beneath the stern look she threw upon him, but then the sudden recollection of the men he had at hand roused him from the dread he had displayed, and fixing upon her a look of scorn and hatred the most malignant, he cried, in a triumphant tone of malice —

"We have met again, as thou sayest, and for the last time; but not because my hour is come; it is thine. Mark me, Joan, the weakness I have displayed is gone for ever; it is not in thy power, nor in His upon whom you pin such faith to daunt me; but ere we part, never more to behold each other, thou shalt know who killed thy brat. Listen: when you consigned it to my care, I took it that same night, and within a hundred yards of the hut where t was born, I twisted its neck."

Joan shrieked convulsively.

"I cursed it as I killed it," continued he, in a voice which sounded scarcely human; "for I knew it was likely to bring me as much annoyance and trouble as it had already. I scooped out a shallow grave and thrust it in, stamping down the loose earth, I shovelled in over it, and I wished at the same time it might be my lot soon to serve its mother in the same way. Are you satisfied now?" he concluded, with a brutal laugh.

It was terrible to see the convulsive agony which passed through Joan's frame—every muscle, every nerve quivered with the intensity of her feelings; she panted for breath, and pressed her chest with her clenched fist, as though her heart would burst its boundary with the violence of her emotion. She gasped fearfully: at length she spoke; her words were uttered in a harsh guttural tone, and with difficulty forced from her throat.

"Holy God!" she exclaimed, "that ever I could have loved a wretch so execrable, so infernal! Thou remorseless, sanguinary monster," she cried, addressing him with bitter emphasis, "thou heartless fiend, I would myself leap from this dread height into the raging sea beneath if I did not know that death would drag you to the flames of eternal fire ere thou'rt many minutes older. I would not survive one second if I had not sworn to gaze upon thee with mocking triumph in the hour of thy death; but ere you perish, if thou canst feel a torture deep as that thou wilt hereafter be the victim of, let me be its inflictor—be mine the mouth through which it is conveyed. Listen to me, villain, and let my words sear thy brain as thine have mine. Know, wretch, that when your vile hand struck down your brother I was in the green lane—know that thou wert scarce out of sight with thy fainting burden when I reached thy brother's side; I raised him, and found the blood flowing in a stream from his temple, where thy murderous weapon had fallen. screamed for assistance, but no one came; I ran to the spring and brought back some water; I bathed his bleeding forehead, and then bound it with my scarf: he revived, but not to speak, only sufficient to show me that he was not dead. I lifted him, and, with a strength I knew not myself to possess, I bore him to our hut; I there essayed everything to bring him back to life, for he had again fainted as I carried him home. My efforts succeeded in restoring him to life, but only for a few minutes; he told me then who had struck him down; he told me why you committed the deed, and in his bitter agony he invoked the most fearful curse man ever uttered upon thy head; as the last words faded from his lips, he expired in my arms."

"Hell and death!" muttered Jasper, terribly impressed with what he heard.

"Aye, thou mayest well invoke thy coming doom," she exclaimed, in a tone of mockery; "a brother's dying curse is a fearful yoke to bend under; but terrible as it is, there is worse to come."

"I'll hear no more," he cried.

"Thou shalt," she returned: "thou canst not escape me—thou shalt know all. Thy fiendish acknowledgment of the murder of my child hath crushed me, and if thou hast one link of humanity remaining, my last words shall wither thee. Hear me: I was alone in the hut with thy dead brother—what I thought, what I felt, I will not repeat. I was some time ere I could decide on what course to pursue, but my woman's heart triumphed over my woman's weakness. I endured the horror for your sake: I kept the secret to screen you from justice—*you*, wretch, who had trampled my soul to dust. Alone, unaided, I dug a grave at the back of the hut, and with a few prayers I laid him in his cold resting place, without a mark to show where was buried one whose only crime was being as noble and full of worth as thou wert despicable and barren of all honour—and now, fiend, hear the consummation of thy murderous act. From the moment I swore to thee I would haunt thy footsteps, I sacrificed every other consideration to fulfil that vow. I fought with nature a fearful struggle to carry it out: until now I have succeeded; but—though I am loath to confess it to thee, for I know it will yield thee delight—I can no longer continue the struggle: my heart is broken, my frame is its victim—I perish, but thou shalt perish with me."

"Thy threats are idle boasting, hag. Stand aside, or I will fell thee to the earth," cried Jasper, knitting his brows, and speaking fiercely.

"Move not, stir not," exclaimed Joan, with extreme energy; "there is more for thee to hear—there is that to tell thee which shall blast thee as a lightning's shaft, when thy ears have drawn it in. I stopped thee in the defile of the mountain near Trusty Tom's hut: I left thee—a swift horse bore me to thy father's house; I stood before him and thy mother—I related to them all thy villany—I told them what thou wert, with whom thou hadst leagued thyself. I told them thou wert my destroyer, thy brother's and thy child's murderer, were still striving to dishonour the maiden thou hadst torn from thy father's roof, and was prepared to murder all who stood in thy path to prevent thee. I unfolded to them all thy villany, thy blackness of soul; I disguised nothing, and made thee stand before them the monster thou art."

"Damnable fury!" cried Jasper, grinding his teeth with vindictive passion, and his eyes like balls of fire rolling wildly.

"They were paralysed at my disclosure," continued Joan, unheeding his exclamation; "and when recollection came again, your father raised his right hand to heaven and added his curse to your brother's; it was an awful invocation, and a terrible sight to see the grey-headed old man call down so tremendous a curse upon the head of his only living child. He finished, Jasper—Almighty heaven! my blood, already chilled, was frozen to ice at the deed—he finished it, Jasper, by seizing a pistol which lay near him, and in an instant he was in the presence of his Maker, scattering his brains and blood upon thy mother, and I——"

"Hell and furies!" shrieked Jasper, standing as if turned into stone by what he heard.

"Your mother uttered but one shriek," continued Joan, as scalding tears rushed down her pallid cheeks, "and her heart-strings snapped asunder, her spirit joined thy father's, and one grave will hold them both. The sight drove me almost mad: I fled; but it was to find thee—to shriek in thine ears the horror——"

"Accursed fiend! spirit of hell!" shouted Jasper, at the top of his voice; "you have accomplished your worst; you have withered me, soul and body—but I'll be revenged: thy death shall be added to my crimes, thou torturing witch."

He rushed forward as he spoke, and seized her by the throat. She screamed violently, but he heeded it not—he drew a long curved dagger with which he was armed from his belt, and buried it to its hilt in her bosom. She uttered a piercing shriek as she received the blow. He drew it forth, and the blood spouted out like the jet of a fountain—he stabbed her again and again, with the madness of passionate revenge, and then, dragging her to the edge of the cliff, he flung her from that terrible height to the sea beneath. She was dashed to pieces in the fall, and the waters closed over her remains for ever.

With a sensation of horror at his own act, with a dread influence which he could not shake off, Jasper watched her body toppling down until the foam of the lashing waves hid it from his sight. A dreadful shudder ran through his frame—he felt sick and cold, and turned, with a groan, from the spot to encounter Churleigh. The old man stood towering over him, his whole person swelled with convulsive passion; he glared on him frightfully, and never earned his appellation of "tiger" so truly as at that moment, when, with a savage ferocity of expression indescribable, he stood ready to leap upon his victim. His appearance was so sudden, so unexpected, and so awful, that Jasper actually screamed with terror, and shrunk back, though he had scarce a foot between him and the verge of the precipice—the next moment the powerful hands of the old man were twining, with an iron grasp, about his throat.

"I have you at last, you bloodhound," he exclaimed slowly, and in a tone of voice terrible to hear; "thou'rt mine now, and Hell's hereafter. If I thought you would utter a prayer, I would beat out your brains before you could breathe a word. Damned ruffian, you ruined my daughter, you murdered her child, and now you have murdered mine. I saw you stab her and fling her below before I could get near enough to prevent you. I had marked you for a dreadful death before you murdered that poor girl, whom you have drowned in misery. I know of no way to make your death more fearful, or I would do it. I would do it right gladly. Down, devil, down, and prepare for hell!"

He forced Jasper to his knees as he uttered his words, and the miserable wretch, with all the agony of suffocation upon him, struggled hard to release himself.

"Help!" he shrieked, gutturally: "help!"

Churleigh compressed his fingers tighter.

"Call not for help, there is none near to help you," growled he. "While Joan held thee in converse, I went among the crew of the Scud. I knew their lurking places, snug as they were stowed away, and despatched them back to the cave, telling them you and I would overtake them!

Ha, ha, ha! if they would overtake you, they must to the devil at their best speed."

"Then to hell we'll speed together," uttered Jasper, striving to rise, with the purpose of throwing himself and Churleigh from the cliff.

The strength of a man in the jaws of death is usually tremendous. Jasper, without any hope of escaping, exerted his utmost power to have a companion in his dreadful fate; he gathered strength from his despair, and rose to his feet despite Churleigh's efforts to keep him down. The struggle that ensued was most deadly; both were desperate—both held life as nothing, so that he could destroy and triumph o'er his foe. The hatred of each to the other was most malignant, and their exertions kept pace with their animosity; it was a fearful sight to see them on the verge of a precipice three hundred feet in depth, struggling and striving with each other, dragging one another to and fro, now on the edge of the cliff with the earth crumbling beneath their feet, and then with bent bodies within two feet of the ground. Jasper still held the dagger with which he had murdered Joan, but hitherto he had been unable to use it; but a terrific exertion of strength, the effort of mad despair—for his back was bending over the frightful gulf on whose verge his feet held insecure footing, placed his hand at liberty, and he stabbed Churleigh deeply in the side; he repeated the blow—it was his last. The next moment, with a growl like the roar of a wild beast, Churleigh twirled him round and threw him; the dagger was wrested from his grasp, and a few heavy blows with the hilt upon his forehead rendered him insensible. Churleigh was bleeding frightfully, but he heeded it not; he staggered to a cleft in the rock, and brought forth a large coil of rope, a hundred feet in length; he attached one end to a stake which he had that morning driven firmly into the earth, and then he made the other end fast by a slip knot or noose round the body of Jasper. When he had completed his work, and saw that each knot was firm, with his little remaining strength he dragged Jasper to the edge of the precipice, pushed him over, and lowered him until he rested upon a ledge which projected from the side of the cliff, above ninety feet from where he stood. He then fastened the dagger firmly to the brink of the cliff, where the rope came in contact with it, resting upon its sharp edge, so that every wave of the rope to and fro, when the weight below pulled it tight, would have the effect of sundering the strands; that done, he crawled to where his gun lay, and obtaining it, and obtaining it, he dragged himself to the stake where the rope was fastened, determined to shoot any one who attempted to raise Jasper from the frightful situation in which he had placed him. The blood still poured from the wound Jasper had inflicted upon him, and as he made no effort to stop it, he grew feebler ever moment; yet he sat there like a grim spectre of horror—a spirit of revenge, watching and gloating with delight over the destruction of his victim. Hours passed away, and still he sat there, though death's icy hand was upon his heart. Evening drew on—a film was over his eyes, and his pulse was so low, life had scarce a tenement in his body. He heard a shriek rise from beneath the summit of the cliff; it was repeated, and he smiled a horrid ghastly smile. At intervals this cry uprose; it was not the scream of a bird—it was not the wail of a wild animal—it was too fearful, to unearthly; he knew it to be the shriek of one who felt that he had but a straw between him and an awful death. He listened eagerly for its repetition, and when it came frighting the still air with its shrill sound, he smiled, though his features were growing rigid, and the mist of dissolution was over his sight. Again and again that fearful shriek was heard by him with dreadful satisfaction; he laughed grimly as he recognised it, and once he muttered—

"Joan, my poor girl—my child—thy wrongs, thy misery, and thy murder have been revenged."

As the words quitted his lips, the edge of the broad moon uprising touched the level of the cliff: and when it was above, it shone on the corse of old Churleigh!

The fresh sea breeze blowing upon Jasper as he lay upon the narrow ledge on to which he had been lowered, restored him, after a lengthened lapse of time, from the insensibility into which the severe blows from the hilt of the dagger, delivered by the heavy hand of Churleigh, had thrown him. It was some little time before he recovered sufficiently to be alive to the full horror of his situation; but when he did, his heart died within him. The full fear of death was upon him with a force he had never before experienced; to look beneath him made his head dizzy, and his soul faint. The ledge was large enough to support him, and only large enough; above him the cliff rose perpendicularly for some distance, and then stretched outwardly until it reached the summit; beneath him it shelved inwardly, in a manner which terrified him to pursue its course with his eye, and more so to imagine. By his side was the nests of some sea birds, which in his descent he had disturbed, and they now flew round him screaming as if in anger at being dispossessed of their home, and were more than inclined to attack the intruder. So small was his resting-place, and so dread the depth beneath him, that his brain whirled at the thought of driving them away; and they darted past him to and fro, almost close enough to touch him, without receiving from him any indication of a desire to rid himself of their presence. He clung to the little patches of herbage which grew on the spot, as though the wind alone could sweep him off; he dared not suffer himself to gaze beneath him, fearing he should grow giddy, and fall; he dreaded to gaze above him, anticipating some evil chance, some unseen gap unconsciously moved into, might precipitate him into the gulph yawning beneath him.

There he sat motionless, every nerve thrilling with intense fear: his eyes rolled widely from side to side, yet neither above nor beneath him: he dared not trust them. At a distance he saw a vessel; he was afraid to remove either of his hands from the grasp they had of the turf, that he might wave one in order to be seen and rescued by the crew; but he shouted, shrieked to them, and felt as he did so that the very exercise of his voice would tend to hurl him below. The vessel, however, stood on; he was unseen, and he watched it, with a despairing heart, gradually vanish from his sight, leaving the sea bare of craft — then in blue misty indistinctness, on the edge of the horizon, he would see the dim trace of a ship glide along—but it approached no nearer, and went out of sight as it came, leaving him to envy the meanest wretch on board. Once, and once only, he cast his eye upon the rope fastened round his body, and followed it with his eye until it reached the brink of the cliff; but though he could not see Churleigh, he *felt* that he was there, and surmised that if he attempted to raise himself, and succeeded in gaining the summit, it would be fighting against dreadful odds to battle upon the verge of the cliff with the remorseless old man: he would not attempt it. He remembered that he had stabbed Churleigh deeply—he hoped that the wound would compel him to quit the spot and seek for help, or cause his death, and he resolved to wait for hours ere he tried the only mode of escape that presented itself to him. And now, thoughts the most terrible began to creep upon him: the murder of his brother, the dreadful death of his father and mother, and the more recent murder of Joan, presented themselves to him, clothed in vestments of horror, and made him groan with torture. It was in vain he tried to dispel them and think of other things, of mere common place indifferent matters; his memory was not so subservient to his will: think of what he would, those terrible remembrances were ever present to him, inflicting the most direful agony. An hour, which seemed a long day, dwindled by, and his mind had been distracted almost to madness by fearful thoughts and recollections. A new source of fear arose upon him, destroying almost the only hope he had. The sea, which had risen by the tide, struck the cliff with its heavy waves with more force than before, and every successive blow made the rock vibrate--each minute it appeared to increase in violence, and with affright scarcely to be described, he fancied the ledge which supported him was crumbling away, and by these repeated shocks would be broken from the mass to which it belonged, and falling into the sea, leave him hanging. He screamed with terror as the conviction came upon him, and repeated his cries in the faint hope that he might be heard by some persons near who would assist him—but no help came. Hours passed on, and he was still in his frightful position, without a prospect of being relieved from it. Twilight arrived, and his fears increased; he grew frenzied—he shouted madly; the birds echoed his cries as if in mockery; his brain wandered. He believed the spectres of those he had murdered, and those whose deaths he had caused, stood before him taunting him. The spirit of Joan seemed to gaze upon him with the same wan, frightful visage she had worn in life, from the sea grave into which he had hurled her. His brother confronted him with his white, ghastly face and bleeding forehead—his father and mother were there to curse him, and Churleigh sat over him like an evil spirit who had summoned these dreadful apparations to drive him to the wildest insanity. When the moon rose, his brain was in a state of frantic delirium; he raved and blasphemed, howled, committed all the extravagancies of fearful madness. He sprung to his feet, unconscious of his position—he uttered incoherent words and yelled forth peals of fiendish laughter—he addressed the wild sea birds as enemies, and defied them. He seized the rope—which, being of greater length than from the ledge to the summit, lay in loose coils at his feet—where it was firm above him, and attempted to climb: he swung to and fro, and but for his madness would have looked with horror upon his situation. He shouted and called it bonny pastime; he continued with vigorous arms to raise himself, hand over hand, until he had left the ledge some distance below him, but he grew fatigued, and slid down again with tremendous velocity: he missed the ledge in his descent, and fell ten feet below it. There he hung, swinging to and fro, and making desperate efforts to regain his former footing; his exertions restored him comparatively to his senses—at least, sufficiently for him to know the danger in which he was placed. He strove to recover the ledge more earnestly than ever: to be suspended at a terrific height, with a full knowledge of its tremendous hazard, almost paralysed him; he grew blind with fear and sick with horror, yet he strove to deliver himself from his impending fate; he swayed to and fro, and when he neared the ledge he felt one of the strands of the rope part. He knew what it was, and shrieked more madly than ever—he made another effort to raise himself—he felt another strand sunder! How he he raved and screamed, prayed, only to follow his prayers with horrible blasphemies. He essayed once more, and felt the rope evidently giving way. What was there now between him and certain destruction? between him and hell? Nothing. He tried again, the rope cracked and stretched with his weight; he tried to reach the cliff, but it shelved so far inwards it was impossible to accomplish it, and consummated the very thing he desired to avoid. As he swung himself forward the last strand snapped, and he felt himself suddenly flying down to perdition. One fearful shriek arose from him, and turning once in his descent he entered the foaming waves, struck against the sharp edge of a rock, and the next instant a mangled corpse was all that remained of Jasper Chough.

CHAPTER III.

"O! thou foul thief, where hast thou stowed my daughter?
Damned as thou art, thou hast enchanted her.
For I'll refer me to all things of sense
(If she in chains of magic were not bound)
Whether a maid so tender, fair, and happy,
So opposite to marriage that she shunned
The wealthy curled darlings of our nation,
Would ever have, to incur a general mock,
Run from her guardage to the sooty bosom
Of such a thing as thou!"

OTHELLO

HAM.—"You do but dally;
I pray you pass with your best violence.
I am afear'd you make a wanton of me."
LEAR.—"Say you so? come on."

HAMLET.

JOHN PAUL followed the advice of Churleigh, and took a circuitous path to the spot where he had left Gasket and Andrew waiting his return. He was

successful in avoiding the band of men whom Churleigh, as he had told Jasper, had induced to return to the cave to await the arrival of their leader; and when he joined the two sailors he immediately steered for the cottage where he had left Eustace, whom excitement and excessive fatigue had rendered too ill to proceed. He was, indeed, in a violent fever, and was delirious when Florence arrived. Paul had acquainted her with his proximity, and had prepared her to find him on a sick couch, but not to the extent to which he had been reduced; however, although she was much grieved to find him in this state, the shock had not come upon her so suddenly and with such ill effects as it would have done had she unexpectedly discovered his dangerous condition. She devoted herself readily to the task of nursing him; albeit the mistress of the cottage possessed considerable skill in all matters of this description, and added to it a kindly heart. The attention which the maiden paid her lover was as unceasing as it was tender and affectionate, and she soon had the happiness of finding that her ministering had the effect of restoring Eustace to his senses, and shortly afterwards to health. It was during her attendance upon the young lieutenant, that Gasket one night drew Paul's attention to her, as she leaned over him.

No. 45

"There," he whispered, "there, Paul, that's just the way her spirit looked the night it appeared to me, when Mr. Sheave's cutlass laid Mr. Prior in his hammock—and she looks as much, poor cretur, like a ghost now, as her ghost did that night."

Florence overheard his remark, though uttered in a low tone, and, with one of her own sweet smiles, she told him that the being he saw on that night was no spirit, but her own real fleshly self, who, having by accident discovered the dangerous illness of her lover, had contrived to elude the watch placed upon her, and finding her way to her lover's residence, succeeded in bribing the porter to let her see his young wounded master, if only for a moment: she confessed that on discovering Gasket in the room as she entered, she was surprised ; but perceiving by the expression of his countenance that he took her for a supernatutal being, she took advantage of his hallucination, saw her lover, and retreated without uttering a word, or making herself known to any one.

Paul smiled at Gasket's mistake, and joked him upon it. He, however, retorted upon him to the best of his ability, and with a gallantry, too, scarcely to have been expected from a rough sea bird like him. He told Florence that she looked so like an angel always that it was no wonder a simple fellow like himself should have mistaken her for one then. She raised her finger at him with a reproving smile as she turned away; and the honest fellow acknowledged to Paul, that if it hadn't been for Mr. Prior's being before him he should have been more than inclined to have sided up to the young lady, dear and—having a clean shirt and shave—have asked her to make the long splice with him. He turned his quid and sighed as he said he was "awar" there was no chance now for him, so he should sail on the old tack, but he confessed it was a pleasure to know that she wasn't her own ghost; for now he did believe that Mr. Prior was likely to make a long voyage before he dropped his peak, and there was almost as much comfort contained in that reflection, as there would have been if Miss Florence had made the port of matrimony with him.

With simple remedies the kind hostess soon reduced the fever which had seized Eustace, and when he became lucid, the sight of his beloved—oh! how glad a sight it was!—quickly restored him to sufficient strength to be remove from the cottage, and from the Isle of Man to Cumberland—where at his earnest appeal, backed by her own remembrances of the many narrow escapes she had of being lost to him for ever, she gave her hand to him. They were wedded privately at a little retired village church, no one being present save their companions and the two daughters of the landlord of the inn at which they stopped. As soon as the ceremony was completed, Andrew lamented in doleful accents that Martha was not with him, that the same kind office might have been done for them, they went direct to Grasmere. Upon their arrival, instead of meeting the good Squire Chough and his kind lady, they were horrified by receiving the same intelligence respecting them which Joan had communicated to Jasper. The effect upon Florence was terrible; for though her residence at Chough Hall had not been of very long duration, yet the affection with which the old lady had treated her, and the kind respect the squire had always paid her, made a deep impression upon her heart, too great for her not to be most painfully shocked at their dreadful fate. She would, though persuaded not, go to the Hall, where they lay waiting for interment, after being the subjects of a coroner's inquest, and there encountered Doctor Gray, who, perceiving the state of nervous hysteric excitement she was in, peremptorily refused to suffer her to remain. He insisted upon her instantly accompanying him, with her husband, to his dwelling in the village, and there await the funeral, and also the arrival of her friends. Eustace added his strong persuasions to the good doctor's, and Florence suffered herself to be guided by them. The worthy physician administered to her some quieting medicine, which he proffered with such admirable tact, such unaffected kindness of purpose and manner, that she could not refuse, and was thus spared an illness which, in the weak state of her system, caused by all she had undergone, might have proved fatal to her. During their sojourn, the doctor bruited the subject which he had once slightly touched upon to Mistress Chough, respecting the resemblance t[illegible] Florence's features bore to one with whom his early life had been connected, and found with some satisfaction that she was the niece of the young lady whose sudden and dreadful death prevented him from being united to her. This fact created fresh interest in him for her, and finding the stories he had heard respecting Eustace to be false, he offered to be the mediator between them and her family, if they proved incensed, which they fully expected they would, by their clandestine marriage—a kindness which was eagerly and gladly accepted by both.

Marthy Bell, 'John Andrew's own,' resumed her situation with Florence as soon as she arrived, evincing the greatest joy at her restoration, exercising her tongue with a perfect conviction that incessant use could neither tire nor wear out that nearer-than-anything-else-to-perpetual-motion member. She was glad she (Florence) had come back; she was glad she had, after all her trials, escaped unhurt; she was glad to see her, glad to serve her again, and would be most glad of any opportunity in future of being of service to her; in fact, what was there she was not glad about, save the dreadful deaths of the squire and his lady? But not least was her gladness occasioned by the return of John Andrew, her particular, own dear, delightful darling, not-to-be-thought-of-by-anybody-else John. She attributed Florence's safety to his courage and skill. They might SAY as they did say, that Paul, finding Mr. Prior too ill to proceed, had, accompanied by Andrew, Gasket, and Lucky George, set off without him, and despatching his three companions in different directions, had himself hit upon the right, and by his bravery had rescued her. Even John himself substantiated this statement; but she was not going to believe it, not she. No, no, that was the dear fellow's modesty, and not the truth; nobody in the universe was so likely to have accomplished the desirable and gallant feat, and, therefore, nobody in the universe should or could convince her that he had not. Perhaps she strutted rather more like a peacock in consequence, and perhaps she thought Alexander the Great a wonderful fellow; but what was he in comparison with her John, after he had brought sweet Miss—no—Mrs. Prior back? Poh!

One morning, full of gabble and importance, she arrived with a little girl whose pale and haggard face betokened her a mental sufferer. This little maiden, she stated, had been brought to the Hall by a gipsey woman, who, after making some inquiries respecting Florence, had requested the girl to be forwarded to her, and then disappeared. This child was Letty Nehemie; the moment she saw Florence she screamed with joy, ran into her arms, and sobbed as though her little heart would break. She was not easily restored to placidity, but when the efforts made to console and soothe her were successful, she related in simple terms the dismay which had seized upon her and the whole tribe of gipseys, when the prolonged absence of Florence on the night Nehemie had captured her induced them to search for her, only to discover that she had been carried forcibly away—a conjecture they arrived at by discovering an ornament she wore lying in the defile where she had been seized. Their natural shrewdness made them fix upon Nehemie as the man who had perpetrated the outrage; and after a few questions to Letty, which she answered in terms sufficient to satisfy their speculations, they departed instantly in various directions to endeavour to overtake him and rescue the maiden. The issue of their labours is known. It was communicated to the child, who felt no great cause for sorrow at hearing of the death of one who had made her brief life most unhappy, but was much grieved that no intelligence had been obtained of Florence. Tom Cooper did not survive the effects of his wound, and when he was interred, one of the female gipseys had taken her in charge, and conducted her to Chough Hall. She told her little tale artlessly, and on its conclusion begged of Florence not to forfeit the promise she had made her of keeping her, and Eustace, much interested by what he had heard, added his request to her entreaties; but there was no need of persuasion, Florence had conceived an affection for her, and gladly promised to keep her word. Martha, who, under other circumstances, might have looked with an eye of jealousy upon the new comer, was about to get married, a reflection which was, as John Andrew asserted, "uncommon pleasant," and therefore with a good grace prepared to instruct Letty in the duties she had hitherto fulfilled; and the affectionate girl, as happy now as she had been wretched, with a heart overflowing with joy, received thankfully her instructions.

Doctor Gray dispatched a messenger to the friends of Florence, stating her arrival, with a summary of the events which had occurred—concealing, however, the act of her marriage; trusting to his power of persuasion, when he broached the matter, to produce a reconciliation, where a cold announcement only might be an insufferable bar to an opportunity of attempting it. The messenger was accompanied on his return by the father and brother of Florence. They met her kindly, but there was a want of that affectionate gladness, which rather chafed the Doctor's warm heart to witness. Eustace had studiously kept out of sight—it had been so arranged; and when Florence's father proposed her immediate return to London, the Doctor interfered, by stating he had a few words to say privately to him, and requested his attendance in his laboratory. No man situated as he was with regard to the parties could have accomplished the task he undertook better than he did, and but for the bitter animosity which Mr. Stanley unfoundedly bore Eustace, he would have succeeded. No sooner, however, did the elderly gentleman ascertain that his daughter was actually married, than he stormed furiously; he uttered a thousand wild things in his rage; he summoned Florence and her brother to him, and acquainting the latter with the fact of her marriage, he launched forth a perfect hurricane of vituperation upon the unfortunate girl, who stood shrinking and trembling at the violence of his rage. Once she clasped her hands in the midst of his wrath, and begged his forgiveness in tones which should have moved a harder heart than his; but in a whirlwind of passion he vowed he would never extend the hand of amity towards her, or look upon her as his child again. He had intended high connections for her; he had calculated upon her wedding a noble of high rank— a matter due only to her descent. She had destroyed all her hopes for his aggrandisement, and he discarded her for ever.

"Do not say so, dear father," she said, weeping at his harshness; and turning to her brother, who had not uttered as yet a word, but stood a haughty and cold spectator, she exclaimed, "Intercede for me, dear William. I have stood often between you and our father's wrath—will you not say one kind word for me now?"

"You have acted on your own responsibility, madam," he answered in icy tones; "you must take the consequences."

"Ay, beggary and a garret," roared her father, passionately.

"With whom?" said a clear stern voice.

They all turned instantly and saw Eustace Prior standing before them, Florence threw herself sobbing in his arms. Mr. Stanley almost howled with passion.

"Scoundrel, vagabond, beggar!" he shouted; "you have stolen my child from me; but I will be revenged, beggar, I will."

"Were you not the father of my wife," exclaimed Eustace, his voice trembling with rage, "I would compel you to retract your words in a degrading posture. Look how you repeat them even to this lady, who is now my wife. I am a nearer relative to her now than you, and beware how you insult or reproach her."

"Insolent villain," cried William, sternly; "dare you thus beard us after your base clandestine act? Another such a speech, and I strike you where you stand."

A glance of lightning flashed from Eustace's eye; he clenched his teeth, and his chest swelled, as, looking at him contemptuously, he exclaimed—

"Boy! thou strike me, boy!" He then turned to Mr. Stanley, and said, proudly, "My escuctheon is as unstained and noble as yours—may vie with a prouder line of ancestry than thine; dishonour was never cast upon it by one branch of my family—I shall not commence it. I have loved your daughter for years, honourably and fairly sued for her hand, I have been so blessed as to gain her affection, and by her own frank and unconstrained will have been given her hand. I am her husband, and am prouder of that title than I should be of a dukedom. For your scorn, sir, I hold it as nought; I deserve it not, and return it as it is bestowed, and in discarding her for ever fear not that you will ever be sought by abject appeals to forego your harsh and stern determination. I swear I will be to her more than you or your son have ever been, and she shall never know, through act or word of mine, one tithe of the anguish your harsh conduct has occasioned her.

"Villain!" cried Mr. Stanley, having impatiently listened to him; "you carry your rascality with a high hand, with an unblushing front, but you shall be brought down—you shall be lowered to the dust until you are trampled upon!"

"By whom?" cried Eustace, sternly.

"By me, by me, dog!" roared he; "by me. There is a way to punish you. I will take it. You shall be crushed, scoundrel. Your marriage shall be set aside; it can, and shall, though I expend my whole fortune in accomplishing it. Resign my daughter, villain, into my hands at once, and hide your head in obscurity, or dread what is to come. Florence, quit him instantly, and accompany me to London, or you, too, shall suffer from my vengeance."

As he concluded, he advanced to lay hold of her, but Eustace thrust his hand back, and exclaimed, fiercely—

"She is my WIFE! Do you hear, old man? she is MY WIFE, and the first who dares to lay a hand upon her I'll fell him to the earth—old or young—I will, so help me Heaven!"

"Then do it," cried young Stanley, at the instant springing forward and seizing Florence by the arm. At the same moment Eustace fulfilled his word and levelled him, by a severe blow, to the ground. Florence shrieked, Mr. Stanley drew his sword, and Doctor Gray, seizing him, called for help. Paul, who was near, hearing the uproar, immediately appeared, followed by Gasket. Eustace, the moment he saw him, resigned Florence to his care, bade him lead her away, which he complied with at once, and, though prayed and entreated by the doctor to depart also, stood firm and confronted the infuriated parent and his son. The latter would have again attacked him, but Gasket held him back, while Mr. Stanley, almost mad with fury, cried—

"You have contrived your scheme well, scoundrel; you have your bullies too, but you and your hired ruffians shall smart for this. You, too, Doctor Gray, shall not pass unpunished; you, if not the contriver of this vile affair, are an abettor: you shall account for your conduct rest assured."

"I am quite prepared, Mr. Stanley, at all times to render full satisfaction when required," returned the Doctor, coolly; "my acts will bear inspection, and my motives also. My conscience is free from self-reproach."

"No doubt," retorted he, sarcastically; "I have not the least doubt of it; it is a remarkably accommodating conscience, and never troubles you at all, I dare say; but it *is* not one I choose to repose faith in. You shall answer for your conduct, sir."

"When and wherever you please," replied the Doctor.

"It shall be shortly, and in a place which will make you quake," roared the old man.

"I have never seen or heard of it yet," replied the Doctor.

A kind of hyena-hysteric laugh was all Mr. Stanley responded to the Doctor's reply, and then he said to Eustace—

"Your smuggling piratical ruffians surround you now, and the conquest for a time is yours, but not for long. When you see me again, you will wish you had never seen me at all."

Gasket, who had been listening with undisguised wonder to all that had transpired since his entrance, now raised up his voice and said, a little excitedly—

"It's my opinion, with a little more length of line you'd go to the devil, old gentleman. Now if I may be allowed an idee, I don't think any one would wait till they'd seen you agin afore they wished you'd never hove in sight at all; and you'll be doing me a favour if you'll tell me who you mean by smuggling piratical ruffians? 'cos if you means me and John Paul, and for the matter o' that, our messmate Andrew, why —"

"Silence, Gasket," cried Prior, as soon as the tar's volubility began to subside into his regular smooth manner of speaking, and gave him a chance of being heard.

"Come, William," exclaimed Mr. Stanley at the same moment to his son, "we will not compromise our honour or respectability by remaining here a moment longer."

"You might be in a more splendid mansion, and do both," cried the doctor warmly.

"I must have the means of satisfaction for the blow I have received ere I depart," exclaimed William Stanley.

"This moment," cried Eustace, eagerly.

"No, sir," returned the young man, with cutting irony, "your eagerness does your ingenuity credit; you know, were we to make the attempt here, we should be interrupted. You shall hear from me, fear not."

Eustace bit his lip, and bowed his head.

"Your friend will find me here whenever he pleases to call," he said.

"And think not we leave Grasmere yet," uttered the old man, menacingly. "No, your every movement shall be watched, so attempt not to quit secretly."

"I am quite prepared to meet all your animosity can devise," returned Eustace, haughtily.

"And don't let me catch one of the spies, that's all," cried Gasket, as Mr. Stanley and his son quitted the room. "If I don't treat 'em to monkey's allowance, why I ain't a blue jacket, and never been on blue water."

The incensed old gentleman made no reply, nor did his son, but they both wended their way to Chough Hall, where Mr. Stanley took upon himself the management of Squire Chough's affairs, which, of course, were in the greatest confusion. Eustace sought Florence, whom he found in an agony of grief turning a deaf ear to all the efforts which Paul was making to console her; and it was not until he roused her spirit of self-respect and independence, that he succeeded in the task. In the course of the afternoon he received a note, conveyed by a village boy; it was from William Stanley, and ran thus—

"There is no one here on whom I can depend; I must, therefore, request you to meet me alone—you will not object—I shall be unattended. There is a quiet spot at the back of the Hall, where it is unlikely any one—UNLESS POSTED THERE—will intrude. You bear His Majesty's commission, I must consider you as a gentleman. I repeat *I* shall come unattended. Ten minutes before five to-morrow morning, will be early enough; any time after that too late." W. S.

Eustace read it, and hastily scrawled—

"I shall be there, and alone!" E. P.

He entrusted it to the lad who had brought Stanley's note, and scrupulously avoided saying a word to a soul respecting the matter. By four in the morning he arose, dressed himself, and kissing earnestly the forehead of his fair young wife, who lay sleeping, unconscious that him she loved dearer than life itself was about to stand before her brother, who would raise his hand to shed his blood, he departed; he left upon the table, ere he quitted, one line, stating that if he returned not before noon, he should be found in the grove of trees behind Chough Hall. He was but a short time reaching the spot appointed, and was first upon the ground. He had not been there a minute, before he was joined by William Stanley.

"You are punctual," he exclaimed; "I must request your pardon if I have kept you waiting."

"I have but this moment arrived," returned Eustace.

Stanley looked pale, and his teeth chattered a little; he saw that Prior's eye noted it, and said quickly—

"I have had an ill night's rest—the morning air is chill,—'it is an eager and a nipping air,' as Shakspere says. Are your pistols loaded?"

"No," returned he; "I waited for you to be present."

"I thank you," said Stanley; "you will, perhaps, favour me by loading mine, while I do the same to yours; we may want both brace, and will fire with each other's loading."

"As you please, replied Eustace; "what distance would you like?"

"Say fourteen paces," said Stanley; "I can snuff a candle at twelve or sixteen; it would be an unfair advantage were I to choose either."

Eustace bowed.

"You are generous," he exclaimed; "it matters little, however, in my opinion. Each of the three is a good killing distance."

Stanley smiled but returned no reply. He loaded the pistols and gave them to Eustace, who having completed the like task returned Stanley's to him. They agreed to take the paces, turn, and fire instantly. A loud report ensued, but no effect was visible. Stanley's brow lowered.

"We will try the second brace," he said.

Eustace assented. Again they took their stations; a similar result ensued. Stanley muttered an oath.

"I do not feel satisfied," he exclaimed; "we will fire a third time. Shall I load your pistols again?"

"They are loaded," returned Eustace.

"Loaded! did not you discharge them?" inquired Stanley, hastily.

"No!" answered Eustace; "I have no desire to take the life of my wife's

brother; but I am here to give you satisfaction. You can fire again, if it pleases you."

"Not unless you return my fire," cried Stanley, haughtily; "I would not commit murder, sir. If I charge my pistol again, will you return my fire?"

"No," replied Eustace, decisively.

"Then there remains but one way," he replied, gnashing his teeth, and striking Eustace with the back of his hand across the face. "You will not hesitate now?"

Eustace's brow became instantly as red as fire.

"Load!" he cried instantly; "you shall have your wish."

"Both the pistols you hold are charged; I will take one of them," said Stanley, his face a trifle paler than before, and his hand a little trembling from excitement.

Eustace tendered both to him; he chose the nearest to him. They took their positions, both fired, and both fell. Eustace, however, was quickly on his feet again, and ran to raise Stanley, who exclaimed feebly —

"You've hit me, Prior; I have done the same to you, I see, by the blood trickling down your arm; we are neither of us much hurt. I am satisfied; are you?"

"I am," replied Eustace, quickly; "but are you not deeply wounded? Shall I get assistance?"

"No, no, leave me here," he replied, hastily; "the reports of our weapons will speedily bring some one to my aid. I am not much hurt; you take my advice and fly. I think you are not so bad as I have been led to believe you, and you are a gentleman. Lose no time, take Florence with you, and, if you can manage it, quit England for a time. I cannot be friendly with you, but I will not be your enemy. Go; tell Florence time may soften her father's anger, but nought else. Away, man, stop not; here comes some one — do not be seen — I will account for my wound. Exert your best speed and quit this place. Fly!"

Eustace heard approaching footsteps, and wringing the hand which Stanley tendered him, hastily quitted the spot and returned to the Doctor's dwelling. He aroused the Doctor and had his wound dressed. The ball had passed through the fleshy part of his arm, close to the shoulder, but had not injured the bone; it was quickly dressed, and when he related the cause, and the parting words between him and young Stanley, the Doctor advised him strenuously to follow the advice. Paul was called to the consultation, and agreed with the Doctor.

"I intended returning home to Kirkcudbright this evening or to-morrow," he said to Prior; "you can accompany me, sir, and stay at my father's house until you have decided what course to pursue. A few hours earlier will be more agreeable to me, and if you decide upon following our counsel, before the sun is three hours older we will be upon our journey."

The safety and happiness of Florence being urged by both as his most important consideration, he acceded to their advice; but he did not like thus quitting, as though he feared Mr. Stanley, or aught he could do; however, when he had consented, he acted promptly. Florence was awakened, and his intention made known. The Doctor procured a carriage, and before eight o'clock everything was ready for their departure. They took their leave of the kind Doctor, with sincere thanks for his hospitality; of John Andrew and Martha Bell, with presents and kind wishes, reiterated warmly by the honest couple. Lucky George they had already parted with, he having resumed his professional duties as soon as he had accompanied them to Grasmere; and with Eustace, Florence, and Letty, in the inside of the vehicle, and Paul and Gasket out, they started for Whitehaven. After something of a fatiguing journey, they gained it, entered on board a schooner, and were soon wafted to the Scottish shores. Upon reaching Kirkcudbright, a few words from Paul to his delighted family, who flocked round him to greet his return after a long absence, obtained for Eustace and his sweet wife a warm welcome. Gasket found himself included in it, and Letty was speedily made almost one of the family.

CHAPTER IV.

"Adieu, my native land, adieu!
The vessel spreads her swelling sails,
Perhaps I never more may view
Your fertile fields, your flowery dales.
* * * *
* * * *
Rise, billows, rise! blow, hollow winds!
Nor night. nor storms, nor death I fear;
Unfriended bear me hence, to find
That peace which fate denies me here."

THE day succeeding the arrival of Paul at his father's house he sought the shipowner to whom he had been apprenticed, with the intention of obtaining a post in a vessel bound for New York. He had marked out a course which he had determined to pursue, to raise himself to a position to aspire to the hand of Alice, and sternly resolved that no difficulty, however great, should prevent him accomplishing his object. Mr. Younger received him kindly and gladly, and immediately he became acquainted with his wishes, he gave him the command of a brigantine, a vessel in which he had once served as third mate, and had displayed his professional ability by taking command of her on her passage from New York to Scotland, in consequence of the sudden deaths of all her officers. The manner in which he had handled her, and successfully completed her voyage, under circumstances exceedingly embarrassing, had obtained for him great praise, as well as a high opinion of his skill; it was, therefore, with great readiness, on his application, that Mr. Younger installed him commander of the brigantine, and professed his willingness to serve him in any way which he could point out. Paul thanked him heartily, and expressed himself perfectly satisfied with what he had already done, and returned home to communicate to the young lieutenant what had transpired, at the same time offering him, if he felt disposed to accept it, a passage in the vessel for a trip across the Atlantic, until the wrath of Mr. Stanley had abated. This kindness, however, Eustace did not accept, although he did not positively decline it, because he awaited the result of some letters which he had dispatched to his friends, briefly relating his marriage with Florence, and the enmity with which her parent had visited him for wedding her. A month was the time appointed for the brigantine to be ready for sea, and before a fortnight had elapsed, two events occurred which made it a matter of policy, if not of necessity, for both Paul and Eustace to quit the mother country.

Eustace received answers to his letters, which contained the unpleasant news that the vindictiveness of Mr. Stanley, so far from abating, had increased; that his influence with the Lord's of the Admiralty had been exercised, and was suffícent to obtain from them a document to Eustace, stating that they were ready to accept the resignation of his commission; with which order, as it was less disgraceful than being dismissed the service, he was forced to comply: he was also given to understand that proceedings were instituted against him in the Ecclesiastical Court, and there was little doubt, from Mr. Stanley's connections and influence, that he would obtain a verdict in his favour; he therefore at once availed himself of Paul's offer, and resolved to quit the land of his birth, perhaps for ever. Among his letters was one from Doctor Gray, who had gathered much of the foregoing by perseveringly following the movements of Mr. Stanley, and forwarded the intelligence to him, accompanied by a postscript, which deeply affected both him and Florence. When they perused it, it ran thus:—

P.S. I had almost forgotten, my dear young friend, to tell you of a matter which caused me some little anxiety until I had seen it completed. I am not exactly an OLD man, though not particularly young; I had mental sufferings to some extent and for some years. I should not mention this, but to tell you it is most improbable we shall ever meet again. 'Constant dripping will wear away a stone,' says the old gossip; in my case her saying is verified. A sorrowful remembrance, too freely indulged in, has contrived to wear out my frame. My professional knowledge tells me that my stay on earth is very limited, and therefore my wants are few. Those of young people, my experience teaches me, are many. Do not, my dear young friend, deem it a piece of impertinence, if, looking upon your sweet young wife in the light of a relation (for her mother was the sister of her who should have been my wife), I have settled upon her my little stock of property—a trifle, some four or five hundred a year—commencing from the present date. I have reserved sufficient to last me and see me comfortably disposed of by the sexton. There, it is out now, and I feel much happier. Remember, the whole matter is arranged and completed, beyond the power of any interference from any one, so don't you or your pretty bargain attempt it; and if you mention it when you write to me, you shall never have another word from,

GEORGE GRAY."

Eustace, though the younger branch of a large family, poor, but highly connected, had a property of his own, approaching the kind bequest of the good Doctor, and thus was placed in comparative affluence--at least, in the position he intended to assume when he arrived in America; he therefore cared little for the steps his bitter father in-law purposed taking against him, so that he succeeded in quitting the country in order to retain his beloved wife. He replied to the Doctor's letter in a manner which delighted the kind man, and received in return another agreeing with the step he purposed taking, and advising his immediate departure.

Paul, on his part, had attended closely to the outfitting of his vessel, to see that she was seaworthy in all her parts; and during this period he became acquainted with the return of Alice and her father to Scotland. The desire to see her again before he quitted the land, perhaps for years, which held her, was too strong to be resisted, and he made known to her his proximity. She with joy met him, and many brief but happy interviews had they. At length the time approached closely for his departure. He met her one evening in a small wood which skirted her father's estate. It was two nights previous to the day appointed for the sailing of the brigantine, and as the time for their being in each other's society waxed shorter, their meetings were of deeper interest. Their hearts were full of hope, though tinctured with sadness. Paul expressed his proud and fond expectations in language so fervid and sanguine that it seemed to Alice a short probation only would be her lot ere the dearest wishes of both their hearts would be realised; and with this glad feeling they conversed until the world, and all it contained save themselves, was vanished from their memory. They gazed in each other's eyes and saw their world shining their, and seemed as though they drew life and all the impulses of their being from what they looked upon: their words were low and passionate, and the tone of their voices soft and rich, for their soul was in all they said; and while they were happy in this delicious community of thoughts, a heavy tread disturbed them, an angry exclamation followed, and their hearts sunk to see her father standing before them, attended by four men. He was white as marble, but after the first ejaculation he displayed no outburst of temper. He seized Alice by the arm and drew her from Paul's side, saying in a low tone—

"Are you to be the disgrace of my house? Are you to be my curse? Get you in! Pause not an instant for a word or look, or I fell you to the earth before your minion and these menials."

Alice wrung her hands, but stood as if rooted to the spot.

"Let not my presence be the cause of pain or harshness to you," ejaculated Paul quickly, in an under tone. "Farewell! we shall meet again—"

"Silence, fellow!" exclaimed her father, and then resumed to Alice, "Will you depart, or shall I put my threat into execution?"

Alice threw her head back and looked him proudly in the face—her pale features and her flashing eyes making her resemble Cassandra of old.

"You may strain your power too far, sir," she exclaimed in firm tone; "the honour of our house is as dear to me as to you, and as safe in my keeping as in thine. Understand me, you may guide me to your wish by gentleness easier than compel me to your will by arbitrary conduct. I return to my apartment not so much at your command as to spare indignity to one whom, but for his timely aid and skill, you would not now be standing there to insult." She extended her hand to Paul as she concluded, and said, "Farewell! may heaven guard and keep you."

Paul took her hand and pressed it, but her father instantly struck them apart.

"Not in my presence," he exclaimed bitterly to Alice, "shall you thus degrade yourself and me; away! Gregory," he added, addressing one of his followers; "attend my daughter to the house."

With one fond earnest gaze upon Paul, her lips breathing a prayer for his happiness, she departed. When she was gone, Paul exclaimed to her father —

"I dare not trust my tongue to express my thoughts to you, sir, or I should utter some truths which might smack of bitterness. I leave you to the satisfactory reflection of having caused much misery, and proved yourself unjust and ungrateful."

"Stay," cried the old man, as Paul was turning to depart; "not such will be the fashion of our parting. This is your prisoner," he cried to two of the men who accompanied him.

"Prisoner!" ejaculated Paul. "Prisoner!" he repeated, and as the men advanced to seize him he retreated a few paces, crying, fiercely, "Stand back; by heaven I'll level to the ground the first who dare lay hand upon me. Prisoner! Upon what charge?"

"That you will learn anon," exclaimed the old man. "Officers, do your duty."

"Stand off!" shouted Paul; do not drive me to desperation, or blood will be spilled. Who dares impugn my character? By what right or authority do you attempt to seize me as your prisoner?"

"By this 'grace of God,'" exclaimed one of the men, holding up a long strip of parchment. Your name is John Paul, isn't it? John Paul, son of John Paul of Arbigland?"

"It is," returned our hero.

"Then I arrest you," he exclaimed, suddenly tapping him on the shoulder, "for the sum of one thousand five hundred pounds, at the suit of this gel'man here. Are you prepared to pay it?"

"Pay it, villain? I do not owe one fraction to any one in the world," cried Paul, in a state of bewilderment.

"O' course not," replied the man; "nobody owes nothin', nobody gets into debt, and all them as goes to prison isn't in for debt, but ony through the willany of a friend. Do you mean to pay the 'mount here speshefied?"

"You have not descended to this vile lie, this base artifice, to crush me, have you?" demanded Paul, fiercely, of the old man. "Is this man mad, or are you the scoundrel he declares you to be?"

The old man directed a malignant smile of triumph towards him, but made him no reply; he turned contemptuously from him, saying to one of the men—

"I have seen your prisoner safe in your charge; let him escape at your peril."

He then quitted the spot hastily, leaving Paul overwhelmed with astonishment.

"Now then, young man, if you please, we are ready to go," exclaimed the man to him.

"Where?" asked Paul, mechanically.

"To Edinburgh, to my crib there; it's a snug place, I can tell you," returned the man. "I was in London, in this vay, for a good many years; ah! almost since I war a boy; but there was nothin' I had there, or that any other of our calling had, as could ekal the one I've got now."

"I shall not go," exclaimed Paul, sternly.

"Oh yes you will," returned the man; "don't be obstropolous; don't compel me to use wiolence, 'cos that aint doing things in a genteel vay. I don't vont to use darbeys, but I must if you don't come kevietly; I've a brace of bull-dogs, too, and if you comes any nonsense I shan't be very pertickler about using on 'em. Come."

He produced a pair of pistols as he spoke, and placed the muzzle of one close to Paul's temple, by way of a hint. Our hero saw that it was of no use to resist—at least at present. The men were deaf to his assertions that he had not contracted the debt at any time or under any circumstances; they told him he must prove that in court; they had nothing to do with it, they were but fulfilling their duty, whether the arrest was illegal or not, and come with them he must, unless he paid the money down on the nail, an alternative which the principal speaker, with a very sigificant grin, said," he sposed he worn't a'zactly goin' to do." He saw there was no hope of escape, but by stratagem, and even that must be done speedily, if done at all. There was one thing in his favour, the night bid fair to be dark, the sun was down, the moon rose late, and heavy masses of clouds, threatening a storm, rose up; he determined to take advantage of the fast spreading darkness the first opportunity that presented itself, and, to disarm suspicion, he said, in a frank tone of voice, shrugging his shoulders—

"Well, if I must go, I must. I shall, however, appeal against the illegality of the arrest."

He was told he might do as he pleased about that, so that he came quietly with them. This he consented to do, and walked on, conversing in a light manner with his captors, until he reached nearly the outskirts of the wood through which their path lay. Here fortune seemed to offer a mode of release; a tree had been felled, and a quantity of the small branches were lying about. Before the men could have the smallest suspicion of his design he sprung forward, seized a branch which had been trimmed to about the size of a quarter-staff, and dealt one of the men a tremendous blow upon the head, which hurled him to the ground completely stunned. The other eluded the blow made at him, and, with an oath, fired a pistol at our hero; it missed him, and the second was instantly discharged. The ball slightly grazed his shoulder, but no farther harmed him; the man, perceiving his failure, hurled his pistol at Paul; it struck him between the eyes, and made them flash fire. At the same moment the officer seized his staff, and, with a celerity and strength for which Paul was unprepared, twisted it out of his hand, and aimed a blow at him with it; his advantage was but momentary—Paul rushed in and closed with him; in the struggle the staff fell to the ground. The officer still held one pistol in his grasp, and tried to use the butt end upon our hero's head; but Paul flung him heavily and then pinned him to the ground with his knee. The man, however, succeeded in drawing a short sword, with which he was armed, and thrust it at his foe, wounding him in the side. Before he could repeat it, Paul obtained possession of one of the pistols, and grasping the muzzle, he beat the stock violently about the man's skull, until his silence told him that he lay insensible. Casting the weapon from him, he sprung to his feet and fled.

When he reached his home he related what had occurred, and by daylight in the morning he had an interview with the shipowner, stating the facts exactly as they had transpired. Mr. Younger's advice, on hearing the circumstances, was, that he should lie hid until the vessel was ready for sea, and then join her at some obscure point on the coast.

"It is not known," continued the shipowner, "at present, that you are to have command of the brigantine. Captain Richard Jones was to have had her, but his dangerous illness will prevent him leaving London for some time. You had better take his name; no one will think of finding in Captain Paul Jones the John Paul who has given the bailiffs the slip."

Paul consented to follow his counsel, the more particularly as Mr. Younger shewed him forcibly that in the event of surrendering himself and proving by oath that he did not owe the money, that the arrest was a base conspiracy to wrong and injure him, a long dreary time would ensue before he could clear himself; he would be involved in expensive litigation with one who possessed a long purse, and would ruin his prospects in endeavouring to right himself. An action for assault and battery would also lie against him for maltreating the sheriff's officers, and imprisonment almost certainly follow the trial, accompanied, perhaps, by a fine—Justices of the peace were more easily influenced at that period than now—and as he knew that his relentless enemy would leave nothing untried to ruin him, he felt conscious he should not stand a chance if he remained, and boldly met the vile contrivances put in practices to ruin him. He therefore at once hastened to a retired spot near the coast, where he could join his vessel in a small boat, and remained at a hut until the ship worked round the point.

The officers, though stunned and severely beaten, were not dangerously so, but recovered sufficiently in a few hours to commence a hot search after their escaped prisoner. Warrants were obtained, every stringent act against him which could be obtained by bribery or influence was put in force, every hole and corner was searched for him within the neighbourhood, his father's house was rudely entered, and one of Paul's sisters was insulted by a fellow, who outstripped his duty considerably. Gasket, who was on the spot, handed him out of the house and thrashed him so soundly, and so thoroughly, he was scarcely able to crawl from the spot, an incident which acted as a salutary lesson to the rest. The vessel was not ready until the expiration of a week, and in that time a sentence of outlawry was obtained against our hero; every thing was done in fact, which could degrade and crush him, but, with all their efforts his hiding-place was undiscovered.

At length the vessel was ready. Gasket, was made her first mate, carried her out of the harbour in good style, and with a fair wind soon reached the spot where Paul was to be taken on board. He had been anxiously on the watch for her, and when she hove in sight a fisherman's boat put him on board without a moment's delay; he was warmly greeted by Eustace, who, with Florence, was on board, and was by him made acquainted with the endeavours made to capture him, as well as the low decrees issued against him, placing him almost on a level with a common felon; it was with a bitter heart he listened to the detail, and, in the impulse of his passion, he swore to be revenged upon all, upon even the country itself, which had thus basely and unjustly wronged him.

"In John Paul," he exclaimed acrimoniously, "they had a warm true friend; in Paul Jones they shall meet with a bitter enemy!"

He turned from Prior with a burning bosom, and paced the deck with the restlessness of one labouring under the influence of strong emotion. Presently he stopped, and, in a loud stern tone, ordered all sail to be made on the ship, and was obeyed by the hands with alacrity. The bustle attendant upon

increasing the canvas having subsided, he walked to the quarter, and looked upon the land, which was fast receding from his sight; he gazed upon it with a lowering brow and compressed lips, and after a moment's pause, he said aloud, in a tone of contemptuous mockery, unconscious of being overheard—

"Farewell, Scotland, my native land—the land of the free and enlightened, farewell. Adieu my home, my birth-place; farewell my native shores, we are sundered in spirit for ever. I tear thee from my heart and curse thee for the injustice of thy laws, for thy iniquitous partiality, for thy scourging the poor, and thy cringing to the rich. Land of my forefathers, proud mother of a Bruce, a Wallace, a Macgregor, and a Douglas, how thou art sunk and debased! The foot of man may traverse ye from Caithness to Wigton, from Aberdeen to Argyle, and look in vain for thy old honour, thy stern justice. Thou hast driven me from thee with scorn unmerited; I drive thee from my soul with hate and contempt. Another land shall claim my hand, my heart my service; I abjure thee. I have within me high thoughts and great resolves; the smallest opening shall bring them forth, but not for thee. If I raise my arm and do deeds of daring it shall be to support thy honour or advance thy fame; henceforth we are separated. Oil and water shall be easier mingled than I reconciled to thee, thou drivelling abject remnant of honour and glory! But for the mother who bore me, and for her who loves me, I would erase all remembrance of thee from my mind, as a thing of baseness, a spot of infamy and scorn. Yet, though I hate thee, I will revisit thee; thou shalt dread my second visit when thou knowest of my first. There shall be fear and trembling on thy shores when he who was discarded as John Paul returns to repay his obligations as Paul Jones. With a heavy hand shall Paul Jones pay the debt of John Paul; the hunted shall be the hunter, the chased shall be the pursuer, and he, the instigator of thy injustice to me, shall well remember him whom he outlawed from thy soil. Farewell, Scotland: as one of your sons I look my last on you. I return only as an enemy, and may my dearest hope fade from my grasp if I forgive or forget the injury thou hast inflicted on me. Adieu thy shores recede from my sight as my love for thee fades from my heart. Being gone, no tie can or shall unite me to thee again."

He ceased, and waved his hand as a token of parting; his eye still fixed itself upon the diminishing land, and he stood like a statue. Sad and painful thoughts crowded upon him, a weight like lead was upon his heart, and, despite the hot rancour with which his bosom burned against his native land, be could not witness its disappearance without a foreboding that in parting with it for ever, he parted with all hopes of future happiness. While he was in a fit of abstraction, after his soliloquizing, Eustace Prior and Florence were engaged in the similar occupation of watching the blue land as it grew smaller and smaller; though they looked not upon it with the same feelings as our hero, they both felt they were leaving their home behind them, to seek a strange land, to dwell among strangers, and look in vain for the friendship and affection of kindred, which they naturally expected would have been theirs, had they remained. Florence was overcome by her emotions, and wept: Eustace cheered her to the best of his ability, although he felt depressed at thus quitting his countiy almost as an outcast; still a tinge of resentment mingled with the feeling, and enabled him to bear the separation with more firmness than he might under other circumstances have done.

"Why do you weep, Florence?" he exclaimed, tenderly. "You should not shed tears to be rid of a thraldom which would have caused you unhappiness while you lived; you should be proud, and bear with resolution a change which the tyranny of others has produced. Follow my example, dearest, and bear lightly wrongs which you have not deserved, and which, bitter as they have been, have failed in destroying our love, and in preventing our union. What if we do leave our native land behind us? it is not for ever, and are we not securing the impossibility of being separated from each other? You should smile and be glad, my love, to think you are delivered from a fate you shuddered at, and which you once feared must be thine. Cheer thee, my sweet Florence; suppose, as Shakspere says—

'Devouring pestilence hangs in our air,
And thou art flying to a fresher clime;
Look what thy soul holds dear, imagine it
To lie that way thou go'st, not whence thou com'st.'

Come, love, remove that kerchief from thy sweet blue eyes, and let me see that thou'rt less unhappy to be with me than to leave the world behind thee."

"My dear, dear Eustace," answered Florence, in a low soft voice, "I do not grieve to leave our country, for I am with you; your home is my country, my hope, my desire: to be with you is all I ask of Him who gives all. I do not sorrow to quit my family or my friends, but I grieve that the act of those who are my kindred, who call themselves my friends, should conspire to drive you from your country, honour, and from fame—"

"No, Florence," interrupted he, "my honour is beyond their reach, my fame is in a considerable degree in my own hands; they may have compelled me to quit England, but that is all; and are not you the price of my absence?" he added, affectionately; "should I repine?"

"The sacrifice required an equivalent of greater value," she exclaimed, with a smile.

"Not had it been a thousand times greater," he replied, fondly; "I esteem that smile of thine beyond price: what, then, my love, must I deem thy value? I know no equivalent."

"And will you always think so, dear Eustace?" she asked, archly, and yet earnestly too.

"Will I not!" he exclaimed, with fervour.

And thus did he contrive to lead her mind from dwelling upon melancholy subjects and giving way to gloomy thoughts; and when, shortly afterwards, they were aroused from their fond converse by the voice of Paul giving orders to reduce the canvas, their eyes in vain sought the land: it had vanished.

For a fortnight nothing of any consequence transpired; the ship ploughed its way across the Atlantic with a speed which, if it did not quite equal their expectations, was, nevertheless, not to be despised: the wind was fair, but there was not enough of it to make the advantage considerable, but they found that when it blew a little fresher than usual the performance of the Kirkcudbright was admirable—that with a stiff breeze, and on a easy bowline, she could move along like a race-horse. The monotony of their progress was, however, relieved by falling in one morning with an American brig, bound to Philadelphia, waterlogged; she had sprung a leak, and her people were unable to discover where; she was sinking fast when the Kirkcudbright hove in sight, and there was but little time to save anything beyond the lives of the crew, when she went down. Her captain, whose name was Hardy, was an Englishman, a fine hearty fellow, and his men were part Americans and part English; they were fourteen in number, and readily assisted in the duties of the vessel, too glad to have escaped the dreadful death which would have been theirs but for the timely arrival of Paul's vessel. Two days subsequent to this the wind freshened and became more fair than ever, and our hero packed all the sail he could upon his vessel to make the most of it. Towards the afternoon of the second day they came in sight of a frigate standing on in the same direction as themselves; she was under easy sail; she had her top and top-gallant-sails set, and was moving along as though her object was pastime rather than government service; there was a little backing and filling in her movements somewhat unnecessary, and shortly after the Kirkcudbright hove in sight, her top-gallant-sails were struck, her top-sails close reefed, and her courses hauled up as though she was preparing for a gale. Paul surveyed her with his glass most attentively, and Eustace, who, with the captain of the American brig, stood at his elbow, said to him—

"What do you make her out?"

"I think she carries a French commission, though she has an English ensign at the peak," he replied; "she is of French build I am sure, and the rake of her spars, as well as the cut of her sails, are French, she never came out of an English port, I am satisfied. Look, sir, and say what you think of her."

Prior took the glass: the moment he cast his eye upon her, he said—

"I know her; it is the French frigate, *Le Diable.* When I was on board the Audacious we had an engagement with a seventy-four, *Le Destructeur,* this very frigate, and a corvette: we took the seventy-four and the corvette, but *Le Diable* escaped. I know her well, she carries heavy metal, and can throw it a long distance; if we cannot escape her with a pair of light heels, we shall be carried to a French port, and enjoy the comforts of a French prison."

"Damn her, can't you fight her?" exclaimed Captain Hardy.

"We only mount six guns," answered Prior, "with a stern and bow chaser; we can, with all your men, only muster four-and-thirty hands, and the frigate carries sixteen ports of a side, and eighteen pounders: her complement of men is little short of two hundred, if not more; what chance should we have if we hazarded a conflict? let us make use of our heels first, then, if they overhaul us, fight while we can."

"And when we can't, blow up the vessel—what say you, Captain Jones?" cried Hardy.

"The Kirkcudbright is not much adapted for fighting," replied Paul, "but before I resign her to yon Frenchman he shall burn his fingers, and every hope or chance of escape shall be taken from us. We must, however, trust to stratagem rather than force. If I can contrive to get to windward of him, he shall find I have not obtained the weather gage of him for nothing. Ho, there! Gasket, let the colours be brought out—we will hang a French ensign on our naked gaff; it may make him acknowledge himself."

Gasket produced, from a small locker which contained a number of flags, the white flag of France; it was run up to the peak of the gaff, and spread out gracefully in the wind. It hung there but a minute ere a similar one was displayed from the French frigate, on the spot an English one had so lately occupied; her topsails were backed, and she lay-to for her supposed countryman to run under her lee. Such was not, however, Paul's intention: the guns were shotted quietly and without display, the hands were turned up, as if with the intention of sending down the loftier sails, but in reality to set whatever light duck could be brought into play. Paul kept the ship to windward of the frigate, and drew on her fast. A private signal was now made by *Le Diable*, and Paul bade Gasket make a signal flag fast ere he run it up, so that it would not shake out, in order that he might gain time before the Frenchman perceived his error. Gasket obeyed him admirably, and a boy was despatched aloft as if to clear the signal halyards, which, to those on board the French frigate, appeared to be foul. The boy, obeying his orders, appeared to do his work clumsily, and took a long time to do that which at another time would have been accomplished in a few minutes. They were now nearly on a level with the frigate, and now came the chance of their discovery. Paul took the glass and surveyed their movements anxiously; he saw that he was not less closely watched by the people on board the frigate, and found their suspicions were aroused by topmen being despatched aloft to shake out the reefs. When they got sufficiently near, *Le Diable* hailed them, inquired their name and destination, to which Prior, being able to speak French fluently, replied. He stated their vessel to be *Le Kirsch-wasser*, from Havre, bound to New York, with a general cargo. The Frenchman bade him lie-to and instantly send a boat on board, but before a reply could be obtained they swept out of hearing. The French commander roared angrily through his speaking trumpet, but obtained no answer; and the first lieutenant with his glass discovered that the stern of the passing vessel displayed in bright letters the name of the Kirkcudbright instead of the *Le Kirsch-wasser*, which Prior had given as bearing a resemblance to it, which, with a casual observation, might have passed. A gun was fired by the Frenchman, and unheeded; a second followed with a similar result, and a third was prepared to be despatched in the same direction, while hands were turned up in droves to spread the canvas; but the frigate, though capable of doing great things, was neither smartly manned nor well handled. The Kirkcudbright was a good mile a-head of her before she was properly in chase, but then her superiority of sailing was manifest. Notwithstanding the speed of the Kirkcudbright, *Le Diable* went two feet to her one, and was blazing away from her bow ports all the time, expending a great deal of powder, but doing no mischief. In less than an hour the distance between them was lessened half, and there was a prospect that the balls, which fell so far short, would speedily find a resting-place in the hull of the brigantine. Paul perceived it would be useless to continue his flight, with the hope of distancing his pursuer; he therefore determined again to resort to stratagem. The hands were piped to reduce the sails; top-gallant and top-sails were struck nimbly, almost everything was taken in, and in a few minutes, where there had been a cloud of canvas, not a rag scarcely was to be seen. This unexpected change astonished the Frenchman; he scarcely knew what to be at; his people were once more sent up to execute the same manœuvre, but displayed such a lack of skill in their movements, that the frigate run some distance past the brigantine before she could bring up.

"By heaven!" exclaimed Paul, warmly, as he watched their actions, "with such a frigate as that, and a crew of my own picking, I would fight anything from a seventy-four cut-down to a first-rate: she s lost in the hands of such lubbers."

It had been agreed that Eustace should go on board the frigate, represent himself as a Norman in command of the brigantine, which he was to still aver was in the French service, and invite the commander on board to satisfy himself. A late dinner was intended, during which he should be made intoxicated, his gig's crew served the same in the forecastle, and when night arrived an attempt made either to get rid of their unpleasant companion by giving her the slip, or fighting her. By the time their arrangements were completed, the command for them to send a boat on board was again made by the commander of the French frigate, and complied with. Florence did not like parting with Eustace—it seemed as if something dreadful was to happen to him; but necessity overruled her fears, and she separated from him, trying to be cheerful—but it was a very lame attempt. Paul sent four picked men with him, and bade him use his wits to the furthest limits to induce the captain of the frigate to come on board the brigantine, for upon that depended all their hopes of getting clear. Eustace promised to do his best, and the boat left the vessel's side to speedily gain that of the frigate. The captain of *Le Diable* received him in his state' cabin, making as much display as though he were an admiral. He was a young man, and very foppishly attired; he bowed politely as Eustace entered, and said—

"*Comment vous portez vous, Capitaine—?*" he paused.

"*Edouard Etienne Eustache,*" replied Eustace, readily. "Who may I have the honour of addressing?" he continued, in French.

"*Philibert Hercule Rossignol Landais,*" replied the Frenchman, in a coxcombical affected tone.

Rossignol d'Arcadie!" muttered Eustace, perceiving a striking resemblance between the captain and a certain long-eared Jerusalem pony.

"You were in a hurry to prosecute your voyage, Captain Eustache," continued Landais; your conduct was certainly droll, to view it in the most favourable light: you were aware I ordered you to send a boat on board after my first hail—why did you not comply?"

"The order was unheard," replied Eustace. "I thought you were satisfied with my reply, and kept my course."

"Yes, and fatigued myself and men to death, by having to spread canvas after we had taken it in for you to come under our lee," said Landais. "You are a Frenchman—no!"

"I have to thank Normandy for a birth-place," returned Eustace.

"Normandy—horror! I should execrate it instead of being thankful to the low province," cried Landais, applying to a scent-bottle. "Paris or strangulation at birth, say I. You have your papers with you, I presume, Captain Eustache?" he added.

"I have not," returned Eustace. "I hoped to have the honour of a visit to my poor vessel from you, monsieur."

"A visit, why—hem! I can't say—really—a—what is your cargo, monsieur?" drawled he.

"Silks, jewellery, articles of vertu, and wines," replied Eustace, without recollecting what there really was on board.

"If it were not for the trouble, half an hour might be, perhaps, agreeably trifled with in the inspection," yawned Landais; "you keep the hands employed, Captain Eustache, and with such a cargo a clean ship is indispensible."

"You might not, without trouble, find a cleaner vessel in any service," ejaculated Eustace.

"Except '*Le Diable*,'" rejoined Landais—"I mean, of course, the frigate, not his satanic majesty. By-the-way, I was lately decoyed on board an English brig, bound to London, from St. Petersburgh, with Russia hides and tallow on board. *Mon Dieu!* I thought I should have died with the horrible odour; I have been bilious ever since. I let the rascals slip, for to have captured them and carried them into port would have been to ensure myself a year's illness. They scented the air for miles; I prayed for it to rain *eau de millefleur*, but the powers above were not beneficent."

Eustace was growing strangely disgusted.

"I will return," he said, "and have the side manned to receive you."

"You are too complaisant," exclaimed Landais, "I will not trouble you so much; you shall remain here while I go—nay, I know what you would say. Ho! without there!" a man appeared at his summons. "Expedite my barge," he exclaimed: the man touched his forehead and disappeared.

"You will surely permit me to attend you?" exclaimed Eustace.

"Not for any earthly consideration," he replied. "I can satisfy myself without your presence. I do not think you are playing me false, nor do I believe you wish to do so, but in these stirring times we naval men must be scrupulous. Amuse yourself until my return, I entreat you; there are books, here is wine; if you are dull my first lieutenant shall keep you company. I am sorry I have no *jolie fille* to introduce, but you know such a thing is not possible. *Au revoir*."

He rose, and before Eustace could address him, he quitted the cabin, leaving him rather bewildered; he would have followed, but a sentry opposed his departure.

"You cannot pass!" he said.

Eustace explained that he would speak further with the captain; the man was, however, not to be moved, and nothing was left but to remain quietly and await the issue of this adventure. As soon as Landais was upon deck he summoned his first lieutenant to his side.

"I have a young Englishman in my cabin," he said; "he would pass himself upon me for a Norman, but his round face and blue eyes, as well as bluff manners, tell his nation more plainly than his tongue. I expect his vessel will be a rich prize; I shall go on board and take possession. You, Fauber, can go into my cabin to the Englishman and entertain him. Let him not know, however, that his artifice is discovered—await my return for that disclosure. You can serve out an extra allowance of grog to the men and pipe them to dance—a prize such as this, and accomplished with such ease, deserves a little rejoicing. How has my villain dressed me, Fauber?"

"To perfection," exclaimed the lieutenant, in affected admiration.

"By the way, there is a pair of gold knee buckles, set with brilliants, which I have," uttered Landais; "they appear monstrous upon my knee—they will suit your brawny limb—may I request your acceptance of them?"

"Oh, you are too kind, sir," murmured the lieutenant. The captain protested he was not, and after bowing to each other several times, Landais descended the ship's side, and was borne swiftly to the Kirkcudbright. He was received by Paul, who could speak French well, and when upon the deck he asked several questions, was answered readily, and with the same story Eustace had told him. Paul's coolness rather staggered him, yet a glance at the people satisfied him that the vessel had an English crew, whatever her port of departure. Paul invited him to the cabin, he entered, and threw himself upon a sofa: he requested to see the ship's books, and in answer to Paul's query requesting Eustace, he acknowledged that he had left him in custody of his lieutenant, until he had perfectly ascertained the truth of his story. Paul quickly discovered the foppish fool he had to deal with: he made an evasive reply respecting the books, and ordered some wine to be placed before him, to remove a portion of the fatigue he vowed he must have endured; and Landais, who was no fop at the bottle, whatever he might be in everything else, was not slow to partake of it when presented to him: the wine happened to be very choice, and he discussed a bottle before he proceeded to any other matter. Paul, who possessed a good flow of wit when he chose to exercise it, kept him in a good humour, and nearly two hours elapsed before the Frenchman found that he had other things to attend to besides drinking wine. At length, with a flushed face, and an unsteady motion, he spoke of returning to the frigate, and requested the production of the books. Paul, however, told him that Captain Eustache had provided dinner for him, he trusted he would not therefore do him so great an unkindness as to decline partaking of it. More wine, cool and sparkling, being placed before him, and just hitting his palate, he took a few draughts, and thought now he was on board he might as well have a snack. Paul uttered his thanks, and added—

"Captain Eustache will dine with us—another glass of wine—he would be unhappy not to do the honours of his own table; you do not empty your glass. Captain Eustache can present you with something more choice than this; you could perhaps find room for a case in your cabin."

"With the most infinite delight," hiccupped Landais, somewhat drunk. "Where is Captain Eustache?—oh, ah, I forgot—send for him by all means; say I shall expire if he declines attending."

"Shall I send your boat for him?" inquired Paul.

"Certainly, certainly," was the reply.

The word was passed for the French captain's cockswain, and when he made his appearance, Landais gave him the necessary order. Paul placed the wine more immediately within Landais's reach, and making an excuse to quit him, followed the cockswain in order to see the effect the return of the

boat without the captain would have upon the people of the frigate, and whether Eustace would be suffered to return; he did this that he might better know how to act, when the important moment for a second attempt at an escape arrived.

During his absence, Florence, who had remained in a side cabin during the interview between Paul and Landais, imagining from the silence that ensued that the Frenchman had departed, come forth to see whether Eustace was in the cabin, and confronted Landais; she did not perceive him until she was in the centre of the cabin, and then with a slight scream of startled surprise, she was about to retreat, when he sprung from his seat, placed himself between her and the door, and with an impudent stare in her face, made her a bow.

"Pardon me, my angel," he exclaimed, "for intercepting you; I cannot permit such loveliness to shine upon me for a moment only. Pray be seated, beauteous saint, and let my eyes be refreshed by gazing upon thy ravishing charms. Positively my soul has been languishing, and withering for so delicious a sight, just as flowers fade for need of sunshine."

Florence did not answer—she was alarmed; he placed his back to the door, and thus barred her egress.

"You do not answer," he exclaimed, the wine making him speak thickly; "speak to me, my angeld. Doubtless your voice is as full of music syrenic strains, and thy words abound in honey, all sweetness, as thy face is a paragon of beauty. Why art thou silent, my charming maid? Ah! you are English, and do not speak my language, and I do not speak yours. Cruel fate! to thus deny our souls communion; to thus rob us of the delight of imparting to each other the excessive bliss we enjoy at meeting. Envious mischance; why wert thou not of my nation? but we will strive, by endearing actions, to counteract—"

"You will oblige me by permitting me to retire, sir," exclaimed Florence, in French, when she found that he continued to regard her with a rude gaze, and was preparing to advance towards her.

"Aha! this is very good," he cried, with delight; "you speak French. Listen to me, my angel; you must not leave us, not for a million existences, unless you would see me expire upon this spot, my sweet girl—my charming Miss — Ah! you have an enchanting name, I know. What is this it is? Celeste—eh, is it not? Ha! what is that I see upon your white hand, a ring, surely you are not married?"

"Allow me to pass, sir," exclaimed Florence.

"Ah! no. Do not drive me to despair, my dear," he cried, attempting to take her hand, which, however, she avoided, retreating from him rapidly. "Be not frightened, my pretty little dove; you will find me tenderness itself. Are you really married?—so young, so very fair. Ah, the wife of Captain Eustache? *Mon Dieu!* what a happy fellow he must be. What can Paradise be to him hereafter? Will you not permit me to salute the tips of these fairy fingers, or will you plunge me into inextricable bliss, dissolve my whole being into the essence of rapturous, ravishing delight, by honouring me with the permission of pressing my lips to thine. Nay, look not so frowningly nor so pale, my enchantress; life was given for love. By the mass! your face looks lovely, even in frowns. Be not hard-hearted as you are fair. May I not have a kiss—not one; remember, sweetest, a female at sea is a spring in the desert to we who parch for their refreshing presence."

"Your conduct, sir, is unmanly and ungentlemanly," exclaimed Florence agitatedly, as he endeavoured to seize her; "suffer me to pass to my cabin. Do not compel me to call for help."

"Help! madame? help!" he retorted, with a laugh. "Ha, ha! you forget this ship and crew, captain, lady, and all are in my power."

"Thine?" repeated she, contemptuously.

"Mine," he rejoined. "My frigate, you must be aware is on the weather-bow, and, if I chose, could sink this craft in ten minutes. The people aboard here, even your husband, for I presume Monsieur Eustache to be the happy fellow, are conscious of my power; more so than you appear to be. You might have cause for frowns, *Ma belle Anglaise*, if I were to order your husband to be run up to the main yard-arm of *Le Diable.*"

"You could not be so cruel as to entertain a thought approaching it," she cried, earnestly.

"Ah! madame, your cruelty is greater," he replied, languishingly; "you deny me happiness, while I should be conferring it upon him; for do not our priests say there is happiness in the grave? Come, you relent: keep your own secret—I will preserve it religiously. You can be kind to me, and I will invite you, my charmer, and your husband, on board my frigate. We shall find many opportunities to be happy."

"If you will not let me pass, I must seek protection upon the deck," cried Florence, with a flushed brow.

He staggered forward and seized her by the waist as he uttered his words. She screamed violently, and broke from him; he pursued her and seized her again. A rapid footstep on the deck was followed by the companion ladder being almost leaped down; a figure rushed into the cabin—it was Paul. The next instant Landais discovered himself upon the floor of the cabin, almost insensible from striking his head against the bulk-head. He was surrounded by fallen chairs and broken glasses, and was at the extremity of the apartment, quite convinced that every bone in his body was broken. Paul was standing over him in angry excitement, and Florence rushed, weeping, to her side cabin.

"Knave! murderous villain!" cried Landais, as soon as he could recover his breath; "you have converted me to a jelly; but you shall walk the plank for it, you ruffian, you shall. A yard tackle shall sway your fellows to the devil, and yon jilt's husband shall—shall—curse me if I know now, but his fate shall be tremendous, whatever I may devise. Now raise me up, you ill-looking, ros' beef, John Bull—you *bretteur*—you have shaken me to death, you monster; I shall keep my berth for a month, and be compelled to make the interests of France suffer accordingly."

Paul did not raise him up, but instead, presented a pistol to his head, telling him in a stern tone that if he made a single outcry he would blow his brains out.

"*Mon Dieu!* you would not dare to murder me, monster," Landais exclaimed, growing very white.

"I will most certainly shoot you if you attempt to move or make a noise," returned Paul; "remain quiet, therefore; I never make a promise that I do not keep, as you shall discover if you attempt resistance."

"*Le scelerat*," murmured Landais, hiccupping, and half rolling over.

Paul summoned one of the men, and bade him send Gasket aft, and in a few minutes he made his appearance.

"I have a prisoner here," said our hero to him, "a little ratlin stuff will prevent his moving uneasily about."

Gasket laughed, and disappearing speedily, returned with some small line, with which he dexterously bound the Frenchman's arms firmly to his side; he then lifted him from the ground by Paul's command, and seated him close to the table. He had scarcely accomplished this act, when the boat which had been sent for Eustace returned, bringing him with it. The French seamen, according to the orders given, were to be taken to the forecastle, and there plied with grog to an unlimited extent, while Eustace made his way to the cabin: he seemed surprised to find Landais in such a condition, but Paul quickly explained the reason, and then had much difficulty in preventing him from inflicting severe chastisement upon the prisoner. They had still a difficult game to play, and if, as Paul told Eustace, they succeeded in winning it, he would find it an ample substitute for the disciplining he wished to bestow on Landais. They quitted the cabin, after Eustace had seen Florence, and quieted her fears, and proceeded to put into execution the scheme which Paul had devised for getting clear of the frigate. Landais was left to himself—a decanter of wine was within his reach, placed purposely there, and one arm left by design free from the elbow; his first object, on finding himself alone, was to endeavour to unfasten the knots of the rope confining him, but his delicate fingers were too weak to undo the work of the iron hands of Gasket, who had "bowsed all taut" with a strength beyond any the poor Frenchman possessed to cast off again. He muttered a number of oaths of the most patrician order, and then paused, uncertain what course to pursue; presently he heard some one moving in one of the side cabins—perhaps it was the fair wife of Captain Eustache. Landais was probably one of the vainest coxcombs in existence. Although Florence had so decidedly spurned him, he could not believe that she really intended it in her heart. It struck him she might have known of the proximity of Paul, and, fearing discovery, had acted as a very dragon of virtue. He looked at his figure—he remembered his face—he was satisfied of the piquancy of his attractions—he was aware of his fascinations, his blandishments--and his unfailing successes with the beauties of Paris poured in a stream upon his recollection; was it likely, was it possible, that one who had gained such conquests among the fair of his own nation should be scorned and despised by an English girl?—it was not in nature. A Frenchman—and such a Frenchman—and not loved by every woman he came across—bah! He listened attentively, there was certainly some one moving in the side cabin. If it were the captain's wife, and he could but persuade her to cut his bonds, he would gain the deck, summon his people, signal the frigate, and whose turn would it be to tremble then? He resolved to try what sweetness of voice, and the fairest promises could accomplish, and commenced by crying, "Hist!" several times: at last a voice in a whisper, exclaimed—

"Hallo!"

Landais thought the reply not altogether feminine; but, perhaps, it was an Englishism, he continued—

"*Approchez voux, ma chere Madame; j'ai besoin de vous parler.*"

What are you talking about?" responded the voice, still in a whisper.

Landais could not catch a work, but he thought he would make the most of his time, and ran on with a rhapsody, in which he declared that celestial beings fell short in a comparison with "his pretty English;" he knew her, he said, to be the kindest creature under heaven, but he knew also it was not possible always to show that kindness of heart which she possessed in such an eminent degree: he vowed he would forgive her the ungracious repulse she had favoured him with, and make her a princess if she would only look in upon him—only deign to turn those soft eyes towards him—"

"What's the use of your talking that gammon?" returned the voice, "I can't parley voo—say what you've got to say in a reg'lar strait down manner, and then somebody can make you out; but I'm reg'larly slewed now."

"*Quoi?*" cried Landais. "*Comment?*"

"Quaw!" repeated the voice. "Quaw! Don't make a row like a parrot, but talk like a man, though you be like a monkey," and the head of the speaker protruded as he uttered his words through the door-way—it was Gasket who had been performing some duties in the opposite side cabin to that which contained Florence, and expecting to gain some intelligence which might prove of use to Paul, from the bound Frenchman, had acted in the way described, but finding they did not understand each other's language, he dropped all disguise and made his appearance.

"Come on," he exclaimed, repeating in his own fashion, the word "*comment*," which Landais has used; "come on—yes, you are in a pretty condition to cry come on; d'ye want to fight with your arms tied? I did'nt think you had so much pluck in ye; howsomdever, you can't be obliged, so stop where you are and be quiet, and don't be trying to pitch any palaver to the loo'-tenant's lady, because if you do, your gib-stay will be flattened in, and your sky-scraper white swab of a wig will be put out of shape afore you could cry hold on!"

With this admonition the seamen departed, and Landais in a fury of despair, seized the decanter, filled his glass, and drank its contents to drive away his care; he repeated this act so frequently that ere long he slid from his chair, and lay upon the floor beneath the table in a blissful state of oblivion—a state of speechless, helpless intoxication, into which his gig's crew had likewise been placed.

Paul ordered them to be kept below, and commanded his men to be on the alert to lay out on the yards at a moment's notice. Everything was done quietly and without making any display calculated to excite the suspicion of the people on board the frigate. Captain Hardy was for at once putting sail upon the ship and giving them another chase, or for boarding them and taking possession of their vessel; he estimated one Englishman as equal to five Frenchmen, and one brigantine to two frigates.

"We are more than a match for them," he cried, testily, "we can beat them at the odds of five to one; look here, we number thirty, don't we? Well, five times thirty is a hundred and fifty, isn't it; very well, that makes us a hundred and fifty to two hundred and fifty, don't it? very well, then, five times a hundred and fifty makes us—"

"Yes," cried Paul, with a laugh "but that progression would soon make our brigantine a first-rate of a hundred and twenty guns, and a thousand men her complement. Rest assured, Captain Hardy, I will not disgrace my vessel.

"Your country," exclaimed Hardy.

"My vessel," repeated Paul.

"And your country," persisted Hardy; "why don't you say your country, old England?"

"It is not my country," replied Paul.

"No?—not England? Why where did you spring from?—America?" ejaculated Hardy, with surprise.

"No," said Paul, "Scotland gave me birth, but that is of no consequence; I will never disgrace the flag I fight under."

"You won't fight under that white rag at the gaff, will you?" almost roared Hardy, "because I'm damned if I do. I'll fight like a sea dog, but curse me if I handle a weapon with a Frenchman's colours flying at the peak, not to be made Lord High Admiral of their nation, or any other. No; I'm true blue, I'll stick to the old country while I've a pin to stand upon."

"If we fight it will not be beneath this flag," exclaimed Paul; "it is not however, my intention to give battle to the frigate if I can help it. The most daring courage, backed by the best skill, would not enable us to carry the day now—we must try stratagem."

"I don't like it," grumbled Hardy; "it ain't ship-shape and Bristol fashion; it ain't sailor like, it ain't—but what's the odds of what I say, you've a right to the command in your own ship, and if you haven't the pluck why you can't help it."

Paul smiled, and laying his hand upon his shoulder, said—

"I have all the courage to attempt a greater enterprise than tackling yonder frigate, though she were the finest that ever swam, but I must not forget the owner's interests. If I lose this vessel through a foolhardy engagement, I lose his property, and sacrifice that which is not my own. Were this a ship of war, and I its commander—were it simply a brigantine, properly armed, I would not run from yon frigate without giving her a little hot talk, but I am in a trading vessel, and while I do nothing to injure my honour, I must do my best to preserve my employer's property."

"Ay! ay! that's all fair enough," exclaimed Hardy, "I had forgotten that; perhaps you are right a'ter all: but let me tell you one thing, it's a matter as goes against my heart to hoist any other flag than that of the land I was born in—it goes against me like sailing in the wind's eye, to be quietly on blue water under the bunting of a nation which, rather than be a native on, I'd hang myself from the cro'jick yard; you ain't partic'lar enough, young man, about the flag of your country. England is your country, though Scotland was your birth place, and her flag is the one you ought to carry at the fore, main, and mizen; you may tell me it's policy and all that, that's your opinion—but in mine there's no excuse for sailing under false colours at any time. 'Tell truth and shame the devil,' said my old mother, and so I will till I go down with the anchor; if you can't show your own colours, don't show any. Why, damme, if I was in a woman's wash-tub, and a seventy-four was bearing down upon me, I'd up with the blue and have a slap at her, if her first shot scuttled me. I would, damme."

"Such reasoning, Captain Hardy, has lost his Majesty's navy many a gallant ship," returned Paul. "I would fight anything, however my superior, if there was a single chance of success, and I would sink my ship rather than strike; but I would never be guilty of the madness of opposing a vessel so weak in all things, for the purpose of war, as this, to a fine frigate like *Le*

Diable. She shall not capture us without a struggle, and I shall do my best that she has not the opportunity of making a prize of us."

"They won't have me at a gift, I'll lay a hundred guineas to a dog vane," cried Hardy; "they won't have me, unless they can take me without cutting me down first, and they shall try hard at that, the rascals, they shall."

Gasket now approached, and after mentioning what had occurred in the cabin, drew Paul's attention to a fog which was rising. Evening was also approaching, and in the darkness our hero hoped to effect his escape. He went himself among the men to see that they were ready, at a moment's warning, to go aloft and set topsails, and then coming aft again bade the man at the wheel keep as wide a berth of the frigate as he could without exciting notice, although there was so little movement in the vessel as scarcely to have steerage way upon her. And now those on board *Le Diable* observed the fog rising too, and they having drawn some distance a-head, made signals for the Kirkcudbright to near them; every eye was blind to their bunting, and it was not until Paul observed preparations made for sending a boat on board of him that he appeared to notice the wishes. The hands weie then sent up and ordered to be concealed in the rigging, save those who were to set the main-topsail, until the word was given to "Let fall" and "sheet home."

The glass had been busy on board the French frigate: the protracted absence of their commander, and the continued disappearance of the gig's crew from the deck, caused the first lieutenant to have some suspicions that all was not right. The people of the Kirkcudbright were too quiet; it had a bad look; their caution was too great to be unsuspected—then it was a violation of etiquette and duty to act without the captain's orders, and there was hardly sufficient grounds of suspicion to justify him in doing so; still he resolved to be on the alert to counteract foul play, if occasion arose. He observed the men go aloft when he was about sending the boat to inquire the reason of their not answering their signal, and countermanded the order, intending to hail them as they came alongside, and despatch a party of seamen on board with a respectable message to Landais. He watched the main and mizen-topsail set, and saw by the white curl of the sea at the cut-water of the brigantine, that she had way upon her; he saw her falling off before the wind without much surprise, expecting her, as soon as she was "held in hand," to round-to; but she gradually fell off more and more, until she displayed nothing scarcely but the broad stern, and was, with only her topsails set, but drawing well, moving rapidly from her dangerous neighbour. The lieutenant rubbed his eyes, and could not understand the manœuvre; he at first attributed it to bad seamanship, and supposed that they would still come round; but no, they kept on, increasing the distance between them every instant, and then the lieutenant ordered a gun to be got ready forward, waiting still a few minutes to see if a change took place, but no, there was no alteration, and they had really made a considerable distance—almost alarming. The gunner reported the gun to be ready; the lieutenant ordered him to fire it, and the white smoke wreathed up as the flash and report transpired together. The shot skimmed along the surface of the water without nearing the fugitive, but, as if the discharge had been the stroke of an enchantress's wand, the brigantine almost instantly appeared covered from heel to truck with a cloud of canvas, and shot forward, like an arrow from a bow, making, apparently, deliberately for the fog bank, which, like a dense mass, rested, at some distance, upon the sea. There was now no longer any doubt of the intention of the brigantine. The lieutenant turned up his hands aloft to spread sails, and the drummer beat to quarters: all was confusion. The men slid down the rigging, and were turned up again. "The captain is run away with," went from mouth to mouth, and scared them all. The want of smart discipline was now wondrously apparent in the handling of the sails. The Kirkcudbright was a long way a head before *Le Diable* would answer her helm, and farther still before she had all her canvas set and was fairly in chase of her. The Frenchman blazed away from his bow ports at the flying brigantine, as an earnest of her future intentions, forgetting that every discharge retarded his progress, and did no damage to his enemy. The guns were loaded as fast as they were discharged, and the brigantine in consequence, with everything set that could hold a capful of wind, maintained the advantage she had obtained by her stratagem.

Both vessels held on their course with undiminished speed for an hour or two, and then Paul succeeded in running his craft into the fog bank. In a few minutes the pursuing vessel was lost sight of, and the brigantine careered forward, plunged in an artificial night. The fog was dense to a degree; the forecastle could scarcely be distinguished from the quarter-deck; every precaution was, therefore, taken to prevent accidents. The man at the wheel was relieved, look-outs were stationed in various parts of the vessel, the lead was kept in readiness, and then the course they had hitherto pursued was altered. They could still hear the reports of the frigate's guns, although they could not see her, and judged that she had not yet succeeded in lessening the distance detween them. Night now fast came on, and made the darkness much greater. The fog had lessened the wind to a considerable extent, but they still made good progress, and hoped before morning to have dropped their unpleasant companion altogether. The brigantine was now sailing on a bowline, and was running parallel with the edge of the fog bank, dropping into the proper course to make the port she was bound to; it seemed as if the frigate had discovered their movement, and followed still in their wake. The flash of their guns might still be dimly seen, and though the report was fainter than ever, still it was to be heard.

Paul had nothing to gain by carrying his prisoners to New York; he therefore resolved to put the captain and his men into their own gig, and, supplying them well with provisions, a mast and sail, in the case of accident, sent them adrift. If they were picked up by their own frigate so much the better—he should gain time by their stopping to do so; if not, it was a hundred chances to one but they would be picked up by some vessel outward or homeward bound. The fumes of the wine and grog had nothing like

worn off when Paul descended to the cabin, and, with the aid of a couple of hands, brought Mousieur Landais upon deck. The Frenchman was too drunk to understand what was going on; and his crew, save two—who were sober enough to be aware of their position, and howl their horror at it—were in a similar plight. They were lowered with the gig, which had been hauled up not to impede their progress, into the water, the hooks cast off by one of the hands, who descended for the purpose, and was hauled on board again, and then they were left to themselves. All night they drifted along; the two soberest towards morning set the sail and put their little vessel before the wind. When daylight came, there was a speck upon the horizon, but whether it was the chase or chaser, or a stranger, they had no means of determining.

CHAPTER V.

" Still onward, fair the breeze, nor rough the surge,
The blue waves sport around the stern they urge ;
Far on the horizon's verge appears a speck,
A spot—a mast—a sail—an armed deck !
Their little bark her men of watch descry,
And ampler canvas woos the wind from high ;
She bears her down, majestically near,
Speed on her prow, and terror in her tier."

THE CORSAIR.

" The launch is crowded with the faithful few
Who wait their chief, a melancholy crew ;
But some remained, reluctant, on the deck
Of that proud vessel, now a moral wreck.',

THE ISLAND.

THE first lieutenant of *Le Diable*, with a shrewd suspicion, calculated upon the course the brigantine would be steered, and promptly resolved upon following it ; he found, soon after his vessel had worked into the fog, that firing at a blank was an unprofitable employment ; it made a great noise it was true, but, like loud talkers, and people who profess much, it was all it did. The guns were therefore kept quiet, and a sharp look-out was established. The first grey streaks of morning had, however, faintly illumined the surrounding sea before they emerged from the dense night, and the look-out at the main top-mast head gave notice of a sail far away on the weather beam. Sail after sail was now added, from a " cursed god" to the lower studding-sail booms, and the walk of the frigate materially increased. It was a noble frigate, and flew through the water in obedience to the sail upon her like a racer to the spur, and now the Frenchmen hugged themselves to find the hull of the stranger lifting up. What vaunts and boasts there were, to be sure, and what invidious comparisons they made between themselves and the brigantine, upon which they were drawing fast. They saw with glee that, although the chase had hung canvas wherever there was room to place it, that they gained upon them, and the drums once more beat to quarters, while a few hands were sent up in readiness to shorten sail the moment it was necessary.

They were correct in their expectations ; it was the Kirkcudbright they still held in chase, and those on board of her viewed with no great satisfaction the gradual, but certain, approach of the frigate.

" We shall have to fight her after all," exclaimed Hardy, rubbing his hands ; " she will soon be within a mile of us. She's a frigate, by the Lord ! and the shipwrights that made her had a slice of luck they never dreamed of. Lord ! lord ! to see how accident will assist even Frenchmen."

" They draw very fast on us, Paul," exclaimed Eustace, turning an anxious glance at our hero, who wore a calm, indifferent air, " What do you mean to do ?"

"Run while I can," he replied, calmly.

"Run! um!" growled Hardy. "Damn me if I wouldn't sooner have a shot between wind and water than run from the biggest Frenchman of 'em all; it ain't like an Englishman to run from anything; it ain't in his nature to do it. He can run after an enemy as fast as any craft, or with a friend as far as he'll go, but, damme, he don't often run away; for my part, I don't see the use of a back at all—not to a honest man; for a lying, jumping monkey of a mounseer it may do very well, but not for an upright fair and above-board Englishman; he has on use for a back—he always, at all times, turns a full front to an enemy, and damme, you wouldn't turn your back on a friend. I tell you what, young man, I'm older in the service than you, and know what's what; take my advice, turn your back on nothing under heaven, nor in it for that matter, and pipe the hands to in stun-sails, and strike to'gaunt-sails, we'll round-to until the frigate comes within gun shot of us, and then we'll pepper away at her while there's a shot or powder aboard; and if we don't hammer the dust out of her then, we will board her on the quarter, and carry her in the turning of a handspik'."

Paul smiled at the earnestness with which the hot but honest sailor spoke, and replied—

"You shall not find me wanting when the important moment arrives."

"Then you will fight?" cried Hardy.

"Yes," he returned; "if I have no other chance left; but," he added, addressing Eustace, "for the sake of your fair wife—who may not meet with the respect due to her should we be captured—I will hold on to the last."

"By heaven! Paul," cried Eustace, fiercely; "if any villain dared to lay hands on her I'd cleave him to the deck, though I was sent to the yard-arm the next instant."

"Providing you had the chance," said Paul. "If, as I suspect, Landais has not been picked up we shall be treated as his murderers, and, with a short prayer, be run aloft by the neck. We have nothing to do, therefore, but to sell our lives dearly. Still, I think it no act of cowardice to keep out of the frigate's reach; she has sixteen ports of a side, and carries eighteens, I dare say. There's no vessel, I believe, that ever fought her guns upon one deck, to surpass her. She has at least two hundred men on board, though, from the swarms clustering about her rigging, I should more inclinedly say two hundred and fifty; if we grapple, can the most desperate bravery hope to succeed in such a contest? Rashness is not courage, and, despite Captain Hardy's experience, which I confess I respect, I must still continue in the path I have chosen, and will not resign it until I am compelled."

"I don't mean to say, young man," cried Captain Hardy, as he concluded, "that you are not doing your best to preserve the ship and the people: I don't mean to say that you are not acting well and wisely. No, damme, though I wish you to do differently. I don't mean to say that you are flying dishonourably, for it's natural that a child couldn't lick a man, or a man a giant. I only mean to say that I never willingly ran from any damned Frenchman in all my life."

"I do not run willingly," said Paul.

"I mean I never ran from one in my life; never," he returned; "and never would, if I could help it."

"I cannot help it," said Paul, drily.

"Damme, then I wouldn't at all, come what might," he roared, hotly.

Paul laughed, and directed his glass to the frigate.

"Whatever you think best, Paul, do," exclaimed Eustace, "and count upon my help to the death."

Paul pressed his extended hand as he removed the glass from his eyes.

"I will do all that can be done, for *her* sake, be assured," he answered; then, turning to the steersman, he said, "let her feel the helm a little more; we shall have to fall off presently, and we may as well have as much of our course out of her as we can. They are about to talk to us with an iron mouth. Aha! here it comes."

A blaze of fire from the bows of *Le Diable* followed his words; it was accompanied by a ball, which did not reach its destination by a considerable distance. Paul watched it as it skipped along, and fell short, and then cried—

"Forward there! send Nat Spanker aft."

A weather-beaten seaman appeared, and touching his hat respectfully, he waited for orders. Paul, who was gazing at the motions of the frigate, as soon as he was aware of his presence, said hastily to him—

"You know the merits of the stern chaser; could you touch yon frigate with her metal?"

The man looked a moment, and then said, as he slapped the breech with his hand—

"I know Long Tom pretty well, your honour, seeing I've tried him many a time afore he was put aboard this wessel, and I'm bold to say that there ain't a piece cast as'll carry so far as this."

"That's not my question," said Paul. "Do you think, as we are running now, you could make a mark in the frigate?"

"I'll forfeit a month's pay, your honour, if I don't knock one of her eye teeth out," answered the man, coolly; or, if you likes it better, sir, I'll lodge it in her for'mast. I'll mark the ball, and if it ain't there when we boards Johnny Crappo, why you may put a black chalk agin my name."

"Then it's your opinion we shall fight her," said Hardy, hastily.

"A' course it is, and that of all the people for'ard, sir," returned the man.

"And you think we should lick them if we tried it?" said Hardy.

"Lick them!" replied the man, with surprise; "most certainly, sir, I ain't a doubt on the matter. I never knowed a English ship's crew that couldn't lick the crew of any foreign craft."

"I owe you a glass of grog, my man," exclaimed Hardy; "you're a blue jacket and talk sense. You hear, Captain Jones," he said, addressing Paul, 'what the people's wishes are."

"Yes," replied our hero; "still I shall think and act for myself until I see fit to take another's advice. I say it with all respect to your opinion. Is that gun ready?'

"Ay, ay, sir!" was the reply of two or three men who directed its movements.

"Stand by the weather-braces," he cried.

A number of men sprang to obey his orders, and Nat Spanker having carefully sighted his gun, the word was given to fire; and with a stunning report the Long Tom delivered its contents. The progress of the ball was watched anxiously; it proved itself to have been well aimed by hitting the frigate in her starboard bow, and throwing the splinters in all directions; a loud cheer from the men accompanied it. The next moment, in a startling voice, Paul cried—

"Fall off one point, and haul on the weather braces!"

It was done, and at the same moment an English ensign was floating from the peak of the gaff; for a few minutes it hung there, and the voice of Hardy exclaimed with a chuckle—

"Now the rascals know who and what we are!"

His words directed Paul's attention to the flag, and in an instant his brow became the colour of scarlet; he stamped his foot and cried sternly—

"Who has dared to hoist that flag?"

"It was I!" exclaimed Captain Hardy, bluffly; "I did it with my own hands to tell the mounseers they had a tooth of Johnny Bull in their lug."

"You will remember, Captain Hardy, you are not on board your own ship," observed Paul, angrily; "another such uncalled-for act, and I shall be compelled to order you into irons."

"Order me into irons! Damme, order me into irons for hoisting the colours of our country! Damme, that is beating to windward with a wet sail. Order me into irons, why—"

"You are on board my ship, sir; I am captain here, and will suffer no man to interfere with me and my duty. Gasket, haul down that bunting."

"What, strike the colours! avast," roared Hardy, jumping before him. "No, damme, no! not haul down a flag I have borne at my peak since I was a stripling; not while I am here—not while I have a stick standing; damme if they shall be hauled down!"

"Stand aside, sir," cried Paul, advancing; "I will be commander in my own ship; your conduct is inexcusable. Unless you remain quiet you shall be confined to your cabin."

"But you don't haul down the colours!" shouted Hardy; what ho, there! Tigers; you are all true blues; will ye consent to the hauling down of our flag to a lubberly Frenchman, though he does carry heavier metal, and a few more guns than us?"

"No! no! no!" cried the men; a number of Paul's own crew joining with Hardy's followers.

"No, to be sure! stand by me, lads," roared Hardy, "and heave him overboard who attempts to lay a hand on the haliards."

"We will! we will!" shouted the men, pressing aft.

"Stand back, on your lives!" shouted Paul; he drew a pistol from his belt. "This is mutiny! The first man who dares to come aft without orders, I'll send a bullet through his head," he cried. "Gasket, do your duty. Captain Hardy, I place you under arrest."

Gasket by force put Hardy on one side, and Paul seized him by the collar! the ensign was hauled down, and then the men set up a shout of defiance, and in a body came aft. Eustace drew his sword, and Gasket seized up a handspike; Nat Spanker laid hold of the rammer of the gun, and half-a-dozen or so of the brigantine's crew ran up and sided with them; everything was in confusion. Paul, however, kept his hold of Hardy, and said bitterly—

"Is this your return, old man, for saving the lives of yourself and crew? Is this a captain's example of discipline and order? Is it by exciting mutiny and disobedience that you wish to show your title to a honourable name? I thought better of you, sir; and you, ye rascals," he cried fiercely to the men who were threateningly closing round; "must you be mutinous at a moment's notice, too. What deficiency of food and grog have ye had that ye should throw up your duty and turn yourselves from good seamen into brawling knaves?"

"We'll do no duty under a French ensin'," cried a voice from the mob: it received a murmuring approval from the rest.

"But you have already, and gloried in it, ye knaves, not many hours since," cried Paul; "if it is my will to show a naked gaff, or the colours of any nation, I shall not consult the ship's company for their permission to do it. My will is your law, and you shall obey it while I hold command—"

"Captain Jones, I am wrong; I beg your pardon," exclaimed Hardy, suddenly. "I have done wrong, and I am sorry for it. Back, fellows, to your duty; I forgot myself and set you a bad example, for which, Captain Jones, I freely render myself your prisoner to do as you please with me. I have stirred up a mutinous feeling, when in a moment like this the utmost harmony should prevail between the captain and his people. I am an old fool and deserve to be punished; I am not a boy, but have acted like a hot-headed one. I ought to have known better—damme if I could not deliver sentence upon myself to be run up to the yard-arm without any grace—"

"Say no more, Captain Hardy; let us forget it," observed Paul, relinquishing his hold; "our danger is more critical than ever. We shall have the iron of the Frenchman about our ears in a few seconds; then you will see that French metal and a French frigate are not to be sneered at by an English brigantine, however lion-hearted its crew. To your duty, my men; you will have plenty of work to do presently, whether you have a flag or no at the gaff."

"You are a generous fellow, Captain Jones," cried Hardy, with warmth; "and whatever you say, henceforth, shall be as strictly obeyed by me as by the meanest of your crew."

As he concluded, the people all turned away, and returned to their respective stations like men who were ashamed at having been guilty of an error, and awaited in silence the orders of our hero, resolving to prove by their alacrity in executing them, their contrition for their momentary mutiny. Still there was a dislike prevalent among them at running from the Frenchman; and though certain destruction awaited them, they would rather have encountered it than not have given battle to their hated foe. The frigate had altered her course as well as themselves, and was now running large; she displayed the same superiority before the wind as she had on a bowline, and neared them fast. It was evident by the silence of the starboard gun, that Long Tom's shot had displaced it, and as Le Diable was once more within range, Ned Spanker was directed to make it tell over their "nose and eyes;" he did himself and gun credit by the execution; but as it retarded their progress, without much effectual damage, Paul refrained from using it. The frigate was now within shot of them, and he gave his orders for the men to stand by with the braces, and the helmsman to steady the helm, but be prepared to sheer hard away to port when he gave the word; he did this because he guessed the frigate would come down and endeavour to rake him, and the event justified his suspicion. He saw the alteration in the sails and the stern of Le Diable begin to appear, and gave his orders in a voice of thunder; the breeze, fortunately, was brisk, and his vessel obeyed her helm to perfection. Once more, as quick as thought, she was on the wind, but was only just able to clear the destructive effects of a rattling broadside, which the French frigate, as soon as she could come round, discharged; a few of her shots cut some lines, and pierced the spanker, but did no great harm. Paul ordered Gasket to up with the English flag, which he did, and the crew cheered lustily. The Frenchman loaded again and discharged another broadside, but with less success than before; while Ned Spanker pointed his Long Tom, and with a well directed shot cut the maintop-mast shrouds, struck the topmast, nearly severing it in half, and killed two men. A hundred hands sprang aloft to repair the disaster; the topmast was secured as well as possible, and she still held her course in pursuit. Her rapid approach now rendered it impossible longer to continue a flight, and Paul prepared to meet his adversary to the best of his ability. A few hands were despatched aloft to furl the lighter sails, while the rest cleared the decks for action. The crew were provided with boarding pikes and cutlasses, and were delighted at the thoughts of being opposed hand to hand to *Johnny Crapeaud.* Paul knew it was a desperate effort, but he determined to do all that could be done ere he suffered himself to be taken, though the numbers were so superior to his own as to render the last expectation scarcely doubtful: the guns were all brought to bear on one side, the yards were slung, the hammocks placed in the nettings, and everything done exactly as if the brigantine was really a vessel of war. Captain Hardy was especially busy, but proved himself of service, as did Eustace, whose knowledge and habitude of command rendered his abilities desirable at such a moment. The Frenchmen imitated their movements; the superfluous sails were taken in, and the wind brought the roll of the drum beating to quarters to the ears of our hero and his crew. Paul held the vessel in hand, prepared to avoid the sweeping effects of the broadside, and return the fire from his feeble display of guns as rapidly and effectively as he could. *Le Diable* bore down upon them with the intention of coming to close quarters, and withheld her fire until it should be sufficiently near to have a withering effect; and just as Paul expected to receive the Frenchman's fire, a man at the mast head sung out—

"Sail ho!"

"Where away?" shouted Paul.

"On our starboard bow!" the man replied.

Our hero turned his glass in the direction, and saw, sure enough, a vessel beating up towards him. He surveyed her a moment anxiously, and then hailing the tops, inquired of the look-out what he made her out.

"She looks like a frigate, sir, he returned; "she's a clipper, and rises like a bird. She's standing dead on to us."

"If this should be another Frenchman, there is no hope left," exclaimed Eustace.

"I am afraid not. We must see what is to be done when we have properly made her out," replied Paul: "I will hold Monsieur *Le Diable* in chase still until I know a little more. Away! aloft, there!" he cried to the men in the waist and forecastle in a quick tone, and gave them the necessary orders to set the sails they had previously reduced. They instantly obeyed, and again the brigantine flew forward at her old pace. As if the Frenchman, from previous experience, had expected some such manœuvre, she was as quickly covered with canvas as her chase, and with renewed speed followed her.

"Upon deck, there!" cried the man aloft, a few minutes afterwards.

An answer was returned, and he conveyed the intelligence that the approaching frigate on the starboard bow looked English in her build, and in the trim of her sails: that she was packing sail upon her, and shewed a brave line of teeth. A broadside from the French frigate, who had yawed round, followed this speech, and Paul, who met the manœuvre by a similar one, returned the fire. Two of his men were wounded; the forecourse and main sail were almost torn to ribbons, braces and sheets were cut asunder, and a splinter torn from the main-mast: but the men cheered and worked their little stock of guns with great rapidity, doing considerable mischief, though from so miserably an inadequate source. Another broadside from *Le Diable* would have done terrific damage, but Paul, taking advantage of the heave of the sea, escaped a great part of it. Again their little battery was discharged, and Nat Spanker did some service with his Long Tom. The men cheered as they fired, and almost believed themselves on board of a sixty gun-ship instead of a six. The noise of the firing seemed like a spur to the advancing frigate, for she neared so rapidly as to make her approach look like magic. But the mystery was solved in the brigantine's maintaining a running fight, and her movements towards the new comer were equal to shortening the distance between them one half. The fire of the French frigate was fortunately not delivered with the rapidity or precision for which the English have so long been famed, or the brigantine would ere this have been a wreck, if left above water at all. Paul's management and skill had much to do with the safety of his vessel: though ardent and youthful, enthusiastic and highly daring, yet he had sufficient judgment to cool that

fervour down when the exercise of it would have brought destruction upon him without the smallest success. He was prepared to fight, feeble as his opportunities for opposition were, and would have nailed his colours to the mast sooner than strike—but he could not deceive himself as to the issue of a contest with the frigate, and it was, therefore, with no little pleasure he heard it announced from the mast-head, that the stranger had hoisted English colours. He turned his glass to her—her royals were taken in; he saw her shrouds manned. He heard three roaring cheers come from her, and then found himself within hail of her. A stentorian voice from aboard cried—

"Hoy, ship ahoy! what brigantine's that?"

Paul replied, and in the same breath the new comer shouted—

"What frigate's that?"

"*Le Diable*—Frenchman. She has chased us since yesterday morning!"

"Thankye, thankye!" was the Englishman's reply, and the vessel swept by, Paul just hearing the exclamation, "Round-to till the fun is over."

Hardy set up a lusty cheer, which was echoed by every man on board the Kirkcudbright, as the English frigate ran up alongside of the Frenchman, and poured a terrific broadside into her. Even here *Le Diable* had the advantage in size, number of guns, people, and weight of metal. The English frigate only carried twelves, and, in fact, was smaller in all ways—but what she wanted in calibre she made up in resolution. The Kirkcudbright stood off and on, witnessing the fight, and Hardy could hardly restrain his impatient desire to be in the fray at the head of his fellows. Paul too felt his bosom burn like fire, and more than once was tempted to steer his vessel into action, but that he disdained to place the Frenchman at unfair odds. The rigging was clustered with his men, and on their eager faces might be read the interest they felt in the issue of the contest as well as the stern determination, if fortune went against their countrymen, to lend their aid to gain the victory, or perish with them. Eustace brought Florence upon deck to see a sight which afforded him and all the men such unmixed satisfaction; but the tremendous discharges of artillery, the cheers of the men, the flashes of fire, and the dense masses of sulphureous vapour which arose from the successive discharges terrified her, and instead of evincing any gratification she cowered and trembled, and clung to Eustace, and speedily was glad again to seek the cabin and the society of Letty Nehemie.

The clouds of smoke from the guns of the two vessels enveloped them so thickly that it was impossible to tell what success was attending either. Paul steered his vessel nearer and nearer every board he made, until there was some danger of his getting a little of the flying metal. At length they saw the maintopmast of the *Le Diable*, which they had damaged, go by the board, followed speedily also by the fore-topmast, with all the yards and rigging; then there was a cessation of the heavy firing; quick and short discharges of musketry ensued; figures were to be seen, in the dimly visible hulls, flitting to and fro; then came three tremendous hurrahs, and when Paul ran under the stern of both vessels he saw on the peak of *Le Diable* English colours flying over French. At the earnest request of his men, he permitted three-fourths of the number to lend their aid in clearing the two frigates of their dead—the destructive effects of the action—and securing the prisoners. The contest had been a severe one, both vessels having suffered severely, the English frigate particularly in her cordage and sails, though her spars and masts had fortunately, as well as singularly, escaped without very considerable damage. It was evening before both ships were in sailing order, and then an invitation on board the *Reckless*, which was the name of the English frigate, was tendered to our hero, and extended to his friends, which he accepted. The captain happened to be an acquaintance of Eustace, and the meeting was, therefore, less constrained. He complimented him upon his wife, but expressed his regret that the service had lost so gallant an officer. He expressed also his surprise, as well as commendations upon the ability and nautical skill Paul must have displayed in being able so long to elude

Le Diable, and acknowledged that his own affair with her was a warm action, spiritedly maintained, and full of hard work to bring to a fortunate termination. A few inquiries of the French lieutenant, who was present, though slightly wounded, respecting Landais, made him acquainted with his fate, and satisfied Paul that in the fog he had not been seen by the people on board his frigate; he was, therefore, unless picked up by some passing vessel, still floating about in his gig upon the waters of the wide Atlantic.

The moon had risen ere our hero prepared to go on board his own vessel; he almost envied the English captain as he heard him express his intention of shaping his course for England, his cruise having expired; and his expectations of being flatteringly received by his countrymen, he having sent home no less than four merchant ships, richly laden, as prizes, besides gaining the honour of having captured the finest frigate that ever swam on salt water.

"Honour and fame such as I hope for, such as I look forward to attain, can never be gained in commercial vessels," thought Paul. "A ship of war must be mine, and then, Alice, then—" he paused—a remembrance of her father crossed him like a blight: it was a bitter check to his hopes—he sighed, and with a feeling of despondency quitted the *Reckless*. He was accompanied by his friends and people, save a portion of Hardy's crew, who volunteered to enter in the frigate, and were accepted in the place of those who had fallen in the action. When Paul gained his vessel, the two ships cheered and parted company, each taking different courses.

After a run of twelve days, when they were still about twenty days' sail from their destination, Paul was on deck one evening, engaged in conversation with Eustace and Florence, their discourse had taken somewhat of a melancholy turn. It was a calm night, there was little wind stirring, and but slight movement in the sea, save the roll and swell peculiar to the Atlantic; the sails drew lazily, and the seamen—unoccupied by the duties of the vessel—were lying about the waist, forecastle, and galley, in little knots and groups, reciting marvellous yarns, or making comments upon the late action. It is probable the serenity of this scene, with a somewhat heavy atmosphere, gave the tone to the pensive thoughts of our hero and his companions. Home had been the chief subject of their converse, and the similarity of their cases had brought recollections which threw a gloom of their minds; gradually, however, they ceased talking, and each fell into a deep fit of musing, the silence only being broken by a loud laugh from the galley or forecastle, drawn by some unbelievable assertion made by one of the crew, and even those sallies became less frequent, until a solemn silence prevailed. Suddenly there was a noise arose from below, one of hurry and confusion, then a bright flash, accompanied by a heavy volume of smoke rushing up the main hatchway, followed by a shrill, startling, piercing cry of—

"The ship's on fire! The ship's on fire!"

It was echoed by twenty voices, and in an instant the serenity was destroyed, and the whole deck so peaceful a moment since, became a scene of the wildest confusion; some men ran to and fro shouting different orders, others remained still, almost paralysed; some mounted aloft to take in the canvas, others cried out for water, and "all hands out buckets;" but amidst the disorder no one did aught to see to or attempt to put a stop to the flames, until Paul, in a voice which he made to be heard from every part of the vessel, commanded silence, and then gave orders for the courses to be hauled up, a band of a dozen to "out buckets,' and a few to follow him to see where the danger existed and the means of staying it. He descended the main hatchway, and encountered a boy whose duty was to wait on him; the lad was crying, and said, that while drawing some spirit, the light he bore somehow—he could not tell how—set fire to it. Paul waited to hear no more, he made for the spirit hold, but the flames burst forth with a fury which, in spite of all his courage, drove him back; there was a large quantity stowed there, and several barrels were on fire; the woodwork of the hold was blazing fiercely, and the flames were licking up everything in their way with a rapidity which defied every attempt to arrest their progress. The men arrived with buckets of water—others were bade assist them; they poured bucket after bucket with great quickness, but it had no effect; the fire increased, and the men were obliged to give way before it in all directions. The men worked manfully, sparing no exertion, but in vain; the fire spread fearfully, and Paul perceived that it had gained too great a hold for human means to stop it, and turned his attention, as he could not save his vessel, to saving their lives; he gave the necessary orders, and the men sprung to obey them; fortunately they were well supplied with boats, and well stocked with provisions. They had saved the boats of Captain Hardy's brig, and now their use was invaluable; they were at once lowered to the water, and food and water handed in, with such property belonging to our hero, to Eustace, his wife, Hardy, and the people, as could be collected, was placed in the boats while it was safe to remain; but soon the heat became tremendous, the flames roared, and the wood crackled; the fire communicated to the rigging, and ran up it in wild, snake-like wreaths, devouring and destroying all that came before it. The foremost, for the wind blew in that direction, was the first to begin to totter, and then Paul gave the order for the men to enter the boats; the same order and propriety of conduct was observed as though they were about to land in port, under favourable auspices; there was no rushing nor crowding—each man went in his turn and took his place till the boat was full, and then they pulled away, giving room to the others, until the last boat, the pinnace, and largest of them all, was filled; and then Paul, finding there was no one else left, quitted the deck of the Kirkcudbright, which no human foot was ever to tread again, and took his place at the helm: a small sail was raised, and he gave the order for his men to give way, which in silence they obeyed, taking long and vigorous strokes with their oars to get a wide offing—for every man knew there was a large quantity of powder on board, and could not tell one moment from another that it would not explode, and if they were within its reach, hurl them to destruction. When, as Paul believed, they were beyond the range of the fragments when dispersed, he bade the men cease rowing, and turned the burning vessel; there she lay where he had left her, fast hastening to her doom; the flames were burning the shrouds, and stays, dancing and leaping to and fro like demons or fiends delighting over their destroying work. There being no command over the helm the ill-fated vessel was yawing about in the wind as though frightened at her position; it was, however, not for long—the flames had communicated to the fore part of he vessel, and soon the masts and top-mast fell, followed by the main-masts top, and top-gallant masts; then the guns, which were all loaded, were discharged, with a startling report, and ultimately a tremendous blaze of light flashed across the eyes of the gazers, almost blinding them, and illuminating the sea around to the verge of the horizon; it was accompanied by a stunning crash, which seemed to deafen them; there was a shower of coruscations shot up into the air, long blazing trails of fire, like the tails of a thousand rockets, and then all was dark and silent—the Kirkcudbright had blown up, and had disappeared for ever.

Paul still gazed upon the spot where she had walk'd

"The waters like a thing of life,"

even after every vestige had vanished which could have told how fair a fabric had there existed: he stood like a statue, his eyes fixed upon where she was not; he seemed rooted to the spot, scarcely breathing, as though he expected to see her once more in all her pride and beauty: at last, he turned his head away with a heavy sigh, and dropping it, covered his eyes with his hand; it was but for a minute; but though so brief, the agony was intense; he dashed his hand across his eyes, and then his face, though pale, wore an air of calmness, blended slightly with sternness. He summoned the boats containing the chief part of his people to his side, and communicated with them his intention of steering for Newfoundland; and giving orders to the people in his pinnace, he led the way. For a long time a dead silence prevailed, until at last it was broken by Eustace, who, in a low kind voice, endeavoured to console Florence, and rouse her from the affrighted unhappy state in which she was plunged. Paul added his endeavours too, and spoke so cheerfully, so full of hope—which, in reality, he did not feel—that she dried her tears, and for the sake of him who was more than all the world to her, endeavoured to appear calm and resigned—an effort which had the effect of raising the spirits of Eustace in a manifold degree, while Paul, to infuse confidence in his men, who were wearing gloomy brows, addressed them in a light inspiriting tone, expressing his firm conviction of being speedily seen, and picked up by some vessel whose destination was the same as their own, or one, at least, who would take them on board until they met with one bound to New York. His words, and his manner of delivering them, succeeded in creating the effect he desired, and speedily the laugh and careless gaiety of the light hearted sailor was displayed by the men, who seeing they had fair weather and plenty of provisions before them, soon forgot the unpleasant predicament into which they were plunged.

Paul, by the aid of a compass, which he had saved from the Kirkcudbright, kept the track which he knew vessels to take passing between England and New York. Two or three days, or even a week, might elapse without his being fallen in with by a vessel bound to one or other of the ports—still he did not despair that by that time at the furthest he and his companions would once more tread the decks of a ship. The provisions were served out at stated times, and occasionally Captain Hardy, who took command of one of the boats, as Gasket did of another, would cause his men to pull alongside of the pinnance, in order to have a "crack" with Captain Jones, that he might do his part to keep up their spirits, by evincing his natural jollity and kindness of heart. He had jokes to tell, sprightly remarks to make, and would have almost made his hearers believe they were bound on a party of pleasure, if they could have forgotten the fearful event which had happened to them; his efforts were warmly made, and by the readiness with which his mirth and humour was met and returned, it was easily to be seen were as kindly appreciated. The night, and day succeeding, notwithstanding, seemed long; for despite the attempts to cheer each other, the horizon was watched with anxious eyes in search of a coming vessel, but in vain—nothing appeared to gladden their eyes; still, whatever the thoughts reigning in their bosom, there was no display of sorrow and despondency—hope in its fairest garb hovered over them, and pointed to the future with a sanguine smile, and they trusted all to its promises. The second day passed, and the next, and fourth, still they held their course, without having obtained the sight of a craft; the fifth and sixth day came, and passed, and then the conversations respecting their position increased: speculations began to pour forth, and despondency to creep in. It was true they still had a large quantity of provisions and water remaining—it was true, save some showers, the weather had been fair, and the wind never beyond a little fresh; but they could not expect it to last, and if a storm should come, the most sanguine had no hope that their light craft could live in the heavy seas of the Atlantic in wild weather. As the cheerfulness and merry sayings abated, Paul's exertions to sustain the drooping hearts increased; he set the example of bearing manfully that which could not be avoided, and of not despairing until all hope was taken away. His was the voice which now sounded clearer and firmer than any other—his the speech which made mirth follow, or hope come again where it had fled. He spoke of their deliverance with a confidence which had the effect of conviction, so that the faint hearted were revived, and the trustful strengthened in their hopes. When the seventh day came, they were still the only living things in sight, and despite Paul's warm language, gloominess prevailed among them; the men were weary of rowing, and grew selfish in their despair. It had been in the first instance discovered that the pinnace, with her sail set, would soon have run out of sight of her companions. The jolly boat had a sail; but the third boat was not possessed of one, hence it was agreed that in order not to part company, neither of the two boats should hoist a sail, but now when so long a time had elapsed without falling in with any vessel, a man in the pinnace proposed that they should hoist the sail, and make for land as quick as they could, without waiting for their companions: his proposal was instantly seconded, and three or four murmured their approval. Our hero, however, fixed upon him a flashing eye, and cried—

"You are a cowardly and a mutinous dog; I marked you on board the brigantine as the foremost to break duty and discipline. Who and what are you, you whining knave, that you should prefer claims to be saved superior to the humblest hand in the sternmost boat? What are your merits that you should occupy a place in this pinnace, advise running a-head and deserting to a dreadful fate men who are worthier than yourself? Are you not a mean, selfish scoundrel? Are you not a base fore-and-aft skulker? Are you not at a coward and a slave? The ever ready with an oath and never with a hand; the blusterer and swaggerer, but licker of every man's feet! Who is there anxious to have you in his mess, or desires to swing his hammock near yours? Who cries for you to take a berth beside him in the galley, and readily makes room for you when yarns are spinning and grog is passing round? When did the first mate send you aloft if a smart hand was needed to hand or reef? *You* propose that we should hoist sail and run a-head! Who suffered you to enter the pinnace, when half a dozen hands were stretched forth to hold you back, and at a word would have hurled you into the blazing hold? Why I--I, you knave, that I might have you in my sight, for I expected some such ebullition of single-heartedness from you, as you have displayed, and it has come; from you, whose life—but that is *a* life—is not worth saving. *You* propose to sacrifice a dozen or fifteen men, the meanest of whom is double your value! *You!* Look you, my fine fellow, take my advice, and keep thy tongue from wagging; I am still your captain, though the vessel I command is reduced to a pinnace, and I will exert my power while I have breath in my body: another such proposal or one word alluding to it, and you shall be placed in the sternmost boat; there are a few there, as you know, not exactly friends of yours, and likely to be less so when they hear of the honourable as well as generous proposition you have made, which if you earn for yourself a place among them, shall be told them. I think you will not doubt the warmth of your reception; you will have a hot welcome most certainly, and shall receive it as positively as I am in possession of this tiller, if another such wish crosses your lips. I am ashamed to think you have found others to echo your infamous suggestion. Men who are worthy of better things—men who, but from some strange blindness, would scorn to associate or agree with you on any point; but one bad sheep will taint a flock: I ought, therefore, scarcely to be surprised at it; however, to you and to them I say let me have no more of this."

When Paul finished, the man looked miserably abashed; his fellows shrunk from him, and those who had echoed his words were the first to turn their backs upon him. Without support or countenance from any, the fellow fell to his own level—a considerable depth to fall—and had there been a hole or corner into which he could have skulked out of sight, he would gladly have availed himself of it: there was, however, no escape, and he sat in his place scowling at our hero, feeling himself, as he was looked upon, an object of scorn. A silence followed this incident of some duration, until an exclamation from Letty Nehemie drew the attention of all; the girl was directing her eyes to the edge of the horison in the rear, and said, suddenly—

"Is that a tree a long way off?"

"Where?" asked Paul, quickly.

"There!" she cried, pointing to the spot on which she was gazing.

"A tree—no, a sail, by heavens!" exclaimed he, loudly—every one looked anxiously in the direction; "it is the spars of a ship rising fast—hurrah, lads!" rescue comes at last!"

"Hurrah!" shouted the men.

A signal from Captain Hardy's boat told that they also saw the vessel, and the boat commanded by Gasket also made signs of perceiving it.

"If it should be a Frenchman?" exclaimed one of the men.

"Why we shall have a French port and a prison," returned our hero, "instead of an American one and liberty."

"We shall escape death for a fate less desirable," exclaimed Eustace, bitterly.

"Let us see that she is French before we cry out," cried Paul; "I hope she is an American or English vessel; but let her be what she may, we are in a helpless position."

He gave orders for the men to cease rowing, and made a sign for the other two boats to join him, which signal they obeyed; as soon as they were alongside, Captain Hardy cried out—

"Luck for us, yet, Captain Jones; we are sure of being picked up; as far as I can judge by the look of her spars as they rise, the vessel is standing dead on to us."

"We are sure of being picked up," answered Paul, laughing, "but how much ought we to rejoice if she proves French?"

The change which passed over the captain's features excited a smile even in those who most feared the supposition being verified.

"Damme," he cried, "I never thought of that; it never struck me, as sure as the sea keeps salt water fish. Phew! there'll be the devil to pay, and no pitch hot, if she is. What's to be done? fight her we can't, for we have neither ammunition, guns, boarding pikes, nor cutlasses; and we can't run, for a breeze is springing up, and she would soon tire us out; but I tell you what, the sternmost boat ain't of much use, and it's my proposition that sooner than surrender to a damned Frenchman, as many of us as have got the stuff in us do crowd in that boat, hoist the black flag, scuttle her and go down to Davy with a cheer, eh? What say you, Captain Jones?"

"I reserve my reply till I see what colours the stranger carries at her peak," he replied.

"And you, lads?" exclaimed Hardy, addressing his men.

A slight cheer was responded, but it was faint, and rather select; the men, perhaps, had rubbed shoulders with the Grim King too recently to desire a further acquaintance for the present. Hardy seemed nettled, and cried crustily to them—

"Why, what the devil! you ain't growing white-livered, are ye? Why if this sail had'nt hove in sight, what would ye have done? You must have been hove over the side, mustn't you? There ain't more grub than can be served out twice, and you can't live on glaz'd hats and oak thow'ts, can ye? Very well, then, what's the difference between going down to a deep sea grave now, fat and full of meat, and going down a week hence, all ribs and

trucks, with your slops hanging about you like pursers' shirts on hand-spikes? Why none, except it is better to slip your wind now than to wait and have old hunger knocking at your bread kit, and nothing inside to keep out the hollow sound: but do as you like, lads; let every man die his own fashion say I—only afore I'll veer out my breath in the black hole of damned Johnny Crepeaud, I'll go down to the bottom like a double-headed shot."

The enthusiastic old man slapped his thigh earnestly as he spoke, and flapped himself vehemently down upon his seat in the stern sheets, out of breath with his exertion. No answer was returned, save a slight murmur, which gradually died away in the absorbing interest the quick approach of the ship occasioned: her topmasts were now plainly visible as low as the mast-head, and soon after her courses became visible, and then her hull. The distance they were from her, made it impossible to decide whether she was a vessel of war, or one in the merchant service, or what nation she belonged to. Half an hour decided her being in the merchant's service, and in the same time the eye, experienced in nautical knowledge, asserted her to be of English build. This was cheering news, and it was a sight still more glad for them, to perceive they were seen, and the vessel bearing down directly towards them; when nearer, English colours were perceived floating from the peak of the gaff, and all the men at the agreeable discovery set up a tremendous cheer, and then pulled towards her; they soon gained her side, and she proved to be a barque, bound to Halifax, from London. They were received by the captain, on learning their situation, in the kindest manner. Accommodation for them all was made by those on board in the most liberal spirit, and they were not a little glad at their escape. The vessel was a clipper, and was not long in performing the remainder of her journey; but to none on board was the news of being anchored in port more welcome than to Florence.

CHAPTER VI.

" And fought away with might and main, not knowing
The way which they had never trod before,
And still less guessing where they might be going;
But on they marched, dead bodies trampling o'er,
Firing, and thrusting, slashing, sweating, glowing,
But fighting thoughtlessly enough to win,
To their TWO selves ONE whole bright bulletin.

Thus on they wallowed in the bloody mire
Of dead and dying."

BYRON.

THE distance from Halifax to the residence, in Virginia, of the brother of John Paul—or Paul Jones, as we shall for the future designate our hero—was still considerable, and as the readiest route was by sea, he found a vessel, bound from Halifax to Philadelphia, carrying passengers, in which he secured berths for himself, Eustace, Florence, Letty, and Gasket, and after a brief voyage, unmarked by any particular incident, they reached it, and journeyed by land to the estate on the banks of the Rappahanoc, possessed by his brother; he was warmly received, and a glad welcome presented to his companions.

When somewhat recovered from the fatigue which he had undergone, he despatched letters to Mr. Younger, stating the loss of his vessel, which he deeply regretted, but which was attributable to no fault or mismanagement of his own; and after thanking him for the favours he received, he stated his intention of quitting the merchant service, and entering the royal, that he might have a chance of carving for himself a name as well as a fortune. He enclosed letters for his family also, and a number likewise for Eustace, who had written to his friends in England, informing them of his arrival, and requesting to be made acquainted with the proceedings of the elder Mr. Stanley, and the prospect there was of an abatement in his resentment, which would enable him to return to England.

Paul Jones, when the letters had departed, looked out for an English vessel of war which, from some cause, might have a vacancy for a midshipman; he knew the rules, and was content to take a subordinate situation until he could rise higher, trusting for his advancement speedily to occur, by his strict attention to his duties, and by taking every advantage of bringing himself into notice as a thorough seaman and active officer. His original intention had been to embark in government service in the Colonies, and by energy and enterprise to attract the notice of the governor, so as to be advanced to a confidential post, and ultimately to rank and station, determining to toil and slave in the path he had marked out until he had accomplished his resolve; but the incidents of his voyage from England, his chase by the French frigate, the sight of the action between the two frigates, and the knowledge of the honour which the English captain had reaped in the contest, inflamed his imagination, directed his ambition into this channel, and now his whole soul was bent upon following the course, and arriving by it to the end and aim of his aspiring. It was in vain he made every exertion by personal application, by recommendations, and such other means as lay in his power; he was neglected, unheeded, and, in several cases where he compelled notice to be taken of him, was rejected almost with contumely: these repeated failures blistered his heart, but yet he would not cease his efforts. In several cases where vessels of war arrived, some from South America, some from the Bahamas, others from England, where a loss had occurred by death, sickness, and other causes, and he the very person most fitted to supply their place, his most urgent appeals and endeavours were fruitless; there seemed a fatality about his applications, for they were all scornfully declined. Why, he could not ascertain, it might have been that his sore-heartedness at his rejection might have magnified the manner with which his services were declined, but to him it appeared as though he were looked upon by "these proud English," as dust, and treated accordingly. He now grew gloomy and discontented, and in this frame of mind, to pass away his unoccupied hours, he sat himself down to read a series of works of a revolutionary character, at that time emanating from the French press in large quantities, and which were circulated among the colonists by those who were disaffected towards the government of England. Franklin and Paine also sent forth their works at this period, which were boldly written, and conveyed strong and sound arguments calculated to inflame and lead a weak mind, and make a strong one look at what he had previously considered Gospel. Paul's brother, of a strong political turn, had gathered these works and placed them in his library, and Paul's was a mind which could with avidity devour them. He applied himself also to other studies rigourously, in order to fit himself for any position or station. During this period he, through his brother, became acquainted with a Mr. Transom, the captain of a schooner, who made voyages to Vera Cruz, a province of Mexico, for gold. As the cargoes were exceedingly valuable, the schooner was fitted in every department as an armed vessel, and was built for swiftness as well. Her captain doated on her, and was never exhausted in praising her. He took a fancy to Paul, because upon one occasion he took a trip with him to Philadelphia purposely to see this paragon of schooners, and when he had seen her, and inspected every part of her, he pronounced her worthy of every panegyric the earnest seaman had bestowed upon her. Paul raised himself an hundred-fold in his estimation by his praise of her; and when he said she was equal to anything he had ever seen of her class, the captain seized his hand, and vowed eternal friendship to him. Paul was to sojourn with him a week or ten days in Philadelphia, at the expiration of which time the *Trackless* (which was the schooner's name) would be ready for her next voyage. One morning Paul accompanied Captain Transom upon a shooting excursion: a double-barrelled gun, which lay upon the ground, just loaded, and which Captain Transom accidently kicked with his foot and discharged, burst into a thousand fragments, and shattered the captain's leg fearfully; he fell with a dreadful groan. Paul raised him in his arms and carried him to the nearest cottage, and then, borrowing a horse, galloped to the city for assistance. He obtained the aid of a clever surgeon, and came back with him instantly. The fractured limb was dressed, and the captain was conveyed to his lodgings, where amputation took place. Paul attended him constantly, and had the satisfaction in a few days to learn from the medical attendant that he was progressing well. The *Trackless*, it was suddenly stated, would be ready for sea two days before her time, in consequence of a large order which her owners had received, which was required to be executed with the greatest expedition. The surgeon said it was impossible for Captain Transom to take the command, and he swore he would if he died in doing it. The doctor made the owners acquainted that death would certainly ensue if he attempted it, and they, therefore, hesitated in trusting their vessel to one in so dangerous a condition; his death at sea might lead to the seizure of the vessel by her crew for piratical purposes. Transom, however, when he learned this, was furious; he contested he was quite well enough to take her, and if they suffered another to have command of his beautiful swan-like craft, he would shoot himself and haunt the schooner. He had been a trustworthy and able servant, the owners were, consequently, loth to part with him, or act directly in opposition to his desire—nay, prayers; they, therefore, met him half way, by saying he should have the command on condition of his taking with him a person upon whom he could depend, and who was competent to take the command in case of anything happening to himself. He gladly agreed, and named our hero, without consulting him whether he would undertake the office or not. He was too glad of an opportunity of emerging from the state of inactivity in which his inability to get a berth had placed him, to decline; he therefore accepted it, and at once returned to his brother's residence for his outfit and articles necessary for his voyage. He laughed as he invited Eustace to accompany him, for he saw, by the solemn face Florence instantly drew, that her influence would be exerted to prevent it; and a woman's influence, everybody knows, is a power of no trifling magnitude. Eustace was about to acquiesce most gladly, but his rapture was checked by a glance at his little wife's pretty face, and he dropped his enthusiastic tone, spoke of the pleasures of such a trip, but concluded by saying, under the circumstances, he did not feel justified in accepting the invitation. Florence's face was radiant with smiles as he finished, and she wound her arms round him, saying—

"Besides, dear Eustace, this place is very lovely; Mr. Paul is very kind, and I do not think if you were to go and part from me for a long while that you could be much happier than if you were to remain here with me."

"I am afraid my little place," said Paul's brother gallantly to Florence, "is less attractive to your husband than the fair lady who graces it; but, whatever its charms, while you remain it shall be my study to make it as comfortable as you find the situation beautiful."

"My brother wants to lay out an anchor to windward of you," said Paul, laughing, to Eustace; "I would have you beware. You had better take a trip with me. What say you, Gasket, eh?"

Gasket's face grew fiery red, then almost white; it flushed again, and he said, rather confusedly, and a little vehemently—

"If I was like Mr. Prior, commander of the prettiest craft Dame Nature ever launched from her stocks, there isn't the island in the world I'd go to see, or the voyage I'd make either for pleasure or money, if in doing it I was to be parted from her. She would be my pinnace, my barge, my yacht, my yawl, my galley, gig, and jolly-boat; my sheet anchor and best bower; and when I parted from her with a will, I should expect, and deserve, to heel for'ard, and go down head first; that's all."

"Ah, Gasket! you were always my good friend," exclaimed Florence with a sweet smile. "It was you who gave me one of the most delightful pieces of news I ever received, and I have never forgotten it."

"Nor I, ma'am," said Gasket, with a close inspection of the nails of his left hand; "I told John Paul o'that; it was then when I first saw you."

"Ay," said Paul, with a smile; "he said if ever he saw an angel that was the time."

"Steady," cried Eustace, joining in the laugh; "I can't suffer you to make love to my wife, Gasket. I think you had better join Paul in his trip."

"I mean to do it, sir," he said, seriously, his colour in no degree abated; "I mean to do it, sir, whether he's bound to the gulf of Mexico or to the Baltic; or, for the matter o'that, to Greenland."

"What have you no pinnace, jolly-boat, or best bower to keep you here?" inquired Paul, laughing.

"No, sir," he replied, in rather a sad tone; "them's not for the likes o' me. I never know'd my mother, or father, or brother, or sister, uncle, or any other kin, and never had a friend in the world to care for me, except one Tom Lanyard, your brother, and Mr. Prior. Why should I e'er expect any lass with plenty of relations to cast a kind eye on one who don't know who he belongs to, or where his family came from. No, sir; I was alone when I was picked up at sea, and, if it please the Lord, I'll die a seaman's death, without leaving a wet eye behind me; I will, sir."

"But, Gasket, you have left me out of the number who care for you," said Florence, kindly, taking his hand as she spoke, "you must think me as warm a friend as any you have; and with respect to meeting with a young maiden, loving and loveable, take a woman's word for it, there is many a fair damsel who, to know you, would love you, and think you no jot the less worthy because you were an orphan. If she loved you, it would be for herself, and not for your relations; and if her affection could be guided by such a consideration, it is not worth the having."

"Come, after that, what say you, Gasket?" exclaimed Paul, laughing. "Shall you go about on the other tack, and hang out signals for a *tender?*"

"No, John, my ship doesn't head that way," he returned, with a faint attempt at a smile; "I shall make the voyage with you. Matrimony is a port I shall never enter, it's my belief, and to say truth, it isn't my wish."

As he concluded he walked hastily out of the room; his conduct was looked upon as a little strange; but he was rather eccentric in his manner, and this behaviour was attributed to the same cause.

Paul soon had everything in readiness for his departure, and as time was precious, he did not wait a moment; he took his farewell of his brother, Eustace, and Florence, and accompanied by Gasket, set out for Philadelphia.

He scarcely paused on the road, and arrived just as the schooner was ready to get under weigh. Captain Transom was on board, confined to his cabin, and was delighted to see our hero. He declared he felt considerably better since he had exchanged his lodgings for his cabin, and expressed his conviction that he should very shortly be well, and be able to stump about upon his wooden pin as well as he had previously upon his fleshy one. He readily entered Gasket upon the ship's books, rating him as a petty officer, and said any other service he could grant he would be delighted to confer, if the way was pointed out to him. Paul thanked him, and promised to avail himself of the kind offer, if occasion arose. Everything being ready for departure, the fore-topsail was cast loose, the anchor was hove up the bows, and the schooner quitted the harbour. During her voyage Paul had every opportunity of discovering that she fully deserved the praises the captain had bestowed upon her; she was beautifully built, her hull lay low, and with an amazing clear run; her fittings were perfect, her rigging was neat and trim, her masts and spars slim and taper, and with a saucy rake, her sails were large for her size, but of the most admired cut; and she was kept as clean and looked as perfect as a nobleman's yacht of the present day. Her crew were picked men, thorough seamen, well-disposed, and well-behaved; Paul found them obedient to his command, and smart in their duty. He made it his pride to make her in all things like a vessel of war, instead of trade, and exercised the men in gunnery practice, until he had made them as competent to work their guns as the ablest seamen in the king's service. Captain Transom did not interfere with any of his operations; for he quickly saw that he was making improvements, and though he thought there was scarcely room for them, yet he was wise enough not, from a feeling of pride, to prevent his executing them. The crew of a vessel soon became acquainted with the merits of their commander, and the people of the *Trackless* quickly found they had not only a thorough seaman, but a good active officer second in command; they were more than pleased with him. They had their duty to do and no more, and yet the vessel had never been in better condition than she was at that time. They found themselves treated as men, not as slaves: and though nothing like freedom was permitted between them and our hero, there was yet a kindly feeling which would have gladly made them follow him through any danger, however great. Their port of destination was gained in the shortest time they had ever made the trip, and without an accident or incident, until their return. The exported articles were discharged from their hold, and an immense amount in gold was taken on board, as well as a small cargo of pepper, cocoa-nuts, cedar and brazil-woods, and nutmegs. No time was lost in completing her freight, and she started on her homeward voyage. They had to touch at Merida on their return, to take in a few things which were consigned by one of their agents to their owners in Philadelphia. And while here they fell in with a large brig, the owner of which, a Mr. Casley, who was also captain, was an old and particular friend of Captain Transom: he likewise had a valuable cargo, but his vessel was not so well fitted for resistance as the *Trackless*, and he took advantage of the sailing of the schooner to keep company with her as far as it was possible; he had, however, to touch at Trinidad, in the Island of Cuba, while the *Trackless* was to make the passage from Merida to Philadelphia direct. The inferiority of the sailing of the brig compelled the schooner to carry much less canvas than her, until they were off the Island of Cuba; and then the time having arrived for them to part, the captain of the brig invited Transom and Paul to take a parting dinner with him, which they accepted, and it being found that the *Trackless* by some accident was short of water, the schooner was run close into land for the convenience of the men obtaining it on shore, and conveying it in the water-casks to the ship. While they were thus occupied, Paul and Transom, leaving Gasket in command of the schooner, paid their visit to the cabin of the brig. They had some distance to be rowed before they reached it, for the two vessels were several miles apart, divided by a headland, so that they were not in sight of each other. The dinner passed off pleasantly, for there were several passengers on board, ladies and gentlemen, who joined the party; and with songs and pleasant stories the hours flew by very agreeably. Night came, and Transom sounded the note of departure; but his friend would not hear of it for another hour or two. After a little contest, Transom yielded the point, and they continued their hilarity. A very short time subsequent to this, the party was disturbed by a sudden uproar on deck—shouts and clashing of weapons; immediately afterwards the cabin was entered by the chief mate, bleeding from a wound in his head, and to their consternation he told them the vessel had been boarded by pirates. Before he had finished his communication, a party of men descended the ladder and crowded, with fierce oaths, into the room—a fearful attestation of his words. The men sprang from their seats, the females shrieked, weapons flashed through the air, and a vigorous attempt was made to expel the intruders from the cabin; but their numbers increased, until the cabin was thronged, and all resistance was useless. The captain, his guests, and passengers, were unceremoniously commanded to go on deck, and their weapons were taken from them before they departed, with the exception of Paul, who, as quick as thought, secreted a brace of pistols and a large carving knife which lay upon the table, in his pea coat. When they reached the deck, they found a number of the men murdered, several bleeding from severe wounds, and the remainder bound. The captain of the pirates, a ruffianly-looking villain, spoke English well, though his accents and pronunciation of certain words proved him to be a Spaniard: he surveyed his prisoners with a sparkling eye, and leaning upon a sword, whose hilt was gold magnificently chased, he exclaimed—

"Who calls himself captain of this brig?"

"I am," replied Captain Casley.

"You have a valuable cargo," said the pirate.

He returned no answer.

"Ha!" ejaculated the pirate, with a coarse, taunting laugh. "I know as well what you have on board as if your bill of lading had been given to me, so your silence will go for nothing: but, captain, with such a freight, you ought to have kept a brighter look-out. Your people were asleep while you were carousing, or they would have picked out my fire-eater," he said, pointing to a vessel which lay at some distance, almost hidden by the shadow of the land upon the water, "and given you notice to spread your canvas, so as to make me have a run for my prize. However, I am infinitely obliged to them and to you for saving me the trouble: it is a pleasant thing to get twenty thousand dollars without exertion. I should have made you walk the plank, but since you have been considerate to me, a whip shall send you to the yard-arm to look in the face of God instead: then, with the utmost coolness, gave the order to "clear the turn," and launch the unfortunate captives into eternity; and seizing by the waist the youngest of the females, a girl of eighteen, daughter to one of the passengers, he said to her—

"Come to my heart, my dear! Tell me how you should like to be a rover's lady? or say should you like to be queen of the seas, eh? thou pretty one."

The poor girl struggled violently with him, but in vain; he imprinted a number of kisses upon her lips, and she screamed bitterly for help. Paul, put his hand upon his pistol at the moment the maiden's father seized a capstan bar, and struck the pirate a tremendous blow upon the scull that it precipitated him to the deck, and the girl burst from him and flew to her father for protection. Several of the pirate's men, with oaths, ran to pick up their captain, while Paul advancing hastily to the maiden, said in a low voice—

"Descend instantly to the cabin; our boat hangs close under her stern; the height is not great. At all hazards get from the window into it, and, if discovered, cast off. It is too dark to be easily seen; I will follow as quick as I can."

The maiden and her father profited by his advice. There were two other ladies who also followed them, but there were two who had run and hid themselves in their fright at the fore part of the vessel, who lost the benefit of this movement. The confusion which the fall of the pirate had occasioned, especially as he was discovered to be insensible, prevented the withdrawal of the four persons being immediately observed, for all the attention of the pirates was directed to his recovery, which as soon as accomplished, was followed by his commanding the destruction of the gentleman who had struck him down, and swearing a fierce oath that the maiden herself should be

subjected to the most horrible treatment. In obedience to his orders, his men turned to seize the father and daughter, and their absence was at once detected; the forepart of the vessel was searched, and two trembling females dragged forth, but those searched for were undiscovered. Three or four men were about to descend to the cabin, when Captain Transom stopped them—

"What the devil do you want below?" he cried. "Didn't you see them go down the main hatchway?"

The men, who were Spaniards, did not understand him, and pushed him rudely on one side, very nearly upsetting him, as he was not quite practised in the use of his wooden leg. He was naturally passionate, and when arouse was not over prudent. He retorted the thrust by delivering a smart blow over the ears of the man who pushed him aside, with a stout crab staff with which he supported himself; he used all his strength in the delivery, and the recipient roared with pain. In the height of his rage he attacked Captain Transom with his cutlass, and the gallant commander defended himself with his stick as well as he was able. Paul sprang upon a fellow who was gazing with open mouth on this unequal combat, wrenched his cutlass from his hand and interposed between the captain and his foe, whom he resolutely attacked; at the same time he exclaimed, rapidly—

"Make for the boat, you know where she lies, cut her adrift and get aboard the schooner as quick as you can, then work her round here."

He uttered this in broken sentences, for as he spoke he combated the pirate fiercely. His antagonist was joined by two or three others, and Paul was almost surrounded; he, however, gave no ground, but parried and cut and thrust with an agility and skill which defied defeat. Captain Transom chuckled with delight, and, flourishing his stick, cried out—

"Give it 'em, my lad; down with the roving rascals! I'll never leave you. Give it 'em right and left! Hur—"

He was suddenly stopped short by a pistol bullet, discharged by the pirate captain, who fired at Paul, but missing him, hit the captain; the ball passed through his heart; he leaped up in the air, and then fell dead. Paul saw it, and with a shout of rage he slashed one of the fellows he was fighting across the eyes, making a terrific gash; the man shrieked and fell, and our hero, with a bound, leaped beyond the reach of the others, who were pressing forward to revenge their comrade, and drew his pistols from the pockets of his pea-jacket; he fired at the fellow nearest, and shot him through the head; twenty shots were fired at him in return. The pirate captain, whose belt was crowded with pistols of various shapes and sizes, fired them in succession at hi n but missed him every time. Still he was not altogether disappointed in his aim, for as he had killed poor Transom in shooting at our hero, so he managed to slay two of his own men in making efforts for a similar purpose. Paul was a better marksman, he had already hit one opponent, and as soon as the man was down he leaped upon the taffrail, discharged the remaining pistol at the pirate captain, wounded him in the shoulder, and then flung the pistol at him; it struck him in the eyes, nearly blinding him, and he howled with passion and pain. The next instant Paul leaped into the sea; directly he reached the surface of the water, after having penetrated far into its depths, he swam to his boat, which still hung astern of the brig. There were four men in it who belonged to it, they hauled him into the boat, and, being unable in the darkness to distinguish his features, they asked him who he was. He told them.

"Where's the captain, sir?" said one of the men in a whisper.

"Shot dead," he replied, in the same tone, "I have only to thank bad marksmen that I have not been served the same. Ah! I see you are here," he exclaimed, on perceiving the young lady, her father, and the two females in the stern sheets.

"Yes, sir," cried one of the men, "they hailed us from the cabin window, and said they were to be taken into the boat."

"All right, Sampson," exclaimed Paul, "shove off the boat; don't wait to cast off the painter, cut it adrift, and give way. I'll work the schooner round if I can reach her, and teach these rascals a lesson."

The colloquy did not take a minute; the boat was shoved off, and the men stretched out with all their strength. As they emerged from the shadow of the vessel, they were seen by the throng of fellows leaning over the taffrail of the brig, who had been watching for Paul to rise, little thinking he was so close beneath them, and a shower of bullets were dispatched after them, but without hurting them. The men raised a shout of defiance, and Paul, making those he had saved lie down in the boat for fear of receiving a stray bullet, urged his men to pull with their best power.

"They will give us chase," he said, "and with their light boats soon overhaul us, unless we get a good start a-head of them. I would not for all the wealth in the world lose the chance of revenging poor Transom's death, as well as those injuries which those now on board will be made to suffer. Give way, my lads; pull with a will—pull together; make her leap out of the water."

The men, animated by his words, put out their strength, and almost made the boat fly.

"By heaven!" suddenly cried Paul, who was watching the brig, "there come the scoundrels over the side; they will run us hard. If we can but get in sight of the schooner it is all I ask; pull lads, never mind the roll, we can spare the music to speed—pull together cheerly, cheerly."

The men took "a long pull, a strong pull, and a pull altogether," they bent their backs to their task, and made the oars bend like whalebone in their efforts. Fortunately, the gig they were in was a very light one, modelled in shape and character to resemble the schooner; it was long and narrow, and fashioned for swift progress; the men got as much speed out of her as it was possible to do, and quickly left the brig some distance behind them although there was not the light of a moon to guide them, yet the night was not at all dark; they could see their pursuers following closely after them, and by the shouts they heard, though faintly, but distinct, and the number they saw crowded into the long boat of the pirates, they judged the worst fate to await them if overtaken. They were without any defensive weapons, save one pistol, which Paul had, and that was discharged; he had no powder or ball to reload it. The cutlass with which he had fought upon deck of the brig he had flung away when he leaped into the sea. There was no hope for them, therefore, but in flight, and that was doubtful, from the great advantages which the pirates possessed, in having a boat lighter for its length than theirs, impelled by eight strong fellows, and the remainder of its crew armed with muskets, and pistols of almost equal length, and well supplied with ammunition. "True hope ne'er tires," it is said, and although the condition of Paul and his companions was desperate, the men exhibited a degree of calmness in their strenuous exertions, which showed they had still expectations of out-rowing their enemies and gaining the schooner. Paul steered them, and by short exclamations cheered them on to their work, as he observed that his pursuers gained a little upon him: he noticed, too, that they kept in shore considerably more than he did and guessed instantly that there was an advantage attendant upon it, either arising from a current or slack water; and as they drew into the land, he did so likewise, to find he had guessed correctly, and that they had diminished the distance between them at least a third—a fact of which they were aware as well as himself, and commenced firing at him; the bullets did not reach them, but dropped alarmingly near. The men in the gig pulled harder than ever, and the pirates also increased their exertions to bring them within range of their shots. The speed of both boats was extraordinary. Paul found he had got into a swift current, and the rapidity with which the boat progressed, raised in him stronger hopes than he had yet possessed that he should be able to reach the schooner before he was overtaken. The pirates, enraged to find that with all their exertions they failed in coming up with the fugitives as quickly as they anticipated, fired their muskets and pistols as fast as they could load them, and as they were really drawing on the gig inch by inch, at every discharge the bullets fell nearer and nearer; several struck the blades of the oars, and one grazed Paul's arm, cutting through his coat sleeve, and passing into the water on the opposite side of the boat. The keen eyes of the pirates detected that they were now withing range, they, therefore, redoubled their efforts—the shots flew like hail, and splashed the boat as they fell in the water around them.

"If we had but a twelve-pounder filled with grape and canister, damme we'd show them what pepper meant," said one of the men, laconically.

"But we have not," ejaculated Paul, "so never mind talking about what we have not, let us look to the only chance we have; they are drawing on us fast—there is no time for talking. Pull, or you will be with the fishes in a few minutes—give way, my lads, let them see you have got strength enough in ye to run a-head of them: pull together, strong and long; that's it, again so—now we leave them!"

But, in despite of Paul's cheering exclamations, the bullets fell around them in all directions. His coat was rent in several places by them, but fortunately he had escaped without a wound. They were making fast for the headland, on the other side of which they expected to find the schooner at anchor, and if they could but continue as they had kept on already, they would speedily have the satisfaction of frustrating the hopes and endeavours of their blood-thirsty pursuers. One moment more, and one of the men received a bullet in his arm, which prevented him from rowing; Paul shouted to him to come aft and take the tiller, as with a groan and an oath he declared himself incapable of holding the oar, and at the same time Paul supplied his place. He was very strong, and pulled vigorously; but, with all his exertions, he was not able to remove the boat out of the reach of the shots, which the pirates shouting and execrating, dispatched after them, and which kept pattering around them without cessation. Another of the men was hit in the shoulder, and the man in the bow of the boat received a shot in the side, but, though wounded, they kept on bravely; their chance had however dwindled almost to hopelessness, but Paul ,tillalmost madly exerted his strength. A shriek from one of the females told she, too, had received a wound, and a shot, discharged with a better aim than usual, passed through the back of the man who had taken

Paul's place at the helm, struck a vital part, and he dropped forward a dead man. With a roar of triumph the pirates observed his fall, and with a frightful perseverance continued their firing There was now but a short distance between the pirates and the gig; the man in the bow of the latter, faint with the loss of blood, was compelled to relinquish his oar, and fell back almost insensible. Paul resumed his place at the helm, and with a desperation little short of madness, the two seamen left plied their arms, in the vain hope of still keeping up the chase. The pirates now came up with them hand over hand; they saw they were in their power and ceased firing, but urged their boat at the swiftest pace, shouting, and roaring, and promising the most dreadful fate to all, which, as it was delivered in Spanish, was rather guessed at than understood. Paul saw that, though within three hundred yards of the headland; it would be impossible to gain it before the pirates overtook them, and, in a despairing voice, he told his companions this, advising them to sell their lives dearly. Those who could swim to the shore—there was a possibility of escape that way—but for himself he would not desert the females, come what may. The men, however, said they would stand by him, and with stern but calm determination awaited the moment when the pirates should run their boat alongside; they, however, held out to the last, and kept their boat going as swiftly as the strength of both would permit. The pirates now were close upon them; two minutes more and their fate would be decided: all hope was gone. Paul drew his knife and compressed his teeth together. The pirates shouted joyously, and at this moment the bows of the schooner were round the headland. Paul could scarcely believes eyes, but sure enough it was there. He shouted with all his strength, hailing her, and then turning with a triumphant laugh to his companions, he cried—

"We are saved! we are saved; Here comes he schooner!"

The men echoed his shout, and the timid, affrighted females burst into tears of joy to learn their deliverance was effected. A minute more and they ran alongside the schooner; two or three men were ready to hook on to the boat, and they were quickly upon the deck. The pirate boat now found they had quite as much to fear as their fugitives had, and as quickly turned to run as they persued. They made for the land, but Paul did not intend to let them escape so easily.

"Forward there!" he shouted.

The usual reply was returned, and he cried—

"Get the bow-chaser, ready."

"All ready with the bow-chaser," replied the man in charge of the gun instantly.

"See what sort of a target you can make of yon boat and the murdering thieves in her— fire away!"

A flash and the report followed —a wild shriek arose in the air.

"She's blown out of the water, sir," said Gasket to Paul, instantly.

"A just retribution on the villains," returned Paul, perceiving with a glass that the shot struck the pirates' galley amidships, between wind and water, and literary cut her in half. He could perceive a few dark heads struggling in the water, and that was all that remained of her crew.

Paul's attention was now directed to running the schooner alongside the brig or the pirate vessel, whichever the scoundrels were aboard of, and giving them battle. In a few brief words he explained to Gasket what had occurred, and inquired of him how he came so opportunely to bring the Trackless to his rescue.

" Some of the men who went ashore for water," he replied, " were missing, and as it began to grow late without their returning, I dispatched some of the hands to look after them. They hadn't got far when they fell in with them and a party of natives, coming towards the sea. It seems that they knew where these pirates had anchored, for the blackguards had carried off a lot of their native women, and they not being strong enough to attack them, they were going to seek for assistance. When they met with our men they told their tale, but our people would not believe it until they showed them the pirate's vessel at anchor; while, however, they were watching her, they saw some people on board heave up the anchor, set the foresail, fore and main topsail and jib, and creep along the shore; there were three or four boats hanging astern ready to be filled with a crowd of black muzzled rascals who were abaft waiting for to get into them. Now our people knew Captain Casley's brig was lying in the course they took; suspected foul play, and crowded all sail for the schooner. When I heard their yarn, after a little boxing about, I thought, as I could rely on the truth of men, that it would be done, if no good came of it; so I roused up the anchor and stood round the headland, and directly I heard the firing I knew no good was going on, and so I set more canvas—and that's all."

"You did well: you saved our lives," exclaimed Paul, warmly shaking his hand. "Poor Transom, I wish you had been in time to save his. Poor fellow!"

" He's gone aloft, John, if ever a seaman has," said Gasket; and I dare say, if we could know his opinions of the matter, he would rather have dropped his peak in that fashion than have slipped his cable in his cabin berth."

He shall be revenged" said Paul, with clenched teeth; " summon the men aft."

Gasket obeyed; and when the men were assembled, Paul exclaimed, in a stirring voice—

" My lads, Captain Transom has been shot dead by pirates, who have taken possession of the brig aboard which the captain and I dined to-day.

They are not far from us, I am bearing down upon them. I have only to say, that I believe every man on board honoured and respected Captain Transom; you will not let him be shot dead like a dog, without striking a blow in revenge, will you?"

The men gave a loud shout, saying—" Down with the pirates! Revenge the captain's murder. Down with the thieves!"

One of your messmates has lost his life, too; one is badly wounded, and one slightly. You will give them something for that?"

" We will, we will! No prayer, and a clean run aloft!" cried several voices.

" By the death of poor Transom, the office of captain falls upon me; I may count upon your obedience to my orders, as though I had left port as your commander?"

The men readily returned an unequivocal assent, and gave him three hearty cheers; they then dispersed to their quarters, and Paul directed the vessel's course towards the brig. He was not long in coming up with her, and found, quick has he had been, she was deserted and on fire in three places—the flames bursting out with the greatest fury the moment of his arrival. He concluded that the pirates had seen him bearing down, and had resorted to these villanous means of preventing him rescuing the vessel from their clutches. There was no person on board—the decks were clear—the bodies of those who had been slaughtered were cast into the sea, and the fire raged too furiously for him to throw any of his people on board to search below for friends or for property valuable enough to make its being saved a matter of consideration, and he now turned all his attention to the point where the pirate's vessel had been laying at anchor, and saw her suddenly emerge under a cloud of canvas, with the evident intention of flying or making a running fight. Paul knew the virtues which nearly all pirate vessels possessed, of swiftness of heel; they were built for speed, and that one point made the essential consideration in every plank that was laid—the long, low, black hull of the pirate, as it came like a bird skimming the waters, told him that this vessel possessed the qualities in an eminent degree— the raking masts and spanking sails were all evidences of it; she was schooner-rigged, and was of beautiful shape and make. Paul scanned her with the eye of a seaman, and though warmly admiring the schooner he commanded, he could not be so prejudiced as to view the fair proportions, the exqusite symmetry, and the superior trimness of the pirate with a feeling of indifference as to her merits, or an underrating of her powers. He saw her shoot across his forefoot and take the very course he was quitting; he instantly gave the necessary directions to put the schooner about and spread all the canvas they could set, which was accomplished with the greatest expedition the men as eager as himself to overhaul her; they were now running in parallel lines, save that the Trackless was some distance astern. The pirate was seemingly not disposed to keep the race silently, for such guns as he could bring to beat upon the schooner he fired. Paul, however, took no heed of them, as they did not succeed in reaching their destination. "I shall not play at bowls with him," he said; "but when I can depend on the water, I'll run in his wake, and if I can get near enough I will rake him."

Gasket quite agreed with the policy, and to the best of his ability seconded the efforts made to carry it out. The cargo of the schooner acted as a drawback upon her speed, but even at such a disadvantage she flew along with such rapidity as quite to delight the people on board of her, and elevate her in their opinion beyond any craft of the sort ever built. She soon was in the wake of the chase, and shortly afterwards the pirate began to shorten sail; his topsails were clewed up, and his mainsail was hauled up, but the after-sail was not diminished.

"What does he mean by that?" said Gasket, who stood at Paul's elbow, watching the movements of the pirate.

"He will show fight," replied Paul; "there goes his red flag to the peak; he sees we have a full freight, he knows, too, that we are in the merchant service; he can boast double our number of crew, and he thinks if he tackles us he may stand a good chance of making a prize of us. The fellow's bold, but I think he will find himself mistaken. What is our distance, think you, now?"

"Our metal will cut his decks and rigging to pieces," replied Gasket, instantly.

"So I think," said Paul. Then taking his speaking trumpet, he cried, "All ready with the larboard guns."

"All ready," was the reply.

"Stand by," he cried; and then turning to the man at the wheel, he exclaimed, "Give the ship a wide sheer to starboard."

The man obeyed—the stern came rapidly round, presenting the broadside to the stern of the pirate, and the moment it was in the desired position Paul, at the top of his voice, cried, "Fire away!"

The report of the guns drowned the last word, and he watched with anxiety the iron, with the speed of lightning, fly towards the retreating ship; they heard a wild shriek follow its arrival—they saw fragments fly in all directions, and a vain attempt made, too late, to sheer the vessel out of its track. The next moment all the sails which had been reduced were spread, and by the time the *Trackless* had her head round she was flying away at the same speed as before. She reached the headland, wore round it, and succeeded in making a considerable distance before they could get round the point.

"The pirate doesn't like fair fighting," said Gasket, with a smile. "That broadside made him feel a little queer at stomach. He'll run for home in one of the islands here-away you'll see."

"If he does not run us too much out of our track, I'll follow him to his hole. Get the bow-chaser ready; a shot may reach him."

The gun was got ready and fired, but the ball fell short.

"We'll try that again presently," said Paul; "he had too much pull upon us to repeat it just now. We will set the studding sails, and see what advantage that will give us."

The studding sails were set, and the walk of the ship increased; but the pirate schooner was very swift, and kept her advantage, part of which had been gained by a better knowledge of the water. The *Trackless*, however, flew along with the swiftness of a curlew; the pirate could not spare her a sail, or a minute, everything which an accurate knowledge of the sailing qualities of his vessel could devise was put in practice by the rover, and his most arduous efforts were made to get, as Gasket had prophesied, to his home in an inlet of one of the small islands which abound in this part of the world. After a further chase of three hours, when day was beginning to dawn, without the *Trackless* having been able to get within gun-shot of the fugitive, the latter suddenly performed the same manœuvre which had cost her rather dearly—the shortening sail; but this time presented a broadside to the schooner, and placed herself in a position to rake her fore and aft. Paul lost no time in giving his vessel's head a different direction; the pirate did not, however, fire, and Paul, at all hazards, stood towards him, turning up a few hands to shorten sail. One of the men in the tops, however, quickly explained the mystery of the pirate's preparing for action, by giving notice o.

a vessel in sight bearing swiftly towards them, which by his description of her, was another of the marauding class. Paul, therefore, expected he should have to fight both; he, however, disdained to haul off, and whatever the odds against him, resolved to have a rap at the fellow he had been pursuing. He bore down swiftly to where the rover was waiting for him, stationed his men at the guns, commanding them not to fire till he gave the word. He placed two men at the wheel with strict orders to attend his slightest gesture, all the lofty sails were handed, and the vessel made as clear and snug as it was possible to accomplish. The rover, as soon as the *Trackless* approached near enough, fired a broadside, Paul, however, anticipated it, and by a dexterous movement avoided, in a great degree, its effects; the next instant his vessel ran alongside her, and in a voice that went to every man's heart he cried—

"Fire away!"

A rattling broadside followed his words, accompanied by a loud cheer from his men: it did considerable execution: and now was apparent the benefit of the instructions and practice in firing broadsides which he had made the crew undergo; they loaded and discharged their guns with twice the precision of their opponents, making every broadside tell in the beautiful fabric to which they were opposed. The crew of the rover were double their number, and the captain perceiving that his craft was being cut up fearfully, resolved to try what numbers would accomplish against the dauntless courage of a few; he, therefore, called the greater proportion of his men together, and gave the order to board the Trackless. It was immediately attempted, for the two vessels were yard-arm and yard-arm. The pirates poured over the quarter with impetuosity, but were repulsed with pikes and cutlasses by Paul and part of his crew, who quitted their guns to repel boarders; they fought with determined courage, and in spite of the rover's efforts, his people were driven back with considerable loss. Another attempt was made in the bows, but with the same ill success. The near approach of the other pirate rendered Paul's situation critical; he kept his people now to their guns, en deavouring, by rapid and well directed firing, to crush his present foe and tackle the other. His people seconded his wishes with an admirable perseverance, and his shot scattered death and destruction upon the decks and rigging of his enemy. One more attempt to board was made by the pirate, who found his vessel likely to be soon disabled from the tremendous effects of the quick firing of the Trackless. He divided his men into two bands, and with the prospect of assistance from his advancing friend, he resolved upon boarding in two parts at the same moment; his lieutenant took the command of one band, and himself of the other, and, at a given signal, they rushed to their respective posts. Paul, whose quick eyes watched every movement on board the pirate, detected the arrangement, and instantly prepared to meet and defeat it. As the quarter was likely to sustain the most tremendous assault, he stationed himself there with some of his best men, and sent Gasket with the remainder to the bows. With wild cries and furious movements the pirates rushed to the attack. Paul briefly cried to his men, as the foe came rushing on—

"Remember Transom, my lads, and strike home in memory of him; do not throw away a blow—think of him—revenge him, and strike surely. Hurrah for Transom and the Trackless!"

The men replied with a stentorian cheer, and met their foes with the steady determination of men resolved to part with life rather than give an inch of ground. The pirates shouted and swore and fought fiercely, but gained no footing: they were pushed from the bows and quarter as fast as they attempted to get on board: some were cut down, others shot, and not a few pitched back into the sea without a single blow. The steady fire of musketry and pistols maintained against them, as well as the immoveable tenacity of the crew of the Trackless, cost the pirates a large number of their brethren, and as they did not possess the sturdy firmness which their opponents displayed, they gave ground, and, after a feeble rally, which failed, they returned to their vessel. Paul was not yet in a position to board the rover, for his numbers were more than twice those of Paul; he, therefore, ordered his men to their guns again, while a hand was sent aloft to watch the movements of the coming pirate vessel, that she might be met if she joined the fray. The man was no sooner aloft than he gave notice that she was hurrying in for the land, and that there was a sloop of war in chase of her. The pirate captain became also acquainted with this fact, and as the vessels, during the last assault, had got separated a short distance, he sent his people aloft at a moment's notice to spread the canvas. His crew, seeing the necessity for instant flight, pushed in clusters to obey the mandate, and in a few minutes everything was set, and the rover shot a-head of the Trackless before almost those on board of the latter knew what was going on. The smoke of the guns, which hung about them in thick clouds, prevented an accurate observation being made, but no sooner was their canvas seen to fall, than the men, enraged at the chance of losing their prize, scarcely waited to hear Paul's command to set the canvas before they spread themselves over the rigging, and covered the schooner with a cloud of canvas, with a speed which made the change almost appear the work of a magician—they were soon out of the thick atmosphere which they had themselves made, and in full chase of the rover. Paul took this opportunity of removing the wounded, and giving the dead a seaman's grave. During this painful task he narrowly watched the countenances and behaviour of his people—to see if they wavered, or were desirous to prosecute the affair further, but could not detect in one of the heated, bronzed countenances the smallest indication of a wish to end the contest were it stood. He did not feel in his own mind satisfied, or anything approaching to it, with the retaliation made for the death of his friend, and he determined, while the people would support him, that he would revenge him to the utmost.

A light wind prevailed, and the superiority of the sailing qualities of the rover, in such a position, remarkably displayed. The Trackless might, with a good breeze, have contended with her, and a difficulty have been raised to decide which sailed the fastest; but, being under the disadvantage of cargo she was not able to reach the speed which the peculiar build and light draught of the rover obtained for him. The advantage which the latter obtained was not so great as to prevent our hero having a rap at him with his bow-chaser, which, if it did not do the damage he intended, had still the effect of making the pirate yaw about, and lose distance to avoid its effects. Land was now not above four or five miles off, and Paul surmised that his enemy could not gain so much on him in that short distance as to escape when they were close in shore before he could get up with them; with this idea he stood steadily on, without adding to his sails, knowing that he should have to reduce them suddenly. The sloop of war which had held the second pirate in chase was covered with a cloud of canvas, and had added to it immediately the vessel Paul was chasing and the Trackless had been discovered by them; she was bearing down, straining every point to come up to her chase, which, like Paul's antagonist, was remarkably swift. The pirates were alarmed at so dangerous a foe as the sloop, and that was not at all decreased by the evident intention of the schooner to take a share in the contest. In the height of their anxiety, both making for one point, and each keeping a sharp look-out after its own pursuer, they contrived to run foul of each other. It was only by great exertion that the collision was prevented—being of a violence sufficient to have sunk one of them; as it was, some damage was done, and the rigging got entangled. Paul, as soon as he observed it, ordered his guns to be double shotted, and the men to stand by their guns, while a few were sent up to be in readiness to shorten sail; he now was overhauling both, hand over hand; their efforts to get disentangled materially impeding their progress. They were still above a mile from the shore and made desperate attempts to get free and run close in; they succeeded in getting separated and about twenty yards apart, when Paul ran in between them, and getting fairly level with each, gave the order to fire both broadsides. With cheers his people obeyed him, continuing their discharges with the same systematic regularity and rapidity which they had before displayed, and which occasioned such great havoc. This species of fighting, in the present state of affairs, was not at all suitable to the pirates' interests; they had no time to spare for a succession of broadsides, they must carry what they had to do as a *coup de main*, and, therefore, determined to each pour as many men as they could into the schooner—crush her at once, and then make for their cave—the natural advantages of which would enable them, they hoped, to hold out successfully against the crew of the sloop of war. Paul guessed by the slackening of their fire, that they would attempt some such manœuvre, and hastily gathered his men where he expected the attack to be made, and, fortunately, a puff of wind lifted enough of the smoke to show him that the new enemy's deck was crowded, and that a murderous fire of musketry was about to be poured in upon him and his crew. He ordered them instantly to lie down, just as a shower, as thick as hail, flew about them. Then the pirates came leaping in all directions—swearing, threatening extermination, and trying their best to fulfil their threats; but they were met manfully and gallantly opposed. The crew of the Trackless fought with a skill and courage far beyond what Paul could have expected them, and made their foes dread them at every turn. It was in vain that the pirates crowded and endeavoured to bear down the numbers of their high-couraged opponents; they were mostly stalwart seamen, possessing great strength, and powers of no ordinary description; they fought desperately, yet coolly, and by their firmness made themselves almost as formidable as did their skill and agility in the use of their weapons. They followed to the letter the advice which Paul had given them, and wasted not a blow, nor gave a flourish uselessly. They husbanded their strength, and when they did strike, he upon whom the blow fell had cause for sorrow if he survived the wound. The sloop of war, which had been four or five miles distant, was now approaching very near; she began to take in her canvas, and fired a couple of bow guns to announce her intention of joining the sport; and those discharges were sufficient to clear the decks of the Trackless of her foes. They flew like children at the sound of thunder—it was devil take the hindmost, for the strangers were cut down or shot as they attempted to fly. Their object in this sudden desertion was soon displayed in their boats being got out and as instantly filled. Paul gave the order instantly to toss out his boats and give chase, and with three boats' crews he started in pursuit, leaving a few hands to guard the schooner and to take possession of the two pirate vessels. His men were armed with pistols, muskets, cutlasses, and as much ammunition as they could find time to throw into the boats. Away they went—the men rowing as if they had endured no fatigue whatever, anxious only to achieve the conquest they had striven so arduously for against such odds. The last boat of the pirates had scarcely grated on the beech, before Paul got the first of his boats grounded also. His men leaped out with him in the midst of them, and followed, in hot pursuit, the rascals, who fled in the utmost disorder. He was speedily joined by the crews of his other boats, and in a body they proceeded to follow the fugitives, firing at them as they fled, and exerting their best speed to come up with them. The beech upon which they had landed was high, and composed of shingle, until it reached a long, narrow fissure in one of the rocks which formed the coast, and then it became rocky and difficult of progress to an unpractised foot. The adventurous seamen, however, heeded it not, and made up their want of skill in surmounting it by perseverance. By degrees the pathway narrowed so as to suffer only two men to pass at a time; Paul was the first to pass along it. On one side the rock rose high and precipitous—on the other was an armlet of the sea, fifty or sixty yards in width, skirted by ridges of rock of such a shelving character that many parts of them were hid in darkness, forming excellent places of concealment for the foes, who could fire from those recesses without being retaliated upon, excepting from their own side. It was a fortunate occurrence for Paul, that, in darting swiftly along, he stumbled, fell, and only by muscular exertion saved himself from falling into the sea; for as he slipped, a shower of bullets passed over his body and flattened themselves against the rocks; a shower followed them which wounded two or three of the latter party, and Gasket, who had followed Paul and succeeded in placing him upon his feet, cried out—

"We must fall back, or else we shall all be picked off like barnacles off copper sheathing. We must force this passage in the boats."

Another rattling discharge of musketry followed his words, but, luckily, without wounding any of the men; and Paul, who saw there was no chance of returning the fire with any good effect, followed, though reluctantly, the advice of Gasket. They hastened back to the spot where they had left the boats, and found they should have to proceed a short distance along the coast to come at the mouth of the armlet. No time was lost in speculating; the men took their places in the boat, and then observed that the sloop of war had run as close in shore as she could, had clewed up and furled her sails, and was despatching her boats for the same purpose which our hero was pursuing. When Paul saw them leaving the side of the sloop, he signalled them to follow him, and said to his men—

"Give way, my lads; let us have the post of honour—we must be first."

The men answered with a cheer; and away flew his light gig, followed by his own two boats, and, at a distance, by those of the sloop, whose crew longed to share the glory with the gallant hearts of the Trackless. They gained the mouth of the inlet, which, by the artifice pursued by the pirates in not taking their boats up it, they had not noticed, and soon made their way along its smooth water to where they expected to meet the attack of the enemy; but all was silent as the grave; there was no sound, save the echo of the noise made in their own progress, and the very silence made them more on the alert for treachery. They found that the fissure terminated in a cavern, which was dark and gloomy in its entrance, and pitch dark as it proceeded. To sally down it without lights would have been a rashness which nothing could have excused, and they had no torch, nor anything which would serve as such; to remain undecided was to expose them to a fire which they could not return; and to retreat was an idea which no man for a moment entertained. What, therefore, was to be done? Paul decided upon proceeding as far as the water would carry him, and then trust to circumstances. Accordingly, forward they went, more cautiously and slower than they had hitherto done, and before they reached very far, they were overtaken by the first boat belonging to the sloop of war, the captain of which sat in the stern-sheets.

"Hallo!" he cried, as he came up with them. "What boats are those? Speak before we fire into you?"

"The boats of the Trackless schooner," replied Paul.

"The same schooner that has been hammering at the pirates?" he inquired.

"The same," returned Paul; "I am her captain."

"I give you joy," he cried; "you are a lucky fellow. I have been after the damned scoundrel I have chased into here ever since yesterday afternoon, He's been kicking up a rare bloody piece of work, and he shall go aloft with a whip, or my name's not Jack Helm. Where have they stowed themselves?"

"That I can't discover; they are not far from here," replied Paul, "I expect; as soon as we get a little farther into the dark they will rattle away at us."

"As soon as they like," cried Captain Helm. "But I've a remedy for their darkness; I'll ferret them out. Jolly boat there!"

"Sir," cried a gruff voice, in a boat a little distance astern.

"Up with a blue light, and throw a little more daylight into this darkness."

In a moment he was obeyed, and the place was illuminated with a brilliancy almost dazzling. Every eye was turned anxiously in the direction it was expected the ruffians had secreted themselves, and with a stentorian cheer, they discovered, at a little distance, a band of pirates quietly planting a number of brass guns intended for their light vessels, so as to form a battery, and by well-directed discharges to blow the boats and their foes out of the water. Paul's men gave a few short but strong strokes with their sweeps, and sent the boat grating upon the shore, which they found shelved suddenly. The gig was followed by the rest of the boats—the expiring blue-light was supplied by another—torches brought by the sloop's people were kindled, and every nook and cranny was exposed, displaying a force far superior, in point of numbers, to the crews of the schooner and sloop combined. This discovery with "discretionary" persons, would have roused them to exercise "the better part of valour," and have shown as much by a retreat as speedy as their advance; but the sturdy sea-dogs knew of no discretion which counselled flight, and in the difference of numbers against them saw only more fun. Paul and his gig's crew were not out of his boat before the other boats grounded; and the pirates, either for stratagem or panic-stricken, fled rapidly up the cave. They were followed instantly, and with swiftness, but they had the advantage of a start, and a perfect knowledge of the locality, and were thus enabled to improve upon the distance they had obtained. The cavern, after the pursuers had proceeded a little way, they found branched into various passages, and as not a trace of one of the fugitives was visible in any of them, they were for a minute or so perplexed, until Paul detected a whisper, which determined the course the pirates had taken. He rushed down the passage, followed by his crew, and before he had gained a hundred feet he heard a voice, which he instantly recognized as belonging to the pirate captain, cry loudly—

"*Todos a sus sitios.*"

A scrambling round followed this order for the rovers to take their respective positions and again all was still. The sailors bearing the torches, however, arrived, and the light making the hiding places no longer tenable, the leader of the pirates shouted—

"*Fuego a ellos! Avanzad muchachos! A ellos! Viva!*"

A fierce discharge of musketry followed his words, which was instantly returned by the pistols of the sailors. Paul would not wait to suffer them to reload, but instantly led them on to the attack with the cutlass; the sailors cheered and rushed at the pirates, who, though they had the vantage ground, had not the courage to stand the charge, they gave ground, and their captain, who possessed more courage than any of his crew, roared, shouted, and blasphemed at their cowardice. He was a little man, but evidently fearless, and stood his ground firmly, calling upon his men, in good Castilian, to do the same.

"*Viva!*" he shouted. "*Guerra hasta la muerte.*"

But his followers seemed little inclined to fight till the death, for they retreated more rapidly than ever, leaving him to bear the brunt of the fray; but he jumped about with such agility, acting upon what prize fighters call the hitting and getting away system, that, with the exception of a slight wound he had received from Paul, he remained unhurt. Brave as he was, he did not see the policy of continuing the affray single-handed, he, therefore, exerted his nimbleness in retreating, and overtook his flying partizans ere they had retreated any particular distance, and as soon as they found that he acted upon their example, they took to flight pell-mell. It was in vain that he called them "*vil cobardes,*" they were not to be stayed by being endowed with the degrading epithet, and kept on at full speed, tumbling over each other in their hurry to get away. The sailors shouted and followed, led by Paul, hotly; they groaned and roared at the pirates as their nimble legs bore their faint hearts away, and tried their hardest to come up with them, either to capture them or cut them down if they resisted. A few minutes' chase, with the occasional discharge of a gun or pistol, brought them to the opening of the cavern that had connection with the mainland. The only path which now presented itself was a narrow pathway formed up the straggling side of an irregular pile of rocks; the footpath was not wider than was sufficient for two to pass abreast, and the little captain, with a valour and determination worthy a better purpose, rushed to it, gained it first, and, presenting his pistols, he shouted, in the Spanish language, to his men—

"*Carajo! Esperad!* stand your ground, fight like men—*Santiago!* I will shoot the first man through the head who attempts to pass me. *Animo! mio companeros.*"

Whether it was his language or his threat which infused courage into his men it is difficult to say, but they turned and met their assailants with more bravery than they had yet displayed, and kept up their beating hearts by liberally dispensing oaths, and their captain lent them good aid in that as well as fighting.

"*A los infiernos con los Ingleses!*" he shouted. "*Que maldito sean ellos il Viva! viva!*"

"Hurrah!" shouted Paul coming up with them, and dashing impetuously into the midst of them. "Down with the roving rascals! down with them!'

His men echoed his cheer, and with their boarding pikes and cutlasses made a terrific charge. They were accompanied by the crew of the sloop, who were not backward in their efforts, or in having a leader to animate and direct their movements; and the Spaniards, having an exaggerated idea of their prowess, fancied themselves opposed to an army of giants. However, fight they must, and they did so in frenzy and desperation; men on both sides were cut down, but the pirates suffered most severely. They were no match for their foes hand to hand, and after a short and tremendous struggle their eyes were anxiously bent on the means of escape; but their leader guarded the pass, and showed no symptom of suffering one to retire, but fought bravely, and, to the best of his ability, endeavoured to infuse sufficient bravery into his men to enable them to defeat their foes, or, at least, retreat with honour.

"*Viva!*" he roared, "*Hacer correr la sangre de aquellos malditos.*"

His men responded to his shouts, but not to his actions. At first, they fought fiercely; but the groans of the wounded, the shrieks and shouts of the sufferers and assailants, cowed them; the steady perseverance of the English sailors, who advanced step by step, and never lost an inch of ground, was too much for their nerves, and they rushed for the pass with one accord, upsetting in their progress their captain, who swore a thousand oaths, and cut at them madly with his sword as they swept by him. Those who were not lucky enough to be first had still to fight to cover the retreat, to preserve themselves from being captured until the coast was clear for them to make their escape also. To their aid, however, came the captain; and, with a face glowing like a brick, he roared at his retreating crew—

"*Vil cobardes! Hijos de perras—Borachons—Puercos—Bestias!*" and every epithet degrading to them he could light upon.

Foaming with the rage which their despicable behaviour had created in him, he fought like a tiger, and was really the only dangerous one amongst them. Paul picked him out, and rattled at him with a determination of revenging the death of poor Transom. The pirate, however, with all his courage, was prudent; he had already had one encounter with our hero, and

received a wound; he therefore avoided him, and fought with others possessing less skill. But Paul was not to be denied in this way, and made at him, absolutely cutting his way to him. The vigour with which he wielded his cutlass soon gained him an opening and when the pirate perceived him close upon him, he looked anxiously at the pass through which his men were still crowding, and muttering—

"*No hay ningun remedio,*"

He dashed in amongst them, and scrambled up the rocks.

"*Estamos perdidos,*" shouted twenty voices as he fled; and his example was speedily followed by others.

"Devil take the hindmost" was now the word, and the pirates one and all rushed up the rocks, the sailors, with a shout of thunder, following. Paul would not lose sight of the captain, and dashed after him, followed by Gasket and the remainder. Successively, but not successfully, the pirate fired his pistols at him, and flung them also, but without a correct aim, and therefore without doing damage. The rocks up which they advanced were rugged and irregular masses, and the pirate and our hero leaped from one to another, in desperate chase and retreat. The agility of the captain enabled him to elude all Paul's efforts to capture him; and, in a fit of rage, he drew a pistol and fired at him, but missed him. He was more enraged by his failure, and made fresh efforts to overtake the flying pirate. He was more successful; and delivered some fearful blows with his cutlass, which his foe found it difficult to parry. They had now reached a considerable height; beneath them lay the bay into which the pirates had been chased. The sea lay calm and placid: a strange contrast to the bloody contention going on so near it; there were the vessels, lying as they had left them, looking like immoveable objects on a plate of glass. There was still a greater height to gain; but there was more room for those flying and those following, and, accordingly, the men spread themselves in all directions, where they had the best chance of overtaking a foe. Paul heeded no one but the pirate captain; him he followed; him he attacked. A high mass of rock stood between him and escape; and before he had time to spring upon it, Paul leaped up from a cluster beneath and stood level with him. He saw that he must now fight, and, compressing his teeth, he muttered an imprecation, and turned to face him. The conflict speedily became terrific: they cut and lunged and thrust with fearful rapidity, and tried every manœuvre to inflict a death-blow. Their swords clashed as though they would break; there was no pause for consideration or breath; the weapons flashed and glittered here and there, like lightning. At length the pirate received two severe gashes, and fought wildly, in hope to repay them; but he only laid himself open to receive fresh wounds, and became frenzied. He gnashed his teeth, and poured forth frightful imprecation; the blood streamed from him, and his exertions, those of maddened rage, became greater as his chance of bringing them to a successful issue became less. Paul received his blows with skill; and, thinking only of Transom, he gave no chance away; and gathering his strength together for one tremendous effort, he, with a violent swing of his sword, sent his weapon flying out of his hand; and in an instant the pirate lay upon the ground, mortally wounded. He shrieked as he fell, and then raised himself half up, the blood pouring from him in torrents.

"*O Dios mio!*" he muttered; "*o soy muerto! Que desgracia! O Madre de Dios! me muero. O Padre nuestro—oh!*"

He tried to cross himself but fell back exhausted. His face grew white and his lips bloodless. He raised his arm feebly, and beckoned Paul towards him; he obeyed the summons, and kneeling down raised the expiring man in his arms, while his companions, led by Gasket and the captain of the sloop, continued chasing the remainder of the pirates. Large drops of perspiration rolled down the dying man's forehead, and a violent shiver ran through his frame; his eyes rolled wildly to and fro. At length, with great exertion, he said in a husky tone of voice.

"*Me muero, senor capitan,* the victory is yours. It is all over with me; but I have a favour to ask of you: will you grant it?"

"Name it!" said Paul, surprised by the accuracy with which he spoke English.

"But will you grant it?—say, will you grant it?" cried the pirate earnestly.

"Let me know what it is," returned Paul, "and, if consistent with my honour and my means, it shall be done."

"It is consistent with both," replied the pirate, eagerly. "You will grant it, I know. Say it—swear it. I am dying. Let me not into hell until I hear you swear to grant my prayer."

"Speak it, man," exclaimed Paul, "if it can be done with truth and honour, it shall, I swear."

"It is enough," murmured the man; "you are Inglese, you will not break your word. *O Dios mio!* that pang. Listen, Senor Inglese. About ten years since I captured a brig; and put to the sword every one on board, save one girl—an English girl, fair and lovely as an angel. O, Santa Teresa! she was very lovely. I kept her as my prize. An island in the Bahamas was my home. I took her there—I married her."

"Married!" echoed Paul, with surprise.

"*Si, Senor*," returned the pirate. "I loved her with all my soul, and I would not have my children come into the world with disgrace upon them. A priest, who was a prisoner, performed the ceremony with a pistol on each side of his head. The girl was not willing to be my wife, I confess. O, Santa Teresa! she was weeping and fainting all the while, and when we were married, hard and fast, many's the time she tried to murder herself; but I prevented her. At last a child was born—a girl—and when she grew big enough to look at, I took a liking to her. She was very pretty, and had a child's pretty ways with her; but she would cry and shrink when I attempted to take her, and run away from me with fear in her face. I told her mother she taught her to hate me, but she denied it, by saying that though she hated me herself, she would not teach her child to hate any one. I didn't believe her, and grew enraged with her. She was always weeping and looking wretched, and would shudder when I took her in my arms, as if a snake embraced her. She always repulsed me when I would kiss her, though she was my wife, and at last I grew weary of this; so one morning, in a passion, I shot her."

"What!" cried Paul, recoiling with horror.

"*O Madre de Dios*, be merciful to me! I sent a bullet through her brain," returned the wretch, groaning; "I was sorry for it afterwards, and lavished all my fondness on the child; she is grown up a fair, beautiful thing, but now she has nobody left to take care of her in the world—not one living soul. *Senor capitan*, will you take her, and make her your child? Will you swear to make her happy for ever?—say you will—swear it before I die. Quick, Inglese, there is mist before my eyes; I grow cold—will you take her? There's gold enough to make her a queen. Speak—quick."

"I will, returned Paul, rapidly, as he watched the death hues passing swiftly over the miserable wretch's features. "Where shall I light upon her?"

She is in this island," returned the pirate; "half a mile to the north of this, in a deep cranny in the rock, facing the sea, there is a small building;

she is there. Take this ring from my finger; those who keep the place will give you free admission, and assist you to remove the wealth. I—*O Dios mio* —water, Inglese—I faint—water, water."

There was none at hand, and no one to fetch it. Paul could only part his hair from his forehead, and watch his ghastly face as it grew livid with the approach of death; his eyes were closed, and the short pants of his chest told vividly that his hour was come. For a minute he lay still, then suddenly he sprung from Paul's arms. and raising himself to his knees, he shouted, with an expiring effort—

"*Viva! Guerra hasta la muerte! Fuego a ellos! avanzad mis campaneros viva! Mas pulvora! O Jesus! el Buque se hunda! Estamos perdidos! Carajo!* —Ha! ha! ha! *Trae, vino! O Dios! me muero agua—agua, por el amor de Dios.*"

He paused a moment, and fell back in Paul's arms, rolled himself uneasily from side to side, and then with difficulty he muttered—

"*O Padre nuestro que estas en los cielos sanctificado sea el tu nombre—O, ave Maria!—Santiago—carajo—es muerto—y no nos dejeis caer en la tentacion—O Madre de Dios! pero libra nos de ma—l.*"

The last word faded upon his lips, and, with a frightful convulsion of his limbs, his spirit fled. Paul witnessed the falling of his jaw—the quiver of his limbs—heard the heavy groan which accompanied these movements, and he knew he held a corpse in his arms. He laid him gently down upon the rock and drew from his finger the ring of which he had spoken; and then, grasping his sword, he ascended the rock, following the course the pirates and their assailants had taken; he heard the discharges of fire-arms still, shouts and the noise of battle yet continued, and with hasty strides he advanced to the scene of action. It seems, in the hurry of their flight, the pirates had taken a direction which led them to the verge of a tremendous precipice, from which there was no escape; the approach was narrow, and the crews of the schooner and sloop were more than sufficient to guard it. They had, therefore, but one alternative—to submit: but as death would meet them that way—for every man of them would be hung if captured; many of them resolved to try and cut their way though the opposition vessels, to stand their ground and really try and defeat their foes; while a few determined, if the worst came to the worst, to leap from the cliff into eternity. Thus the battle assumed a fiercer aspect than it had hitherto done. The captain of the vessel the sloop had chased, came more prominently forward than before, and cheered his men to resistance. The struggle was hotly maintained, and courageously supported on the pirates' side, much to the astonishment of those who had made them fly so easily before, but not more to their surprise than pleasure, for they would rather have had a little trouble to gain the victory than have obtained it without a blow, for the sake of honour. Paul quickly entered the fray; his men welcomed him with a cheer, and rushed after him, as he, at once, with inspiriting cries, plunged into the midst of the rovers. His blows fell quick and heavily, and the animation which he displayed, caused him not only to be well seconded, but to be given way to by his foes, who deemed him too formidably an enemy to stand firmly before. As he encountered the pirates one after another, a few short desperate cuts were passed between them, which ended in the pirate seeking another foe, or falling miserably wounded. Those who were near, saw and noted Paul's prowess, and hesitated ere they crossed his path; several retired precipitately, rather than fight with him; and the giving way of a few who were resolutely followed up, ended in a similar display of conduct by the rest. They retreated rapidly until further progress was arrested by the precipice; then some fought madly, regardless of all consequences; others leaped into the fearful gulf, and the rest threw down their arms, screamed for quarter, and were made prisoners; a few minutes more and the contest ceased—the refractory were slain, and the captives bound.

"When the fight was done," the prisoners were marched off to be taken on board the sloop, and the captain congratulated Paul and himself upon the successful issue of the affray. He mentioned the prospects of a rich haul of gold and merchandise, which he expected to discover in the cavern; and told him that as he had mainly contributed to the capture, his share would be proportionably great. Paul replied, and declined accompanying him immediately in search of the anticipated prize, saying he felt satisfied that whatever was discovered would be faithfully accounted. He had another object at present, which demanded his immediate and exclusive attention, and, that completed, he would lose no time in joining him. The captain acquiesced and departed with his men, and our hero dispatched his own people with their wounded on board the Trackless, and with Gasket and four sturdy fellows he went to search for the dwelling which contained the pirate's child.

He proceeded, as directed, along the north side of the rock for rather more than half a mile, until he reached a ravine which was of considerable depth. He looked down, but discovered no signs whatever of a building, or anything approaching to it, and looked round him, but with no better success. The spot on which he stood commanded a view, on three sides of him, more than a mile each way, and the fourth was the sea; there was nought on which his eye could alight indicative of the place he expected to find, and he began to surmise that in his agony the pirate chief must have misdirected him. He could not for a moment entertain a thought that he had done so purposely, or why tell him of the child's existence at all—the more especially as the relation conveyed a frightful instance of his villany. At last a thought struck him to descend the ravine; the overhanging masses of rock presented, on a first inspection, a terrible impediment to this design; but a more scrutinising and closer examination showed him a spot where such a feat might be attempted; he resolved to try it, and communicated his intention to Gasket, who expressed his readiness to follow him anywhere. No objection was made by their companions, for the matter was made optional to them, and therefore, the descent was commenced. At first it was but blind work, and required strong nerves, for they dropped from clump to clump of rock, where a slip would precipitate them two hundred feet; they were, however, all used to frail footing on giddy heights, and thought less of their proceedings than most landsmen would have done. Down they went, occasionally stopping to gaze down the chasm beneath them, or to look at their leader, who skipped from rock to rock, with the agility of one who had passed the greatest part of his life chamois hunting. After they descended at least fifty feet, Paul paused to rest, and, while gazing intently around him, he discovered a more regular path than that he was taking, leading to an opening which appeared more the result of an excavation than a work of nature. It struck him that this led to the place he was seeking, and with a little exertion he contrived to get into the track, followed by his companions, one of whom, from an accidental stumble, nearly met with his death; he was saved by Gasket's catching him by the collar as he rolled swiftly past him, and trusting his whole weight to a rushy twig that grew from a nook in a slab of rock by where he stood; the sudden jerk which the stopping of the falling man's weight caused, nearly destroyed his equilibrium; but the toughness with which the twig's root's clung to the rock, preserved them both. After this little, but not very agreeable, incident they proceeded with alacrity after Paul, who not having seen what transpired, gained some distance a-head of them, and quickly perceived that he was in the right track, by lighting on a path hewn in the rock. He hastened down it, and found himself shortly stopped by a huge block of stone, fixed perpendicularly in the rock across the path. This was a barrier which there was no means of passing or surmounting, but by some special contrivance of which he was not aware. He felt perfectly satisfied there existed a passage, but was totally at a loss to imagine where it was situated, for the minutest scrutiny did not enable him to ascertain its whereabouts. After a short consultation, Paul raised his voice, shouted, and tapped with the hilt of his cutlass against the rock; to the surprise of all they beheld the rock of stone move inwardly, as if on hinges, and gradually opened a passage for them. Paul took advantage of it and rushed on, followed by his comrades. When the last was through the block closed with a loud noise, and he found himself in a spacious quadrangle formed in the rock, confronted by a dozen fierce-looking fellows, armed to the teeth. They appeared quite as much surprised to see him as he them, and for a minute they gazed on each other without speaking or moving; at length finding they were two to one, the pirates—for they were part of the band—with tremendous oaths, attacked our hero and his companions. They knew, however, well how to defend themselves, even against superior numbers, and returning a taunting laugh to a summons to throw down their arms, they entered with animation into the conflict. It was fierce and bloody while it lasted, but sturdy courage will always prevail against mere enthusiasm, and after a brief struggle the pirates called for quarter, when the dexterity of their opponents had reduced their numbers to an equal amount with their own. Paul granted it, and then showing the ring, he demanded entrance into the dwelling, which was not yet visible. The man to whom he showed the glittering hoop stared at it and then at him, and after elevating his eyebrows, and opening his mouth, exclaimed—

"*Carajo!* why didn't you show that at first, we would have obeyed it, and saved our blood."

"You did not give me time, answered Paul; "you must, therefore, take the consequences of your own rashness. Come, no more words; lead me to the building which contains the young maiden, the captain's daughter."

"*Adonde esta el capitan?*" asked the man, sullenly.

"He is safe," he answered, evasively. "It was at his request I came; you will do well not to refuse my bidding."

"*Vamos, siguiendo!*" returned the fellow, with a gloomy countenance, and walked on.

Paul followed him, after he had given directions to Gasket to secure those they had conquered, and passing through a narrow gallery cut in the rock he came suddenly upon a narrow archway, excavated by nature, beneath which they passed, and entered a serpentine passage, ill-lighted and so full of turns and diverging corridors, that to one unacquainted with the road it would have proved an inextricable labyrinth. Paul looked to his weapons expecting foul play, but his guide kept on his path without turning a glance towards him. After they had progressed a considerable distance, and no change in the character of the place evident, Paul was about to stop his conductor and make him give some proof that he was not misleading him, when he unexpectedly encountered a blaze of light, and found himself, by a sudden turn in his path, upon a broad surface of rock in the open air; to his left was a small building, looking more like the exterior of a natural grotto than a dwelling-house, and to this building, from which there was an extensive sea view, his conductor advanced, opened a door and admitted our hero, who saw the interior, like the passages through which he had just passed was excavated out of the body of the rock; the man led him to an upper apartment, and when they reached it the man said—

"You must wait here a few minutes, senor, while I send for Senora Rita."

"I will see that you do send for her," replied Paul. "And mark me, Spaniard, if you attempt to put any trick or foul play upon me, a bullet from this pistol shall cut itself a road through your skull."

"You need not be alarmed, Senor Inglese," returned the man; "I shall not quit you. I will summon Senora Rita's duenna, Madre Jacinta hither; you shall give her the order. What ho, Jacinta! *Ola, Madre Jacinta! Ola, Jacinta!*" he bawled at the top of his voice, until a shrill screeching voice answered in Spanish—

"Jesus! what is all that noise? *Borachon!* Do you think you are swilling in the cave? Out upon you. *Bestia!* you want a cudgel do you not, *hijo de perra? Madre de Dios?* a strange senor!" cried an old woman, checking her scolding language as she entered on perceiving our hero.

"*Si,*" returned the pirate; "*el Senor* would speak with the senorita; fetch her."

"*Puerco!*" cried the woman; "is that the way to address her duenna? learn manners, *borachon. Adonde esta el capitan?*"

"Ask the senor," returned the man.

"*Es muerto!*" exclaimed Paul.

"*Es muerto!*" they both repeated, with astonishment and horror.

"*Si,*" replied Paul, "he is dead. He has bequeathed his daughter to my care; produce her, and quickly, for my time is precious."

"What proof have we that senor is not playing some wily trick upon us?" said the old woman, cunningly.

"This," returned Paul, producing the ring; "and this will ensure your obedience to my commands," he continued, drawing a pistol from his belt, and presenting it at the old woman's head.

She shrieked, and retreated to the further end of the apartment and mumbled a few prayers, crossing herself devoutly at the same time.

"Stand up," said Paul, as she crouched at his approach: "you have no cause for alarm, if you do as I command you. Bring the young senora here, or lead me to her; and be speedy in whatever you do, if you desire to live.

"I will bring her to your excellency this instant. Jesus be gracious to me! you shall not have to wait the telling of a bead," replied the old woman, hastening away.

"*El capitan es muerto, senor* tells me," observed the pirate, when the duenna had left. "Where and how did he die? at sea by fighting or by fever."

"He died, and lies a quarter of a mile from hence. Heard you not the firing?" said Paul in reply.

"No," replied the man, with surprise; "we have heard nothing, we can hear nothing, buried as we are."

Paul eyed him doubtingly.

"It was short, and hot too," he said, "and the sound might have penetrated a deeper recess than this. However, as you appear to know nothing you shall know all; you will better understand what you may expect from any ill behaviour on your part. Know that I am commander of a schooner, and in conjunction with the captain of a sloop of war, have chased the two vessels belonging to your gang, run them in here, captured them both, and have slain part and taken the rest of your crews; a view round yonder point would shew you I have spoken no more than truth, for there your vessels lie under the lee of mine and the sloop."

"*Que desgracia!*" muttered the man, with a chopfallen countenance; "*Que maldito!* Senor will be merciful to me. I swear, by all the saints, that I will prove a true and loyal subject, if he sets me free."

"Let me have a proof of it in your future conduct, and I may be induced to comply with your wish," said Paul; "but once give me cause to deem you treacherous, and nothing shall save you from the yard-arm."

"*Gracias senor,*" exclaimed the man, with a brightening countenance, and was about volubly to declare his truth and devotion, when the governante entered, bringing a young child about nine years of age; she was tall for her years, and very fair. Paul was much struck with her beauty—it was wonderful. Her full, deep blue eyes fringed with jet black eyelashes, her pinky cheeks and red lips were almost perfect in their shape and hue, and there was a quiet, timid expression which interested him almost as deeply as her beauty.

"*Come esta V.,*" he said in a kind tone to her, and held out his hand; she took it hesitatingly, she returned his salutation timidly, and, looking round the room in a fearful, trembling manner, she murmured—

"*Adonde esta mi padre?*"

"He is far away from hence," replied Paul, gently. "Will you trust yourself with me for a little while? I will be kind to you and take you to friends who will love you."

"Will you take me to see my father," she asked, in Spanish.

"Do you wish to see him," he inquired, pressing her hand.

"Oh, no, no," she replied, in a terrified tone.

"Senora Rita is not good to say so," said the duenna, keeping a close eye upon Paul's pistol, which he had deposited in his belt; "she should love her father—her good, kind, amiable father; everybody loves her father, do they not, senor?" she concluded, addressing Paul.

Paul did not reply to her, but said—

"Will you go with me?"

"I witl go with you if we do not see my father," she replied.

"Why do you dislike him?" asked Paul, "does he not love you? Is he not kind to you?"

Oh, he *talks* kindly," she replied, "but I cannot love him—indeed I cannot love him," she added with a shudder; "I have always been frightened of him, and hated him, senor—yes," she cried, vehemently, stamping her little foot, "hated him since he killed my mother—"

No. 55.

"Oh, hush; Rita should tell no tales," interposed Duenna Jacinta.

"Silence, hag!" cried Paul, sternly, and then smoothing his brow, he said—"You know he took your mother's life away?"

"Oh, *si senor*," she exclaimed, bursting into tears, "I saw him kill her; he shot her with a pistol. It is a long while since, but I have never forgot it, and I never can. I have never prayed for him since, senor, though my dear mother, when she was alive, bade me pray for him as well as all the world, but I could not do it. Take me with you, senor, I will go anywhere with you, for you are young and handsome, and do not look wicked. I will go with you, if you will promise me I shall never see my wicked father more."

"I can easily make that promise," returned Paul. "If you come with me you shall never see him again."

"Then I will go to the end of the world with you," she said, placing both her hands frankly in his.

"Poor child," Paul murmured in English, "you shall go with me and find a happier home than that beneath a father's roof. I wish it had been my fortune to have rescued your mother."

"Oh, happiness!" she cried, clasping her hands with delight, "you speak English." She said this in excellent English.

Paul looked suprisedly at her.

"You speak it too," he said, speaking the language.

"Oh, yes," she returned, "my dear mother taught me, and sometimes my father would speak it to me. I love English, for it was my mother's native language, and if you are English I shall love you too."

Paul smiled.

"We shall be very good friends, I have no doubt," he said, and pressed her hand; then turning to the pirate he said to him in Spanish—

"Haste to where my men hold your comrades in captivity, inquire for *el Senor* Gasket, lead him hither to me, and be quick about it."

The man made him an obeisance and quitted the room instantly, with a brief.

"*Si, senor*" on his lips.

A colloquy ensued between our hero, the child, and the duenna, in which the latter performed a part which did not advance her in the estimation of Paul, and he felt little hesitation in showing her his opinions upon the subject, in such a manner as to almost make the old crone go upon her knees and beg for forgiveness. While she was yet deprecating his anger the Spaniard returned with Gasket, and our hero acquainted him with his intention of having the dwelling searched, and its contents conveyed on board the Trackless. The Spaniard readily proffered his assistance, and told them of an outlet leading from the house to the base of the rock, which would wonderfully facilitate the transmission of the effects. Paul gladly availed himself of the advantage; he took the child under his charge, and, leaving Gasket in possession of the dwelling, he wound, under the guidance of the Spaniard down the pathway he had spoken of, and, after a short walk, found himself at the mouth of the cavern, which the seamen of the sloop, under the superintendence of the captain, were ransacking of its contents. He did not interfere with them, but proceeded to the spot where one of his boats lay. He hailed it and was conveyed on board his vessel. His first object, after installing the little Rita in his cabin, was to see to the comforts of the wounded, and when that duty was accomplished, he summoned a number of his men, and entering his boat, he bade them pull to shore.

It was his intention to return to the dwelling of the pirate captain for the wealth it contained, but as it was also his determination that the whole of it should be preserved for the benefit of the little Rita, he resolved not to mention a word to the captain of the sloop, because he knew, according to the rules of the service, he would consider it confiscated, and claim it in the king's name, thus depriving the orphan of the only compensation for the loss of her parents which it was Paul's resolve she should possess. Night was fast approaching, and under the cover of its friendly shade, he planned that the property should be conveyed on board the Trackless; everything seemed to favour him in his kind intent. When he reached the shore he encountered the captain of the sloop, who inquired of him his destination, to which he replied he knew that there were a number of pirates secreted in the island, and he meant to capture them. The captain lauded his energy, saying—

"You would have made his Majesty a good officer Captain Jones, and, perhaps, we may yet see you gazetted to a frigate."

Paul bowed, and a flush mounted to his brow.

"I shall be glad to see it, believe me," continued the captain. "With respect to the fellows you are in pursuit of, you will greatly convenience me if you will bring them, when you have caught them, to me round the point. I wish to get under wiegh instantly. One of the fellows here has turned king's evidence, and tells me another of these rascals will be thereabouts shortly, laden with spoils. I wish to catch my gentlemen, but if I do not look sharp he will give me the slip."

Paul quickly assented and they parted. Our hero made for the path which the Spaniard had pointed out; and once more led by him, he sought the pirate's abode. Upon reaching it he found Gasket had made good use of his time, and brought to light wealth to an immense amount, principally consisting of precious stones and doubloons; the pirate evidently leaning towards that species of wealth which was of enormous value in a small compass. The more bulky property was of inferior value, except a few chests of massy plate, all which Paul had carried to the Trackless, and when everything which presented claims to be taken was transferred to the schooner, he caused a heap to be made of the rest and set fire to, leaving only a blackened mass of ruins to tell where the abode of iniquity had existed.

The captain of the sloop had put a number of his men on board each of the pirates vessels, as well as the whole of the prisoners, and, without losing a moment's time had got under sail and made for the place where he expected to obtain another prize. Paul was not long following him; he stood out of the bay, and with a good breeze, which sprung up opportunely, he run for the point at which the sloop was cruising. He examined narrowly the damage which the trackless had received in her engagement with the pirate, and had it repaired fully. He was not sorry to find that she had received no injury sufficient to impair her powers of sailing, and in less time than he anticipated, he hove in sight of the sloop, and the transfer of the prisoners was soon effected. The captain told our hero likewise, that an accurate account of the booty captured had been made, and that his and his ship's company's share should be forwarded to them through the owners of the Trackless at the earliest opportunity. Our hero thanked him for his courtesy, and the two ships' company, reciprocally cheering each other, they parted, and the Trackless made the best of her way to Philadelphia.

During the voyage home, Paul was much interested in his little charge. He found her quiet and amiable—thoughtful and intelligent; she had been accustomed to solitude, her only companion being the duenna, and being naturally reflective she had reached a knowledge and manner beyond her years. From an infant she had been terrified at the sight of her father, and had, with undivided love, clung more devotedly to her mother. Her murder before the timid child's eyes had impressed her with a horror which had nearly deprived her of intellect. The anguish she suffered, knew not, even by years, mitigation, and had preyed with such poisonous effect upon her frame as to become fatal. The sudden change, the revolution of circumstances which Paul's appearance had made—her removal from the place, where, since her mother's death, she had been withering, were too much for the weak state of her system, and Paul perceived, with real regret, that it was doubtful whether she would live the voyage out. He had a clever medical man on board, and he placed her under his charge with more than earnest injunction to do his best for her recovery, but the surgeon at once pronounced her case hopeless. The child seemed to have a knowledge of what was going to happen, but expressed no dread; she talked of death as a slumber in which she should have sweet dreams of her mother. To the last she refused to keep to her cabin she loved the green sea and blue sky, and would pass the best part of the day upon the deck, walking among the strong and sturdy men there like a fairy spirit in a sweet child's form. There was not a man in the vessel who did not look with kind eyes upon her, and there was not one who did not feel hurt when it passed among them that the doctor had said death had her down in his log. Every day she grew feebler, but was never fretful or pettish when her strength was insufficient to suffer her to remain on deck; and one evening when Paul sat by her side trying to make the hours pass unwearily, she talked to him in a higher strain than he had ever known her, and she spoke of her mother—her dear mother; her voice was low and gentle, but very earnest, and she took his hand and kissed it, saying, as she pressed it to her burning lips, that if her sweet mother had not been killed, and she had him for a brother, she should be very sorrowful at the thoughts of dying, but, as it was, it was perhaps the happiest for her. She looked him in the eyes as she spoke, and smiled so sweetly, so affectionately, that the tears rushed into his eyes until he was blinded by them; he turned his head away and hurriedly dashed his hand across his lids, then he turned to her again, and she was dead.

She lay as a child sleeps when fatigued by the sports of a summers day slumbering peacefully and calmly, refreshing her weary frame in sweet repose. Paul gazed thoughtfully and règretfully upon her for some time, and then with something of a heavy heart, he went upon deck. It soon passed among the men that their little favourite was dead, and the loss of a dear friend or relative could not have effected these honest fellows more deeply; they went about their duty in a quiet, almost solemn manner, as though their noise would disturb the dead child in her death sleep: they talked low and gravely of the youthful spirit that had fled—the sweet maiden who had been among them as a flower shows among rocks, and their converse was tinctured with sadness, and they looked as though grief had fallen with heavy hand upon them. The next evening the child was buried in the deep sea—it was a solemn sight to see the body of that young creature consigned to the unfathomable waters. Paul read the service over her in a clear impressive voice; once or twice his voice faltered, and there were those near who fancied they perceived thick tears, but he made a strong effort, and concluded in a firm tone, and then turned sadly from the spot and entered his cabin, while the people returned to their duty something less lighthearted for the loss of a child, whose only claim upon them was interest and sympathy.

Fair winds assisted them—fair weather attended them. Advantage was taken of it by crowding sail, and, notwithstanding the delay which the Trackless had met with, she entered the port of Philadelphia two days before she was expected. Paul lost no time in seeing the owners, and in giving a full account of all that transpired, and had the satisfaction of being warmly eulogised, as well as handsomely remunerated for his services. The property which he had taken for the little Rita from the pirates' dwellings was sold by private contract, and equally shared between the people of the schooner; he generously refraining from taking a single coin. The engagement he had with the pirates soon got noised abroad, and he was gratified by finding that his name was in every one's mouth; this he considered the first step to fame, and inwardly resolved to take advantage of it the first opportunity that occurred. He was offered the command of the Trackless with considerable emoluments; he was also offered several ships of larger size, but he declined all. The merchant service was not the road to glory, and he would not pursue it; he waited for a better chance, he could better afford to wait, for now he was spoken of by men in power; and with no little joy did he hear that it was not improbable he would receive the command of a ship of war: he, therefore, leaving his address with those likely to forward his wishes, left Philadelphia, accompanied by Gasket, had made the best of his way to his brother's estate upon the Rapahannoc.

CHAPTER VII.

"Aloft fair Albion's ensign flows,
As now she gains upon her foes;
Prompt are the signals—quick the fire—
Glad cheers the British hearts inspire!
Through heaven's wide vault the guns resound,
Dense clouds of smoke extend around.
The groups press forward to the shore,
Where a calm stillness reigned before;
And, in a wild suspense, await
The issue of their champion's fate.
Hush'd are the the sounds, the breezes bear
The murky clouds that fill'd the air:
With shattered masts and captive crew,
The foes, dismantled, rise to view;
While the brave victors bear away
The long-sought trophies of the day."

J. H. Lowther, Esq.

Paul Jones remained for a long period at home with his brother, who was seized with an illness of an alarming character. Lieutenant Prior and Florence were still with him when Paul returned, but their stay was not of long duration, for they had received letters from the parents of both stating a full forgiveness had been given by the father of Florence, and a reconciliation effected between the two families; a happy state of things, brought about chiefly through the instrumentality of Doctor Gray, who had been unceasing in his efforts to achieve this desirable affair. Both Eustace and his sweet wife were delighted at the intelligence; and, with no little gratification, they prepared to return to the land of their birth. Their thanks to our hero and his brother for the kindness and services they had received from them were as fervent and earnest as the warmest heart could have wished; and, with mutual consent, they parted. To Gasket they would have shown their sense of his truth and devotion by munificence as well as grateful acknowledgments, but when the hour for separation arrived he was nowhere to be found. His absence created some surprise, but though a rigid search was instituted for him, he could not be discovered, and they departed without seeing him, leaving behind only their thanks and a handsome present. They embarked at Philadelphia, and after a long, but safe voyage, they arrived in England, and were soon happily installed beneath the roof of Mr. Stanley, who, by kindness and affection, endeavoured to obliterate the remembrance of his former harshness. About this time the unhappy differences which led to the separation of the colonies from England took place; the mistaken line of policy which England pursued, accompanied by aggressions which nothing in the conduct of the colonists could have justified, filled every thinking man with indignation. It is not, however, the intention of this work to speak of the causes which led to the American war, but simply to mention its existence, and the connexion our hero had with it. Paul Jones possessed a reflective mind. It has already been stated that during the time he was with his brother he had devoted himself much to works of a political nature, and when the colonies were oppressed by England, he was one of the first who strongly and strenuously sided with the former. There might, perhaps, have been some slight prejudices influencing from his expulsion, for it was little else, from Scotland, and the slights he had received when making application for a post under government. This ill disposition was added to by his not receiving, on the part of himself, or men, a fraction of the wealth which he had assisted—in fact, mainly accomplished—capturing from the pirates; and all his representations, backed by men of established credit, failed in obtaining for him more than a cool reply, that the government only acknowledged the people of her own vessels in the distribution of prizes which were confiscated to the crown. To do the captain of the sloop justice, he had exerted himself to see the claims of our hero established; but his representations, though made with a manly spirit, and candid acknowledgment of the share Paul had taken in securing the success of the affair were unavailable. The enthusiastic hostility which Paul expressed towards England may have obtained much of its asperity from these causes: he looked upon the mother country as a hot-bed of injustice, and panted for an opportunity to testify the hate he felt towards it; mistaking, as did many others, the acts of a few for the deeds of a nation.

At this time his brother, after a long illness, whom he had unweariedly attended, died, and left him sole possessor of his little property; and shortly afterwards, Congress determined upon making reprisals for the maritime aggressions which England had made; a fleet was speedily prepared—a small one, it was true—and men capable of taking command of the vessels were eagerly sought for. Among the first who attracted the notice of Congress was John Paul Jones, whose conduct in the schooner, the Trackless, had excited such admiration; and it was speedily intimated to him, that if he desired to do American service, he had but to make the offer, and he would at once be appointed to the command of a vessel of war. He did so instantly; and the result was, that on the 22nd of December, 1775, he was appointed by Congress to be a first-lieutenant in the American navy. He was at first mortified, that, as he expected he had not had a ship given him; but as it was represented to him that merely individual interests were to be studied in giving vessels to those persons who possessed directly and indirectly a vast influence in the infant state, he swallowed his mortification with the promise that he should receive the first vacancy that occurred. With some difficulty, he got Gasket—who had returned to him about a week after the departure of Eustace and Florence, he having gone on a hunting expedition in the back woods—a berth as a master's mate on board the same ship, the Alfred, to which he was appointed first lieutenant. He said nothing to the honest tar until he had concluded the negotiations; and then, when he proffered it, with an expectation of it being received with pleasure, he was surprised to meet with almost a direct refusal to accept it. Upon inquiring the reasons which led to this denial, Gasket replied—

"I don't like, John, to fight agin my country."

"*Your* country," replied Paul, with a laugh; "how do you claim England as your country?—you were born at sea."

"I can't exactly say that," returned Gasket. "I was picked up when very young, off a wreck; but it don't follow that I was born at sea."

"Nor does it follow that you were born in England," remarked Paul.

"But I *feel* that I was; I feel, John Paul, that I am an Englishman. I was brought up by an Englishman, in an English ship; and I've served under an English flag ever since; and dam'me if I like to fight against old England—it don't seem nat'ral, and that's the truth."

"No man, Gasket, has a right to consider country, where gross injustice has been done," argued Paul. "England has unjustly oppressed these colonies—most indefensibly unjustly—and refuses to acknowledge, in the smallest degree the infamous wrongs she has perpetrated. It is right she should be resisted, and taught that injustice, even from a strong hand, which will sooner or later be punished. Remember, too, Gasket, that if you fight against England, you will fight with those who have English blood in their veins—with those who are as nearly allied to England as you are; and that argument alone is sufficient, I should imagine, to do away with your objection."

"I can't say I see that," replied Gasket; "supposing, John, your mother knocked you down for a sin you did not commit, do you think it would be right and fair to return her blow for blow, and do your best to knock the old woman down because she saw things in a wrong bearing: a mother, John, is a mother, and ought to be treated as such. Mothers love their children, John, even if they do sometimes give a little more punishment than is necessary; but they soon find out they have done wrong, and make up for their flogging by being fonder and kinder than ever. It's my opinion that if the people hereaway consider themselves the sons of England, which, seeing their fathers all shipped from the old country, is no more than they ought to do; I say I think if they do, they ought to wait a little while and try and mix up matters without coming to blows."

"Those are points left to wiser heads than mine or yours, Gasket," said Paul; "and whatever we may think will not affect the steps already taken; but with respect to your reluctance, I think you ought to divest yourself of it, and look upon yourself in the same light as I view myself, which is, as a citizen of the world. You cannot with certainty lay claim to any country as your birth-place—it might have been France as well as Eng—"

"Don't say that, John; don't say that," cried Gasket, with vehemence, speaking with all the bitterness which at that period all English sailors felt towards Frenchmen; "I couldn't have been a Frenchman—no, no, say anything but that."

"Well," replied Paul, laughing at his earnestness, "we will not suppose any country; we will suppose the Atlantic or Pacific, but you have neither relations nor connexions of any sort, in any country—"

"Say no more, John," said Gasket, interrupting him; "it is of no use arguing with you, you can sail round me at will in argument; I see you are bent upon my going with you, and I'll go; but, by the Lord! as here I stand,

had rather lose my right hand than fight agin the old country. I would rather lose my fist, John, and go agin the mounseers, than go whole-handed nto action with those who, until now, have been my messmates."

"If you have such strong opinions upon the matter, my good friend," said Paul, kindly, laying his hand upon his shoulder; "far be it from me to induce you against your will to follow me—"

"It's all done, John," cried Gasket, preventing Paul from speaking further; "I will join you, so say no more of the affair. I am obliged to you for the rank you have obtained for me, and it shall go hard, but I do my best not to disgrace it."

Without another word he wrung Paul hard by the hand and quitted him.

The arrangements for the disposal of the estate and the effects of his brother having been concluded, he hastened to take his post on board the ship of war, the *Alfred*, attended by his honest friend, Gasket; and their first cruise was directed to New Providence, one of the Bahama isles, and with another sloop in company, she made sail for their destination. Never did Paul find more bitterly the want of discipline than upon this voyage; all the men were inexperienced, and would not be taught; they were all equal, they said, and it was with difficulty the men were persuaded to do their duty, while the officers even the most subordinate in rank acknowledged no superior. The captain was next to a nonentity, and the first lieutenant was still less obeyed. With such a state of things it was little likely much honour was to be achieved and, accordingly, upon arriving at New Providence, through gross incapacity upon the part of most of the officers, the landing, which was to have been effected in the night, was delayed till the morning, and thus the very object for which they had come was defeated—namely the capture of a large quantity of military stores, which the governor of the island, aware of their arrival, had contrived to send away in the night. Their landing was not opposed, but as they were disappointed in their object, they had nothing to do but to embark again, and shape their course back again for America. While they were yet off New Providence they fell in with the Glasgow English frigate, and now Paul thought there was a chance of redeeming the honour he considered they had lost: a council was held, and fighting was rather eschewed. Paul had almost to storm before he could get them to fight, and at last, when through his strong representations, they believed the capture of the English frigate was certain, they prepared for action. Paul was given the command of the lower gun deck, and with alacrity he prepared to do his duty, and aid in winning the day, a result he calculated upon as inevitable. The action was commenced, and maintained with some spirit for a short time, but the superiority of the broadsides and discipline of the Englishman was so manifest, that the Americans were astounded ; the effects were tremendous, so far exceeded what they had anticipated, that they at once sheered off to Paul's indignation—nay, almost madness. It was in vain that he urged the captain to continue the contest—his representations by means of which victory might be ensured, were unheeded, and the vessels fairly took flight; their lightness of heels enabled them to distance their pursuer, who chased them as far as it was possible, and they entered their port with the satisfaction of being every way disgraced.

"I expected no other," said Gasket, in reply to a bitter exclamation of Paul; "but if we had an English crew—"

"If we had," interrupted Paul, with vehemence; "if we had, and I had commanded, I would have carried the frigate if she had been thrice her force."

"Ah!" sighed Gasket, "there's nothing like the old country after all."

Paul did not reply ; perhaps, at that moment, he felt as much.

The proceedings of the American squadron gave unqualified dissatisfaction to Congress, and to the American people generally, and a rigid inquiry was substituted, the result of which was the appointment of our hero to the command of a sloop of war, entitled the *Providence*. But the duties imposed upon him were not much to his taste ; his chief employment was to escort vessels from Rhode Island into the Sound, and from Boston to Philadelphia. He was afterwards occupied in cruising, and in six weeks captured sixteen sail—his vigilance, his determination, and his speedy movements, enabling him to gain information as well as success in all he undertook. He acted upon the same principle, which, in an after period, so mainly contributed to Napoleon's unexampled success. He was no sooner heard of in one place, than he was seen in another. There was no guarding against the rapidity of his movements, and merchant vessels who believed him far away, beheld him on their quarter with the astonishment of men who gazed on feats of magic. One important service he did to America was the capture of the Mellish, a a large armed vessel, which had on board ten thousand suits of clothing for the army, under the command of Generals Burgoyne and Carleton. Many other feats of equal value he performed, and at length he reached the Delaware, and received from all parties acclamations and praises. Now, indeed, his star was in the ascendant; and now with glowing thoughts, he saw honours awaiting, and but a short probation to pass ere he was invested with them, and then who should step between him and Alice?—Alice, the pride of his soul, the hope of his ambition, the twin star of his glory!

One night as he lay slumbering in his ship, upon the Delaware, he dreamed that the same tutelary angel who appeared to him when a boy, while sleeping in a cave upon his native shore, stood before him; she still wore the same aspect and form of Alice; she pointed to a steep pathway, which appeared to wind up a mountain to a considerable height; there was a blaze of light at its termination which dazzled his eyes when he attempted to gaze upon it. Once more she waved over his head the flag she had before held above him, and with a smile which made his heart swell with proud joy, she vanished, and he awoke. A man stood beside him, he declared himself a messenger from Congress. He held a packet in his hand, which he delivered. Paul dismissed him, and, with the impression of his dream, powerfully grafted upon his mind, he opened the packet. It contained a flattering letter to him from Congress, with the two following resolutions, the first of which he read with wonder. It ran as follows:—

"Congress, June 14, 1777.

"Resolved—that the flag of the thirteen United States be thirteen stripes, alternate red and white; that the union be thirteen stars, white in a blue field, representing a new constellation."

This was the symbol his dream had presented him with. The flag of his vision!

The second resolution said—"Resolved—That Captain Paul Jones be appointed to command the ship Ranger." The instructions were equally brief, thus:—"We shall not limit you to any particular cruising, but leave you at large, to search for yourself where the greatest chance of success presents." With an honour of this description, he was indeed proud, and he resolved to exercise every means he could invent and adopt, to return the favours Congress had thus showered upon him. His first destination was France; there to mature a project which he had conceived, and offered to Congress, of attacking the coast of England, with which he was well acquainted. His design had been concurred with, and to himself was left the mode of working it out. He quitted the Delaware with the cheers of a multitude, who witnessed his departure, ringing in his ears, and with a strong determination in his breast, that they should have cause to repeat those demonstrations to him on his return. His was the first hand which raised the independent flag in the Delaware. His vessel, the Ranger, was the first that hoisted the Union flag, and upon his arrival at Brest, where the French fleet under Count D'Orvillirs lay, his flag, as he stood into the harbour with his colours flying, was saluted by the French, being the first salute which the American flag received from the representatives of a foreign power.

After he had made all the arrangements he thought necessary, he quitted Brest and made for Whitehaven, determining that his first exploit should be the destruction of the shipping in the harbour. It was not, perhaps, alone the reason for his selecting Whitehaven that it was an important harbour and usually contained between three and four hundred sail, but he knew that his name would be blazoned along the coast—that it would prove a terror to those who had wronged him, and a harbinger of joy to one whom he knew would recognise in his actions the undying desire to win *her* hand, which reigned supreme in his bosom. His voyage was an expeditious one, and made with every precaution for secrecy. He forbore to make prizes, for his work was dangerous and required a clear ship and room to work it—he did not want it crammed with prisoners; but when he neared the Isle of Man he captured all the small boats likely to give information, took the crew prisoners, and sunk their boats. The wind, which had been favourable, increased to a gale, and he was compelled to take the North Channel, which brought him on the Irish coast; this was a casualty, but not an undesired one. He intended coasting round Scotland, and, if possible, endeavour to gain some information of Alice. This intention, however, was for the present prevented by the stormy weather which ensued, which kept him beating about without enabling him to get out of the Channel. While making up towards the Roads, near Carrickfergus, he saw a vessel of war, which he ascertained from a fishing boat he detained for information, to be the Drake, of twenty guns, and he resolved to bring her to action; but through the violence of the winds and a serious accident with his cable, he was prevented fulfilling his desire. A shift in the wind enabled him to make direct for Whitehaven, and he came within sight of it the next evening. The wind, however, dropped materially, until it became so light he could with difficulty keep way on the ship. His intention, therefore, of running close into shore, which he had made, he was compelled to abandon, for he saw that in case of accidents compelling him to retreat, he should be unable to stand out to sea with so little wind afloat. He determined at midnight to man two boats with volunteers, and fulfil his plan of destroying the shipping. His crew were a source of much trouble to him; they were much after the same class as those who had rendered the expedition to New Providence futile—each man considering that he had rather a right to be requested than commanded, and it was only by persuasion, and, in some cases, violent coercion, that he got them into anything like subordination. It was principally through some absurd notions of etiquette, which the officers indulged in, which delayed the embarkation of one and-thirty men, who were to undertake the expedition, and before they reached the outer pier, the first scene of their operations, day began to dawn. A few of the men thought it advisable to retreat, but Paul, with a stern countenance, and a tone which could not be misunderstood, vowed he would shoot the first man through the head, who attempted to abandon the project before he gave the word. This silenced the murmurers, and despatching one boat under the command of the first lieutenant—a man upon whose courage he could place dependence—to the northern side of the harbour, he took himself the southern side. When they reached the first fort, Paul scaled it before any one; he was followed by Gasket and the rest of the crew, save one man left as boat-keeper. Paul gave a vigilant glance around him, but a silence pervaded the place which seemed almost unnatural; he listened with intensity, but not a sound reached his ears; the stillness was unbroken, save by the faint crowing of a distant cock. Paul gave the word, and with cautious movements they proceeded to spike the cannon of the forts; the noise of their implements, in spite of their endeavours to make as little as possible, sounded in the still air, and made Paul expect each moment to see the watch make their appearance, but not a man was in sight. They concluded their work without being discovered, and made for the southern fort. In their way they came upon a small building; they heard voices talking and laughing; a closer glance told them it was the guardhouse. A massive key was in the lock upon the outside of the door, and, with a dexterity which deserved praise, one of the men turned it without being heard by those within. The guard were thus fairly shut in their house, and Paul leaving his men to guard it, in case of outcry or alarm being given, proceeded, with Gasket only, to the southern fort, which was a quarter of a mile distant, and with his aid alone he spiked all the cannon mounted upon it. When this task was finished, Paul looked up for the blaze which he expected to see rising from the shipping on the other side of the harbour; but he looked in vain—there was not even a solitary volume of smoke. He clenched his teeth; he began to fear his lieutenant, yielding to the murmurs of some of the malcontents, had returned to the vessel; he felt sick with disappointment and anger, and resolved to hasten to the point, and if they had done what he suspected, he would follow them and endeavour to compel their return, or else alone attack what they had feared to undertake. He would not have waited even to pursue them, but the combustibles were in their possession, and without them he could do nothing.

It had been agreed that when the shipping on the northen side were in a blaze, Lieutenant Wallingford was to join our hero on the southern side, and, conjointly, they were to set fire to the vessels there stationed; but now it seemed as if none would be fired, and the whole object of the expedition be destroyed. A storm raged in Paul's breast, as, followed by Gasket, he hastened rapidly to the northern side, and he reached it just in time to prevent the departure of the boat, which was, as he had anticipated, about returning to the ship; but not, as he had surmised, from faint-heartedness, but from the light with which they were furnished having burnt out at the very moment it was about to be used. The candles with which Paul's party had been supplied, were also extinguished, and thus, in the very moment of success, their hopes seemed destroyed. A retreat was instantly proposed for day was fast breaking, and as instantly rejected by Paul. His quick eyes detected a house at a short distance from the town, through the windows of which he saw the reflection of a fire; he spoke of it, and Gasket instantly volunteered to go for a light. The party seated themselves while he departed, and preserved a dead silence—each man wondering at Paul's boldness, and the result of the daring attempt. Still not a sound or sight was there to show them they were observed, or that any one even was stirring but the sun, and that began to appear above the horizon rapidly. Gasket's return was now anxiously looked for, and in a short time he returned—he had been successful. The men could hardly refrain from greeting him with a shout of joy, but they restrained their feelings. They at once proceeded to place combustibles among the shipping; the steerage of a large vessel had been filled, and was set on fire. This vessel was surrounded by about one hundred and fifty others, in which combustibles were placed. A barrel of tar was discovered and poured into the flames, making them blaze with unquenchable fury. By this time an alarm was given. An American, who feared the success of the expedition, thought it best to side with the strongest; and while Gasket had gone for the light, he had contrived to desert, steal into the streets, and alarm the town. The people hastily attired themselves and rushed to the pier but Paul, to the surprise of his own followers, refused to embark, fearing that the burning vessels were not sufficiently ignited. He presented a brace of pistols at a number of the townspeople, who came running up, who were more curious than courageous, and they instantly decamped for help. At length when all our hero's people had embarked, and the fire was blazing furiously from the holds of a large number of vessels, our hero stood on the end of the outer pier and watched the people gathering in hundreds. No one approached him—he stood alone in the sight of all, who wondered, who he was, who were their enemies, and what were their number. At length the numbers increased too formidably for him longer to remain; he entered his boat, and, with a shout of triumph, he ordered his men to give way, and they pulled towards the Ranger. When the Whitehaveners found that to two boats' crews they might lay all the mischief that had been done. their rage knew no bounds; they rushed down to the piers and forts, and with a howl of fury discovered all their cannon spiked. They, however, got others, and commenced a brisk firing, the effects of which the men in Paul's boat were glad enough, by a little extra exertion of strength, to get out of the way of. They were soon alongside the Ranger, and Paul put sail upon the ship and left the town, he had often as a boy visited with pleasure, with regret that his design of setting fire to it. in order that "The scenes of distress which they have occasioned in America may be brought home to their own doors," had not succeeded.

Of the consternation his visit had caused it comes not within the range of this work to speak; let it suffice that it Paul's glory was added to by his name being in the mouth of everybody, this event accomplished it. He set sail from Whitehaven, and ran over to the Scottish shore, with, as the reader knows the intention of meeting Alice, or of gaining some tidings of her. This intention he could not exactly explain to the officers and crew, and he therefore mentioned one which he had previously formed, that of endeavouring to obtain possession of the person of an English noble, in order that through his negotiation, the Americans who were prisoners in England might be better treated. At St. Mary's Isle dwelt the Earl of Selkirk, and, with the, double purpose of capturing the nobleman and obtaining information of Alice he—having reached St. Mary's Isle the afternoon of the day on which he had fired the shipping at Whitehaven—landed with a boat's crew, and proceeded to the castle, which was the earl's family mansion. As they advanced he ascertained that the earl was in London ; he also ascertained that Alice still resided with her father, and he resolved to see her. The purpose for which he had landed had in one sense been obtained, and in another could not be obtained. He gave the order for the men to return on board, but to his surprise they refused; they were elated with their success at Whitehaven, and were now as eager to do desperate deeds as before they were loth. Paul at first was disposed to be peremptory, but he found he had those under him who only obeyed him to a certain limit, beyond which they denied his right to control their actions. He remonstrated with them, but they urged in reply that the conduct of the English upon the coast of America had been so barbarous, that they only did their duty to their fellow-countrymen and the Congress in retaliating. Paul would not listen to any retaliation which included the taking of human life in it; and, at length, when, after the strongest arguments against their levelling themselves to the character of mere robbers, he found them still bent upon going, in which determination they were backed by the lieutenant, he waived his right to command them, and quitted them with disgust to return on board, conjuring them, however, as men, to refrain from insult and oppression. It is somewhat singular that his arguments and conduct had, at least, the effect upon the men of moderating the desire for bloodshed and plunder which they landed with, and induced them to be contented with the family plate belonging to the noble earl, and a few coarse jokes upon the lady, who with firmness met them, and granted their demands.

Paul, when they returned with their prize, met them with no welcome. He felt hurt and ashamed that his name had been used for this, to him, disgraceful purpose, and, with the blush of anger as well as shame, he ordered sail to be made upon the vessel, and worked round towards Kirkcudbright, with the hope that he should succeed in seeing Alice before the report of this last transaction had reached her ears. He had taken the precaution to have his guns masked, and gave his vessel as much the appearance of a merchantman as possible, in order that the prying eyes of the fishermen hereaway might not detect him, and run with open mouth to the authorities of the places he purposed visiting, and so frustrate the idea he had conceived respecting them. He was not long in reaching the point from which he started in the Kirkcudbright for America, and leaving his lieutenant in command of the ship, with the order, "stand off and on," he took a boat and went on shore. He had dressed himself with studied care—he wore the dress of a captain in the navy, one which well became him; and remarkable as he was, before he left his native land, for his personal qualifications, no one would have believed, to have now seen him, how much this could have been enhanced by his attire. It acted as a disguise, and, in hastening to the residence of Alice's father, he met with two or three whose faces were quite familiar to him, but none of them appeared to recognise him; he received a respectful salutation due to his rank, but no mark of recognition. He felt pleased at this, and quickened his pace, with renewed hopes that he should, unquestioned, gain the house which contained his beloved, and, by the ministry of the same good fortune which had preserved him from being known, obtain the much desired interview with her. He passed several persons more in his progress, but they were all strangers to him, and he succeeded in gaining the house without the slightest stay or hindrance. There was a handsome shrubbery which surrounded the dwelling, and through this he threaded his way until he arrived at the back, and then secreting himself in a copse from which he could see her chamber window, he began to concert a scheme for seeing her. He had abstained from questioning any one whom he met whether she was in the house, or on a visit to a friend, from a lurking doubt that he might be recognised and his hopes frustrated, and had reached the house without having more than a hope to sustain him that his journey would not be profitless. A few glances at the house convinced him that she was there : the house bore all the tokens of the family being at home, and now came the difficulty of making his presence known. After some little pondering he determined to sing a song which he had written years since, when he first knew her, and which, he having a sweet voice, she used to be particularly fond of hearing him sing. If she was within hearing he knew she would instantly recognise both song and singer, and he might reasonably hope, if she did, that she would not be long in seeking him. With a voice, therefore, which at first was weak and trembling, but which grew firm and clear as he proceeded, he commenced the following:—

SERENADE.

Awake thee, arise thee, my bonny bright love,
On the shore my boat's waiting for thee ;
And the stars with their eyes of sunny light, love,
Now illumine the breast of the sea.
Come forth ! fear thou not ! the rude breath of wind
Cannot swell the proud soul of the deep ;
For the moon, with bright looks and smiles ever kind,
Has charmed him, and kissed him to sleep.

We'll float to the spot where the mermaiden sighs,
Rippling waves into smiles with her breath ;
She's fainting with gazing in the depths of her eyes,
Which the sea mirrors forth from beneath.
And she's warbling a song of such rare melody,
Of such pathos and exquisite tone,
That the sea nymphs are weeping with fond sympathy,
E'en as though her sweet ruth were their own.

Come forth, love ! the sea is enfolding its breast
In a robe steeped in heaven's pale blue ;
And the waves, with a laughing, babbling unrest
Press the beach with a kiss ever new.
Unveil thy lov'd eyes from their light woof of sleep,
Which has flung its sweet dreams o'er thy brow,
To the loveliest cave ever found near the deep,
Swift and free will we sail, I and Thou.

Paul paused between each verse, and watched eagerly to see whether he had been heard, but could not perceive that the slightest notice was taken of his vocal exertion; even under this discouragement he commenced the second verse, and went through the third. When he had finished he remained quiet for a short period, pondering upon what would be the next step it would be best for him to take. While considering, he suddenly detected a foot treading upon some dried twigs near him, making a crackling noise, and giving certain indications that some one was approaching, though it appeared as if the comer wished her approach to be unobserved. Paul peered through the bushes and saw a young girl, in the habit of a waiting-maid, stealing towards him with a stealthy step, pausing every now and then to gaze about her, and listen like a timid doe in a wood startled by the sound of a footstep. Paul rose up silently, and glided noiselessly past her, taking a small circuit to escape her observation, and then placed himself with his back against a tree, in a spot which stood in the path she would take to return. The girl was evidently looking for the singer of the serenade; she seemed half afraid of her task, yet appeared disappointed that she could not see him she was in search of. At first she bore a frightened look, but her extended search failing in satisfying her object, she lost her timid aspect, and bore a frowning, pettish one, and indulged in a few exclamations, which, however, were inaudible to the ears of our hero. She turned to retrace her steps, and with her eyes directed by turns on each side of her, she advanced close up to Paul before she saw him, and when she did she gave a slight scream, and turned as white as death. He caught her in his arms, and said, quickly—

"Don't be afraid, my good girl, there's nobody here to hurt you. What brought you here?"

The girl trembled like an aspen at first, but the soft voice of our hero restored her a little, and then a glance at his face and his equipment quite recovered her.

"Did you sing that pretty song?" she inquired, looking at him a little archly, with a most wicked pair of black eyes.

"What makes you wish to know?" he replied.

"Because I should like to learn it," she answered, with a laugh, having quite recovered the alarm which the sudden sight of him had occasioned; "will you teach it me?" she added.

"Was it only upon your own account that you entered the shrubbery, to find out who sung that song?" inquired Paul, the interest he had in her reply prevented him from answering in the same spirit of badinage with which she addressed him, "or was there any one who counselled you to come hither?"

"Why, the truth is, sir, my young missis knows that song very well, for I have often heard her sing it," returned the girl, "and she heard you sing it as well—in fact, I had just finished dressing her when you began."

"Oh, you are sure it was me who sung?" interrupted Paul.

"To be sure I am," replied the girl, "I can tell by your voice as you speak. Well, as soon as you sung the first line, she caught hold of me, and trembled like a leaf, and seemed to hold her breath until you'd finished it, and then when you had ended, she said, "Lyddy, I know that song well," says she. "So do I, miss," says I; "I've often heard you sing it," says I. "Yes," says she, "Lyddy, that song," says she, "was made by a friend of mine," says she, "who's far, far away, across the wide ocean," says she, "and I thought," says she, "nobody else know'd it but him," says she; "I should like," says she, "to know who this is as is singing of it." "So should I, miss," says I, "for it's very sing'lar that somebody as nobody knows should sing a song as nobody knows but you, miss, and he," says I, and so I did think it odd, and that's truth. So says I, "miss," says I, "s'pose I runs and has a look in the shrubbery," says I, "and if there's anybody there, miss," says I, "I'll soon find out who 'tis as knows your song as you thought nobody know'd but yourself." "You ain't afraid, Lyddy," says she. "Lord bless you, miss," says I, "it ain't in the power of mortal man to fright me; I don't care for none of the sex, not I," says I, which is the truth; the best man in Christendom couldn't make me afeard of him, that he couldn't."

"Well, but what said your mistress?" interrupted Paul, a little anxiously.

"Oh, she said, 'Well, then, Lyddy, you can go,' says she, 'but don't let any one see you,' says she. 'Trust me for that, miss,' says I. 'I mean not any of the servants,' says she. 'I know, miss,' says I, with a wink and a nod, 'nor your father either, miss,' says I."

"Is he at home?" inquired Paul, abruptly.

"Ay, that he is, worse luck," continued Lyddy, not seeming to remember that all his chattering was made to one who was an entire stranger to her; "you don't know my master, I dare say; ugh! he's a nasty, cross, ill-tempered, ill-natured, ill-looking, scolding, grumbling, crusty, rusty, swearing, hollering, cross-grained, vexatious, quarrelsome, fractious, cantankerous, always-out-of-humour, never-to-be-pleased-at-no-time, old, ugly fellow."

"He does not stand very high in your favour, at all events," exclaimed Paul, smiling.

"Nor in anybody else's," said Lyddy, with a toss of the head, almost out of breath with her volubility, "a tartary, peppery—"

"So at your mistress's wish and your own, you came to look for me?" interrupted Paul, as the maid was about to launch forth into another list of invectives against her master's good name.

"Yes," she replied, "and says my young missis, 'If you see the person that sung that song, try and discover when he learned that song, and who taught him it.' 'That I certainly will, miss,' says I, 'or I'll forfeit my ears,' and now, sir, for my young lady's sake and mine too," this was uttered with a wicked look, "perhaps you'll oblige us by telling me—you don't look very hard hearted—in fact, if you was my sweetheart, which you ain't, and, for the matter of that, nobody is, for I don't think the fellows about here worth having; but if you was my sweetheart, I think I should find you very good-natured. I hope I ain't wrong, sir: you won't refuse me, will you?"

"I should be very sorry to refuse so pretty a girl any reasonable request," returned Paul, desirous of currying favour with the girl, in the hope of facilitating an interview with Alice. "Know, then, my pretty lass, that I learned that song on board a ship called the Wildfire. Tell your mistress so; and say likewise that my name is John. And if she desires to know aught respecting him who composed the song, she may learn much from me."

"Oh, very well. Will you stay here?" responded and inquired Lyddy.

"I will," he replied.

"Is there nothing else you would have me carry?" she replied, looking up at him, under her eyelids.

"Nothing, at present," he replied.

"You have a nice face," she said, with an arch smile. "If I was a young man, and you a young girl, with that face, I should have——"

"What?" said Paul as she hesitated.

"Have sent a kiss," she replied, with a merry laugh, and took to her heels.

He did not attempt to follow her, but looked with a smile upon her as she fled, and with a beating heart awaited the arrival of Alice, for he had no doubt that when she learned, from that message, that he was there, she would not hesitate a second, but meet him at once. He was not deceived in his conjecture. Ten minutes had scarcely elapsed subsequent to the departure of Lyddy, when he saw the form of Alice winding cautiously among the trees. She was alone; he sprung forward to meet her; and when her eye fell on him she uttered a cry of delight, and sank into his extended arms. Paul pressed her to his heart with all the ardour of passionate love, for several minutes. Their hearts were too full to speak: Paul was the first to recover his voice.

"Alice," he murmured, in tones which thrilled her; "my dearest, my beloved Alice, my heart leaps at sight of thee! My bosom throbs and pants with delight, to have thy dear head leaning on it once again! What joy, what happiness is mine! A moment like this repays me for all I have endured while absent from thee. Raise up thy head, Alice—dear Alice! and let me look upon thy eyes, my beloved!"

She turned her face upwards, and, with an expression playing over her features which made his heart glow to witness, she exclaimed—

"I have looked for this hour, dear Paul! with the fondest hopes, for a weary time: but I deemed not it was so near. I thought not, while seated, an hour since, in my chamber, that I should hear thy voice—thine, Paul!—oh, to me the sweetest music mine ears have ever listened to."

"Hast thou learned to flatter, dearest, since I have been away?" he exclaimed, with a smile.

"No, Paul," she replied, "it is no flattery; I have thought of thee each day and hour. It is a long time since we met. Every hour have I had a thought, a hope, a prayer for thee; and when, at a moment least expected, though thoughts of thee were ever upon me, thy voice burst upon my ears, never did human voice or music sound so sweet, so dear to my heart."

Paul pressed her fondly to his bosom.

"And no less desired," he said, "has the time for our meeting been by me, sweetest; no less looked for, hoped, and prayed for. In the still night, a thousand miles from land—in the broad glare of day, upon a sunny sea—in the turmoil of the gale, and the crashing of the battle, thy image has ever been present to me; thy spirit that which I have invoked; thy memory that which filled my heart. The hope to gain thee has cheered me on; the hope to see thee sustained me in the weary delays and troubles which I have undergone; and now my duty has brought me to this coast, I have not wasted one moment in fulfilling the ardent desire I have had to see thee—to hold thee in my arms!"

"We should both be glad, Paul; both be thankful," replied Alice; "for an adverse fate seems bent on sundering us. Even now I dread the presence of my father, who is ever roving about the grounds, may put some terrible termination to our interview—as that sad one when last we parted."

"Fear not, Alice; in this garb he would be less inclined to treat me with contumely," said Paul, somewhat proudly; "even, indeed, if he recognised me."

"It is that of a naval officer," said Alice, regarding it for the first time.

"Aye, of a captain, Alice," said Paul, triumphantly; "it is a great step, Alice—I rank with a colonel in the army. Your father will not so despise me now as he has done."

"England hath done justice to you, Paul," said Alice, with a smile of elevated joy.

"England!" he repeated, with bitter irony; "had I waited for the justice of England, I should still have been a captain of the foretop instead of the quarter-deck; still have worn a foul anchor on my arm instead of an epaulette upon my shoulder. Oh, Alice! not to England do I owe my proud distinction."

"Great heaven, Paul! not to France?" she exclaimed with astonishment on her face.

"No," he returned; "I have obtained the honour from—"

Before he had time to proceed further, Lyddy made her appearance, and, in great haste, exclaimed—

"Oh, miss, here's your cross old father coming this way; he has been hunting for you. I met him just now, and I thought he would have snapped my head off. 'Where's your mistress?' says he, 'I don't know,' says I, 'It's a lie, says he; and go fetch her to me, or you shall repent it,' 'shall I?' says I."

"No matter what transpired, Lyddy," exclaimed Alice, interrupting her; "meet him, and if he is advancing hither, stop him, and say that I am coming."

"Very well, miss," replied Lyddy, giving a side glance at Paul as she retired, as much as to say—"I can see whose sweetheart you are."

You must away, Paul, cried Alice, urgently, "without delay; but say where we can again meet, and if it is in my power to accomplish it, I will without fail be there."

"Dear, Alice," exclaimed Paul, earnestly, "it is hard to part thus from thee—let me meet thy father?"

"No; oh, no, no!" quickly cried Alice; you know how vindictive he his—you must away dear Paul. I shall be most unhappy for you to run any such risk."

"As you will," returned Paul; "I would not give you pain for the world. There is a headland on the coast—"

"Near here; I know it well," exclaimed Alice, hastily. "Quick, quick, I hear my father's step. Say to-morrow evening, at nine."

"At nine!" repeated Paul; "I will be there."

"And I, if I live," said Alice, with energy.

The footsteps of the old man were now plainly heard. Paul kissed Alice fervently; tore himself away; darted through the trees, and disappeared before the old man, accompanied by Lyddy, talking with the shrillest accent at the top of her voice, made his appearance where Alice stood. He regarded her with a stern, suspicious look; then his eyes peered in every direction. Again he looked at Alice, and she met his gaze firmly. He grunted and bit his lip, and then rudely bade her enter the house. She made no reply, but turned to obey him; at the same moment Lyddy said to him, with a very knowing nod of the head—

"I told you, didn't I—I tell you a lie now, don't I?"

"I say you did, and you know it, you artful jade," cried the old man "but let me catch him; I warrant me I'll spoil his trolling."

"Will you? If there had been anybody here, you would have had to mind they didn't spoil the shape of your face—if it is possible to do such a thing."

"Silence, you impertinent hussy. How dare you speak with such insolent pertness to me? Another such a speech, and I send you packing."

"You didn't hire me—I ain't your servant," murmured Lyddy, half afraid to be openly saucy. "What do you think he says, miss? He says he heard somebody singing here, and it was too good for a beggar."

"And I did," repeated the old man, with vehemence. "Alice, you must have heard it!" he exclaimed to his daughter; "it proceeded from some spot hereabouts, and I suppose like myself, you came in search of the fellow."

"Don't answer him, miss," cried Lyddy, eagerly, afraid that her mistress's love of truth would induce her to disclose the facts; "it's only the gout got from his toes to his head, and given him a singing in his ears. Let us go to our room, miss; we shan't be interfered with and interrupted there."

Alice took the hint, and retired without answering; while Lyddy, by her flat contradiction and pert remarks, maintained a stormy dialogue with the old gentleman all the way to the house, effectually preventing him from putting any further question to Alice.

Paul in the meanwhile made the best of his way to the ship, deeply gratified with his interview with Alice, and though once or twice the thouhgt crossed him that honours gained in any service but that of England. and the efforts of that service whatever it might be, directed against England, would not be grateful to her feelings, still he dismissed the thought, and dwelled only on the gladness, the joy she had shown on meeting with him. His boat was just off the shore when he reached it, and in a few minutes he was safely wafted on board. The design which he now had was to attack the Drake, which he knew to be near, and he hoped, by conquering her, to strike a decisive blow on behalf of the infant country whose flag he sailed under. His first orders were to let fall the courses; the topsails followed; the topgallant sails, and even royals, for there was not much wind astir, were sheeted home; the spanker, jib, and stay-sails were all set, and away flew the Ranger. Paul, when these evolutions were completed, descended to his cabin, and summoned the various officers of the vessel to his presence, and declared to them his intention of attacking the Drake. To his surprise, not less than his indignation, the lieutenants at once expressed themselves decidedly against it; their strongest argument being, that, off an enemy's coast, there was a species of madness in hazarding a contest in which there existed great doubts of success; and, in the event of defeat, the very worst, from their recent descent on Whitehaven, was to be expected from their foes. Paul could barely keep his temper; he urged most strongly that it was essential for America that they should do some deed which should make the English cease to regard them with such a contemptuous opinion of their naval capabilities; he begged of them, for the honour of their country, for their honour as men, not from a weak fear to abandon an opportunity so glorious of raising the new country in the eyes of all Europe. But they listened to him coldly; they did not like the risk; there was too much of a personal feeling involved to take in much of the honour of their country. They were too ridiculously influenced by some absurd notions of etiqutte also, which completely set discipline and obedience at defiance; and they left the cabin without ceremony, to consult with the men, or rather bias them against complying with Paul's design. Our hero was disgusted with his officers, and he, too, sought the deck to appeal to the crew to stand by him in this emergency. He no sooner reached it than he found the men in the most excited state; the lieutenants, with a want of generosity not very honourable to them, had strongly hinted to them that Paul intended delivering them into the hands of the English, as a price of his own pardon, for taking up arms against his country. They alleged that as Great Britain was his native land—that as all his family were of the same place—that his prejudices and sympathies would naturally be all English; and the whole expedition in which they were engaged was one so rash, so impolitic, so improbable of success, that it was their duty at once to return to the port from which they had sailed, and refuse entering into a similar expedition, unless they had greater support. The men quite agreed with them, and when Paul appeared they were in little better than a state of mutiny. He started when he saw the disrespectful and even threatening glances with which he was greeted; but his was a heart not to be intimidated by any such demonstration. He looked sternly at them, and at once saw it was no time to appeal to them, he therefore commanded them to their duty, for they were crowding aft, and was infringing carelessly the sacred right of the quarter-deck. Shakspere says—

> "There's such divinity doth hedge a king,
> That treason can but peep to what it would,
> Acts little of his will."

The word captain might have been well substituted; for in no position in life, where command is in the hands of one person, is power so absolute as that of a naval commander. Even though these fellows were disposed to mutiny—were even countenanced by their officers—yet the command Paul uttered in a clear firm voice was obeyed, and the men went slowly forward to gather into little groups and discuss the matter among themselves. Paul, meanwhile, paced the quarter-deck thoughtfully, resolving not to give up his project, and endeavoured to devise a scheme which should induce his people to comply with his wishes. The vessel still held on her course, and was steered in the direction of Carrickfergus, off which he knew the Drake to be at anchor, and the cloud of canvas under which he sailed soon brought him into the North Channel, where the Drake, with her topsails set, was plainly visible. The hands were turned up to reduce the canvas, which order they obeyed; and when the ship was stripped of all her light sails, Paul ordered the men aft, and, in a short speech made his intention of bringing the Drake to action known. Before the men had time to consider or be influenced by the stirring words of our hero, one of the lieutenants addressed them, and with some art contrived to completely destroy the effect which Paul's speech was eminently calculated to make: and, as soon as he had ended, they, with one voice, declared they would not fight. Our hero's temper got the better of him; he advanced among them, and, in strong terms, upbraided them. He dared them to deny, or refuse to obey, his authority, and seized the fellow, who had been loudest in the utterance of mutinous expressions, by the shoulder, with the purpose of ordering him to be put in irons; but the fellow, a tall, stalwart man, called to his messmates to stand by him, and throw the captain and his authority, too, overboard. A pistol clapped to the head of the first who advanced to comply with the request made him start back, and our hero received something like respect from the rest of the men; he saw the momentary advantage he had obtained, and he seized it. He appealed warmly and earnestly to them:—he called upon their courage, and told them to assist the call—that the Ranger was superior in metal and numbers, which he believed to be the case, and that success was certain—a success which would bring them the thanks of Congress, and glory in the eyes of the world. He did not wait for their assent or dissent: he concluded his short harangue by bidding the men return to their duty, for so long as he bore the commission from Congress he would assert his rights, and insist upon having them, if he lost his life in the effort. He had the satisfaction of perceiving that the men obeyed him, and once more he trod the quarter-deck with the air of one who would be commander in his own ship. Gasket attended him by order, and a short communication took place respecting the intended conquest, and then they separated. The Ranger worked up the North Channel under easy sail, and was speedily observed by the look-outs on board: and as they failed to answer any signals, the commander of the Drake sent a boat, with a young gentleman in charge to board her, and bring back a description of who and what she was; where from, and whither bound. The boat, deceived by the merchant's look which our hero had contrived to give to the Ranger, pulled alongside of her, and was instantly captured. The success of this manœuvre wrought a marvellous effect upon the men; they were now as ready to fight as they previously had been to fly, and Paul, delighted to see the alteration in them, promised them as easy a conquest of the Drake as they had already made of her boat and the crew. Whether a careless look-out or not had been kept on board the English vessel it is not so possible as it is probable to say; but be it as it may, the capture of the boat was not observed by them; they merely fired a gun to recal it, and hoisting their anchor they quitted the road, and, attended by a number of yachts and pleasure boats, came out towards the Ranger. By this time Paul unmasked his guns, and the Drake found her boats was missing. The warlike character of the stranger was no longer doubtful, and the instant Paul sent the American flag to the gaff end, the drums on board the Drake beat to quarters, and the ship was cleared for action. Paul backed his top-sails and lay to for him, while the Drake crowded sail to come up with him as if afraid that he should lose him. When the vessels were within pistol shot, Paul called to his men to stand by their guns—

"You must fight now," he cried, in a triumphant voice; "you cannot fly—you must fight while a timber floats, for defeat will be worse than death. Captivity, such as the English treat the Americans to, presents horrors which a brave man would cheerfully die to avoid. You have everything to fight for—liberty, life, and glory; let us but beat yon frigate, and the stepping-stone to America's independence will be secure. Think of those at home, and strike home."

The men gave a loud hurrah, and Gasket, who stood close by Paul, said, while the roar of the cheer was sounding—

"Do you, John, think of home, as you give the command to strike home?"

Paul started, and his face flushed, he grasped Gasket by the arm, and, without appearing to be offended at what he had said thus boldly, he replied, in a stern tone—

"I think, Gasket, of those who drove me an outcast from home, and my heart is steeled. I swore to come back a terror to these shores, and I will. Proud England shall learn how her despised sons can pay undeserved contumely."

He turned away, but Gasket could see in his heaving chest that the excuse was not strong enough to deceive even himself. Paul said hastily to him, in a moment after—

"To your post, and remember, old friend, you fight under *my* flag:" the last words were uttered emphatically.

"I remember, John, that I obey orders if I break owners," replied Gasket, and quitted our hero to take his station.

The Drake now ran right up to them, and the commander seeing the Ranger laying to so quietly, came out to know if our hero surrendered; he, however, replied—

"No, I have been waiting for you to come up. It is getting on for eight o'clock, so the sooner we begin the better."

His crew echoed his words with a loud cheer, and the people of the Drake replied with a similar one. Paul, then, in a clear voice, asked if all was ready with the guns, and receiving an answer in the affirmative, he gave the order to "fire away," and the crew discharged a tremendous broadside, which made the Drake quiver from head to heel; it was returned by the Englishmen with an equal force, and was kept up by both with the greatest spirit: the boats and yachts which had attended the Drake out, finding the iron flying about in all directions, retired with precipitation, and kept, for the remainder of the contest, at a distance, where prudence got the better of curiosity. Both vessels discharged their broadsides with the greatest rapidity, but Paul quickly found the precision of the Englishmen's fire, and the admirable discipline they exhibited, would soon sink his ship if he did not manœuvre, and by stratagem counterbalance the disadvantage under which he laboured; he had rather a full complement of men, and could spare a fair number to tend the sails without robbing the guns of any of the people, and he tried what was to be done by raking; he gave the necessary commands, and succeeded in laying his vessel broadside athwart the bows of the Drake, and pouring in a terrific fire, which completely swept the decks with a shower of shot. The Englishman, however, speedily cleared himself from his dangerous position, and laid himself broadside to broadside, again keeping up a steady and destructive fire. Paul now sent a party of men into the tops with hand-grenades, as well as a party of marines, skilled in the use of their rifles, and these fellows hurled down their terrible missives, and the marines with their sure aims killed and destroyed a great number: still the English fought fiercely, and their shots told with a power which made Paul uneasy for the result; but he cheered on the men, and acted with such extraordinary energy that it was impossible for any of his people to be idle, or show the white feather. Still the tremendous discharges from the Drake made his men waver, and it was only by the greatest exertion that he could keep them to their task, and fill them with hopes of victory; the gaff of the Drake had been shot away, and several Americans cried out, with great glee—

"She's struck! she's struck!"

But Paul knew his opponents better; his practised ear detected no slackening in their firing, and the next minute, with a glow almost of pride, a strange anomaly as he was situated, he saw the English colours nailed to the mast, and this act met with a stentorian cheer from Gasket, who was working at his gun with almost all the ardour he would have shown had the foes been Frenchmen. Again our hero perceived symptoms of wavering in his crew, and these unfavourable symptoms were even encouraged by the officers; the men who ought to have done most to have dispelled it; not discouraged by this "heavy blow and great discouragement," he animated the men by his own example, scorning all fear of death; he was everywhere in the thick of the fight, now directing the men aloft, now cheering on his people with a voice which was clearly heard above the tremendous din of the battle; his foretopmast was shot away, and several important stays were cut; the mainmast was riddled, and several of his guns had been silenced, while a mass of dead and wounded lay around, frightful to look at. The Englishmen were not in a much better predicament, their fore and main-topmasts were down with the loose rigging and tackle, laying upon the deck, creating the greatest confusion; the mizen-topmast was also gone by the board, and every mast bore terrible evidence of the execution the Ranger's guns had committed. Three times had she caught fire, but each time it had been extinguished by the gallant fellows, who left their guns to accomplish it, and returned to their duty with all the energy which they might have been expected to have shown if their own individual interest had been concerned in gaining the victory; they had no thoughts of disobeying their captain, and certainly no thoughts of retreating, and fought with a steadiness and courage which ought to have made them successful. Paul, on the other hand, directed the efforts of an unwilling crew; men, who it would be wrong to say were not brave, but whose mistaken notions of equality—where strict obedience to one, if he be a competent man, is so necessary for success—rendered them as difficult to manage as if they had been cowards. They fought desperately, it was true, but they knew it was a matter of life and death, they must either conquer or die; there was no escape unless they proved victorious, and that lent them an energy which, under the circumstances, they might have failed to possess; every advantage which they gained was communicated to them by our hero; every damage which the enemy's shot did to them was carefully kept from them, and thus, without officers, but one, to animate or assist them, they were comparatively bolstered up, and performed wonders: still the effect of the Englishmen's fire was prodigious, and Paul found that his vessel was getting so crippled, that if it continued, and he even gained the victory, he should, perhaps, be so disabled, as to present an easy prey to the next ship of the enemy which might heave in sight; he resolved, therefore, to board the Drake, and summoned his men for the purpose. He ordered Gasket to accompany them, and placed himself at their head, and after addressing a few short words to them, bidding them be firm and bold, and the day would be their own, he leaped into the mizen chains of the Drake, for the guns were almost muzzle to muzzle, clambered up the side, followed by Gasket and the rest of the men, and a tremendous hand to hand contest ensued. The English fought with the bravery and steady resolution which characterizes them, while Paul with his crew, having everything at stake, battled with a desperation amounting to frenzy. The struggle was terrific; the English were cut down where they stood, rather than yield an inch, and the Americans, warmed up into action, behaved most gallantly; neither budged from the other, and the slaughter was tremendous. To Paul, however, the merit of continuing and sustaining the conflict was due; he animated the men both by voice and example. He plunged into the wildest and fiercest points of contention; he opposed the sturdiest and the most skilful, and fortune smiled upon him wherever he stood and struck. His voice was like the sound of a trumpet; and as he occasionally cheered, and called to his followers to support him—to strike for their country with their best ability—to conquer or perish in honour of American independence, the tones went to their hearts, and infused bravery into the souls of the wavering, while it strengthened the resolution of the courageous. Gasket followed, and fought by his side, and did honour to the trust placed in him; but it might have been observed, that when his arm might spare a blow it never gave it. He was recognised by one of the Drake's people, who had served in the Audacious with him, and no little astonishment was displayed by the English sailor. He fought hand to hand with him; and during the desperate moment of their struggle the discovery was made, upon the impulse of the moment, the sailor lowered his sword and exclaimed—

"What! Gasket—ain't you Gasket, who was captain of the maintop in the Howdashus seventy-four?"

"The same, Flying Jib-boom Joe," replied Gasket, calling the man by a familiar appellation given him for the length of his nose, but which was more frequently curtailed to "jib-boom," for ease in speaking.

"And you're a fightin with the Yankees agin us, eh?" asked he emphatically.

"As sure as buntlines and cluelines won't make shrouds," returned Gasket; "come Jib-boom, haul down and surrender."

"I'll see you d—d first," cried Jib-boom. "No, Gasket, there wasn't a hand aboard of the Howdashus, or, for that matter, in any ship I've since been drafted to, that I'd sooner have cut my life-lines adrift for than you. I'd have gone overboard; I'd have given up my kit, and lived six upon two for a year for you—damme, there ain't nothing I wouldn't have done with all my heart and soul for you, for I thought you true blue without a skulk. But now, since I've found you fighting agin your old shipmates—agin them as has fou't and bled along with, and would at any time ha' done it for you—why, damn you from truck to heel, a seaman's curse upon you, here's the hand that once would have shaken to oakum any fellow who had run out any line athwart-hawse your good name, and now it would be the first to clear the turn to run you up to the yard-arm. I tell you, Gasket, that, if you founder in this fight, your hulk shall not go over the side afore a clear whip has run it up to the yard-arm for your shipmates to clap eyes on a—"

"Avast, Jib-boom; avast!" cried Gasket, writhing in agony at his words, for the man was an old friend, and a favourite of his; "clap a stopper on your tongue, and take a sheer to larboard, or port for a foe—I am obeying orders, though I'm breaking the owner of this," he struck his bosom hard as he spoke; "luff up and keep away; I don't want to strike an old friend and messmate."

"Old friend and messmate be d—d; I pitch 'em to the devil," roared Jib-boom, taking his quid from his mouth, and flinging it on the ground, while he stamped upon it with great vigour. "Don't old friend me—I wipe you out of my log; you're aboard here as an enemy, so come on as an enemy. Stand by; for, by the Lord, if I can scuttle you, I will."

Gasket made no reply, but received the attack which was made upon him with a steady courage, but with the regret of one who felt every blow came from he hand of one from whom he had experienced nothing but friendship. As Jib-boom, in the height of his resentment, fought wildly and fiercely, Gasket, who was far cooler, and did not attempt even to return a single blow, received the desperate thrusts and cuts directed at him, parrying and avoiding them with the greatest ease, and, at length, succeeded in disarming him. He forbore to strike him, though Jib-boom expected it, his rage while he was fighting preventing him from seeing that Gasket had returned none of his blows. He, however, stood firm, and did not flinch, though he believed instant death was coming; Gasket, however, only said to him, in a quiet tone—

"Don't be so hard upon me with your thoughts, Jib-boom. Many a man may have cause to lift his hand agin his countrymen (though I may run clear of that, seeing as you know that I was born at sea, or at least I suppose I was), and still not be—"

"I won't hear nothing, Gasket," cried Jib-boom, impatiently; "I've seen enough. You've got my cutlash, so down with me; for if I surrender, may I—"

"You are a prisoner," interrupted Gasket; "haul your wind and save your life."

"I won't owe it to you, Gasket," cried Jib-boom, impatiently; "I won't, and here goes for Davy Jones, and the curse of a lee shore when you're homeward bound upon you; may it wreck you, as you've wrecked my faith in a me smate."

With these words he rushed to the side, clambered over the nettings, and with a wild cry leaped overboard. Gasket watched him for a moment, and then, throwing his sword away, he bounded to the side, and, with a desperate spring, followed him.

CHAPTER VIII.

"Now he's coming,
And not a hair upon a soldier's head
Which will not prove a whip; as many coxcombs,
As you throw caps up will he tumble down,
And pay you for your voices,
*   *   *   *   *   *
CIT.—Faith, we hear fearful news."   CORIOLANUS.

"Alack! or must we lose,
The country, our dear nurse; or else thy perso n,
Our comfort in the country. We must find
An evident calamity, though we had
Our wish which side should win; for either thou
Must, as a foreign recreant, be led
With manacles through our streets, or else
Triumphantly tread on thy country's ruin.'
IBID.

PAUL had been far too actively engaged in endeavouring to make good his position on board the Drake, to hear the colloquy between Gasket and Jibboom, or even to notice the incident which followed it; his energies were concentrated—his whole attention—his very soul was directed towards conquering the English and their ship; in the heat of the combat his eyes were ever and anon turned upon his followers, to keep them, by stirring words, to their duty; still the affair between Gasket and the hardy English sailor escaped him. The battle raged with a fury which made it certain that it could not long continue; the firing—the crashing—the groans and cries of the wounded, mingled with the oaths and shouts of the combatants; the hot suffocating clouds of smoke in which they were enveloped, lit up every now and then by the flashes of fire from the guns as they were discharged with murderous animosity by the foe: all told how desperate was the conflict. Still Paul maintained his ground, though at the expense of the lives of many of his followers; still he fought on, cutting down his opposers with a strength equal to his skill, which, in itself, was great. Muskets and pikes were levelled at his breast—cutlasses gleamed round his person—pistols flashed in his face, still he was unhurt, though in a storm of bullets; his clothes were rent in several places, his hat was perforated with balls; but by some especial providence he had not received a wound. On he moved, though every step he took was severely contested and hardly gained; several times he concluded he had obtained the victory, but as often the determined resolution of the English compelled him to acknowlege that the important object was neither obtained, nor so certain of being so as he could wish. Even in the moment when success appeared least doubtful his men were repulsed, and nearly driven from the vessel; but he rallied them with strenuous exertions, and by hard fighting gained the ground they had lost. Fiercer and hotter the fight raged: the men seemed actuated by the spirit of devils, and with unrelenting fury did their utmost to slay each other; at length one of the marines who still remained in the tops of the Ranger, succeeded in shooting the commander of the Drake; the first lieutenant fell at the same moment, by Paul's hand, mortally wounded. Our hero, with a bound, leaped over the body of his fallen antagonist, gained the quarter deck, and, with his own hand tore down the English colours, and trampled on them, uttering at the same moment a wild cry of triumph. His men echoed his cheer, and the English sailors, seeing they had no commander, surrendered, but such was the state into which the Americans had been worked, that they continued the attack upon many who had declined to surrender until Paul commanded them to hold their hands.

"The victory is ours!" he cried, in a stirring voice; "that glorious fact should more than satisfy ye all. Let there be no more blood shed—we have gained the battle after a fearful struggle, but it is at a sacrifice and expense of life no less honourable to the conquered than to us. Let not this proud moment be tarnished by acts which she would be the first to execrate in others. Remember, those ye have conquered have done nobly in behalf of their country, and deserve nobly of us, who have done our best in behalf of America. Ye have had enough blood to glut the most sanguinary heart among you—let there be no more shed."

There were some loud cheers followed this speech, mixed with some murmers, and when he could make himself heard, he exclaimed, in a stern voice—

"The first man who raises his hand against one of those who are now our prisoners, will make an enemy of me—no light one, I promise you; I am captain, and he who breaks my orders shall have cause to remember it. Now, lads let us make the decks a little clear, both on board our own vessel and the prize."

Three cheers were given at their success, and the men then separated to perform their duty. The first person for whom Paul searched, when this affair was ended, was Gasket, and he, with gratified eyes, beheld him standing a a short distance from him, leaning upon his cutlass with an air of abstraction. Paul hastened towards him, and touched him upon the shoulder; Gasket started, and turned his eyes upon our hero with a mystified look, as though for the moment he did not recognise him; Paul scarcely noticed it, but shook his hand heartily, and said—

"You are not wounded, Gasket; you are not hurt, my good friend?"

"Not in body," replied Gasket, "not in body, John; fortune has behaved pretty handsome as to that; I have not a spar touched, nor a line shot away."

"I am very glad to hear it," replied Paul, warmly, and shaking his hand earnestly; Gasket returned his squeeze, and said—

"Nor you, John, I hope. Fortune has been bountiful to you in giving you the victory. It isn't to be quite expected that she would suffer you to win it, without letting a little of your blood for ink to log the *glory* of the day with." He laid an extraordinary emphasis on the word glory.

"She has been bountiful to me to-day; I have beat my enemy and have not a scratch; but, hey! Gasket, where have you been—overboard? Why, you are soaking with water—what is the meaning of it?"

"One of the people here fell overboard," replied Gasket, evasively, reddening beyond his usual deep flush at the evasion, "and I went over after him."

"Did you save him?" inquired Paul, quickly, and with interest.

"Yes," returned he, "but with a little difficulty, there was a boat dragging astern of the Ranger, as luck would have it, and I got into it; I shoved it round to the side, and then came aboard here to do my duty again."

"What boat was it?" cried Paul, with surprise. "How could a boat be dragging astern of the Ranger?"

"It was the Ranger's gig, but how it came there, those who lowered it can best tell you," answered Gasket.

"This must be inquired into," exclaimed Paul, with knit brows; "there was some treachery intended, and, for what I know, there may still be some. I'll search it out."

"If I might offer an opinion," said Gasket, "I would make no stir about it, but keep a bright look out, and if any foul play is intended, you'll catch 'em in the fact."

"They shall not forget it if they do," returned Paul, bitterly.

"Ah, Paul," said Gasket, shaking his head with a depressed air, "neither crew nor officers aboard the Ranger, are friends of your's; the officers less than the crew, and I think you might do better than fight like a lion, and risk limb and life for a parcel of lubberly—"

"Hold, Gasket, no names," interrupted Paul, with a smile, and a wave of the hand, "recollect I am not of their country, and a suspicion of my truth to them is natural—"

"Ay," replied Gasket, bitterly; "but why take a berth where you can be suspected at all; you don't deserve it, John, that *I* know; but they don't know you as well as I do; hows'ever, the man who turns round upon his shipmates can never expect to find friends among those he's deserted, or those he deserts, for when a man turns traitor to his country, she gives him up to all hands for scorn, and them as pays him for his treason don't think as well of him, whatever service he may do 'em, as they do the commonest loblolly boy in their service. The man's a traitor, John; and those as pays him looks on him as such—just the same—and treats him the same. Though I agrees to this, for I think so myself, I don't see what these lubbers of the Ranger—for that they are lubbers, those as knows an earring from a backstay, or a spanker from a flying jib, may easily see—I say, I can't diskiver why these lubbers should obey your orders with no more respect than a doctor's mate would scud under bare poles to the galley fire at command of a doctor's mate's minister—"

Ere Gasket could proceed further, Paul stopped him. There was an expression hardly of anger, but certainly sternness on his features, as he said—

"Gasket, I look upon you as a stanch friend—one devoted to me through storm and calm."

"And I am, John; I am, back and edge, from spanker-boom end to flying jib-boom end, from keel to truck, fore and aft, starboard to port," cried Gasket, rapidly and with feeling. "It would take a deep sea line to fathom

your stowage in my heart, John; there isn't, perhaps, much room for anchorage for any craft, but what there is gives a good hold, stronger than that the best bower of a seventy-four could get in a good roadstead. I am your friend, John, or else—" he paused.

"I should not have you fighting by my side in this battle," exclaimed Paul, supplying the words he hesitated to utter. "Is it not so?"

"It is, John, and that's the truth," replied Gasket, a little vehemently.

Paul smiled; but it was a melancholy smile.

"I knew you were my friend, Gasket," he said; "a stanch, true friend, or the word traitor would not have been borne by me so quietly. I know you mean me well, though you think me a traitor."

"It isn't that, John. No; I cannot think *you* a traitor," said Gasket, deprecatingly; "for your heart, your figure-head, your hull, your whole trim is not that of a traitor. No; I believe that what you do, is done from the honest feelings of your mind. I haven't much to do with spec'lation; my ship doesn't head that way; my sailing orders always came from the bo'sen, and I never trouble my head about anything but the set of a new topsail, or the rake, the fishing, or the fidding of a topmast. You were always ahead in those matters; and, as it was always my belief, would have made a better captain than a subordinate—the name's as long as foreto'-ga'nt mast-stay—and what I was going to say afore you brought me up was, that you are the best captain the Ranger ever had, and cert'ney, if the Ranger's people are a specimen, the best 'Merikey ever appointed to a ship. And for all this —for all they knows this—for I've heard them on the fork'sel, in the waist, and on the quarter deck, say you're a thorough-built seaman, and knows as well how to handle a ship, as a bo'sen's mate does a cat, when he's paying a man over the back as he owes a grudge to; yet they don't treat you as the capt'en. Why, they arn't worth fighting for—"

"It is not they," said he, "who I fight for," replied Paul, proudly. "I have a trust in me from Congress, which I'll keep faithfully if it carries me to the yard-arm or to the bottom. I am no traitor, Gasket, I fight for principle. I fight for the weak against the strong—the oppressed against the oppressors—for liberty against tyranny; and do you think I would sacrifice the good cause for a few who are too selfish to care for their country's interest?"

"If they don't care for their country who are of it, why should you who are not," asked Gasket, pertinently.

"For the same reason which induced me to undertake the cause—for the honour, for the glory, for the right of it. Remember these few are not all, America; it is not these few who represent the body of the people oppressed. The miserable petty cavils of those whom I am supposed to command, though annoying and betraying a spirit of ingratitude, are not sufficient to induce me to throw up my allegiance to the power I have endeavoured, and will still endeavour to serve; it is not strong enough to betray my trust."

"I am not able, John, to work my ship through all the channels, the narrows, and the straits of argument, because though I might have my port clear in sight, yet, from want of having a clear tongue, I should shoal, or run dead on to a reef, and founder for want of words to explain my meaning. All I have to say is this—in the gale or the dead calm, in the wreck or all a-tant-o, you'll find me the same as you knew me on board the Wildfire. Ah! that was a happy voyage! but no matter, I am the same—*you* will never have to heave for soundings when you want to find my heart; and I would give all I can say is mine—it isn't much, though enough for me—I would give five years of my life if I had only eight to live—damme, John, I'd give *up* all, and go over the side with a happy smile, if that young woman you saw in your dream had waved the Union Jack over you instead of the stripes and stars."

He squeezed Paul's hand hard as he concluded, and he went away hastily to assist in clearing the vessels from the effects of the battle, and to lend his nautical knowledge in repairing the damage which both ships had, to a considerable extent, sustained. Our hero watched him as he hastened and busied himself in directing and assisting the crew, and a shade of melancholy crossed him, as he unconsciously found himself echoing Gasket's wish.

He quickly, however, shook off the feeling in the contemplation of his glorious success, the more especially when he discovered that he had gained the victory against a superiority of guns, of number of people, and a reputation which had made the English in many cases victorious, and always formidable, while the Americans, who had not forgotten the case of the Glasgow, could hardly believe fortune had so favoured their bravery; for whatever bad spirit they evinced towards Paul, that merit, at least, could not be denied them. A large number on both sides were killed and wounded; the former, were immediately committed to the deep, and the greatest attention was paid to the latter. The captain and lieutenant of the Drake were reserved to be buried with honours due to their rank and to their bravery, and when the hour arrived for them to be committed to the deep, Paul made a short address to the people assembled, in praise of those whom he had conquered. He spoke feelingly and impressively; he pointed out the devotion which the English had paid to the honour of their country; how with one feeling animating all, one sentiment, they had fought to the last. He spoke of the high courage of the captain, who had nailed his colours to the mast, and had fallen in his country's service ere he had seen them rudely torn from their place of honour. He spoke, too, of the admirable discipline, the order and obedience which the crew had evinced, and concluded by saying—

"It is only this implicit confidence of the seamen in their captain, and ready obedience to their commands, which makes the English, as a people, invincible. They are guided by a strong mind, and appear to act as with one will—one intelligence; and great as our glory is in thus defeating them, high as were my hopes of success, still in this hour of cool reflection, I have strong reason to believe, that had the captain of yonder vessel survived, the action might have had a different issue. I know the indomitable spirit and resolution of the English while they have a leader, and know they are never beaten until they are cut down—until they are utterly incompetent to continue the contest. Although we meet them as enemies, let us not despise their courage or skill; example may be taken from a bad man, if that man excel in any art it is desirable to attain. Let us copy, then, their good qualities while we eschew their bad; let us deal generously and nobly with a generous foe; let us emulate their deeds, while we humble not to a power existing, but that of the Supreme Being; and if ye will but do this, the independence of America will soon be established, never to be shaken. High and dauntless courage should be honoured in any man, let his nation be what it may; and in doing honour to these brave men we are now committing to the deep, we pay a generous tribute to their bravery, not to their country—to their individual qualifications and merits, not to their native land; and when the sea closes over them, let every man, as he returns to his berth, lay his hand upon his heart, and say, as these men fought and bled, even unto death, for the honour and rights of their country, even so will I for mine!"

Paul ceased, and, with one spontaneous burst, the men gave him a loud cheer; he, however, repressed their loud demonstration of coincidence with him, by pointing to the bodies which were ready to be lowered into the sea, and, in a quiet tone, exclaimed—

"Chaplain, do your duty!"

The reverend man bowed and read the service of the dead at sea; and when he concluded, and a deathlike stillness reigned among those who stood bare-headed spectators of the scene, Paul gave the signal, and the bodies were cast into the deep, and then the men quietly returned to their duty.

Both the Ranger and the Drake had suffered severely in the contest; the latter especially in her mast; the whole of her topmasts were carried away, and the foremast, pierced in several places by shot, was in a tottering condition, the tackle was in almost irreconcilable confusion, being cut and torn to pieces in every part. The Ranger lost her main and mizen topmasts, while the mainmast had a double-headed shot sticking firmly in its side; shrouds and stays were cut adrift, yards splintered, and other damage which almost rendered her unmanageable; the hull, too, was much injured, and presented a very different aspect to the neat trim clipper she went into action. Repairs, however, were soon made—spare spars took the place of the shattered, or shot away; new lines were rove through new blocks; and in a few hours, by great activity, the Ranger was in sailing trim again, looking not much the worse for the severe battle in which she had been engaged. The Drake also was attended to, but having suffered more deeply in the action, she did not present so fresh an appearance after she had been put in order as her adversary. Paul knew that the news of the contest, with its result, would be quickly conveyed to London, and that he should have half a dozen frigates in chase of him. He did not wish to lose the advantage he had gained by being captured with his prize; he, therefore, made preparations for sailing to Brest, but before he started he determined, at all hazards, to keep his appointment with Alice. He made sail for the headland, where she was to meet him. After putting Lieutenant Wallingford on board of the prize, and though not in such trim for speed as previously, they were not long in working round the coast, and some time before the hour appointed, the two ships were off the headland. Paul suffered the Drake to draw ahead, knowing that he could, when he pleased, overtake her again, and kept the Ranger hovering about until near the hour appointed. It was a beautiful night, calm and still, and the moon, which was at the full, rose up from the deep silently, illuminating the shore and sea with her soft mild rays; there was hardly a ripple or a breath of wind, and Paul, who expected to be hotly chased, viewed the serenity of the scene with less satisfaction than he might otherwise have done, knowing that escape was almost impossible, for the light cruisers could draw over the sea fast with hardly any wind, and could pour men in such numbers into his vessel, that any attempt to defeat them would be hopeless. Before he landed, therefore, he ordered his men to be on the alert to make sail at a moment's notice: he stationed look-outs in the tops to sweep the horizon, and to prevent any curious fishermen from making remarks upon what they saw, he ordered an English ensign to be hoisted at the gaff end; he gave orders to summon him by a gun if any strange sail, looking suspicious, hove in sight, and ordered his boat, when it left him ashore, to return to the ship, and a pistol shot was to be the signal for it to come off to fetch him aboard again. These preliminaries being all arranged, he quitted the Ranger, and was put on shore. He saw his boat on its way back to the ship, and then he wended his way towards the point where Alice was to meet him: his anxiety had brought him ashore an hour before his time, and he strolled leisurely along to pass the time away. When he arrived at the meeting place, there was no sign of Alice visible, and he roamed in the direction in which he knew she would come. After he had proceeded a short distance, considerations for her induced him to alter his mind: she might be observed walking with him —might be watched in her progress to the headland by her suspicious parent. There were many other points, too, which induced him to relinquish his intentions: he, therefore, turned back, and arriving at a small green knoll, he threw himself upon it, and waited for the time for her approach to arrive. He had not laid there a minute ere he heard the sound of footsteps and then of voices, and presently he saw two persons approach, and seat themselves near to him, without discovering his locality: he listened, and heard the voice of a young man, with a strong Scotch accent, address a young girl who accompanied him—

"I tell you, lassie," he said, "I hae spoken no but truth; you ken I waur ne'er given to leeing, not e'en when I was a wee bit chiel at Dominie Macnab's, who ye ken used to glower upon we laddies with an awfu' look like the evil one himsel.'"

"I mind him weel," replied the girl, with a laugh, and continued with an arch tone. "But eh, Jamie, ye were a graceless ne'er-do-weel then, though ye're better sin' a leetle, though I ken nothing of the lees you told the Dominie, but dinna ask me to gie you a gude name for speaking truth, for you have told me mony—"

"Not lees," interrupted the youth. "No, Jeannie, ye canna say that and look me in the eyes steadfastly."

"I would na look ye in the eyes at a', Jamie," answered the girl with a laugh.

"Why for no?" he asked.

"For ye jest speer at a body with sic impudence, a lassie dinna ken what to do wi' her eyes for the next hour."

"It's na impudence, my ain Jeannie," returned the youth, fondly. "It is na that, it is because I lo' yere blue eyes sae dearly, it is because I think in the warl' there is none lik' thee, my dearie."

"Ha' dune wi' ye're saft talk, Jamie," replied the girl, in a tone which sounded far more like 'pray proceed;' "and dinna squeeze an' press me so, you'll drive the breath out o' my body. Canna you talk wi' your tongue without using your lips, too?"

"It is sae natural," said the youth, "your lips are sweeter to me than—"

"Nonsense," returned the girl. "Jest behave yoursel', and tell me all about this awfu' pirate."

"He is called Paul Jones," said the youth, complying at once with her request. Paul pricked up his ears and listened attentively. "And folks say he is Scottish born."

"Nae, Jamie, that canna be, for if he was of bonny Scotland he would never turn his heart again the land which gae birth to his mither," said the girl.

"Indeed he has, lassie," returned the youth; "there was one who met him last night here."

"Here!" screamed the girl. "Angels preserve us! I hope not. Oh, Jamie, I should die if I saw the monster," and she shuddered as she concluded.

"Not you, Jeannie," replied the youth, "he is no sae ill-faured."

"An ill heart, Jamie," returned the girl, "maks a body ill-faured."

"An' sae it does, Jeannie," replied the youth, "an' that is why ye're sae han'some, for ye have an ower gude heart."

Jeannie might have given Jamie a press of the hand, or some other little token of kind acknowledgment of this complement, but she did not return any answer verbally. After a minute's silence the youth spoke again.

"It is said that this Paul Jones has destroyed Whitehaven, and a' its shipping, besides murdering the people, and carrying off hundreds of preesoners; he has sunk, too, an awfu' number of vessels, and done ither terrible wark. He has carried off Lady Selkirk's plate an' jewels, and gol' to a very large amount; and, as I was tol', he would a killed her with a pistol which he held to her heed, but for her ca'ing upon the Lord, at which he shrunk away as though he was the dark fiend himself. I wouldna be surprised, Jeannie, to hear o' some terrible wark hereabout before morning; for, as I have told you, Sandy M'Math saw him hereabout last night; and he says that he is the same John Paul, of 'Kircoobree,' that was 'prenticed to Mr. Younger, and was thought sae weel to do till he run awa wi' Mr. Younger's ship, an' burned it, and now has some back to burn a' Scotland."

"Let us gang, Jamie; let us gang from here—I dinna like the place," said the girl, in a tone of alarm. "Eh, sirs, he must be a sinfu' man to hurt those who never hurt him; the curse of Scotland will be upon him for turning agin the land that gave him birth and the mither who bore him, and a' his relations and friends. Eh, Jamie, I knew him a cannie laddie; he must be unco' sinfu' and wicked, and if the curse of a simple lassie like myself can do him hurt for a' his evil deeds and thoughts to our land, I—"

"Hold!" cried Paul, springing to his feet, and standing before them.

Had a ghost, or a thunderbolt, or a cannon-ball, or anything fearfully startling suddenly made its appearance among them, it could not more effectually have startled them. The girl uttered a piercing shriek, threw herself upon her knees, and buried her face in her hands, while the youth staggered back with a face as white as ashes. Paul waited for a moment that they might recover from the effects of his sudden appearance, and then said, in a mild and sorrowful voice—

"Be not afraid; I am not the monster or evil one you think me."

The youth shook off his apprehension in a moment, and hastening to the side of his sweetheart, he raised her, and placed his arm protectingly round her. He eyed Paul from head to foot, and then, in a voice hardly steady, he exclaimed—

"What are ye, sir? who are ye, sir? We may seem startled, sir, but ye come in such an unco' fashion ye may not wonder that simple folk should start; but ye'll ken that, though started a wee bit, we are not frightened—

ye ken that, sir." The last words were said bolder than the previous ones.

"I ask your pardon for breaking in upon you so abruptly," said Paul, with a smile, though a sad one; "but it was important to me not to delay a moment. Look up, maiden, and cease to tremble," he said, addressing Jeannie; "you have no cause to fear me."

"What is your wull?" said the Scott, not exactly relishing the idea of a smart-looking officer addressing his best beloved, and speaking, therefore, rather haughtily.

"To you," said Paul, in reply, "simply this—do not believe all that you hear; do not condemn any one until you are so well possessed of the circumstances connected with him that you are sure he deserves condemnation. Remember it is man's nature to strike again when struck, the more especially when he has not deserved the blow he has received. The humblest, meanest insect that crawls, the earth-worm, will turn if trodden on—it is nature. Quarrel not with a man—despise him and condemn him not—because he obeys a natural law. And for you, maiden," he said, taking Jeannie's hand which, with a little distrust, she suffered him to hold, "before you form your lips to utter a curse upon any fellow-creature, be convinced of your own knowledge, and not of hearsay, that he deserves no less. A curse may not be recalled, although it may be your lot to discover that the anathema was prematurely invoked; and one who appears so simple and good as you would rest ill if you discovered that you cursed where you should have pitied."

"I was wrong, sir," said Jeannie, raising her soft blue eyes timidly to his. "I was wrong, sir; I should na curse any one—the minister has told me so at kirk; the evil minded and the evil-doer will be cursed of God. It is our duty to pray for our misguided fellow-creatures. I was wrong to attempt a curse, an' I hope our Lord will forgive me the sin."

"Amen!" replied Paul. "You are both young—both likely to be happy; I hope you may be so, sincerely. And, in other years, whenever a man's name comes across you with an evil brand, remember to-night, and be not too ready to think him so bad as report makes him. Crimes are not to be palliated; but the circumstances which lead most men to their commission are chiefly those which should excite our commiseration for them, not our curses. The man is sufficiently cursed having commited the crime. It should be our duty to pity and pray, not to help in hurling them deeper into perdition then they are already doomed to fall. You were speaking of Paul Jones when I interrupted you; one day you will hear a far different account of his present deeds—reserve your curses, your ill opinions, till then; and then if you see cause to register in heaven your bad opinion of him, do so; you have his free permission!"

"His!" they both exclaimed with surprise.

"Even so," he returned. "*I am Paul Jones!*" They started, and drew back. He stayed them with a motion of his hand. "Hear me, ere you depart," he said, speaking with strong feeling; "Scotland spurned me—cast me out from her bosom—degraded me unjustly. She did it, I swear, as here I stand, by all that is holy! I deserved not the ill I received at her hands. I swore to repay it, and I will; but not on the weak and defenceless; not—

but no matter for this ; time will explain my motives as it will display my deeds, and all I ask is justice from those who may be taught to hold my name in execration. All you have heard, youth, and related respecting me to the maiden, is falsely, basely, and infamously exaggerated ; and when you are among those who *were* my friends, do not add to the number who, without knowing the truth, speak with evil tongue of my motives and actions; and if you should see my—my mother, whom I dare not venture to visit, for her sake more then my own, tell her—for God's sake tell her to listen to nothing—to believe nothing of me until she hears from or sees me; tell her that I have not forgotten all that she inculcated in me; tell her that to her I can justify every act I have committed; tell her that I am still her son—her dear boy—as she fondly called me long ago. God bless her! God bless her, for ever! Bless her—" He dashed his hands across his eyes as he spoke, and would have continued, but nature would have its way, and, turning his head aside, he wept like a child. The sight of a man in tears is a terrible sight—not your mere weak-minded driveller, but he who has a bold heart and a strong mind : he from whom you might expect tears of blood instead of water. To a woman especially is this a sight that at once touches her heart, and Jeannie turned her head upon her lover's shoulder and sobbed bitterly. Jamie, too, was affected. The silence which ensued was broken by Jeannie, who murmured, mingled with sobs, so as hardly to make her words distinguishable—

"God save us! I am ower sorry I spake sae ill o' ye, John Paul,' and sair am I that I should hae brought a curse agin ye to my lips: I hope ye will forgie me—I hope ye will, John Paul—"

"Say no more, Jeannie Cameron," said Paul, who by a strong effort had recovered himself. "I knew ye, Jeannie, when you were a little child, and I was just starting upon my first voyage. I have not seen you of late years, but I knew your voice when I heard it. And now I have a favour to ask of you—time presses, and I must away. Convey my blessing and my message to my mother; tell her I am well, and that she shall shortly hear from me. Do not say to-night to mortal that you have seen me; to-morrow you may tell whom you please, save that you say you saw Paul Jones, not John Paul. I would not have my family's situation compromised by England or Scotland's opinion of me, and in one name they will not recognise the other. Farewell—you will shake hands with me?"

"I will," said Jeannie, extending her soft hand. "Aebody kens their ain gate best; an', John Paul, I doubt na you ken ye're's better than folk who talk so mickle about thee, but if you see fit to do bluidy deeds, oh! remember Him who died to save us, and be merciful to your fellow men."

"Jeannie, I would not shed the blood of the simplest thing in nature if I were not compelled," said Paul, solemnly, "and be assured whatever desperate circumstances fate may throw me into, I will think of you, and hold my hand where I am able to spare ; though I believe I need not do more than follow the dictates of my feelings. Farewell! heaven bless you, and you, youth—may you both be happy."

Jamie and Jeannie took a kind farewell of him, and hastily quitted the spot, while he, full of thought, hastened to the headland.

Alice had not arrived, and he stood gazing upon the sea, while his thoughts were far from the scene on which he was looking. He sunk into deep abstraction, and remained oblivious to all around him for some time; he was, at last, aroused by a hand laid upon his shoulder—he started, and found Alice by his side; she smiled as she returned the fervent greeting with which he welcomed her, and said—

"Your caution slumbered with your thoughts, Paul; my footstep was not so light as to be noiseless, and yet you heard it not; neither did the inward monitor in your breast, as the novels say, acquaint you with the approach of your mistress."

"In truth, Alice, I was in deep thought," returned Paul, "or I should have heard your step, I should have been looking anxiously for thee, and should feel ashamed that you should have approached me unseen or unheard, but that it was thoughts of thee which engrossed my attention so completely—"

"As to forget the original of your reflections," she added, jestingly.

"Not so," he returned, "you are merry to-night, Alice."

"I am in better spirits," she exclaimed, "than I have been all day, for I have succeeded in persuading myself out of a foolish fancy I had formed—one which pained me deeply."

"May I ask what it was, Alice?" he inquired.

"Oh, I am ashamed to mention it. Do not ask me—it was a weakness; I ought to have known better. I do not wish to think of it again, so let us say no more about it."

"As you will, Alice," returned Paul, tenderly; "I would have you do nothing which should for a moment distress you. Let us remove from hence to the beach, we are too exposed here; there may be those abroad who, seeing thee here alone with me, may make thy father join us—a favour I would gladly dispense with."

Alice laughed at his remark, and replied—

"You would not be more loth to see him than I, at the present moment. Your caution slumbers not now, Paul," she added.

"No," he replied, fondly, "for you are by my side."

They walked on, talking affectionately and tenderly as they wound down the cliff to the sands, and then, as they stood there half embracing, Paul pointed out his vessel, which was lying off for him

"There, Alice," he said, "is the vessel which I command; there she lies—the glorious bark who will bear me upwards until I have attained the height my ambition aspires to—the pinnacle upon whose summit thy dear hand rests, the reward of my exertions, the prize for which I would dare the greatest danger, defy the extremest peril; there she floats, Alice, trim and graceful, looking in this light, aye, and in all lights to me, a bright spirit; her clear white topsails are the wings by which she glides her graceful form through waters—she is a thing of beauty—of delight."

"You are enthusiastic in her praise," exclaimed Alice, smiling.

"Should I not be so, dear Alice?" replied Paul, earnestly. "Is she not the means of my approach to the felicity of calling thee mine? Is it not by her aid that I shall stand among men honoured and eulogised? Will she not be the cause of thy proud father meeting me with open arms, though now he spurns me from him with contumely?"

"Thou hast wondrous faith in her powers, Paul," returned Alice, pleasantly. "Had I not as great faith in thee as thou hast in you vessel, I should be jealous of her."

"Not thou, Alice; thou couldst never be jealous of my viewing with fond eyes any object which brought our union nearer," said Paul, warmly.

Alice looked fondly on him, but did not reply; she presently turned her eyes upon the vessel, and, after regarding it attentively for a moment, she observed, with some surprise, the English flag flying from the peak of the gaff.

"Paul," she exclaimed, "you told me that you owed not your distinction to England, yet your vessel carries her colours."

"And though the English ensign floats there, Alice, and will while I hover on this coast, yet is there still as vast a barrier between me and the haughty insolent nation, as the sea which divides the American continent and the spot on which we stand. I hate her, Alice; and rather than serve her I would be again a drudge in a collier," cried Paul, speaking excitedly.

The brow of Alice lowered, a shade of sadness crossed her beautiful features; but she remained silent.

"You do not speak, Alice," exclaimed Paul, after a moment's pause.

"Oh, Paul," replied Alice, with considerable emotion, which she vainly endeavoured to suppress; "I have told you that I have all this day been oppressed with a horrible foreboding—with a fearful surmise which fixed itself in my brain with an agony I have no words to describe. It was in vain I sought to drive it away—it would return with tenfold vigour, until the time drew near for our meeting; then I succeeded in chasing it away, for I thought I knew thy heart, thy high and honourable principles too well, too surely, to have one doubt of thee; but now thy words have brought it back again with terrible force."

"What is it, Alice? speak love," said Paul, eagerly; "tell me what this surmise is which has led thee to doubt me? Let me know at once, that I may grapple with it, and rid thee of so foul a phantom for ever."

"I feel ashamed to confess it, fearing I have wronged thee," she rejoined, with feeling; "and if I have, Paul, you will forgive me, and attribute it solely to the strong desire that your fame should be free from spot or blemish."

Paul pressed her hand affectionately, and she proceeded—

"There has been, I am told, a descent upon Whitehaven by the commander and crew of an American vessel, the commander bearing the name of Paul Jones. He came meanly, and like a dastard, in the night; and while the whole town was buried in sleep, basely set fire to the shipping; and when the inhabitants were alarmed by the intelligence of his wickedness, and ran half-dressed, unarmed, to behold the flames, this Paul Jones and his crew fired upon them, slaying many, and then retreated with their best speed from the wrath of the survivors, not daring to attack the people whom, under cover of the night, they cruelly attempted to destroy. I have heard, also, that they crossed over here to St. Mary's Isle, and by force broke into the castle of the Earl of Selkirk, who was absent in London, and stole, among many other things, the whole of the massive family plate, and then hastily slunk away with their booty."

The face of Paul Jones glowed like a furnace as he listened to her words. She paused, and with a powerful exertion, he mastered his feelings, and said—

"Well, Alice, and you have surmised—"

"That—that Paul Jones might—" she hesitated.

"Be John Paul," he exclaimed. "Is it not so?"

"It is," she returned. "Oh, Paul, dearest Paul, it is in your power to rid me of this miserable suspicion. I pray you, as you love me, say but one word, that my heart may be at peace."

"Will you tell me, Alice, why you imagine that I should be the actor of these deeds?" he inquired.

"I will," she replied. "When yesterday I suggested that England was the power which had elevated you, you denied it, as now you have, strongly. You also said France was not the donor, and in remembering this—in remembering your destination when you quitted Scotland—it crossed me, and with a withering force, that America might have bestowed these honours upon you—that, indeed, the vessel committing these outrages might have been the one you command, and that, under an earnest desire of gathering honour for my sake, you might have been misled into acts, which, so far from meeting with my approbation, would break my heart. The difference of name, and my knowledge of your honourable nature, have assisted strongly in divesting me of the idea, that Paul Jones and you are one person; and it only remains for you, Paul, to put the strange fancy to flight for ever."

"I should first tell you, Alice," said Paul, speaking with assumed calmness, "in justice to the crew and commander of the American vessel, that the reports you have heard are greatly exaggerated; in the first place, but few of the shipping were burned, and not an inhabitant was destroyed—not a shot was fired but what was done in derision, in return for the discharge of a few cannon, which the people of Whitehaven, having obtained from one or two vessels, the cannon of the forts being spiked, drew to the pier and levelled at us."

"Us!" echoed Alice. "Oh, Paul, my worst fears are realised; you are the man—the pirate upon whom the execrations of Britain fall so heavily."

"Alice!" exclaimed Paul in a grave tone "it is the custom of a tyrant master, when his servant or child will no longer submit to his oppressive despotism, to style him rebel. The Americans have been oppressed by England, and because they would not suffer themselves to be trampled upon, they are termed and treated as contumacious rebels. I am Paul Jones—I have enlisted in the cause of America, and in her behalf will do my best; for your sake do I aspire to glory, but the glory I reap shall be America's too. I am no pirate—I am the servant of a state who would still have been loyal to this country if she had treated them as men, not slaves—as children, not as the conquered natives of a foreign soil. I have raised my arm on the side of justice and virtue."

"To commit acts of blood and rapine upon the coast that gave you birth," said Alice, bitterly.

"Alice! Alice!" cried Paul, stung by her words, "do not judge me too hastily, I have done no more than is my duty to the country I serve. The monstrous conduct of the English upon the American coasts—their terrible treatment of their prisoners—all—all justify reprisals, that we may compel them to treat those who have fallen into their hands with more leniency, even with the same consideration which they display to prisoners of war. Hear me, Alice," he continued with considerable anxiety in his voice, seeing with pain that she averted her face from him. "I have served England as you know—since I have parted with you, also, have I done her service. I sought to be in her navy—I tried hard and anxiously to be admitted among her officers—I had interest—I had acknowledgments of my capacity from those whose opinion and recommendation were of great value, yet was I rejected—not only rejected, but with scorn added. From Scotland am I outlawed; for what Alice? for a debt sworn by your father against me, which he knew was never incurred."

Alice shuddered, and Paul continued speaking wi much excitement—

"Thus has Great Britain driven me from her with scorn, which I have never deserved. Think you Alice I am of a constitution so cold, so indifferent, so feeble, that I cannot feel this contumely with burning indignation; the greater, too, when its effect is to shut me out of all hopes of you—debarring me from the opportunity of winning the fame which was to be accompanied by your hand. I learned, Alice, to curse the land in whose defence I would once have gladly died; the oppression she displayed to me upon a small scale was extended to the colonies on a large one. Injustice had made me reflect—reason; it made me a hater of oppression and oppressors. I became in my principles a citizen of the world, I eschewed country, land of birth, all such feelings, and united myself in heart, at least, with the oppressed of any nation. The conduct of England to her colonies made me side with the American people. I have enlisted in their cause, I have already gained honour and fame, I shall still rise higher, I feel that I shall stand on a proud eminence in the world's opinion, and be then able to offer thee, with my heart, a name which even thou mayst be proud to share."

Alice shook her head mournfully.

"You deceive yourself, Paul," she exclaimed; "the contest in which your are engaged is unnatural, and can never succeed."

"Unnatural, Alice!" exclaimed Paul. "Is it unnatural for those who are oppressed to endeavour to cast off the yoke of the oppressors? Is it unnatural to resist a tyranny which would trample you to dust? I would not strike a blow, with wanton malice, upon any object, however mean or humble; I would not be guilty of an unprincipled or unjust act, knowingly, to any creature upon the face of the earth; but I confess I have not the meekness prescribed in the Christian law, to turn, when one cheek has been struck, the other to the smiter; so far is my blood rebellious, in so much has it power over my prudence; and such, perhaps, is my obstinacy, that I do not hold this a weakness, for though I acknowledge prudence is an estimable qualification, especially in men in whom great trust is placed, yet I believe your prudent over-much people are rarely so pure in principle, so free, or possess such honesty of purpose as I believe myself to be endowed with. I have been struck deeply, bitterly, and I must strike again."

"There is an especial difference, Paul," returned Alice, "in retaliating an injury upon one to whom you are bound by no ties, and one who possesses claims upon your heart. Would you deem yourself justified in flying in the face of the Almighty, because he has visited you with misfortunes, disappointments, and hard trials? Would you have me curse my parent, and be a contumacious rebel to his authority, because he has treated me harshly and unjustly?"

"This is not a parallel case," said Paul.

"Oh, Paul, it is!" exclaimed Alice, earnestly; "indeed it is. Do not set your heart against the pleadings of nature. Great Britain is the land of your birth—you are one of its sons—you are bound to it by ties sacred to all men, even as I am bound to my father the author of my being. The most wretched serf of Russia loves the land which gave him birth; the volatile Frenchman, who is in love with every new object he sees, constant to nothing living, is still true to the land of his birth; still, in all his wanderings, believes no place in the world like *la belle France;* and it has ever been the boast, the proudest, heartiest feeling of Englishmen; their toast in a foreign land—their idiom—their open saying—their bye-word, that "there is no place like *home.*"

"Alice, you are advocating one of the most illiberal prejudices mankind possesses," observed Paul, gravely.

"Illiberal!" echoed Alice, with surprise.

"Even so," he returned, "the native of every country believes all that is good, great, and talented exists in his native land alone. No land can be so fertile as that where first he drew breath—no people so generous, brave, and virtuous as his countrymen—no science or art so high as that which distinguishes his fatherland, and with this prejudice in his mind he views all other nations—their position, their talents, and abilities—their resources, their advancement, all are measured and seen through this medium, and rated accordingly."

"Paul, I have loved you," said Alice, with strong feeling, "and—"

"*Have* loved me?" echoed he, laying a strong emphasis on have.

"Have loved you," she repeated, dropping her eyes to the sands; "I think you have cause to know it. In preferring you to all men, in esteeming you in all things superior to all I have ever seen—in loving only you, have I been illiberal to others?"

"Love of country, Alice, and the love you feel for one of the opposite sex are two different feelings," answered Paul, with some emotion; "one is a love of place, and the other a love of kind."

"You are deceiving yourself with sophistry, Paul," returned Alice; "they are both love of kind. The associations which lead us to love of country are chiefly remembrances of the relatives, the friends, the happy hours spent in thoughtless childhood with youthful and dear companions in spots and places and familiar haunts—the memory of each serves to endear the other. Those places would have been nothing without the merry faces; those faces are still dearer from the remembrance of the pleasant places. It is the love of home and friends which makes a man love his country, simply because his happiest hours were passed there. An Englishman will love Devonshire better than Middlesex, because the former was his birthplace, the home of his youth: but he will love England better than all the countries in the world, because it contains the county where he drew breath, and where all his dearest ties exist· that land in which all his best feelings are centered *is* better and lovelier *to him* than anyother place in the world, and is he to be deemed illiberal, because, knowing it, he openly asserts it to be so? You are silent, Paul;—oh! let me urge you, as you love me, not to raise your hand against your country—my country!"

"Scotland shall not receive a blow from me," replied Paul, with energy, "although deeply as she has injured me, for your sake I will hold my hand."

"England and Scotland are one, Paul," urged Alice; "one king governs us, the same laws rule us, we act in concert, we are as one nation; you must consider us as one, although I was born in Scotland. My mother was English, all her family were so, and many of my father's relatives also. My sympathies are connected with one as much as the other; my sweetest remembrances belong to both. A happy childhood was passed in England, in Scotland I met you—to both am I true; and Paul, every blow you strike against either will fall upon my heart."

"Nay, Alice," exclaimed Paul, with great earnestness, "do not so blind yourself to my motives; judge me not harshly if I have espoused the cause of a new people—a people who are English in all their assocciations in their origin; who have equal, if not greater, claims upon the mother country than those residing in it, and yet are treated infinitely worse, even as though they were an inferior order of beings, almost as low in civilization as the red people whom they have displaced. I fight only for right against might, justice against the vilest oppression; do not judge me coldly or harshly. I have been wronged, but I have not raised my hand in retaliation in the service of a nation utterly foreign to my own; I have not stained my name or my sword with the deeds of a villain in the cause of tyrants."

"Whitehaven and St. Mary's Isle, Paul, are not the noble deeds of one aspiring to high honour," exclaimed Alice, not in so satirical as in a sorrowful tone.

"By heaven!" cried Paul, vehemently, "you wrong me, Alice; I swear by all that is sacred you do. At Whitehaven I expected opposition—such opposition as would have crowned me with glory if I had defeated it, and the acts of my people at St. Mary's Isle, were done in despite of my wish to the contrary. I sought only to capture the Earl of Selkirk, that the barbarous conduct of the English to the Americans might be checked. The design failed through his absence, and though no outrage ensued, I regret that an act in which I had no share, nor any control—which I reflect on with shame, followed; but it shall be fully repaired and the stain eradicated—but let us talk no more of this, Alice, let us speak only of our next meeting."

"Nay, Paul, it is this subject alone that we must speak upon ere we part; your future conduct will decide whether we ever meet again."

"Alice!" exclaimed Paul, starting as if struck with an arrow.

"'Tis even so," she replied, sadly; and then exclaimed, with considerable fervour, "Paul, I have loved you long and devotedly; all the energies of a heart capable of strong feeling have been centered in that passion—all my hopes, my fondest thoughts, cherished in secret, my prayers have been thine. Even under the cruel tyranny of my father, in hours when his harshness has made me wretched, and one word to him against thee would have rendered them at least peaceful, my love for you has never swerved—never wavered."

"I believe it,' exclaimed Paul, fervently.

"It is in your power only to change the tenor of my wishes," she continued; "and by your perseverance in the cause of America, to effect an eternal separation between us."

Alice!" he cried, urgently.

"Hear me yet a moment," she rejoined. "I look upon your conduct in this struggle between the colonies, as I would upon that of one who lifts his hand against those he is bound, if not to love, to reverence. Your mother, your sisters, your father, and your brothers, live upon a land upon which you would seek to bring fire and sword; they were born upon that land, are bound to it by the same ties which made their ancestors prize it above all others, and risk their lives in its defence; and yet, among them and theirs, you would come with strife, with thoughts of blood and vengeance, to repay only a few injuries which you have received from a handful of unworthy men, who no more represent the people of England than a grain of dust can its fertile soil."

"Alice, America sought not the war with England," urged Paul; "she seeks only to be free and independent—to keep her own which she purchased, and which, therefore, is her's, fairly and justly. Let England acknowledge her independence—which would be but rendering her mere justice—and she will lay down her arms."

"You speak of justice," returned Alice, quickly; "from whom did the colonists receive the lands? From England. Who kept armies to protect them from the red men, from the real possessors of the soil, but England? Whose institutions governed them? Those of England. Whose power did they swear fealty to when they purchased their lands, but to England. They held them only from and under England, and having grown to a certain strength, they cast aside justice, and claimed the right to govern themselves—they cast down the ladder which had reared them, and supported them as they rose, and then cried they were acting justly, and would be free."

"It is the privilege of a people, when improperly governed, to displace their existing rulers, and place over them those whom they have reason to believe will rule them more justly," observed Paul; "but, Alice, you reason as an Englishwoman, and with the prejudices of one; in America, you would find they reason differently."

"Doubtless," she exclaimed, laconically.

"And as strongly," he rejoined. "But this is a subtle question, Alice; it is one which we view differently; but it is a road for me to gain the honours, the name, the wealth, which shall gain me your hand."

"No, Paul," cried Alice, with startling energy, "though the refusal break my heart. No, not though America raised you to the highest point of rank and fame in her power to bestow, were you then, Paul, to seek me upon your knees, loaded with medals and crosses, to unite my fate to thine, I would refuse you, though the chords of my heart snapped asunder as I uttered the negative. Oh, Paul, dear Paul, if you love me you will quit this service. I

will forego my promise to my father, and be thine even in the humblest circumstances. I will follow you round the world. I will be all a faithful, loving wife can be to you, and in the greatest poverty, if it should please Heaven that such should be our fate, I would smile and cheer you, solacing you ever, and never repine. I would cling to you, Paul, as a faithful wife should cleave to her husband, in weal or woe, in misery or in happiness. Quit this service; let your vessel sail without you, and I am thine even unto death. Now on this spot will I join my hand in thine ; now will I give up home, father, everything, and be your's, and your's only."

She pressed her hands convulsively together, and looked with agitated anxiety in his face for an assent. His lips quivered as he attempted to reply ; a thousand conflicting emotions were at war in his breast. Here was the prize he had looked forward to as the summit of his wishes, of his ambition, ready to be his, if he would but utter one word, and abjure America; the sacrifice of refusing to utter it was to relinquish the only object which had made him thirst for glory. On the one hand, he was bound in honour to be true to the service he had accepted; on the other hand, his happiness, while he lived, depended upon his union with Alice; he knew her to be strong-minded, and not to be diverted from a line of conduct which she felt it right to pursue. To adhere to America was to lose her, and to desert the Congress was to compromise his honour most fearfully. Either course was fraught with anguish to him, and he groaned aloud as the struggle between love and duty raged in his bosom. Alice waited for some time to receive his answer; but as he remained silent, she clenched her hands agonisedly, and, dropping her head, she exclaimed, in a low, mournful voice—

"Your silence pronounces my doom—"

"Stay, Alice, for God's sake! be not too hasty," cried Paul, excitedly; "pause one moment ere you decide. You know, Alice, my love for you is a religion; it is the whole object of my life, to which my every act has tended. Even in this struggle, Alice, the thoughts of honours and distinction have been only desirable for you, and you only."

"Paul, I am not to be won by their aid, were they great beyond conception," exclaimed Alice, decisively.

"But remember, Alice," continued Paul, almost franticly, "that I am pledged to the performance of a duty. I have enlisted in the cause of America. I have *taken an oath* to be true to her, she has placed a great and sacred trust in me, she has faith in me; and would you, Alice—who love honour as the breath of life, have me break the pledge I have given her—forfeit the truth placed in me, and have my name held up as a thing of scorn—a wretch devoid of honour, of trust, of truth?"

"America knows you only as Paul Jones, your name is John Paul," returned Alice; "you had already broken your faith with England when you enlisted in this cause, and think you, Paul, implicit confidence is placed in a renegade traitor?"

"Alice!"

"They are strong words, John Paul, but truth is ever strong, and titles, however deserved, are hateful, when heard by those who have earned them. As Paul Jones, you have been a traitor—as John Paul, never. Believe not that Congress places faith in your *disinterestedness;* think not they trust the purity of your motives in joining the weak against the strong. No, they know you have wrongs, real or fancied, to charge to England, and they trust to your desire to revenge those wrongs, rather than a *pure desire to serve them.* Do your crew treat you as a friend to their country—as one upon whom suspicion cannot light?"

Paul started and bit his lip.

"Do your officers show an eagerness to obey your lightest command, knowing that they are furthering the views and earnest exertions of one devoted to their cause from the pure principle of carrying out what is just? No, Paul, your changing countenance tells me you are mistrusted and suspected in the very ship you command; you have not, I believe, one friend on board."

"You mistake, Alice, I have one," he interrupted hastily; "one true as steel—Gasket, my single-minded, honest friend of the Wildfire."

"An Englishman, and does he join the cause with avidity?" she inquired.

"No," he returned; "to do him justice it is with reluctance—it is for my sake only he serves America; it is simply to be in the same ship with me."

"But no *friends* hast thou amongst thy followers. Oh, Paul!" she cried, even with anguish, "a traitor to his country is the despised of all parties—thou wilt not gain honour even if thou dost earn it; the envy of those whom thou servest will keep it from thee. Art thou prepared, years hence, if the nature of thy occupation will grant thee so long a term of life, to find thyself the deserted victim of the ingratitude of those whom thou hast served so well, without a friend, without even I to console thee; poor as mine might be, it would still be sincere—art thou prepared for this?"

"Alice, Congress will not so reward those who have served her," returned Paul, emphatically.

"It is enough," exclaimed Alice, mournfully. "We must part, Paul, for ever."

"No, no; oh, say not so, Alice," cried Paul, bitterly. "Be just to me."

"I am, Paul," she replied, a little proudly, "and to my country too, even at the expense of my own happiness—but let that pass. You have taught me that a public trust should rise superior to private feelings; my country places a trust in me as in all her children. I will not betray it."

"And you reject me, Alice!" exclaimed Paul, his lips so parched he could scarcely articulate his words.

"Not so," she returned, "it is you who resign me for America—to join a contest, the success of which injures my native land, my friends, my countrymen. Every victory of yours strikes a blow against them, and your ill success, your captivity, would bring wretchedness, agony to me. It is in vain to argue the subject further—I am yours if you relinquish America, the Almighty's if you refuse. I await your reply."

"Alice, I have received a trust; I have sworn an oath to be true to it, and I cannot break it, though your decision crush my heart to powder."

Alice grew white as death—her limbs trembled, her lips quivered; but by a strong effort she threw off the faintness that was stealing over her, and, in a calm tone, she exclaimed—

"The dream is fled, the vision is chased away—I have awoke from the slumber, and the cold reality is mine. Paul, I am my country's child, though—though—" she would not say his determination was death to her; she finished hurriedly, "Farewell, farewell, Paul, for ever; may God bless you, and make you happy," she burst into a bitter torrent of tears, and staggered from the spot.

Paul stood like a statue of stone as she spoke; but when she concluded, he sprung to her side, he flung himself upon his knees at her feet, and, with wild energy, he cried—

"Alice, hear me this once; 'tis all I ask, Should a time come when your opinions respecting this struggle alter, and you may be led to believe America was in the right, will you rescind your decision against me? Should

I find America ungrateful, and throw off her service, will you receive me? Answer me, alice, one word—but one little word."

She tore her dress from his grasp, she waved her hand and fled, while he covered his eyes with his hands, and, bowing his head to the ground, wept like an infant.

CHAPTER IX.

"Came there a certain lord, neat, trimly dressed,
Fresh as a bridegroom; and his chin new reaped,
Showed like a stubble-land at harvest home;
He was perfumed like a milliner,
And 'twixt his finger and his thumb he held
A pouncet box, which ever and anon
He gave his nose, and took't away again.
* * * *
He made me mad,
To see him shine so brisk, and smell so sweet,
And talk so like a waiting gentlewoman,
Of guns, and drums, and wounds."

FIRST PART OF KING HENRY IV.

"This is Signior Antonio,
How like a fawning publican he looks;
I hate him."

MERCHANT OF VENICE.

WITH the Ranger, accompanied by the Drake, with American colours flying over English, Paul Jones entered Brest. Guns were fired, flags waved, people came in crowds to welcome him; shouts of triumph were raised on all sides, the bells of the church sent forth a merry peal. Had they been Frenchmen entering with an English captured vessel the joy could not have been more universal. Yet there were two men on board the Ranger who did not partake of the mirth—the gladness with which every other brow seemed smiling, the one stood upon the quarter-deck surrounded by his officers, the object of general attention, the object of every cheer given of congratulation from all parties of respect and homage. His breast was burning with a blighted hope—with the bitterest disappointment fate could curse him with. The other was seated in a small cabin, he was without his coat, which was beneath his feet, his arms were folded, his eyes were fixed upon the floor, his teeth were set, and at every salute of guns, at every cheer his brow fell lower and lower, and his teeth ground against each other; and then he said, clenching his fists and speaking with singular bitterness—

"And this I helped to do—I—I. Jib-boom, your curse is on me!"

He said no more, but sat until the noise ceased. It was a long time ere it did, and when all was quiet again, and had remained so a little while, some one entered his cabin. He looked up—it was Paul; he started up as if from a dream, and raised his hand with a seaman's salute to his head.

"How is it, Gasket, I find you here alone," said Paul; "I missed you, and have been seeking you? Why were you not upon deck to receive the cheers and congratulations showered upon us by the people of this city?"

"Because every cheer was like a marl'spike through my heart; because the sight of them stripes and stars over the union jack was blinding to my eyes. I know if I'd been upon deck and heard these French mounseers hollaing and shouting at a thing they never seed afore, I should have forgotten you and myself, and made clear decks; it wouldn't have been the right conning if I had, and so I came below to be out of harm's way."

"I know, Gasket, you are doing your feelings violence by serving in this ship; I know that for my sake you are living on board here, when you would rather be—"

"Don't say a word about it, John," interrupted Gasket; "I've slung my hammock in your ship, whatever it be, even though it might be a French frigate, and it isn't friendly in me to show my likes and dislikes to you in this fashion; but I shan't any more. I'll stand on the same tack as the others, for a short or long leg, and you shan't know but what the service is pleasanter to me than even old England's."

Paul squeezed his hand and said—

"Let me see you upon deck, and let me see you the same light-hearted, gay messmate you were when I first joined the Wildfire: you have been so dull and thoughtful ever since we quitted America, and even before that, you are not like the same man—"

"Well, John," exclaimed Gasket, "when the hands are piped to mischief I'll make one among 'em."

"That's kindly said," cried Paul; "follow me on deck; we will go ashore and take a stroll through the town."

"I want to ask you one question," said Gasket, hesitatingly. "You—you—when you were ashore on the Scotch coast, did you happen to hear anything about Mr. Eustace and Flore—I mean Mrs. Prior?"

"I was going to tell you, as we strolled along, Gasket, that I have received a packet of letters from America, which have followed me here; among them is a letter from Captain Prior—"

"Captain," echoed Gasket.

"Yes," replied our hero, with a smile; "he has been restored to the service, and through Mr. Stanley's interest he is posted; he commands a fine frigate—the Lightning."

"Hurrah!" cried Gasket, with a cheer, "that's the best news I have heard since we sailed from Philadelphy."

"He has heard of my joining the Americans; he speaks gravely and sorrowfully," said Paul. "He thanks me warmly for what little kindness I and my poor brother were able to show him, and would now more than ever wish to make me some return; for he says he knows my spirit, and when next we meet, it may be upon the sea as foes. He's a noble fellow, and I feel warmly the generous manner in which he speaks of the motives which he believes induced me to fight for America, and the delicacy with which he mentions his own adherence to the flag of his native land, imposing upon him the necessity, if ever we should cross each other on the Atlantic, of fighting, although, privately, he is so well disposed towards me. He tells me he is very happy—that Florence is also; indeed, she has herself written a few lines in his letter to me, and to you—"

"To me?" echoed Gasket, with a sort of hysteric laugh. "To me—has she though! has she? The Lord bless her! What does she say? Overhaul it, Paul; overhaul it and pay it out to me."

"She says—'My kind friend, Gasket, I have not forgotten you. I regret that your absence when we quitted America prevented my seeing you to bid you farewell; the time, perhaps, may come when I may meet you here in London—I hope it will, and shortly, that I may show you the services you have rendered my husband and myself have not escaped my memory, or, that I cease to esteem one whose devotion and services have made him a valued friend. Believe me, wishing you every happiness, yours sincerely, Florence Prior.' That is all," concluded Paul.

"All," replied Gasket; "all!—it is an Indyman's freight to me. All! God bless her! Ha! ha! I didn't expect this; it has made me feel all abroad. If it don't make any difference to you, Paul, I should like to have that small bit of writing."

"Here it is," replied Paul, tearing off the portion of the letter addressed o Gasket, and presenting it to him.

Gasket took it, and surveyed it with eyes expressing the greatest delight. He could not read it, but he looked attentively at every word, and presently, with a chuckling nervous laugh, he said—

"Lord love the dear little fingers that pricked that out so prettily. Ha! ha! the stitching of a dandy sky-scraper ain't so neat by a whole latitude—no, nor the log of an admiral within hail of it either; talking with bunting is a pretty fashion of hanging out your ideas to them as can read 'em, but there isn't a signal in the service could hold a light to windward of this. I shall stow it away snugly, and only when I want to do my toplights good, I shall overhaul it; it will come like a breeze when the ship is making stern way."

"It has struck me said Paul, eyeing Gasket stedfastly, "that you would like to join Captain Prior in his frigate, the Lightning."

Gasket's eyes glistened.

"If you should," continued Paul, "say but the word; I will give you your discharge, and obtain you a passport for England. I see too plainly that all your feelings are enlisted against the cause which I have undertaken and that all your sympathies are with Prior. I shall not think unkindly of you, Gasket, for following the dictates of your heart; you would rather die in the service of England than live loaded with honours awarded to you by America, and you would sooner serve under Eustace Prior than any captain in the English navy; speak the word, and you are free to depart."

Gasket, when Paul awaited his reply, sat thoughtfully; it was evident his inclinations, his impulses, all tended in the direction of an acceptance of Paul's offer, and yet there was something which withheld him from making the acknowledgment. That the proposal had filled his mind with pleasant thoughts was plain from the satisfaction which pervaded his countenance, but that there was an under-current struggling with the tide was perceptible by his thoughtfulness. Paul watched the changes his features underwent, and after a short pause, exclaimed in a kind tone—

"Let no thought of me intervene with your desire to join Eustace Prior. He is your oldest friend; he has done you many services; he is attached to you as you are to him; he can confer favours and honours you will be proud to receive, and he will be ready to bestow them the moment an opportunity offers. I have no favours to grant in the shape of honours, but what you would receive reluctantly; because though I direct the gift, the hand of America would present it in the way of friendship. I have little in the shape of a heart to bestow on you—all I have is yours; but, Gasket, though the only being I ever loved with the truest devotion has parted with me, upon my adherence to the cause of America in this quarel between the two countries—"

"What—Alice—Miss Alice—wore ship!" cried Gasket, springing to his feet and expressing his astonishment in broken sentences.

"Even so," returned Paul, "I honour her still for her devotion to her country; though I am the sacrifice; I stand alone. Life has little that I care for; nothing to bestow worth receiving. I have nothing in common with the people on board this vessel, and *now* I am fitted to rule them as their commander. As my friend, you have been treated by them with distrust and suspicion; the little my heart has to offer you is inadequate to the want of courtesy of those who have none of your knowledge and not a tithe of your worth. Go to Prior, Gasket; you will be happier with him. I shall neither be offended or hurt at your quitting me. I shall regret it, but it will be because I lose the last friend which links me to old thoughts, old remembrances, and old ties. Go, and I shall stand alone to battle with the world."

"If I do may I be damned!" roared Gasket, grasping Paul's hand, as though he would crush it to powder.

"No, John; I'll stick by you till I lower my peak to death. Now say not a word about it; the offer of the finest frigate that ever swam upon salt water would not make me alter my mind, so it's no use to think about it. I won't hear a word. Hang out the signal for sailing, and I follow in your wake."

Paul tried to remonstrate with the honest seaman, but he would not listen to him, and the subject was therefore dropped, and Gasket, with a delicacy which did honour to his feelings, refrained from putting a single question respecting Alice to our hero, having observed the allusion made by him was made with considerable pain. They took the stroll proposed by Paul round the town, and were everywhere, as soon as the person of Paul became known, greeted with cheers and the greatest enthusiasm; whether it was gratifying to the feelings of Paul it is difficult to say, the thoughts of Alice were too strongly mixed up with his successes to let his reception give him unmixed satisfaction, but Gasket took this popular favour as anything but what it was intended, for he was so convinced that he had done wrong in helping to beat and capture an English vessel, that he would have been delighted if they had met him with threatening brows, gloomy and scowling looks, and indications of hatred and disgust, so that he might have gratified his antipathy to the clamorous Frenchmen, by fighting as many as would stand up to him. Their friendliness to him, their demonstrations of joy, their hurrahs, and endeavours to shake his hand, he took as an insult—a cool, deliberate insult; a barefaced exhibition of delight, for his having raised his hand against his countrymen; he, therefore, received the applause showered upon him by the men, and the bright glances of the women, with neither goodwill or encouragement, and was not long in expressing his anxious desire to return again to the quiet solitude of his berth. Paul complied with his wish, and with the cheers of the noisy multitude, ringing in their ears, they once more took up their abode on board the Ranger.

One of the first acts which Paul did upon his arrival at Brest, was to write a long letter to Lady Selkirk. He exonerated himself from any participation in the seizure of her family plate, and stated the motives with which he landed. He spoke very strongly of the tyrannous and inhuman acts of the English in America, rendering retaliation necessary, in order that the cruelties exercised might be put a stop to. He begged her acceptance of the plate, unrestricted by any condition, expressing his intention of forwarding it to her by the earliest and readiest conveyance. The letter was well dictated, well written, and bore strong evidence of a superior mind. It was sent to her ladyship through the postmaster-general, and was forwarded open, that it might be read by the ministers of England, and even royalty itself; though, in the latter case, there was no hope that any appeal to the heart, however energetic or pathetic, would soften the obduracy of the bigotted monarch towards the American people. It is but just to Paul Jones to say, that it *did have the effect* of making the parliament renounce its sanguinary acts, and exchange, as prisoners of war, those they had deemed and treated as rebels, for the prisoners whom Paul had captured in the drake. Out of his own private purse our hero purchased the plate at the price affixed to it—a heavy one. It may be as well here to state, that although it was not until some time after this that he was enabled to send the plate, yet he did accomplish it, and received a letter of acknowledgment from the Earl of Selkirk, who declined to *accept* it, but was afterwards prevailed upon to alter his determination.

The victory which Paul Jones had achieved over the English vessel, not only created a sensation among the lower orders and middle classes of France, but among the higher orders also. Admiral the Count D'Orvilliers, who was in Brest when Jones arrived, forwarded to the Minister of Marine at Paris, not only a notification of the arrival of our hero at Brest, but also a brilliant account of his achievement, and a handsome panegyric upon it; this was communicated to the King of France, and Louis—the unfortunate Louis XVI., afterwards beheaded by his own people—conceiving an idea, which was afterwards a favourite scheme of Napoleon's, of a descent upon England, sent for Benjamin Franklin, who was then residing in Paris, and requested him to desire Paul's presence at Versailles, expressing his intention of giving him the command of a fine frigate to hoist his flag on board, several frigates to be entirely under his orders, sloops and other vessels conveying troops, in fact, a small squadron. Dr. Franklin obeyed the king's command; he forwarded a very flattering letter to our hero, and in conveying the king's intentions to him, requested him to keep them a profound secret until he was allowed to mention them. It was with pride that Paul received this letter from the great and good Franklin: with a glowing heart he read his warm eulogiums;

praise from him was praise indeed, and the only alloy Paul felt in receiving this mark of approbation and favour was, that Alice would not share it.

He departed from Brest for Paris, Gasket accompanying him, and when he reached the renowned city he was met by Dr. Franklin in the warmest and kindest manner. He was immediately introduced to M. de Sartine, the Minister, who lavished on him the most flattering encomiums, and promised him—too much to be realized. The Indienne, a supurb frigate, was to be instantly put in commission for him, a quantity of frigates and corvettes were named to accompany him, wonders were to be accomplished, and France was to have the honour of purchasing immortality for him. All men, possessing a rather large share of ambition, have their weak points, the point to which their ambition tends being the most particular one; Paul Jones, with as sensible a mind as most men, with a clear and forcible judgement also, was not proof against praise which was not actually undeserved; flattery, which was too well managed to appear fulsome, or promises which held out such prospects of immediately realizing all his expectations. It was natural that he should have been highly gratified—it would have been unnatural if he had not; cold-heartedness was not one of Paul's failings, he was by nature sanguine, and somewhat against his better sense, he fancied that Alice might yet be induced to renounce her resolution against him, might yet receive his hand when she found him standing on the proud pinnicle to which he aspired, covered with honours, the cynosure of all eyes. Once again the ambition, which his separation from her had caused to decline, sprung up again with renewed vigour, and he now longed for the moment to arrive which should place him in command of the squadron, and the troops destined for the descent upon England. But he had to learn the bitter lesson which shows the value of the word or promise of a man in power; in the heat of his enthusiasm he proposed a number of plans to the French goverment—as they were the acting naval power for America, to cripple the power of England. Out of them all, one only was received, which one, even the delatoriness of the French cabinet, did not hesitate upon deciding in favour of. It was to capture the Baltic fleet, richly laden, and escorted only by a single frigate.

Paul obtained his information from some fishermen whom he had captured off the Irish coast previous to his attack on the Drake, and whom he had, with presents, set at liberty, on condition that they gave him information of the above nature. As soon as they obtained it, and for which they were to be remunerated, they sent him the intelligence; he communicated it to the Government, and was instantly dispatched to Brest, but what was his mortification, after travelling there at his greatest speed, to find on his arrival that a notice had been sent to the admiral, and he had dispatched an officer with several frigates. Paul thus anticipated, lost what he calculated to be a glorious opportunity of distinguishing himself, and returned deeply vexed to Paris. It was, however, some satisfaction to him to hear afterwards that the Baltic fleet had been missed through the French officer not having hugged the English coast sufficiently. Paul found himself excessively courted at Paris; everybody desired to make the acquaintance of "he who had beat the English." Among those who sought and strove to gain his acquaintance was the celebrated Marquis de la Fayette—he was young at the period, but of an enlarged mind; he quickly perceived that Paul was as much to be admired for his brains as his courage—for his mental qualifications as well as for his mere dashing bravery, and he became much attached to him. The friendship of the Marquis brought him that of many others; and a young nobleman wrote to him requesting *the honour to serve under him*, protesting that he would rather fight by the side of our hero than in the ranks of the first nobility of France. On all sides was he flattered and caressed; the ladies vying with the gentlemen in seeking his society; but though he behaved with courtesy to all he met, and with gallantry to the ladies, yet there was a canker within which made many of the females view him as cold as the rest of the northerns, little thinking that a volcano raged in his breast beneath. Gasket attended him everywhere, and the glances and sweet sayings which were directed to our hero, but fell short, were recovered and lavished upon his follower, but with considerably less success. Where Paul was cool, Gasket was ice, his dislike to the French was so rooted—so much a part of his nature, his education, his religion, that although he strongly expressed his idea that all women, whatever their country, ought to be viewed as tender, loveable creatures, never to be ill-used, or even thought ill of, yet there was some reservation with regard to the French women, because they were French, for no other reason; he did not deny them their beauty, their sprightliness, but they were French, and that one word was a death blow to their attractions. Their fascinations, their smirks, their pretty ways of courting were all lost upon him; they were French, and his heart was steeled against them. He passed through the ordeal unscathed, and once declared, emphatically, that he "would rather be keelhauled for trouncing an Englishwoman—not that it was in his nature to do such a lubber's trick, God forbid! —than he would kiss the handsomest Frenchwoman who had dropped athwart him; and it must be confessed, they had all alarmingly lovely figure-heads, and an howdashus way of luffing up short athwart your forefoot, or dropping under your lee." Paul, with a smile, admonished him to be careful, or he would find the broadsides from their eyes hotter firing than any he had ever been in.

"I should not be surprised to see you haul down your colours yet to one of these black-eyed, white-teethed, smiling damsels," concluded Paul, with a laugh.

"Ah, John!" said Gasket, shaking his head and looking seriously, "you needn't be afeared of that, they don't carry heavy metal enough to make me strike my colours: mine are nailed to the mast, and I'll sooner sink my ship than haul 'em down to another."

"Another!" replied Paul, with surprise. "I never knew you carried a maiden's colours at your fore. Who is she?—what is she?—where is she?"

"Avast! avast! Paul," cried Gasket, with a face of scarlet, "I—you—that is I meant that—"

"You have been in love a long time and kept it secret," replied Paul, laughing.

"I was going to say, Paul," said Gasket, redder than ever, "that it isn't a Frenchwoman as would make me haul down my ensign or jack. I—when in saying I'd sooner sink my ship than haul down my colours to another, I meant that my colours were nailed to the mast for Englishwomen—that was it, John, I am true to the Eglishwomen, they was what I meant by another.'

"Oh," replied Paul, with affected gravity. He would have proceeded, but he saw there was a strange mixture of painful seriousness in the effort which Gasket made to laugh it off and though he could not account for it, he, from a kind motive, dropped the subject. Gasket a minute after spoke of the sultriness of the weather, of which his face presented a tolerable sample. Paul did not remark it, but Gasket made it an excuse for taking a walk in the air.

A few days subsequent to this, the Marquis Lafayette begged to introduce to the notice of our hero a French gentleman, who had recently been appointed to the command of an American vessel, then fitting out. By some strange accident the name did not transpire until the ceremony of introduction took place, and then both started, for both perceived they had encountered an old acquaintance; Paul, that he saw before him the veritable *Philibert Hercule Rossignol Landais*, and Landais, the Englishman who had tricked him out of his frigate, and consigned him to a small boat on a wide sea. An exclaimation of surprise escaped the lips of both, and the Marquis Lafayette observing it, said—

"*Parbleu!* you have met before?"

"Yes," answered Paul, "I had the honour of meeting Captain Landais on the Atlantic; he will probably remember our meeting and separation."

This was said in a cool, steady tone, and Landais swallowed all his astonishment as quickly, knowing it to be to his interest to keep Paul from relating the events of their meeting, as he had given quite a different account to the government of the transaction. He had been picked up by an American vessel and conveyed to New York. The story he told was that his frigate had been attacked by two English frigates and a corvette; that he had fought to the last, but finding his vessel sinking, he had, with a few devoted followers, taken to the gig, and thus escaped being made prisoners by the English. He knew Paul could give an entirely new version of the affair, and as he found him in such favour—no little to his surprise, for Eustace Prior was the only name he remembered—he felt pretty well assured that his version would be credited, and he would be ruined; he, therefore, gave our hero a very cordial grasp of the hand, and endeavoured to exert the same coolness as Paul displayed.

"Ay, truly," he exclaimed, in support of Paul's remark; "we have met, and had a pleasant bottle of wine together. I'faith I remembered our meeting for some time afterwards."

"I have no doubt of it," returned Paul; "It was enough to fix it indelibly upon the memory of any one placed in your situation."

"You drank deep, I'll be sworn," exclaimed Lafayette, laughing, "you seamen are rare fellows to drink; one would believe that the sight of so much water around you would be an effectual antidote to thirst."

"Rather say a provocative," answered Landais. "By the long eye-lashes of my sweet cousin Lucelle, which are an incentive to passionate adoration, the very sight of salt water produces in me a fever of thirst."

"It must be the brine, then, which causes it," said the marquis, smilingly, to Paul.

"Possibly," returned our hero; "yet *if* it induces thirst, it is rather to my mind like the Mirage in the desert, which gives the semblance of water, but is not available. The sight raises the desire to drink, but the thirst must be quenched by another fluid."

"Always suppposing that fluid to be wine," exclaimed Landais.

"Always," rejoined Paul.

"It is pleasant," observed the marquis, proceeding to broach another subject, "that you have met before, for Captain Landais will command the Alliance, which will be under your orders. For myself, *mon cher ami*, I shall have the command of the troops, and accompany you on board your vessel."

"I am exceedingly gratified to hear it," returned Paul. "Your ministry are acquainted with M. Landais, and are, doubtless, acquainted with his merits sufficiently to place confidence in *him*; I know enough of you, my dear marquis, to be most pleased with the arrangement."

Lafayette shook Paul's hand for the compliment, and expressed his earnestness to serve under him, and at the same time communicated the intentions and wishes of the French king, which as yet had not been conveyed officially to our hero. As their conversation turned into a private communication, a brief "Excuse me if you please," passing from the marquis's lips to Landais, the latter sauntered round the room humming an air, affecting the greatest indifference, waving his handkerchief, and giving out scent enough to have supplied a whole saloon of ladies. He threw himself upon a chair placed opposite an oblong looking-glass, sufficiently long for him to see the whole of his daintily arranged person, and he admired himself with the greatest satisfaction. There was a set in his cravat, a pattern in his ruffles, a style in his coat, a felicitous hue in his stockings, a texture in his small clothes, a freshness in his wig, a brightness in his shoes, a brilliancy in his buckles, a richness in his ornaments, a clearness in his skin, a whiteness in his hands, a magnificence in his vest, a smallness in his feet, a soundness in his calves, a slimness in his waist, a breadth in his shoulders, a languishment in his eyes, a redness in his lips, a whiteness in his teeth, a pinkness in his cheeks, a sweetness in his glances, and a melody in his voice, which almost entranced him. He gazed upon himself and smiled blandly; the effect to him was irresistable. He thought of Narcissus and muttered—Pshaw! He certainly did not think of expiring at the sight of his own loveliness, but he flatered himself there was rather a considerable number of charming, ravishing young damsels that would. The thought insessibly brought to him the semembrance of Florence; her strange repulse of him who was certainly, in his own eyes, too handsome to be ever resisted by any woman that ever breathed, who had a heart; that it was not any demerit in him he was convinced, but fear only on her side of what she should suffer if her husband discovered she had a preference for the enchanting Landais. These thoughts led him on to the recollection of being flung down with outrageous violence by our hero, and as instantly brought to his memory a vow of revenge he had made when exposed in his gig to the fury of the sea, to retaliate upon, Captain Eustache, our hero, and all the crew of the vessel, should it be his fortune ever to fall in with them again. An opportunity seemed to offer now. In having to act in concert with Paul, it would be easy, he speculated, to make his plans fail—to haul him down from the height in public favour he had gained, without committing himself in accomplishing it; he knew the way to manage it, he was delighted with the thought, and found in his shrewdness another point of personal qualification to admire, He, however, resolved not to show his teeth until he could bite, and lolled upon his chair, ever and anon applying a small gold vinaigrette to his nose, fanning himself with his fairy-looking fabric, in the shape of a cambric pocket-handkerchief, and humming forth the air of the most favourite song in the last new opera, looking anything, in fact, but one who was hatching a villanous scheme.

Lafayette having finished his communication, cast his eyes upon Laadais, and then said in a low tone—

"By the way, Monsieur Paul, what of this *Perroquet* Landais; this *Ensoir*. You have met before? what do you know of his capabilities?"

"He can drink wine to an excess, he can lisp trash, and insult women. I have had no opportunity of judging what further he is able to accomplish."

"I judged as much by your remark on his appointment to the Alliance," observed Lafayette, "and with the exception of his being a wind-bibber, which I confess he does not resemble, I feel quite satisfied that you have summed up all his qualities in your brief account of your knowledge of him; for my part I am at a loss to understand what could induce M. de Sartine to give such a perfuming pan the command of a frigate."

"His recommendation, I dare say, was unexceptionable," remarked Paul.

"Why, yes, he has a remarkably pretty cousin, Lucille; it is said that she is either a sister, or a wife married to him when very young; however, De Sartine is not ignorant of her existence or her beauty, nor is she blind to De Sartine's power. One good turn deserves another, and Monsieur Landais is appointed to the Alliance; however, if I possess any influence with his Majesty, I will see whether I cannot get him drafted to another ship."

"Not on my account," observed Paul; "albeit, a quick shrewd captain to obey my orders the moment they are given, would be an advantage to the expedition of no mean consideration; still, I would not have his Majesty think I made any hypercritical interference with his ministers' appointments."

"As you please," replied Lafayette. "The fellow has a reputation for courage; he commanded, some time since, a fine frigate, Le Diable, and maintained a sėvere action for several hours with two English frigates, both superior in size to himself, and a corvette of eighteen guns; the fight was desperate—the frigate was on the point of sinking—she was boarded on both quarters by the frigates, and in the bows by the corvette; his men were mostly killed, and rather than be taken prisoner at this critical moment, a few daring hands by his desire cut the gig adrift, and with only a morsel of provisions, which in the hurry and confusion they were able to lay their hands upon, they trusted themselves to the open sea in their fragile boat, and escaped."

"How is it they were not seen from the decks or mastheads of the English vessels?" inquired Paul, rather astounded at this version of Landais's loss of his frigate.

"Oh, I believe they were too much occupied to notice it," returned the marquis; "besides, night came on, accompanied by a thick fog, which hid them quickly. If any one had been on the watch, I understand, they could not have discovered them."

"You believe this tough story, Marquis?" said Paul, rather sceptically.

"Undoubtedly," replied the Marquis. "Why not? Aha, Monsieur Paul, you are like the rest of the English; you think us rather a talking than a brave people."

"Indeed, you mistake me," exclaimed Paul; "of all enemies the English have, the least despised foe is the French. They think it a trifle to conquer the people of any other nation, but an honour to defeat the French; and they have cause. No, Monsieur le Marquis, I made no allusion to your people in doubting the story; it was to the man, not the nation."

"You were not, perhaps, far-wrong in having the doubt in that case," returned La Fayette, with a laugh. "It is hard to believe a trim-painted puppet can be a very terribly brave man; however, we shall, perhaps, have an opportunity of judging of the sweet smelling captain's merits when he gets alongside an enemy."

"Not, I hope, to find too late that there was too much cause for the doubt," observed Paul.

"Parbleu, no!" exclaimed La Fayette, quickly, "I will make further inquiry; and if there be cause for mistrusting his capabilities or his courage, Monsieur *Le Encensoir* shall convoy a few spice vessels from the Indies, but not join *our* expedition."

A few more words finished the colloquy, and once more they entered into conversation with Philibert Hercule Rossignol Landias; they were not aware that effected and highly perfumed gentleman had overheard nearly every word of their conversation, nor did he intend to let them have any idea that he had, and therefore when they returned to him, he welcomed them with a soft smile, and hoped that he had not been any bar to their conference, assuring them, if they required further confidential communication, he would instantly retire, and return when they concluded. They begged him to keep his seat; and Paul, with the intention of drawing him out, congratulated him upon his appointment to the Alliance, and being engaged in an expedition in which there would be much hard fighting and plenty of honour to be gained.

"It is that one consideration," returned Landais, "which made me exert with M. de Sartine the most powerful interest I have."

"The eyes and wheedling tongue of *la jolie Lucille*," muttered Lafayette.

"I was satisfied," continued Landais, "that in whatever affair Monsieur Paul Jones was engaged, who ever followed him would be highly distinguished, and have a share of the laurels with which he would be covered. My imagination was fired at the idea of accompanying him, and I rested not until I obtained the appointment."

Paul bowed to the compliment; and the marquis, with an ironical laugh exclaimed—

"Really, Landais, I should have hardly supposed you had an affection for fighting."

"Why, Monsieur le Marquis," inquired Landais, a little abruptly, fancying this a small reflection upon his courage.

"Oh! simply because your exterior befits you, to my mind, more for the bower and the boudoir, the saloon and the promenade, rather than the quarter-deck of a fighting ship," returned the marquis. "Your voice, too, soft and melodious as it is, is rather fitted to whisper tender vows in the small ears of fair demoiselles, than to brawl through the hoarse trumpet to your men when aloft."

"You flatter, monsieur," returned Landais, with a gratified air. I acknowledge my outward appearance is not of a rough seaman. But I cannot, for the life of me, discover why the captain of a vessel should not be as well attired on board his ship as the colonel of a regiment upon parade. He has not the duty of a common man, he has not to lay out upon a yard, or to man a capstan-bar; his duty lies with his head, not with his hands, and consequently requires no disarrangement or disregard of the person to perform his functions. For myself, I acknowledge I carry the feeling perhaps a little to excess, but we are all liable to have some point upon which we are weak—that is mine. I do assure you, messieurs, I am like Sardanapalus, the Assyrian monarch—I am gentle, luxurious, indolent, nay, almost effeminate, in peace; but in war, whether in boarding an English vessel of greater size than my own, in directing the broadsides, in fighting hand to hand with an enemy, I believe, having proved myself already, that I can make as good a warrior as most men who aspire to that distinction. Such, I believe, Monsieur Paul Jones, you will find me. Messieurs, I pray you for the present excuse me; I have a small affair upon my hands which I would not set aside upon any consideration; I am always to be heard of in the Rue St. Honore. Monsieur le Marquis, I kiss your hand; Monsieur Paul Jones, esteem me your most devoted."

With these words upon his lips he ambled out of the room at a gentle trot, followed by the eyes both of our hero and the marquis, with an expression of cool contempt playing in them.

"The man is an ass," muttered the marquis; "we must have one we can depend upon to command the Alliance. This fellow would be thinking of the set of his wig or the shape of his nose, instead of fighting. I will appeal to the king."

"Do not be premature, marquis," said Paul; "let us not sow discord ere we depart. The man has interest with the minister—"

"The most powerful—a woman's!" interrupted the marquis, with a smile.

"It will not be wise, therefore, to interfere with the appointment," continued Paul; "I will place him in such a position that his conduct cannot materially affect the success of my plans, and therefore we will not hazard the warmth the minister displays in the expedition by seeking to reverse one of his appointments."

"You are right, Monsieur Paul," returned Lafayette, "your reasoning is conclusive, I subscribe to it; let us talk no more of this civet cat, Landais, but pay a visit with me to the Tuileries, there are a number of friends most anxious to make your acquaintance. All I ask of you is to beware of your heart, there will be a tremendous assault made upon it; the heavy battery of direct looks, light artillery of smiles and glances, platoon firing of sighs, and a gunnery of innuendoes and sly speeches, which if you have the courage to withstand the attack and come off triumphant, I can only say you are fitted to conquer a world. Alexander would have been afraid to attempt."

"I will do my best to sustain the attack as becomes a brave man," returned Paul, laughing, "and trust that fortune will not be less kind in keeping me clear of these destructive schooners and frigates than she has already those of the English nation."

"Let us hope so," returned the marquis. "*Allons, mon cher ami.*"

No man, especially a stranger, could have been more flattered or caressed than was Paul at this period; he could scarcely himself credit that a simple

action with an English vessel, in which, after a hard struggle, he had proved victorious, should have lifted him up to the admiration of a nation so suddenly, but so completely, and it was with the most sanguine expebtations that he looked forward for the ensuing expedition, to obtain a name as great as renown could make it, to become almost an eighth wonder—would Alice refuse him then? It is not to be wondered at, that he should have entertained these feelings; he was not egotistical, but he was ambitious; he knew what he had done, he fancied what he could do if he had proper support, and there is little doubt if he had been well supported, he would have been a Nelson. He perpetually heard praises from all sides, from men whom he might believe, from women whose looks and actions, at least, proved them sincere; he was applauded and cheered when he appeared in public, and crowds followed him soliciting his appearance at their houses, and pressing for invitations wherever they knew he was to be present; it should hardly create surprise, therefore, that he was affected by all that flattery and caressing, but notwithstanding the brilliant prospects held out to him, he soon discovered that all was not gold that glittered. He found that various excuses and delays were made with respect to the vessels which were to form his squadron—a delay was made in their equipment; some officers refused to serve under Paul Jones, and others were appointed in their place. A cabal had evidently been formed against him, but by whom he could not discover; nothing was said or done against him openly. He was still the lion of Paris and the Parisians; but notwithstanding his popular favour, he was unable, in spite of repeated urgings, to find that arrangements for his expedition were completed; he was put off from time to time with various excuses, and the warmest protestations of regard and anxiety for his interests, but not a step was taken to advance it. At length it got bruited abroad what was the expedition he was about to undertake; he had kept it an inviolable secret, and was much enraged to find it in everybody's mouth. Who the discloser was, it was difficult to ascertain, and, to his considerable annoyance, he more than once heard himself pointed out as the man. This, whenever and wherever he had the opportunity, he denied; but the object of the discloser was gained, for the king finding it made known, declined following up the plan he had laid out for Paul to pursue. This was the more distracting, as the squadron was nearly ready for sea. The first news which Paul received of this disheartening determination of the king was in a letter from the Marquis Lafayette, who was to command the troops with him; he told him the king had commanded him to prevent the embarkation of the troops, and to join his regiment. He expressed his deepest regret at the unfortunate event, and his sorrow that even his regret was of no avail, the king's command was not to be disobeyed, and he must submit to his fate. At the time Paul received this communication, he also received another; it was written in English and ran thus:—

"Sir,

"It rarely happens that a man passes through his life without at some period receiving a great surprise. I believe the hour has come for yours. On perusing this letter I shall be much mistaken if you do not agree with me. I shall not write to you in my own name, for I feel that there are many bitter associations connected with it, both in respect to you and myself; I shall, therefore, write in the name of one who is, I have every reason to believe, as dear to you as to myself—as the father of Alice Manners, I address you."

Paul's eyes glittered at the word, and his hand trembled; he read on with avidity.

"Circumstances, the state of my daughter's health not being the least of them, have induced me to alter my opinion respecting you, and my future views for Alice. I have just arrived in Paris, and am staying at a private hotel, the Hotel du Nord, Rue Richelieu. Your locality was easily ascertainable, and I have lost no time in writing to you, to request the favour of an interview with you at your earliest convenience. I breakfast at ten precisely; if I remember rightly, you are an early riser, and are fond of a walk before your morning's meal. I shall breakfast at home every morning this week, and shall partake of it with an additional zest if you share it with me. For the present, adieu. Believe me yours sincerely; once your friend, once your foe, but now an aspirant for an affectionate tie, which no division of feeling can sunder."

Paul read and re-read this note a hundred times. He summoned the servant, and, upon inquiry, found it had been brought by a servant in English livery, who merely left it without saying a word respecting it. With a beating heart Paul once more perused its contents; the seal he scrutinised; the coronetted crest he could not be deceived in; the handwriting he recognised—it was the hand of Alice's farther. But what could be the meaning of this extraordinary change in his sentiments? He determined, come what might, he would keep the appointment, and at least endeavour to discover his motive for thus writing to him. He accordingly, the next morning—having attired himself with great care—having, with pardonable vanity, dressed himself in his commodore's uniform—directed his steps to the Rue Richelieu, and arriving at the Hotel du Nord, he gave his name, and was instantly, with the greatest respect, ushered into a superbly-furnished apartment. Sure enough he saw the father of his beloved Alice, seated at a breakfast table, and on his entering, the old gentleman instantly rose from his chair, advanced towards him, and held out both his hands with all the warmth of one who met and welcomed an old and dear friend after a long absence. Paul, however, bowed stiffly, kept a firm hold of his hat with one hand, and the other resolutely by his side. The old man was nothing daunted, but welcomed him, smilingly, to a chair.

"I flatter myself, Captain Paul, or, as you are better known here, Commodore Jones, that I have given you the greatest surprise you ever received;" and he laughed gleefully.

"That you have surprised me, and that extraordinarily, I confess," returned Paul, coldly; "but I must first know your motive, and the probable result of our interview, ere I acknowledge you have succeeded in completely surprising me."

"I do not despair," Commodore Jones, of making you acknowledge before we separate, that I have not only surprised you more than ever you were before, and more than you are likely to be again, but that surprise shall be a most agreeable one, too."

Paul bowed stiffly, though barely able to keep the anxiety he felt to know the nature of the communication he was about to hear from making itself visible.

"I have to thank you," continued the old gentleman, "for the immediate attention which you have paid to my request. I yesterday sent to you, desiring your presence any morning this week at my breakfast table; you are here this morning. I expected no less from your generosity, and am much gratified that I am not deceived."

"I school myself to habits of business," returned Paul, still preserving his coolness. "My time is much occupied with matters connected with the American government, and were I not to pay immediate attention to any private affair when the opportunity offers, so long a time might elapse ere I could attend to it, that a charge might rest against me of neglect. I am at your service, sir; whatever you wish to communicate you will oblige me by at once making me acquainted with it."

"Pray be seated, Commodore Jones," exclaimed the old gentleman, pressingly; "you have not breakfasted?"

"I left word at my hotel that I should return to breakfast," said Paul.

"Then, my dear friend, you must disappoint the people," he observed. "Nay, I will take no refusal. Ho, who waits there?" he cried in a loud voice.

A full-dressed lacquey made his appearance.

"We will have breakfast," exclaimed the old gentleman, whom we shall for the future call Mr. Manners; "let it be instantly placed upon the table."

The man bowed and disappeared.

"There has been disagreement between us, Commodore," said Mr. Manners to our hero; "it has been rancorous and bitter; but as sometimes the greatest enemies make the closest friends, so let us hope that I may yet be upon terms of the greatest friendship with you. I pray you be seated; believe me I am sincere in the expression of good feeling towards you; pay me at least the courtesy of sitting and listening to me. I acknowledge you have some reason to doubt me, but I can assure you, in the present instance, you may believe me without a fear of being deceived."

"Mr. Manners, I do not fear your deceiving me; I trust to my own judgment to secure me from that," returned Paul. "I may lay some claim to a right of doubting the truth of your good intentions towards me from past occurrences, and to the same cause you must attribute my inability to meet you with the frankness and cordiality of one who held you in high esteem; but, sir, I will listen to you with patience whatever your proposal may be. I shall be guided only by a strict sense of honour in my assent or dissent to it. Proceed, sir."

He seated himself as he spoke, and Mr. Manners was about to commence, when the servants made their appearance with the coffee, and the old gentleman instantly said—

"I think talking much at meals bad for digestion, especially if the subject be interesting. One is too apt to be discussing the merits of the question rather than the merits of the edibles. We will, if you please defer our conference until we have disposed of the breakfast."

"As you please," was Paul's rejoinder.

A few common-place subjects were started by the old gentleman while the repast was being partaken of, and discussed by Paul with an indifference which his thoughts, constantly tending to one subject, prevented him from actually feeling. The meal was soon despatched; and when the servants were clearing away, Mr. Manners said to them—

"Let me not be disturbed by any one until this gentleman departs; so long as he remains I cannot be seen by any one."

The servants bowed in acquiesence, and quitted the room. As soon as Mr. Manners found himself alone with our hero, he said—

"I know that time is a precious commodity with you government people, and, therefore, I will not detain you very long; let us come to the point at once."

"You will be favouring me by doing so," responded Paul.

"To do you favour or service is my warmest desire," said the old gentleman, "I shall be delighted at any and every opportunity, I do assure you. You naturally think this strange, after having so long expressed myself in such strong terms against you: but to the point. Many years have elapsed since you dragged me from the verge of that mysterious Rubicon which divides life from death. I was upon its brink when you rescued me, and brought me back to life. For that act you merited, and you had, my warmest thanks. I was not lost to the depth of the obligation, nor was I undesirous of rewarding it; I thought of a thousand ways to remove you from the station in which fate had placed you, and instal you in a higher one, in which your natural capabilities, would have found a wide and honourable field for displaying themselves, and raise you to the height it was my opinion you deserved—but of my intentions I will say little; it is enough that they were frustrated in the outset. At the time you rescued me from a watery grave, you saved the life of my daughter, and she was grateful to an extent far exceeding my expectations and my wishes; not that I would have had her feel cool and indifferent to the obligation she, conjointly with myself, was under to you, but the mode she took of displaying her sense cf it was opposed to my designs for her, at that time more particularly, and to illustrate that point efficiently, it is sufficient that I should make an acknowledgment exceedingly humiliating to me."

"I require no such confession, sir," interrupted Paul; "I beg of you to spare both yourself and me."

"Nay; it is necessary that you should know the motives influencing my conduct to you," said Mr. Manners.

"I do not require it," observed Paul.

"But it is due to myself," persisted the old gentleman; "I would not have you believe it was mere caprice, or even that it was the bare dislike to my daughter's wedding with one—you will pardon me—whose blood was not so high as her own, that made me so enraged on discovering your love for each other. No, sir, with shame I confess it; I was one night at the house of a nobleman, a friend of mine, induced to play; I won rather largely; a night or two subsequent, I was desired to give the gentleman, of whom I won, his revenge; I did, and the consequence was, that in addition to seven thousand pounds which I had already won, I rose from the table fifteen thousand pounds more the winner. He came immediately afterwards into possession of an hundred thousand pounds; he still demanded his revenge; I could not refuse to give it him, and still I continued the winner, until, at last, I won sixty thousand pounds of him. I then refused to play any more, but he reproached and taunted me; we continued, until the whole of his fortune became mine. He then staked his house, he lost it; his estates, they became mine—his furniture, library, books, plate, carriages, horses, all became mine—he was beggared. He uttered a wild cry of dispair, and was about to rush from the room, when he suddenly stopped, and cried out—"there is the harness belonging to my horses, stake a single carriage against it." I would have refused, but there was an expression in his face which compelled my assent—it was white to deathliness—his teeth were set together, his eyes rolled wildly, and his aspect was more that of a fiend than of a human being. I consented, I staked the carriage—he won it—again he staked it against the remaining carriages—these he won; he staked them against his furniture—fortune declared for him. To make my story short, the harness won him back his house, furniture, estates, plate—everything, in fact, of that description which he had lost. He stuck close to the table—I would have removed; but no, he was not gorged with play yet. Now he staked *all* he had won back, including the harness, against twenty thousand pounds—he won it. He shrieked with joy—*his turn had come.* We staked sum after sum, both mad. I now began to feel the agony which had possessed him; I staked madly, and looked eagerly for the fall of the dice; fortune was against me—out of one hundred and twenty-thousand pounds, which I had won of him, ten only remained. We threw for the sum—he won. He would now have left off; but no, I was stung by my osse . I demanded the continuance of the play; he won the first stake. I doubled it—he won; again I doubled it, and lost; doubled again, he again was the winner. With frenzy I doubled and doubled my stake; he won, won, won, perpetually won, until I rose the loser of fifty-thousand pounds—all the ready money I had in the world. I did not, though frenzied at my loss, pursue the play, so that my house, estates, and other property were hazarded as his were; the loss of the money was sufficient; for my estates were mortgaged, and yielded me but a scanty income. I will do the gentleman with whom I played, the justice to state that, when I declared I would not play longer, he pressed my reluctant hand, and said that having now given me my revenge, if I would accept the fifty thousand he had won of me as a mark of his esteem, I should be conferring a favour upon him. I could not accede to it, my rank would not permit it; I, however, borrowed twenty thousand pounds, for which he would take nothing but my note of hand, and then, before he quitted the table, he went down upon his knees, and swore a fearful oath that he would never play again. I did not imitate his action, but I made the same oath, and would have kept it, but—"

"I have heard you patiently, sir," interrupted Paul; "but I am at a a loss to discover what connection your confession has with my attachment to your daughter."

"I am just coming to it," he replied; "this affair occurred shortly after you saved my life, and upon one occasion this gentleman called upon me—he saw my daughter, and fell in love with her; he made proposals for her, and I gladly consented, for there was but a puny sickly boy between him and a dukedom. He commenced paying his addresses; but after his second visit, he told me one morning that he must withdraw his pretensions for my daughter's hand, for upon having an interview alone with her, she had very candidly told him her heart was already engaged to another—that she could never love him, and begged him, as a man of honour, to spare her the persecution of addressing her, when there existed no possibility of her rewarding his perseverance by her hand. It was like a thunder-clap to me; for a moment I could not speak; at length I found my voice—I put a thousand questions to him—I asked him I scarcely know what—he could give me no other information than he had already. I vowed that she should wed him, bnt he would not suffer it, and decidedly told me he had passed his word of honour never to repeat the subject to her, and with a few more observations he left me. That night he set off for Italy, and I commenced the attempt to discover who it was who had thwarted my dearest wishes; for, as you can well understand, an alliance with my wealthy friend, bound as I was to him, was most desirable. I questioned Alice at first by hint and inuendo; when I failed by indirect questions I proceeded to direct ones; she did not deny that she had given her affections to another, but she would not discover who that person was—I grew furious, and she firm—the more I threatened, the more decided she became, and then I tried appeals, and then she wept, but still she kept her secret. I tried other means—I watched her—I followed her everywhere, You I never suspected, never dreamed of, until one day I noticed you walking together, it struck me there was something more in the manner of both than mere friendliness—it might, perhaps, have been that I was then suspicious of everybody, and fancied things which had no foundation for my conjecture—howbeit, I followed you to the sitting-room. I then overheard what I will confess made my eyes extend with wonder. I could scarcely credit my ears, for, to the last moment, I could not believe there was really any ground for suspicion, until I actually heard you tell her you loved her, and she acknowledged that she returned it. The most fearful passion shook me, for to her marriage with some wealthy suitor did I look to retrieve my shattered fortunes, and now was that about to be dashed to the ground! How were all my fond speculations of preserving my name and rank without slur upon the verge of being completely destroyed! I waited to hear but little ere I burst in upon you both. What I said you may remember better than I can. I uttered all that passion prompted. I was unable to hesitate at a single expression ere it quitted my lips; and, knowing your courage and spirit, I wonder that you showed me the forbearance you did. I have frequently since been astonished that you did not fell me to the earth; but I can believe it was for my child's sake that you held your hand. After that interview, and forbidding you to enter my house, an evil destiny once more placed me in a position which helped to pluuge me still further in difficulties. I was at a party of nobles—once more play was introduced—I tried to be excused, but a royal duke pressed me to cut in. I dared not refuse—I played—the stakes were high—I lost, and lost until I was engulphed in destruction. I quitted the table a beggar—I entirely mortgaged my estates, and with the wreck left from the sale of a few valuables, I paid a visit to an old friend in Spain, carrying my daughter with me. My title I dropped, and took the name of Manners, for I could not appear as a nobleman without a guinea to keep up the dignity. I had been there a short time when I met with the gentleman to whom I owed twenty thousand pounds; he was now the Duke of D——, and possessed of enormous wealth. During a brief conversation, I alluded to my daughter—I found that he still loved her, and was unwedded. I engaged that my daughter should give him her hand of her own free will—I told him she had been led away by a romantic imagination—that she had seen her folly, and was now ready to confess that she had mistaken a mere flight of fancy for love—that her heart was free and disengaged. He listened eagerly, and declared his readiness to renew his proposals to her, if, after an interview with her, he found that I had not deceived him. I agreed to it; I told him he should judge for himself, and named a time when he should meet her. I hoped so to work upon her feelings by my distressful situation that she would readily consent to sacrifice her wishes to the honour of her family. I hastened to her—I explained everything. I told her we were both beggars, and that I had laid aside my title for that reason alone, and not, as I had previously told her, for the sake of avoiding the impertinent curiosity of persons while we were travelling. I showed to her how my name, as a man of honour and principle, would be redeemed by her consenting to my wish. I placed before her our exact position at that moment—how impossible it was to ever retrieve our position if she did not consent. I exhorted, I implored, and conjured her by every sacred tie to comply with my wish. She was agonized at what she heard—poor girl! she was terribly agonized, her whole frame shook convulsively, and several times I thought she would have fainted; but she had a strong mind, and by a powerful exertion she threw off the struggling emotion, and appeared calm. Her face was white, but it was as calm as an unruffled lake. I believed I had conquered, and I listened with burning anxiety for her reply. It came—how can I describe my feelings when I heard her say in measured tones—

"If my happiness alone were the sacrifice you ask of me, to save the honour of our family I would grant it freely and readily—you should not hear a sigh from me, or know that I repined at a fate which was hourly carrying me to the grave: but when there is another's wrapped up in it, it leaves me but one path to pursue."

"And that?" I asked with a parched throat.

"Is to refuse your request. I do it sorrowfully, with exceeding pain," she answered, "but I cannot, even to save the name of our family from the taunting mouths of the multitude, consent to condemn another to the misery of a broken heart; but, sir, I will promise you this upon oath, I will never marry without your consent."

"To this reply I poured forth a torrent of invectives—a volley of imprecations; in fact, at that moment I was mad, but though my fury seemed to terrify her, it did not move her from the determination she had formed, and I was obliged at last to quit her, having obtained only her oath that she would not wed without my consent. The succeeding hours I passed burnt up with mad thoughts, until evening, when I resolved to have another interview, and try and prevail upon her to see the Duke of D—— without stating to him what her intentions were. I found you with her. I concluded at once that you had followed us—that it was under the influence of your persuasions that she refused to obey me, and I confess I was frantic when I cast my eyes upon you."

"I feel it but justice to myself and to Alice, to state," said Paul, who had listened to Mr. Manners with the utmost attention, "that the decision to which she had come was influenced by no persuasion or wish of mine, directly o indirectly; it sprung from her own nobility of heart. At that time no one

could have felt more deeply the disparity of our positions than did I; and though I confess my heart would have been seared for ever, I tried to induce her to forget me; but as I would not—as I could not acknowledge I should not feel her marriage with another with the most agonising bitterness, she would not give her hand where she could not give her heart."

"I can believe you," replied Mr. Manners. "Well, sir, I was compelled to send a note to the duke; I gave up all hope, after seeing you, of persuading her to obey my wishes. I stated to him, that my desire to have him for a son-in-law, had led me to mistake my daughter's feelings; I begged his pardon, and took a farewell of him as well as I could manage it. At this time I received a letter from an agent, telling me a relation had bequeathed me some possessions in the West Indies, and advised me to send over a person upon whom I could depend to look after them. I determined to go myself, principally because I hoped the time such a journey would occupy would wean Alice's thoughts from you. I quitted Lisbon for Porto Rico, Alice accompanied me, and we arrived safely there. I had not been there long, before an old acquaintance of mine crossed my path; we had been friends at college. He had quitted England for the Indies when young, and the climate had helped to make him an older man than myself, though he was younger in years than I. He was single, and the sight of Alice determined him to wed; he was a millionaire. I could not object, the more especially as my new possessions were far below my expectations. I began gently with her, but there was the same obstinacy as before. My old friend had none of the scruples of the Duke of D———; he cared not about her being in love with any one, so that he married her. He paid his addresses to her; she refused him—nay, spurned him. I trembled for the destruction of this new hope, but he laughed, and said her spirit only endeared her the more to him. A plan was laid, by which it was hoped to induce her to consent. The most plausible story was invented of your death; men were hired who were to swear to the fact of having seen you perish by shipwreck; everything was carefully done; documents forged—even a letter to her was written."

"That alone would have betrayed you," said Paul, smiling, though he could not help feeling a disgust at the villany thus almost coolly acknowledged. "We had agreed never to write to each other, but in such characters as only we knew."

Perhaps it might," returned the old man, "but that we never tried, for all our long laboured schemes were frustrated by your appearance amongst us; a ghost could not have more astonished me than your presence at Porto Rico again. I grossly insulted you."

"And, for Alice's sake, I respected you," said Paul, emphatically.

"I feel it deeply," returned Mr. Manners, with a low bow, and then resumed: "I hastened to my friend, Goldeye; I told him of your presence, and it was then agreed for all of us to go to England. I was to appear to be so deadly offended with Alice, that I would not speak to her. I was at once to ship her off to England, with the understanding that I staid behind to settle some affairs respecting my property there; that Goldeye had given up his claim to her hand, and would remain where he was. At the same time, Goldeye instantly wound up his affairs, put all his property on board the Penelope, which was to bear Alice to England, and he and I were to follow, about a month afterwards, in another vessel. What followed this determination you are aware of; Goldeye accompanied me to England, but his health received a shock by the change of climate, and he hastened at once to Cheltenham. Upon the arrival of my daughter, I repaired to my Scottish estate, which, by funds raised from the Indian plantations, I had redeemed from the mortgages held upon it. Still you followed me, and, to effectually get rid of you, I descended to an act which I have ever since repented of—an act which levelled me in my own esteem, which degraded my honour, and for which I humbly beg your pardon."

"I would to God you had never committed that act!" exclaimed Paul, with vehemence. "Heaven! what I might have been spared if you had not —but no matter, it is done, and cannot be recalled."

"But say you pardon and forgive me!" exclaimed Mr. Manners, in a humble tone; "let me hear you say—even though you can never forget it, for that I could not expect—that you forgive me; for my daughter's, for Alice's sake, John Paul, you forgive me," he concluded, in a solemn tone.

Paul turned his head away, and for a moment was silent. "Presently," he exclaimed, in a voice of deep feeling, "for her sake—by the memory of all that beloved one has endured for me, for which, may Almighty God shower down the greatest happiness upon her now and for ever!—in her name, and for her sake, I expunge from my memory a deed which has done much to render me hopelessly wretched for ever."

There was a pause for some minutes, and then the old gentleman took Paul's hand and wrung it, and, in a low tone of voice, said—

"I thank you from the bottom of my soul. I have but to say, in judging my conduct, place yourself in my situation. I was a father. It is the fashion to look upon all fathers as hard-hearted tyrants; and why? because they occasionally happen to have different views respecting the future position of their children to what those children may have themselves. Is it to be supposed that a father, who shows an anxiety for the welfare of his child is therefore hard-hearted—therefore a tyrant? Is the trouble, the anxiety, the care of rearing, nothing? Is the expense of tuition, of procuring the means whereby they shall appear as the admired of all admirers, nothing? Is the attention, the devotion paid to them in illness, in weakliness, and even in ruddy health, worthy of no reward? Is the heart which has been theirs from childhood to maturity, guiding them through the mazes of ignorance, leading them from the paths of danger, and carefully directing their steps to future happiness, to be stigmatised as hard and tyrannous, because it prevents them following a track which must end in misery? Is all the tenderness with which they have been watched, nurtured, and brought to man or womanhood, to be trampled on and forgotten, because the romantic imaginings of youth are interfered with—because the experienced eyes of one, tenacious of their future well-being, would check their headlong career along a path, which can only be attended with unhappiness? Can he be a tyrant who, forseeing danger to his child, would do his best to save it? Is he worthy of hatred who, having seen through the course of a long life the misery attached to marriages, where the position of the parties are unequal, should endeavour to the utmost to prevent his child forming such a connexion? Is his anxiety, his earnest endeavours to promote such a match as he is well assured will produce, at least, content—a match where want can never be known? for you know the old saying, that 'when poverty walks in at the door, love flies out of the window.' Is his strong desire to place his daughter in a position where she will be respected, and never know the wretchedness attendant upon griping penury, a proof of his obduracy, his harshness, his tyranny? Are all his hopes, his fond speculations, his dreams of her happiness, his yearnings for her welfare, which with such solicitude, he has, from her infancy, looked forward to, to be thrust aside, and treated with disdain, simply because he would have those hopes fully carried out? Is the reward of all his care and affection to be hatred and disgust? Is it natural, sir—is it just? And yet it is almost universally the case. A father rears his child tenderly, he spares neither pains nor expense upon her education, he lavishes his affection upon her—she is his darling, his pride; she is the heiress to his fortune, to a name of honour—she is accomplished, she is lovely, possessing all the attributes of person and of mind, which make her the honour and pride of the family. She is fit for a throne, and the fondness of his heart thinks of nothing but a high destiny for her, where all his care and anxiety will be rewarded by seeing her grace the circle which her beauty and accomplishments eminently fit her to preside over—when lo! he discovers she has formed some attachment with a fel—with a person infinitely below her rank, her wealth; in short, in every degree her inferior. She is young, and, therefore, obstinate. She has been used to every luxury, without knowing how it has been obtained, and she is quite prepared for love and a cottage, without having an idea that it requires something more than fairy hands to stock it. She belives, doubtless, that she could be happy with him for whom she has formed this silly and romantic attachment, even in poverty; but she has got to learn what poverty is, and when the lesson is learned, she then discovers that there was something like a shadow of reason, even of affection, in the endeavours of a father to save her from it; but previous to her understanding this hard truth, she forgets all her father has done for her—she wipes out from her memory every act of kindness, of solicitude, of tenderness and devotion; she looks only upon this one act of his—this really strongest proof of his affection for her—with eyes of aversion; esteeming it the most abominable exercise of despotism, the iron hearted deed of a soul callous to softer emotions, the tyrannous act of one who takes the advantage of his being her father, to effectually destroy the happiness *she expects to have* with this chosen youth of her heart, for ever, and takes the first opportunity of showing her sense of it by abandoning his roof, wedding with her lover, and then expects to be at once forgiven. If forgiveness is denied, 'the inexorable old tyrant,' her father, is viewed with greater aversion than ever his stern hard-heartedness is—perhaps, cursed; the right to exercise natural feelings is denied to him, and he is remembered only by her upon whom he has lavished years of tenderest love and devotion, as one who has ever been a deadly foe to her happiness."

"Your remarks are, to a certain extent, just," exclaimed Paul; "but not entirely. You place too much to the account of the father."

"Indeed! has a father no right to a voice in the disposal of his daughter's hand?" asked Mr. Manners.

"I do not deny that he has what may be termed a prescriptive right," returned Paul; "but of that anon—you speak of the long attention and devotion of years to the child commanding a corresponding reward, by giving you the power to dispose of her hand as you please; do you forget it was an act of yours, independent of any consideration for her future welfare, which brought her into the world? Do you deny a right you have, when she has come into the world, a helpless thing, to foster and cherish her?"

"No," replied Mr. Manners.

"Is it a consideration more for her future welfare than the support of your own pride, that you educate her for the position in which you move?" asked Paul. "Would you, as a nobleman, feel it consistent with your dignity to give her the education of a poor tradesman's child? Would you not be ashamed to suffer her to receive only the plainest tuition, when your station demanded the possession of every accomplishment?"

"Why—a—not exactly," returned Mr. Manners.

"Then," continued Paul, "it is a motive of self-pride which induces you to procure the means whereby she shall be the 'admired of all admirers,' stronger than any consideration for her advancement and happiness, and when she is growing up, supposing these things were tokens only of your esteem and devotion, do you have no reward in her innocent prattle, in her affectionate conduct to you, in her little endearments, even in the progress you see her make in the accomplishments you are bestowing upon her, have you no reward in this?"

"True," replied the old man; "but suppose, by way of example, you had planted a seed in the earth, that seed produced a small flower, green and delicate, but giving promise of a splendid blossoming—supposing that it was the pride of the garden—that you watched and tended it hourly, trimming it, keeping all weeds from it, and raising it with the greatest attention and affection into a beautiful plant—and supposing, when it had just reached its perfection—when it was in its pride and loveliest time, the hand of some rude gardener came and robbed you of it, because he took a fancy to it, are you to be considered a hard-hearted wretch because you do your best to prevent him?"

"Suppose, to continue your simile," said Paul, "that the flower had the power of feeling—suppose that it 'took a fancy' to that gardener, and would rather be with him, and could be happier in his humble plot of ground than in your gorgeous parterre—suppose that, if it remained with you to be transplanted at your will to a hothouse, the very atmosphere of which it hated—where it was sure it would pine and perish—would you be able to justify your affection for it by preventing it becoming the property of the gardener? You have given me an old proverb, permit me to give you another. 'When the dance is to be for life, we ought to choose our own partners;' and thus, I think that, when the future happiness is at stake, for the destiny of a married life embraces it, all the right of giving or withholding her hand should rest with her. I cannot but see that the whole tenor of your remarks apply to my affection for your daughter, and they bring me to this conclusion, that having discovered, by obstinate opposition to the wishes of Alice—by contumely, reproaches, and unjust and oppressive acts to me, you have failed in gaining your object, you have, therefore, resolved to try what mildness and appeals will do to make me give up—"

"You mistake me," eagerly exclaimed Mr. Manners, "I have no such thought. No, no; what I have said has been done with a view of justifying myself in your eyes for my conduct towards you. I would not have you suppose that, after you had saved mine and my daughter's life, I could have been so violently set against you by anything but the complete destruction of hopes I had formed for her—"

"And yourself!" exclaimed Paul.

"A—a—well—commingled with my own views," returned the old gentleman, with a little embarrassment. "I respected you, but you were at that time, the more especially, considering my embarrasments, not exactly in a position to become my son-in-law, as, without meaning offence, you may be aware."

Paul bowed, and said, frankly—

"I was so fully convinced of it, that I made up my mind not, under any circumstances, to wed her until I could demand her hand. Had I not made the resolve, I should have been your son-in-law long since."

"That you have behaved honourably, most honourably, as few young men placed in your situation would have done," returned Mr. Manners, "I am quite satisfied, and that knowledge has led me to pursue my present course with respect to you and my daughter. It may, perhaps, be necessary to tell you, that my old friend, Goldeye, died some time since at Cheltenham, bequeathing to Alice the whole of his fortune; it is an immense one, being between four and five hundred thousand pounds, every sixpence of which she has the sole and undisputed control of."

"He has left you a handsome legacy?" inquired Paul.

"Why—a, not exactly," returned Mr. Manners, playing with his fingers, "some five hundred guineas or so, and a few trifles. Alice has all."

"Without any person having any voice in its disposal?" remarked Paul, eyeing Mr. Manners earnestly.

"Ye—yes, she has it all entirely her own, to do exactly what she pleases with," he replied, assuming an air of frankness; "but that is of little consequence compared with her marriage with you. I find opposition useless; years, change of scene—everything I have tried has proved inadequate to wean the heart from you; no maiden on earth could be more devoted to a man than she has been to you."

"I do believe it," exclaimed Paul, enthusiastically."

"The sickness of hope deferred, is, I find, wearing her constitution out," continued the old gentleman. "She is evidently pining away; she will be happy with no one but you; and, as her happiness, I find, rests solely and entirely upon you, I have determined to waive all my former scruples, and to give my entire and full consent to your union."

"You have!" exclaimed Paul, almost gasping for breath.

"I have," returned Mr. Manners, smiling amiably. "Your rank as a commodore, which is equivalent to that of a general in the army. Your brilliant exploits, which have created such a sensation, both in England and France, and the fame you have acquired, will compensate for any want of fortune on your part, and prevent inquisitive or chattering persons from looking at your descent."

"Sir!" exclaimed Paul.

"I mean no offence I do assure you," observed Mr. Manners, quickly, "I merely meant to observe your present position, which you have right gallantly obtained, will render an alliance with my daughter far less unequal than it would have been when you were less fortunately situated."

"Have you communicated with Alice upon the subject?" inquired Paul, earnestly.

"I have, certainly," replied the old gentleman.

"And what said she?" he asked anxiously.

"At first she doubted me. Being very dutiful, as usual," returned Mr. Manners," she would not credit that I should so suddenly change; but, at last, when I gave her good reason to believe me, then she grew perverse, and I am sorry to say, did did not receive my overtures with the joyful enthusiasm which I certainly expected from her; but it was a mere girl's whim. Because she saw I was ready to consent, she appeared indifferent about the matter, simply to put me in a rage—for no other purpose you may be sure."

"Indifferent, was she?" exclaimed Paul, with an anxious look.

"When I say indifferent," returned the old man, "she did not laugh and dance as I should if I had been a girl; no, she wept and sobbed, and would hardly speak, until I got from her these words—'There is nothing in the world, dear father, would give me greater happiness than to wed with John Paul, but my union with him depends entirely upon himself.' That was all she would say ; I, therefore, at once determined to see you—and now you know all."

Paul was thoughtful for a moment, and then he suddenly asked—

"How knew you I was in Paris? What led you to expect that, in Commodore Paul Jones you should find the despised and execrated John Paul?"

"A short time since, I was talking with the Earl of Selkirk," replied Mr. Manners; "the restoration of his plate brought your name into our conversation; he then mentioned that he had heard—I believe through the Stanleys—that your real name was John Paul, and you were of Scottish parents. I said nothing, but I at once remembered that some time since I had heard a song sung in my grounds which I had heard you sing when we were friends; I searched, but failed in discovering any one. At that time, I know your vessel, the Ranger, was off the coast, and I at once concluded that you and Paul Jones were one man. To make sure, I spoke to Alice respecting you, and, in a confident tone, spoke of the identification of John Paul with Paul Jones. She confirmed it, and knowing you were in Paris—"

"How did you know it?" inquired Paul.

"How, how!" repeated Mr. Manners; "why your name is in everybody's mouth. It is well known you visit the Court here, and your attendance at every party is also publicly known in London. I can assure you, you have a rare name for gaiety; it is said there is scarcely a noble lady, young and handsome, who is not in love with you, and to whom you do not return the compliment, In truth, I fancy it is a little jealousy on the part of Alice, for she has heard it, as well as myself, which makes her weep and fret so when she is alone."

"I wish that rumour would not invent deeds for me which I have no thought of performing," exclaimed Paul, bitterly, his face reddening with anger. "If it were not such a notorious liar, its inuendoes might obtain some credit. This is a base calumny, and I trust, sir, during your sojourn in Paris, you will not only see that it is so, but, upon your return to England, take the trouble to disabuse yur daughter's mind of any belief she may attach to what she hears of this nature respecting me."

"With all my heart," returned Mr. Manners; "but you will have that pleasure yourself, for she will be here, I expect, in a few days."

"And I shall be happy to meet her," exclaimed Paul.

"And as I see no necessity for delay, the nuptials may as well take place as speedily as possible," exclaimed the old gentleman.

"That is a matter which must rest with Alice," observed Paul.

"Of course the lady always names the day," remarked Mr. Manners, with a grin.

"But I allude to another matter," said Paul; "there is a slight misunderstanding between us. Did Alice speak of it?"

"Oh, yes—yes—a mere trifle," returned the old man, quickly. "She did not state exactly what it was, but acknowledged that a very little would set it right. I will undertake to smooth all that away."

"But in the event of my wedding your daughter, in the capacity of a commodore in the service of America, will not you be compromising your loyalty in the eyes of the English Government?" asked Paul.

"That is hard to say. The English Ministers of the present Government are a queer set—what is sauce for the goose is *not* sauce for the gander is their doctrine; they might hang up as a rebel one man for doing it, and say that I had done perfectly right, and *vice versa*. But I will speedily settle that matter. If they make any stir about it, and I find they resolve to inflict penalties upon me, or any nonsense, I will quietly sell my property before they come to their decision, and declare in favour of America. It is easily done, I have friends in England who would manage it beautifully for me if I desired it; that objection, I believe, is met and answered. You are, I need hardly ask, quite ready to marry my daughter?"

"Quite; most earnestly do I wish it, if she will have me," exclaimed Paul.

"Then," said Mr. Manners, "I will guarantee that she will do that fast enough—"

He was interrupted by a hurried knock at the door, followed by the sudden entry of a lacquey, who said, respectfully—

"There is a special messenger without from his majesty, who wishes to have immediate speech with his Excellency Commodore Paul Jones."

"Admit him!" exclaimed Mr. Manners.

The lacquey bowed and disappeared, and immediately afterwards ushered in an officer who tendered a note to Paul Jones, who, with an apology to the old gentleman, instantly perused it; it requested his immediate presence before the King of France upon matters of importance. Our hero instantly acquainted Mr. Manners with its contents, and took his farewell of him, with a promise that he would shortly see him again.

CHAPTER X.

"What boots the oft repeated tale of strife,
The feast of vultures, and the waste of life?
The varying fortune of each separate field,
The fierce that vanquish, and the faint that yield,
The smoking ruin, and the crumbling wall?
In this, the struggle was the same with all;
* * * * *
In either cause, one rage alone possest
The empire of the alternate victor's breast;
And they that smote for freedom or for sway,
Deemed few were slain, while more remain'd to slay."

BYRON.

THE meeting with his Majesty of France, was to make him acquainted with the pleasing intelligence that his squadron was ready for sea, and that he was to accept of a *carte blanche* as regarded instructions, with only the simple command that he was to repair to the Texel by the 1st of October; he had orders to sail the following morning, and having information that there were eight East Indiamen expected on the coast of Ireland, he saw the necessity of losing no time in setting sail. He wrote a short note to Mr. Manners, and stated the position in which he was placed, but that he hoped by the beginning of October, to be once more with him and his adored Alice, never to part.

His squadron set sail the following morning; it consisted of his own vessel, Le Duras, which he had named in honour of the celebrated Franklin, le Bon Homme Richard, not a very fine or strong vessel, having been in the East India service; a new frigate, the Alliance, which was commanded by the coxcomb, Landais; two privateteers, and Le Monsieur of fourty guns; and La Granville of fourteen ; La Pallas, of thirty-two eight-pounders a brig, La Vengeance, twelve three-pounders; and Le Cerf, a remarkably fine cutter, carrying eighteen nine-pounders; with these vessels, Paul hoped to perform far greater feats than he had yet been able to accomplish; he resolved to make a bold effort that he might win Alice with "his blushing honours thick upon him." All he required was active co-operation on the part of the captains accompanying him, and that was the very thing he was not to have. He had a meeting with them in his cabin the day he sailed, and soon found, from the tone they assumed, that very little dependence was to be placed upon any of them, and he broke up the meeting with disgust, commanding them merely to observe his signals and obey them. They returned to their respective ships, and the first proof he had of their obedience to his commands, was the disappearance during the night, of the two privateers, Le Monsieur and Le Granville, who, without assigning any cause, abandoned him; the cutter, Le Cerf, shortly subsequent to this, disappeared also. He was much vexed at their conduct, for their loss was considerable, but he resolved still to proceed to Limerick, where he expected to meet with the Indiamen, and signified his intention to the captains of the Alliance, the Pallas, and Vengeance, who still remained with him; but Landais now began to show his determination to revenge the indignity which he had received from Paul, when in command of Le Diable. He objected to proceed to Limerick; he refused to assign any but a few paltry reasons, that were easily set aside; he talked largely and loudly about having received orders from the French and American Ministers to use his own judgement with respect to paying obedience to all the orders Paul might choose to issue, and he con sidered, in the present instance, that it was necessary he should exercise the discretion he had been allowed to employ. The airs and displays, the fopperies, the affectation of this daintily-dressed and highly-scented person, awoke so large an amount of disgust in Paul's breast, that to prevent losing sight of his prudence, he told him, hastily, that his presence was needed in his own ship the Alliance. As he departed, Paul exclaimed in emphatic tones—

"You will please to remember, Captain Landais, that I am the commodore of the squadron. You will recollect, sir, the powers vested in me by the American and French governments place me in a situation superior to that of any person accompanying or holding any post in this expidition. My orders are a *carte blanche*, and my command absolute. I shall make certain signals to you, which I shall expect you to answer and obey; and remember, sir, that you will have to answer to me, as well as to our respective governments, for any disobedience, any whim, or caprice, may induce you to exhibit. I wish you good morning, Captain Landais."

"Farewell, Monsieur Jones," returned Landais, with a low bow; "I shall not forget what you have communicated to me, nor shall I fail to remember the instructions I have been honoured with from both ministers. As they hold a power superior to yours, you will pardon me, commodore, if I consider it my duty to obey them in preference to you. I have the honour to take my leave of you."

He departed with a skipping step, perfuming the air as he went, astonishing the nose of many of the crew, and producing from one rough fellow a remark expressing his wonder where he would be blown to if he encountered "a sou'-wester." That same night the Alliance followed the example which the two privateers had set, and was nowhere to be seen when the morning came. The Pallas and Vengeance were now the only two vessels accompanying him, and he was obliged to give up the intention he had formed of capturing the East Indiamen, but hugged the Irish coast, with the hope of meeting with some opportunity of counterbalancing the difficulties in which the conduct of the refractory captains had placed him.

The young nobleman who had written to him, desiring the honour of serving under him, was on board Le Bon Homme Richard. With Paul he held no command, not having the requisite knowledge, and his rank forbade him taking a subordinate situation; he was on board, therefore, more as a visitor than in any other capacity. His short acquaintance with our hero had been sufficient to raise a considerable friendship for him, and, as he was rather enthusiastic and chivalric in his nature, he looked with fervent eyes upon the purport of the expedition.

When the conduct of those of the captains, who had so unceremoniously disappeared, prevented the plan being carried into effect, no one could have expressed themselves more bitterly upon the occasion than did he; nor did he hesitate to utter his anathemas both loud and deep. A portion of the crew of Le Bon Homme Richard were Frenchmen, some Americans, others peasants, and some were Englishmen who had been for some time prisoners in France, but rather than be immured in a filthy prison and half-starved, they consented to serve, when a preposition to that effect was made to them. The boatswain was a Frenchman, a big, burly fellow, nearly as broad as he was tall, and, overhearing the young noble speak irreverently of his countrymen, he grew exceedingly restive. He was an irritable, easily disposed to be mutinous fellow, but otherwise a good seaman. He many times felt more than inclined to give the young noble a pretty good hint that their opinions respecting the behaviour of the absent captains were very different, but a respect for his rank, which he could neither account for nor get over, kept him silent until some stinging remarks, which he conceived compromised the honour of the whole French nation, uttered while he was close at hand, roused his indignation, and, advancing close to the young noble, he whispered in his ears.

"Don't you be too free with bunting, Monsieur le Vicomte; those who have hauled their wind know'd why they did it better than you, and will, I dare say, show as clear a log as him who carries his flag on board Le Bon Homme Richard. When men has commands of ships, they doesn't want boys to teach 'em on which side to carry their spanker-boom; take my advice, and give them signal halyards of yourn—"

He was interrupted by a most unceremonious thrust from the hand of the young Vicomte, which, being given with a remarkably good will, sent him staggering away, enraged. The fellow returned and made a blow at the nobleman, knowing that, as he had no command, the punishment for striking him would be comparatively small; he, nowever, missed his aim, and staggered forward to receive a severe blow in the eye from his youthful antagonist. He was maddened at that, and seizing a rope's-end he prepared to lay it about his shoulders. This feat, however, the young Vicomte prevented by drawing a small dirk, with which he was armed, and vowing by all the saints in the calendar, that if the boatswain approached him he would let out his life with it. The boatswain saw no reason to doubt his word, and did not advance, but he held out his fist menacingly to him, and told him, in strong terms, that if it were not for the knife, he would certainly pay him over the sides with the rope, and make him dance like the piper who played before Moses in the wood. Paul happened to come upon deck in the midst of this animating incident, and, upon hearing the case, ordered the boatswain into irons. The man protested he would not submit to be seized, and some of his countrymen supported him in his declaration; but both Americans and English, admiring the spirit of the young Vicomte, voted the boatswain in the wrong, and, in spite of his struggles, and even the efforts of several of his countrymen to rescue him, forced him below, and manacled him. The scene during this affair was anything but creditable to the decks of a man of war; and Gasket, who, with Paul, was most prompt in obtaining order, was compelled to exert himself among tha French sailors, both by coercion and reasoning, to induce them to return quietly to their duty. It was sometime before the confusion subsided; and, what with the notions of equality on the part of the Americans, the offended pride of the French, and the sullen disinclination of the English to do anything beneath the flag which the vessel bore, made Le Bon Homme Richard more like a privateer than a vessel of war, with the commodore of a squadron commanding it. This was not the only case in which Paul found that his command was not likely to produce for him the glory which he speculated upon obtaining; there were many small incidents which, though of a trivial nature, were important, as they showed to what extent his power was respected. Already he began to have misgivings that the expedition would entirely be a signal failure, and instead of returning to France covered with glory, he should go back discomfited and disgraced; and this, too, when for the sake of her, who was now, as he believed, so completely in his grasp, that nothing but the most unforseen circumstances could prevent their union, he would have entered Paris with the voice of Fame trumpeting his name with louder and more praiseful tones than ever. Most bitterly did he reflect on the situation which the ungenerous cabals, and selfish, jealous conduct on the part of those men who left France with him, and who, for their honour's sake, should have stood firmly by him. He resolved, however, sternly and firmly that, come what might, he would not return to France a defeated man—he would go down to the bottom with his vessel first; although all hope of Alice would be swallowed up in the deed, and yet to gain her what would he not have sacrificed? Frequently the strange lteration in the conduct of her father towards him were the subject of his thoughts; he was too generous-minded, too noble in his own motives and actions to at first arrive at the proper conclusion respecting it, until its singularity so constantly recurred to him as to make him go over their conversation, and when it suddenly struck him that the bequest of Mr. Goldeye to Alice, which gave her the bulk of his fortune, subject to her entire control, was the real motive which had made him consent to receive Paul as a son-in-law. The old gentleman was still comparatively poor; he was too proud to ask his daughter to pay his debts; he knew she would not be commanded to it, and, in all probability, would refrain from making the offer out of delicacy. He surmised that if she wedded with Paul, that the latter would command possession of the money; he should feel less compunction in asking him to advance him a certain sum, and he feared not its instantly being granted to him out of gratitude, for having given his consent to the match, which, as far as birth went, was at least very unequal. Paul having once touched on the right chord, was easily able to unworm the whole matter, and the result was, to make him anything but look with a more favourable eye upon Mr. Manners. But for this he cared little, as the selfish truckling of the old man brought him such a prize—that is, if fortune proved favourable to him in his present undertaking. He had sworn to WIN her, and win her he would, or never accept her hand; he would not receive it as a gift which he had been unable to deserve, and thus was he more than ever, by these reflections, strengthened in the determination never to return to France but as a conqueror.

Upon the afternoon of the day when the struggle between the boatswain and the young Vicomte had taken place, the Good Man Richard, with the Pallas and Vengeance, was off the coast of Ireland, and Paul, observing two merchant brigs, apparently deeply laden, made sail in chase of them, overtook, and captured them. A few hands, and a couple of prize masters, were put on board, and they were sent to Brest; this was a beginning, and the prospect of a large share of prize money, produced an alteration in the conduct of the men. They now began to grow more obedient and more respectful; they looked for Paul to lead them into engagements of profit as well as glory, and had no objection to try and earn the latter for him, if for their sakes he would keep a sharp eye to the former. He was quite ready to obtain both if possible, for both brought him all that his ambition aimed at—a glorious renown. The following day he cruised off the Scottish coast, and fell in with a couple of English privateers, carrying twenty-two guns each; after a brisk fight maintained with great gallantry by the English, at very unequall odds, they both surrendered. Two hours after, a brigantine was captured, and the three were sent immediately to Bergen in Norway, according to instructions which Paul had received respecting all vessels of war he might be fortunate enough to capture. These successes added materially to the subordination of the crew, who were now as ready to obey as they had been to mutiny. Several more smaller prizes were captured, and every one was a fresh "turn" in the faith in Paul. He still hoped to be joined by the Alliance, or to have, as had been promised him, a reinforcement from Brest which he had sent for when he sent his first two prizes there, and, as soon as it joined him, he intended to enter the Shannon, where the eight East Indiamen already spoken of were lying, and capture them, a splendid prize, both or his people and himself. But in this hope he was disappointed. for the Channel fleet, under the command of Sir John Lockhart Ross, hove in sight, and he was obliged to make the best use of his heels to get out of his way. He steered for Bantry Bay, and as he knew that many "victuallers" from Cork to North America steered that course, he hoped to intercept and capture them; but after remaining a few days he was not repaid by a sight of any of them, and determined, therefore, to try another scheme. He stood up the North Sea, and his line of progress was more successful than it had been in he Bay; several more prizes fell into his hands, and from some of the prisoners, as well as from newspapers he found in one of the prizes, he ascertained that the port of Leith was left wholly unprotected. It instantly occurred to him that a sudden attack might enable him to lay these places under heavy contribution, returning him, for the hazard necessary to run, both wealth and glory. The more he thought of it, the more practicable it seemed, and he resolved to attempt it. He acquainted the captains of the Pallas and Vengeance with his scheme, and they thought it rash. The crew of Le Bon Homme Richard, to whom he had communicated his intention, softening the danger and magnifying the probable amount of success, were quite ready to undertake it, and one and all desired eagerly that he would at once stand for the Leith Roads. He was himself too much interested in the matter not to comply with their wish, and accordingly for the Roads they at once steered. He signalled his two consorts, but they all along paid too little attention to his signals to be very scrupulous in their observence of those he now hoisted, and they followed his track more because they did not exactly know where else to go, rather than out of obedience to him.

There were two cutters and a ship, mounting twenty-two guns, lying in the Roads, and these formed no very insurmountable barrier to overcome, for, besides his own ship, and the Pallas and Vengeance, he had several prizes which he resolved to make useful, if only in appearance. One of the prizes had a large quantity of soldiers' clothing on board, and he made many of his men, as well as a large proportion of the prisoners, attire themselves in the red coats, and appear on deck, in order that as they went up the Frith of Forth, the inhabitants of the coast might mistake them for transports carrying soldiers. The scheme was well contrived, but whether it would prove successful it is difficult to say, but almost at the very hour at which the descent was to have been made, it came on to blow a tremendous gale; all thoughts of the descent were, of course, compelled for the present to be abandoned, the storm was long and fierce, and blew directly against them. It increased in violence to such an extent, that they were obliged, in order to save the vessels, to run before it, and ere it subsided, one of the prizes, with all on board, fell a victim to its fury.

When the gale abated, they were too far from the Firth to renew the attempt, and Paul, with much reluctance, abandoned it; this did not prevent him forming many of a like nature, but he was cursed with consorts whom the prospect of great wealth, as well as honour could not tempt into deeds out of the ordinary course of courage. It was in vain that he submitted to the captains of the Pallas and Vengeance a variety of plans calculated to forward the cause in which they were embarked most materially, they would not see the force and value of his speculations, and without their co-operation he knew it was useless to attempt them. He, however, hugged the English coast, spreading alarm wherever he appeared. Now he was off Sunderland, capturing vesels, and before hardly it was known he had left there, intelligence was brought that he had made a number of prizes off Flamborough Head; he sailed up as far as the Humber, and even to Hull, where exciting much consternation and carrying off a couple of prizes, he once more made for the neighbourhood of Flamborough Head, hoping to meet with some sign of the reinforcement he had expected, that place being named as a rendezvous for them. He was not disappointed in one expectation, if he was in others. He had heard that the Baltic fleet would speedily appear off here, and he cruized about in the hope of meeting with it, and on the 23rd of September it came in sight; it was convoyed by a fine frigate, the Serapis, which carried forty-four guns, and a twenty-two gun ship, the Countess of Scarborough. He had the wind of it, and hoped to get at it to his own advantage. He was about two leagues from the shore, and he endeavoured to prevent its running in close to shore, so as to obtain protection from the guns of Scarborough Castle. He had, however, been seen from the cliffs, and the signal of an enemy on the coast was hoisted on the highest turret of the castle, the frigate and the twenty-two gun ship stood directly towards him, while the fleet of merchantmen endeavoured to run their vessels close under the guns of the fort. This, with some difficulty, they succeeded in accomplishing, but the Serapis and Countess of Scarborough left their position, intending to bring our hero to an engegement. He was nothing loth to oblige them, but there was little or no wind, and he was unable to get his vessel in the situation he wished.

Night came on, and still they were some distance apart; and, as darkness began to set in, the two English vessels, not believing that they would hazard a battle in the dark, tacked, and stood in for the shore. Paul, with the aid of a night-glass, detected the movement, and instantly altered his course with the hope of cutting them off. The Alliance, which had appeared in sight in the morning, but had not reported itself, now lay-to, watching quietly what was going to be done; and the captain of the Pallas, observing the sudden alteration in the course of Le Bon Homme Richard, concluded at once, knowing the state of disaffection the crew had been in, that they had mutinied, and were running away with the vessel; he, therefore, stood directly out to sea, resolving to get a good start, if, as he expected, he should have the satisfaction of being chased. Paul signalled the Alliance to join him, but not the slightest attention was paid to his signals, and, as he now drew very near to the Serapis, he resolved to run every risk, and commence the engagement. He ordered the drummer to beat to quarters, and something to his surprise, but no little to his pleasure, he observed that the call was obeyed with alacrity by his men. He went among them, and spoke to them individually and collectively, and stirred them up by animating words to do their duty gallantly. As soon as he got within pistol-shot of the Serapis, he received a tremendous broadside, and returned it before the sound was out of the enemy's guns. He now appeared, as he had in all his previous engagements, with all that clear coolness, that command of temper and nerves, so essential in such a situation as this, for the exercise of the discretion and judgment, by which, often as much as valour, the success of a contest is obtained. His commands were uttered in a loud, clear voice, and might be heard, when occasion required it, in every part of the ship, above the roar and din of the conflict. It was about seven o'clock when the fight commenced—the moon did not rise till eight—it was nearly dark; and what with the dim light of heaven and the clouds of smoke from the discharge of the guns, it was almost impossible to see what was transpiring beyond the mere discharge of the cannons. The dense volumes of smoke became almost suffocating, and the heat intense; the flashes from the guns as they were discharged were bright and vivid in the thick atmosphere, and the thunder of the report, were the only things to be clearly made out. Paul dispatched some able hands into the top to keep a look out, and the precaution was not uncalled for, inasmuch as the Countess of Scarborough had been able to draw up into action, and laid her broadside to the stern of Le Bon Homme Richard, and before Paul could alter the position of his vessel he received a terrific raking fire, sweeping the decks, killing and wounding a large number of men. He was, however, prompt and decided in his movements, and succeeded in steering his vessel clear of the Countess, and of sending a broadside into her which shattered her terribly; he then endeavoured to bring six eighteen-pounders, which were placed in the gun-room, to bear upon the Serapis, expecting them to do tremendous execution. The sea was calm, and he made sure of deciding the fate of the contest by the use he would make of these cannon, but at the first discharge, being over-loaded, or old, or unfit for use, they nearly all exploded, and this was the more desastrous in its effects, for Paul, placing so much importance to their proper use, had placed Gasket and a party of picked men upon whom he could most depend, and nearly all of them were killed or fearfully wounded by this unexpected and unfortunate explosion, Gasket being one of those who were desperately wounded. Paul, as soon as he learned the disaster, superintended the removal of the wounded, and among them Gasket, whom he lifted in his own arms, and bore to the cockpit, and bade the surgeon pay him every attention; he wrung Gasket's hand affectionately, and then resumed his arduous and dangerous part in the direction and animating of his crew.

The Pallas, the Vengeance, and the Alliance held aloof, though to do the captain of the first justice, as soon as he saw Paul engaged he did his best to work his vessel into action, but there being hardly a breath of wind, and having hauled off to some distance, he found it a difficult matter to draw near without being a considerable time in accomplishing it. Once more the Countess of Scarborough succeeded in raking Le Bon Homme Richard, and once again Paul returned the compliment with a rattling broadside, which inflicted great damage; but he found that the age of Le

Bon Homme was too great to enable her to stand the terrible precision and rapidity of the Englishman's fire; every shot tore away the bulwarks wherever they struck, as though they were so much paper, and the carpenter reported that she had sprung a leak—most disagreeable tidings at a moment like this. There remained but one course for him to pursue, and that was imminent in its hazard, but he had made up his mind to gain the victory or sink with his vessel. He saw that, unless he ran alongside the Serapis and fought her muzzle to muzzle, that the repeated rakings of the Countess of Scarborough would clear his decks of his men and rid him of all chance of success, but that, if he was yard-arm and yard-arm with her consort, her firing would tell as much against the Serapis as Le Bon Homme Richard, and induce her, therefore, to relinquish her share in the contest, he ordered the helmsman to lay him close alongside the Serapis, and the man so well obeyed him, that the jib-boom of the Richard carried away part of the mizen rigging of the Serapis, Paul himself was the first to jump and lash the two vessels together, and then re-animate his men in their attack upon it. His stratagem in every way answered, the captain of the Countess of Scarborough, finding that he should do serious damage to the Serapis if he continued firing at the Richard, hauled off, and left, as he thought, the numbers on both sides about equal, but the Serapis, owing to the unfortunate accident on board the Richard, had the advantage of guns, as she had a battery of eighteen pounders in the gun-room, which were well manned, and did frightful execution in the hull of Le Bon Homme Richard. To counteract the effects of this, Paul would have mounted some of the guns which had not yet been discharged, in the gun-room, in the place of those which had burst, but he could not get any of the crew to fire them; they had no objection to take their chances of death in the regular way, but they did not like running the hazard of being struck down by the very weapons they had turned against their enemy. He was, therefore, compelled to turn to some other method; he ordered his men to lash the Richard to the Serapis wherever it was possible to effect it, and they obeyed him, and, when the captain of the English frigate perceived this, he was glad to cease his firing, foreseeing that if his attempt to sink the American succeeded, his vessel would, in all probability, be carried down with it. Recourse was now had to small arms, and a sweeping fire of musketry was kept up; the guns of the Richard were still, when practicable, discharged, but several of them had been silenced through the people who manned them being all killed or wounded. Paul having, in his action with the Drake, seen the good effects which had resulted from throwing hand-grenades from the tops on to the enemies' decks, despatched a number of men aloft to fling them down, and also a number of marines, who were good shots, to bring down officers and men indiscriminately. The combat now raged fiercer than ever—the fire of musketry, guns, and swivels was incessant, and the explosion of the grenades deafening. To add to the din, the firing of the cannon of other vessels besides the two engaged took place, and Paul detecting it, despatched one of the men aloft to ascertain which were engaged. The man brought down word that the Pallas was engaged with the Countess of Scarborough, the Alliance was standing off and on, and the Vengeance was laying-to, watching the contest. Paul was glad to hear that, at least, the commander of the Pallas had shown some little courage, though there was not much required in opposing a thirty-two gun frigate to a twenty-two gun ship. However, it was pleasant to know that he should not have the Countess of Scarborough attacking him again, at least for some time, and, with fresh spirit, he continued the direction of his men in their desperate contest.

There were four guns on the forecastle which had been well commanded during the earlier part of the fight, but the officer commanding was wounded in the head, and for a short time they ceased firing. Paul soon discovered their silence, and ascertaining the cause, took upon himself the command until he could place a person on whom he could depend in charge. Situated as the two vessels were, the working of these guns was very important; they committed great destruction, and their silence was for the time a boon to the people of the Serapis; but several men who were employed in firing the muskets, observing our hero commanding these guns, ran to his assistance, and speedily six, instead of four, were brought into play. The moon had now risen, and made everything plainer to be seen than before, and Paul, who did not fail to use his eyes to the best of his ability, saw the mainmast of the Serapis, which was painted straw-colour, plainly brought out by the moonlight, and he directed one of the pieces to be well loaded, and rammed home the shot himself; he pointed it and discharged it, and heard the crash of the splinters as it hit the mark it was levelled at, telling him, though the volume of smoke which rose from the discharge prevented him seeing it, that it had taken severe effect. Again and again he discharged it, and was satisfied that ere long he should have the satisfaction of seeing the mainmast totter and fall over the side.

It is not to be supposed that the English all this while were idle—the bodies strewed upon the deck of the Richard, her severed rigging, her broken spars, her shattered bulwarks, were all too powerful an evidence to the contrary, and bravely they continued their share of the work; they maintained the action with such skill, with such determination, and with such deadly effect, that, as a hasty glance by Paul showed him every now and then the sweeping destruction they were causing, he felt a misgiving that nothing but unexampled perseverance and desperation could gain him the victory. He saw that his only chance was in mowing down the people of the Serapis, and really compel her to strike from want of hands; he despatched fresh hands aloft as he could spare them, and kept them well supplied with hand-grenades. The marines, also, of whom there were a large number, made such use of their musketry, that the English seamen were almost driven from their quarters, but again and again they returned, and their guns were discharged with such rapidity that, unless some means of silencing them were adopted, nothing could keep the Richard from being defeated. A shot destroyed one of the pumps, which had been kept going in consequence of the leak, and the water gained fast upon the vessel. The carpenter came to report this, but not finding Paul, he inquired of a seamen what had become of him, for it was his duty to tell him that the Richard was sinking. The seaman told him it was his belief that he and all the officers were killed, and pointed out the frightful heap of dead which lay upon the deck, in confirmation of what he said. The carpenter grew frightened, and meeting with a gunner, told him what had occurred. The man became alarmed, shouted out for our hero, and at the top of his lungs announced the fact that the Richard was sinking, the two vessels were so close that the commander of the Serapis overheard him, and called out,

"Do you surrender? Do you surrender? Do you strike?"

Paul, who was still serving the garrison on the forecastle, heard him, being nearly opposite to him, and uttering a loud laugh of derision, he exclaimed, at the top of his voice—

"Strike! no—never; I'll sink my ship first—Strike! I'll make you strike ere you are much older!"

A shout of defiance was returned, and the battle continued to rage fiercely. Shortly after Paul had returned this answer to the English captain, an

English seaman on board the Richard, standing close by Paul, and who in the heat of action had forgotten all about country, and was working his gun with as much ardour and enthusiasism as if he had been opposed to a national foe, cried out to him—

"Well, I'm damned if the third lieutenant ain't hauling down our colours!—no striking, Davy Jones or victory!"

"What!" shouted Paul, scarcely believing his ears, and turning his eyes rapidly in the direction in which the man pointed. One glance was sufficient, he saw the man spoke the truth; he beheld the third lieutenant, a man who had always displayed a refractory and insubordinate feeling, deliberately hauling down the flag and calling for quarter as lustily as he possibly could. The sight was maddening. Was it for this he had maintained this desperate struggle? Was it for this the lives of so many brave men had been sacrificed? Was it for this that he had hazarded everything in the world? Was it for this that a lieutenant should, perhaps in the moment of success, haul down the flag, and surrender, destroying name, fame, honour, everything? The blood rushed boiling to his forehead: he called to the man to desist, he shouted in tones which might have been heard above the roar of battle, far beyond the precincts of the two vessels, to hold his hand, but the man persisted, and still called out for quarter, and kept pulling down the flag. In a state of frantic rage, in a mad paroxysm of passion, his whole blood leaping like molten lead through his veins, inflamed too, by the fearful scene in which he was engaged, he dashed forward, springing over the dying and the dead—in tones of thunder he bade the lieutenant remove his hand from the halyards, but he was disregarded. The man had his hand upon the flag, another moment it would have been on the deck, and, in the wildness of his fury, Paul drew a boarding pistol from his belt, and shot him through the heart; the man uttered a frightful shriek, and fell lifeless at the feet of our hero, who ran the flag up to its original place, and calling for another flag, he had that nailed to the mast, vowing, by a terrible oath, that the man who attempted to haul it down should meet with the lieutenant's fate.

The captain of the Serapis, although he heard what Paul had asserted, still believed that the Richard was in a sinking state, and that it required but little more to complete the conquest, which he imagined must be his. He summoned his men, and resolved to board it, and when they were ready the attempt was made, but they were met by such a storm—such a hurricane of shot—that they were compelled to give back and retreat to the gun-deck. The English had barely retreated, when word was brought to Paul that the Alliance was bearing down, and knowing the miserable state the Richard was in, he was not sorry to hear it, although he would rather have done anything than have any portion of the victory owing to Landais. What, however, was his surprise and indignation, when Landais, running past him, fired a broadside directly into the Richard, killing and wounding several men. A roar of execration followed this act of treachery, and the Alliance drew a-head. There was no doubt that this was a piece of the direst villany on the part of

Landais, as there was no mistaking the two vessels, the Serapis having a broad stripe of white along her side, while the Richard had no such mark. Paul vowed, if he escaped the fight, to give him a bitter proof of his remembrance of this monstrous deed, and turned his attention once more to the Serapis.

The state of both vessels was now pitiable; the mainmast of the Serapis was suported only by the yards being lashed to those of the Richard, her rigging was rent to rags, and was on fire. The Richard was in a worse condition; her sides were all but driven in; her stern miserably shattered; her rudder destroyed; her foremast tottering; her yards and sails cut, rent, and shattered in all directions, and there was five feet of water in the hold. The fire on board the Serapis raged with fury, and was communicated to the rigging of the Richard, and all hands on both vessels, were turned from fighting to extinguish the fire.

By this time the Pallas had succeeded, by the help of the Alliance, in conquering the Countess of Scarborough. When she surrendered, the commander of the Pallas asked Landais if he would take charge of the prize, as he had many serious damages to repair, or whether he would sail and assist the commodore, Paul Jones.

Landais replied that he would do the latter, and instantly began to make towards Le Bonne Homme Richard. The Alliance being under topsails only, made rather a slow progress, and as she drew near, Paul, who had already had one specimen of her captain's treachery, warned his people to beware of her approach, but they disregarded his warning, and greeted her arrival with a cheer, fondly believing that she was coming to assist them. The people of the Aliance responded to the cheer by firing a tremendous broadside into their vessel, the effect of which was terrible; several men were killed, others were wounded, and the hull and rigging materially suffered. To depict the astonishment and the rage which took possession of the people of the Richard, would be impossible. They poured forth a volley of invectives and yells which promised Landais summary vengeance if they could get him in their power. He, however, drew past, paying no attention to the cries of the people it was his duty to assist instead of destroying, he was evidently bent upon sinking Paul's vessel, with him in it, crushing fame and life at one blow, in revenge for the treatment he had previously received, and from an excessive jealousy of the estimation in which our hero was held at Paris. As soon as he was far enough beyond Le Bon Homme Richard, he tacked, and once more stood on to her. This time, he was expected; and through the energy of Paul the men flew to the guns. Landais, as they anticipated, discharged another broadside at them. With yells of disgust and scorn they returned his fire with the guns double-shotted, and so well, and with such precision, did they deliver it, that many of the crew of the Alliance were killed and wounded, and the masts, spars, and rigging much damaged. Landais himself had a narrow escape from an ugly shot, which went "between the wind and his nobility," and that quite satisfied him of his share in the fray. For the remainder of the action he kept far aloof, where no shot or danger could come to him, and viewed calmly, indeed gladly, the desperate position to which Paul's vessel was reduced, without having the remotest intention of assisting him in any manner.

When Landais disappeared from the immediate scene of action, the crew of the Richard continued their efforts to extinguish the fire, which still burned furiously, and succeeded almost as soon as the English, who, having got the flames in their vessel under, returned at once to the attack, and once more the fight raged with as much vigour as ever. Paul, although always to be found where danger was thickest, was, as yet unwounded, and what was of as much, if not more importance, was undepressed in spirits. He never for an instant flagged, either in personal exertion or the exercise of mental energies, always powerful. Wherever a disaster occurred he was at hand to repair it, whenever the men grew faint-hearted, or even approached towards a feeling of that nature, he was by their side to animate them in any moment of emergency. If a man holding any important post was shot while in the execution of his duty, he was ready to supply his place, until he could place a man whom he could trust in lieu of him. To his constant exertions—to his unremitting perseverance and industry—to his courage, and knowledge, and discretion alone, was his successful maintenance of the fight up to the present hour owing. Few men, under the disheartening circumstances he had to cope with would have continued the fight as he did; but he had screwed his determination to one point, and between success and destruction, he knew no resting place.

After the many hazards he had undergone, he had yet one to come, which surpassed them all—one which only the greatest presence of mind could have surmounted. It appears that when the carpenter came to report the manner in which the leak was gaining upon the Richard, a number of hands were placed at the pumps, but the water gained so rapidly, that the gunner mentioned, and the carpenter, in a moment of alarm, gave up all for lost, and, opening the scuttles, let a large number of prisoners whom Paul had captured, with his prizes, out of the hold, telling them that the vessel was sinking. These men had but to rush from the Richard to the Serapis, in order to have at once, by their aid, given the victory to the English; had they even set upon the Richard's crew, they might have easily mastered them, but having been so long pent up in a narrow hold, hearing the dreadful crashing of the shots as they tore and wrenched their way through the hull, auditors of the fierce uproar, though they were unable to witness it, unconscious on which side the scale of success was preponderating, they came upon deck confused and bewildered. Paul was astounded at their presence, he knew instantly the imminence of his hazard, and, at the same time, perceiving their uncertainty, he assumed an aspect of fierce authority, ordered them to the pumps, removed his people who were working at them, and made these prisoners supply their place. Under the influence of incertitude—the roar of battle still raging round them—the men, unconscious how near they were to escape, and deciding the issue of the contest, obeyed him, and worked with right good will. This difficulty having been overcome, Paul gathered his men for a last and desperate effort; the hold was half full of water; the vessel was again on fire; the loss of his men had been terrible, and he knew if he failed in his attempt, nothing would be left for him but to sink. There was still a good supply of hand-grenades, and he sent one of his people into the maintop, with orders to cast them wherever he saw men clustered together, upon the deck of the Serapis. Men were sent up also to help the marines in sweeping the enemy's decks, and he remained below with the remainder, to work such guns as were serviceable. Once again he worked one of the guns himself, endeavouring to destroy the masts of his adversary, and his people seconded his efforts with determined bravery. The men in the top poured down a destructive fire. The seaman, who was entrusted with the hand grenades, did his duty with a perseverance and an intrepidity highly creditable to him. He was not content with remaining in the tops, but advanced along the main yard until he nearly reached its arm, and flung his grenades with admirable precision; succeeding, also, with much dexterity, in casting a number of them through the hatchways of the enemy, and setting fire to the cartridge of an eighteen-pounder, which, exploding, injured several of the English who were near it. Paul now tried his utmost; his guns were discharged with the greatest rapidity; the musketry poured in a storm of bullets. He cheered his men, and they cheered again; he found his shots telling, and the fire of the Serapis fast slackening; he increased his exertions, and the English made one terrific effort; both ships were again on fire; the storm of shot increased; it was the last fearful struggle; the men fell on all sides; victory seemed in the hands of both, yet declared for neither—both fought with despair and desperation. The crew of the Serapis was reduced to a mere shadow of what it was when it commenced, but they still fought on gallantly; several of the prisoners who were working at the pumps were brought to man the guns, and this accession of strength was more than the crew of the Serapis could withstand. They, however, fought on; their colours, like Paul's, nailed to the mast, until the main-mast, which for some time had been upheld only by being lashed by its yards to Paul, went over the side with a tremendous crash. The lashings had been cut asunder, and no longer having support, down it went, carrying all the upper spars and rigging with it. The ship was on fire and perfectly unmanageable, and to continue the contest longer was impossible; the commander of the Serapis came on the quarter-deck, and with his own hand lowered the British flag. Paul uttered a shout of joy which was heard on board of both vessels, for he knew that had the commander of the English frigate continued less than a quarter of an hour longer, the victory must have been his, for the prisoners began to see the true position of the combatants, and ere long would have joined the English; the more especially was the moment critical, as at this very juncture a dozen men of the Richard, believing success impossible, had contrived to get on board a shallop belonging to the Serapis, and made off. Paul ordered his men to cease firing and give three cheers for victory, this they did, and instantly afterwards our hero ordered the commander of the Serapis on board of the Richard. He was obeyed, and with his officers, he came on board and tendered his sword. The surprise of the captain and Paul was mutual, when the latter recognised in the captain of the Serapis, Captain Pearson, the captain of the Wildfire, and he perceived John Paul, who, no very long time previous, was his captain of the maintop.

"Good God!" exclaimed Captain Pearson, "can it be possible—you, John Paul—you, Commodore Paul Jones—do my eyes deceive me?"

"No, Captain Pearson," replied Paul, with a smile, "you are not deceived, I am the same John Paul who was captain of the maintop on board the Wildfire, and I am also Commodore Paul Jones. I cannot but say I feel prouder still at my victory, in knowing I have defeated a commander of such great bravery and acknowledged skill as Captain Pearson—a man in every way an honour to the country he serves."

"I tell you what, Paul," returned Captain Pearson, "you have, in beating me, had to do one of the hardest things you ever attempted in your life—I feel it justice both to the frigate and people I commanded to say so; but I, though I cannot admire your fighting against your lawful king and country, yet I am damnably glad that I have not been obliged to strike my flag to a skipping Frenchman, or a know-nothing Yankee. Damme, I would sooner have swallowed my sword red hot."

"It has been my good fortune to add another triumph to the American flag, Captain Pearson," exclaimed Paul, "and in doing so I—"

"The American flag!" muttered Pearson, discontentedly. "Sir, it should have been the English flag. You should never have deserted the flag you was born under; that you had sailed and fought under."

"Captain Pearson, I was a hunted outcast, for no sin or crime of my own, but that of loving one who loved me in return. England cast me out—despised and rejected me. America received me, and to America shall all my best services be given."

"Hem!" coughed Captain Pearson, "England will learn to value those sons of hers who possess merit, when it is too late to repair the error she has made in rejecting them. It is a blessed government we live under, and posterity will have a high opinion of their worth I doubt not. Hem! your consorts are valuable friends, eh?"

"*Very*," responded Paul.

"The captain of yonder frigate," he continued, pointing at the Alliance, "would grace a yard-arm. I think I could give the order to sway away to the line he was bent to with much satisfaction. I should fancy you would not be backward, eh?"

"You can make shrewd guess, Captain Pearson, I know that by former experience," replied Paul, "but whatever I may think, it is hardly politic to mention my thoughts here. I have much at the present moment calling my attention. If you will take up your abode in my cabin for a short time, you will oblige me. You are a seaman, and will not mind the bulk-head being down."

Captain Pearson assented, and, with his officers, descended to the cabin, while Paul turned his attention to the state of his vessel; and the one he had captured. They were both still on fire, and the greatest exertion were necessary to suppress the flames. Water was handed up in buckets, and, by the united efforts of the two crews, the flames were extinguished, but not

until this success was nearly destroyed by the fire penetrating within a few inches of the powder magazine; if it had reached it, nothing would have saved the vessel from being blown up.

For four long hours had the battle continued; it having commenced at seven o'clock in the evening and not terminating until eleven. The whole night was consumed in endeavouring to repair the effects of the struggle—in clearing the vessels of the fragments of spars and rigging by which they were encumbered—attending to the wounded, and consigning to the deep the bodies of the slain. When the morning came, the state of the Le Bon Homme Richard was examined, and it was found that the leak had gained so much upon the pumps, that it would be impossible to carry her into any port. The wounded were instantly moved on board the Sepapis, and so rapidly, at last, did the water increase that there was hardly time to get the remainder of the wounded out before she went down, carrying everything with her, including the whole of Paul's property, which amounted to a very large sum. A few hands remained on board of her until the last, cutting adrift everything in the shape of stores, rigging, or boats, likely to be of any service, and just before she sank, quitting her for the Serapis.

CHAPTER XI.

"His cold long fingers now were pressed to mine,
And his faint smile of kinder thoughts gave sign;
His lips moved often as he tried to lend
His words their sound, and softly wispered, "Friend!"
Not without comfort in the thought expressed
By that calm look with which he sunk to rest."

CRABBE.

THUS terminated a stuggle which was, perhaps, one of the fiercest and bloodiest upon record. Paul Jones gained a victory of which he might be justly proud, and the defeated have still no cause for shame at being conquered. A more desperate, determined, close, and sanguinary engagement could not well have taken place—one which the victors found it so difficult to gain, and the conquered strove so hard not to lose. The amplest praise for courage and perseverance was due to both sides, and Captain Pearson, whose ship was on fire for three hours during the fight, sustained no disgrace in striking his flag, while Paul gained immortal renown. The conduct of the captains of the Serapis and Countess of Scarborough in coming out to meet two frigates—a thirty-two gun ship and a corvette, mounting twelve guns—was worthy the character and honour of Englishmen. The fact of the Pallas only entering into the engagement takes nothing from the merit of the two Englishmen; for they knew not but they should have to encounter all, while Paul, unsupported, fighting at first both vessels, and then having to sustain the treacherous attack of Landais, with a ship inferior in all respects to the Serapis, justly deserved the fame and praise lavished upon him when his success in this action became known. The behaviour of Landais, and the commander of the Vengeance, who kept to windward during the fight, needs no comment; the villany of the one, and the cowardice of the other, obtained for them a place in the obscurity into which, after this affair, they both justly sank. When the Richard went down, Paul actively directed his men in rendering the Serapis manageable. Jury-masts were rigged, new ropes were rove, and fresh sails bent in place of those shot to ribbons, and everything which ingenuity, knowledge, and an active mind could suggest was done to place her in trim again. The morning was hazy, not a vessel was in sight, and our hero, with such unwilling companions, thought fit to attempt no further enterprise; he, therefore, signified his intention to his consorts of repairing to the Texel direct, to which they signified the most ready assent.

Gasket, through all the turmoil, trouble, and anxiety, had not been forgotten; Paul had repeatedly visited him, and had, with most sincere and unfeigned regret, learned from the doctor that his wounds were mortal. He had, with earnestness, conjured him to exert all his professional skill to save him—he proffered him a large reward if he could rob death of his prey; but the surgeon told him that Gasket had been struck in a vital part, and added, emphatically, that there was no hope. Proud as Paul was of his victory, this blow stripped it of half its gratification, he would gladly have consented to part with the best portion of the glory he had acquired if the generous, open-hearted Gasket had been spared to him; but this was not to be, and he was compelled to sustain the loss of the only true and tried friend he had, as best he might.

It is hard to part with the simplest things to which we have formed an attachment—a dog, a bird, anything we have been in the habit of daily seeing and viewing with a kindly feeling we part with with regret. There is something in the very familiarity of its sight which endears it; we have seen it every day for years, we saw it yesterday, we see it to-day, but ere morrow it is to quit our sight for ever, and instantly a thousand fond associations arise. Remembrances which enhance its value—recollections of pleasant hours it shared with us; sweet memories which grow stronger and dearer, as we know they can never be shared again with the object from which we are about to part to meet no more. It is not in dumb animals alone that this regretful feeling is raised. Who would idly throw away a book he loved to read through and through when a boy, tear it up, or burn it? How many a thumbed Robinson Crusoe still dwells in some revered corner of a handsome library? Is not the "old house at home" dear to the heart? Is it ever forgotten? Are not the old walls, the old roof and windows, no matter how shabby their contour may look in the present day of stuccoed fronts, and "remarkably handsome family villas," cherished idols of the heart? And when it is rased to the ground by the remorseless hand of the builder for something newer and handsomer, is there not a feeling of sorrow that the old place, the scene of many a happy hour, shall never more glad the eyes and pleasure the heart? If this feeling of sadness is excited by things inanimate and domestic animals, how much keener is the pang when the beloved object to be parted with is a friend—a tried, valued, sincere friend—the partner of joy, of sorrow, of danger, and every trying vicissitude. He who stood by us in our grief, and hazarded and smiled with us in happier hours—who has exposed his life to shield us from harm, and would share the small remnant of a scanty purse—his all—that we might not want. A heart

"That the world in vain had tried,
And sorrow but more closely tied;
That stood the storm when waves were rough,"

and never knew change, come what alteration in his position or circumstances there might; with such a one it is harder to part, when their destination is to that

"Bourne from whence no traveller returns,"

than to sustain any evil fate may have in store for us, at least to a mind capable of appreciating the full value of such a friend, and those who cannot understand or feel the possession of the regret a loss of this nature must occasion, we can only pity the want of the luxury in having a friend.

To Paul, the loss of Gasket was a matter of anguish, which, until the moment of the simple-hearted seamen's dissolution drew near, it never struck him he should have felt. It at once exhibited how highly he estimated him, how justly he, in fact, valued the undeviating friendship and devotion which he had always shown him, and he fancied now, that they were to be separated for ever, that he had not returned it with half the kindness it deserved. He conjured up many instances of neglect and ingratitude, which existed, however, only in his imagination, and quarrelled with himself for such conduct as he believed he had been guilty of, and this came more severely, as he saw there was no opportunity of repairing his injustice; but, if unremitting attention—if the application of every comfort he could bestow could atone for former neglect, no one could have endeavoured to make the compensation more earnestly than he did, and no one could have been more conscious of it, or more grateful for it than Gasket. Time drew on—the progress of the Serapis to the Texel was very slow; four days elapsed and they were still beating about, having a head wind and tempestuous weather to contend against. Gasket had grown weaker every day, approaching nearer each hour, though very gradually, to his death, and on the fifth morning, when Paul, who had snatched an hour's sleep, after watching by him all night, was again at his side, he said to him in a feeble voice—

" My line is nearly all run out, John—there is not half-a-fathom to unreeve. I don't want to slip my wind in this narrow hammock—let me be going free when I spring my luff for the long voyage; lay me upon deck, John, that when my soul goes aloft, if it pleases the Almighty, it should go up like bunting up the pen'ant halyards—that my eyes may look their last upon the blue water, as they did their first."

" The frigate labours heavily, Gasket," said Paul, in a kind voice; " we are beating to windward with only jury-masts to help us; every third or fourth sea makes a clean breach over the decks—you will not be able to stand the weather."

" You know best, John," he replied, in a disappointed tone; " but that was always a wish of mine when I was only the size of a rigger; I tell you what, you may carry me to the gun-deck—I can look out of one of the leeward ports, the weather will not touch me there."

" You have not strength to quit your hammock," observed our hero, persuadingly; the attempt may hasten what we are endeavouring to prevent."

" Prevent!" echoed Gasket; " don't deceive yourself John, my log's made up. I shall go ashore over the standing part of the mainsheet. I spoke to the doctor, and, like a true seaman, he told me that I'd sprung a leak no pumps could keep under; that I must founder, and he couldn't keep me afloat over to-day. Now there's a strange feeling about my heart and head which makes me sure he gave the true heave of the lead there. I feel stronger now than any time since I've been first struck, and I've seen too many messmates slip their cables not to know that's my signal for sailing to the other world. Now don't you turn away your head John, because my looks upon your face can't be for long, and I don't wish them shortened. Come, rouse me out, John, and lug me to the gun-deck; I must look upon salt water afore I sheer off."

Paul's teeth were set and his brows were knit; he made no reply, but, lifting him in his arms, he carried him to the spot he desired, he laid him gently down, and would have despatched one of the people for a blanket, but Gasket would not permit it. He stated his wish to remain as he was, and our hero suffered him to have his own way. He looked upon the sea from one of the leeward port-holes, and for some time gazed upon it, as it tossed and tumbled in wild confusion, without speaking; at length he said—

"I was very young, as you know, John, when I first looked on the sea; I had seen no land then, and as I grew older it seemed to me the natural element for men to live on. I had the same thoughts of land as long-shore people have of the sea; and I have often thought it strange, when I have known messmates who were born and brought up boys on shore, lay in the bunt of a topsail, and look upon the sea, until they have fancied it green fields, and of a sudden have started to the yard arm, and leaped into it, to have, as they said, a roll in the grass. I have gone overboard after three or four messmates of mine who have done that, and brought them aboard again. The doctor said they were mad, only he called it by a name as long as the fore-to'-gal'nt mast stay. Now, when I've overhauled it in my mind, I have thought there must be something on land which I have never fetched; I have laid and looked at green fields, but never fancied they was the sea—no, no, never; but it wouldn't become me to call 'em foolish as thought so much more about the land than the sea, for there may be something in home, and friends, and birth-places, which draws a man's heart there ahead of all other things. I have never know'd any of this, as I was born on the sea, and I am glad that I shall slip my cable on it; not but what I dare say it is pleasant, as I have heard many shipmates say, to be stowed away in an old churchyard which you played about as a boy, and where your kin and friends may always have an eye on your last berth, and the youngsters come and stick flowers in it. I dare say this is all very pleasant, but it is not a thing for me to look or hope for, for I have neither family nor kin of any sort. No old churchyard that I skylarked about, or youngsters to show their pretty remembrance that it ain't a skulk that is under hatches; and so, with an eighteen-pounder at my head, and a couple at my feet, I shall go down quietly enough, where no one can point out the spot, though, for the matter of that, there is no one to point it out if they know'd the place."

"No one!" exclaimed Paul.

"Why, there's you, John," said Gasket, "who, if you thought you could make my last sleep lighter and pleasanter by pointing it out, or doing anything, you'd do it. I don't speak of you, John; no—I know your heart too well; no—I speak of kith and kin, of which I've none. It's something for a man to say he was picked up above a thousand miles from land, without any log or bucket, or any stray thing to tell whether he was the luff of a mermaid, or whether he had dropped from the skies, or com'd of natural parents, or anything, and I do think I should have been happier if I'd a know'd a mother; but what's the use overhauling that now my grog is stopped, and, with or without family, I must go over the side ; and perhaps its better that I should have nobody to let the tears run out of their lee-scuppers for my sake—it is all the better—it is."

He paused from exhaustion, and his face, which had been flushed, now grew deadly pale; he panted for breath, and a cold clammy perspiration broke out all over him ; he, however, rallied, and with a faint smile, he said, in a weak voice—

"That was the first cast of the lead—there's very little water—the next heave I shall shoal. There's one thing I would say to you, John, afore my glass is turned. When you hoisted the American flag at the peak of your gaff, it was the first making of the port of honour and fame which you had long been steering for, and you was, I dare say, right in doing it. I don't say nothing about that; but I didn't like serving under the flag."

"I know, my faithful friend," exclaimed Paul, with feeling; "I know that for my sake alone you served against your conscience."

"That's it, John," returned Gasket, grasping his hand and smiling kindly; "I had always served under a British flag. England had always behaved well to me, and when I turned against her it went against my conscience sorely, but then I loved you better than England, and I wouldn't have fought against you for any pay or flag in the world. Do you think, Paul, that when I'm reported to the Lord, and he overhauls my log, that he will clap me down on the black list for serving against them as behaved well to me, because I liked you the best?"

"Rest assured, Gasket," exclaimed Paul, affected by this proof of the simple-hearted fellow's love for him, "that if you have no worse forfeiture of conscience to show than this, you need not fear to meet the eye of the Almighty."

"Well, it's cheering to hear you say so, John, for I know you will tell me the truth," returned Gasket, "I confess I have nothing heavier to log, and if you say it ain't bad enough for me to be put in irons, why, perhaps, my berth aloft will be as good as what a true seaman may look for'ard to. I have heard that when the chaplain prays for a hand, he makes it an easier passage aloft, but if you now would say a word or two for me I am sure it would do more than the parson's lingo."

"I will, Gasket, I will. My true-hearted messmate, I will," replied Paul, scarcely able to speak, his heart was so full.

"John, you couldn't have done me a kinder act than calling me your messmate," exclaimed Gasket, with sudden animation; "that has done me more good than all the doctor's stuff I've taken; that's cleared the turn for my run more than all. Ha! ha! it is pleasant to hear you call *me* YOUR messmate. Why, John, we were once, and though you carry wash-boards, yet you make, and have made, no difference since you were in the fork'stle with me. How should I show you I couldn't forget it, but by sticking to you back and edge, hoist what flag you might; though I will say this, John, that you never hoisted the Frenchman's colours. I could have died for you, John, but damme if I could have fought under a French flag, even for you—but what signifies all this now, I've struck to death, and I wished to do it."

"Wished!" exclaimed Paul, with surprise.

"Ay, John, wished it of all things, and if them guns hadn't burst, I would have made for where a bullet would have hit me, and that's the truth, and I shouldn't like to die without you knew it," he exclaimed earnestly.

"What should have made you weary of life?" asked Paul, with some astonishmont.

"Why I felt as if I had a fourteen-pounder in my breast instead of a heart," he replied. "I once heard Mr. Prior read about a man who was turned out of his country and then fought against it, and when he'd conquered all the places, his mother came to him to save the town he was born in. He did, and then he was set upon by his new friends and killed. Now I often thought that would be your case. I don't like these Yankees; they havn't behaved like men to you, and I'd rather give my heart over and over than you should die the death of a dog, which I was always afear'd you would, by treachery, and I didn't like dropping Englishmen as I would Frenchmen or any other foes; it was always as if I was burning myself. When I fired I felt like a dog—I was ashamed to look a tar in the face, and the sooner I slipt my wind I thought the better."

"I have much to answer for," exclaimed Paul, bitterly.

"Not you," replied Gasket, "I needn't have served if I hadn't liked; twice you gave me the offer to quit you and I would not take it. I've only myself to blame; but that warn't the only thing, no, no—that warn't the chief thing that kept me as if I was waterlogged. I hardly know how to pay it out. I—here's the piece of writing which Mrs. Florence Prior sent to me; I wish you to take it, and when you see her give it to her, and say I sent—no I will keep it; let it go down with me. John, do you think if I had had a mother, and father, and sisters living, and had come athwart such a craft as Mrs. Prior, I could have got her to come under my lee and make the long splice with me?"

"Why not?" Paul asked.

"Do you think there is anything in my build that should have turned the heart of such a angel against me?" he inquired.

"Most certainly not," replied our hero, "Why do you ask this?"

"Because, John, Miss Florence, as she was called when I first knew her, and as I like to call her now, was the only creature I ever saw that made me haul down every colour I carried—jack, ensign, pennant, and all. I don't mind now, John, to say to you, I bore for her a devotion greater than for anybody else in the world besides; I could think of nothing, however hard, even if I had my bows stove in in doing it, that I would have stopped at if she wished it done. I would have—what is there I wouldn't have done, or tried to do? Oh, John, when we were in Virginia, and she was staying with Mr. Prior, at your brother's, I couldn't scud, wear, or lie to, she looked so lovely—she had such sweet eyes, and spoke so kindly, I sometimes thought I should have fallen on my knees to her, and told her, that the very sight of her made my heart move up and down like a brig's boom in a calm; but then I thought she'd take it ill, that one so rough as I, who had no kin, should be so howdashus as to love her, and so I clapped a stopper on my tongue, and went out into the woods that she mightn't see how she sailed round me with her beauty; and when she sailed for England, there was that in my heart which seemed as if it would grow larger and larger till it burst, and I felt as if I had a capstan-bar down my throat; I couldn't have said 'Good bye,' not if I had been seized up to a grating, and had six dozen for refusing, so I cruised in the back-woods until she had sailed. Since that I have felt as if she carried away my heart and spirits, and there was a fourteen-pounder left in its place. I know she was far a-head of me in station, I know that when she's looking round I do not come within sight, much less within hail. She would never think of me, and it made a change in me, which even you observed. Well, well, it is over now, and my port is made, though I would sooner have had—but what signifies. When all the hands are turned up on the last day, what I might have hoped for will not be in the log I shall have to give, and then I dare say it will be all the same; but if you should ever cruise in a latitude where you may speak her, you may say that I am under hatches, and afore I died I said that, out of all the world, she was the only woman I ever loved."

The countenance of Paul, during this speech, had exhibited an expression of considerable astonishment. He heard what had never struck him as existing. What, with all his knowledge of Gasket's heart, he never would have surmised, though once or twice he fancied that he would rather have been with Eustace than himself. When he had somewhat recovered from his surprise, he wrung Gasket's hand, and promised faithfully to fulfil his wishes.

"Not if you think she will be affronted, or will laugh at me," he exclaimed, suddenly; "I wouldn't have that—I would rather lie in my deep sea-grave, and she know not whether I had sunk or was afloat, than she should do either."

"No woman feels affronted by the love even of the humblest man," exclaimed Paul, warmly, "and Florence knows your value too well, Gasket, even to smile at your thinking her better than all the world. She is too good, too amiable, to jeer at any one, much less at you, and for such feelings."

"God bless you, John!" exclaimed Gasket, in a husky voice; "you were always at hand to serve out comfort, when a hand needed it. I don't like parting with you, John. We've sailed in many weathers together; we have messed at the same table; we have worked at the same gun together. I have seen you rise from a common man to a commodore, and should like to live to see you admiral of the red; but liking isn't having, as we say of grog, and so we must part company. You have been very kind to me, John—

very; from the first moment you stepped on board the same ship with me until now, and now as I am sheering off for ever, if there was any way I could make you happy, I would pray to the Lord to grant me the power of doing it. As I am a dying man, John, I have tried to be true to you, and afore I have made a spare hammock, tell me whether you think so."

"Before God! as here I kneel," exclaimed Paul, his eyes suffused with tears, from strong feeling, "a better, truer-hearted, kinder friend; a honester, simpler, worthier, nobler heart, no man in the world ever had to stand by him, than I have in you, and in this moment of our separation, my heart smites me bitterly for forgetting this in numberless—"

"Avast there, John, avast," exclaimed Gasket, his voice growing more feeble than ever, "you have never forgotten me at any time. Come, John, John, never turn your head from me—look on me. Why should you show a wet eye, John? Damme, you make my scuppers run over. I—why, we must part some day, and why not now. John, take your hand from your face if you love me. Let me see your face; why, that's it. John, I have looked my last upon the sea; there is a haze over it. You had better send a hand aloft; a smart seaman, to keep a bright look out—its very hazy. John, are you sure the fire was got under? the deck is full of smoke, open one of the ports, and yet I am very cold. John, John—I'm shoaling—have I got your hand—remember Florence—topmen away there—clap on the yard-tackles—stretch along your tackle-fall—toss out. John, God bless you —the pumps are choked." He paused for a moment, and, at first, Paul thought he was dead, for his eyes closed, and his face exhibited the ghastly pallid hue of death; but a moment afterwards he opened his eyes, and tried to gaze around him; they were dull and glazed, but he turned them anxiously from side to side; he knit his brows, and worked his lips about with an evident wish to speak; he passed his hand wildly through his hair, and at length, exclaimed, "The reef has knocked a hole in her which no carpenter can stop, and the seas that make over her will wash everything out of her, as clean as a captain's steward does a stew-pan; ay, you may cut away the masts, but she will not move; you may spare yourself the trouble, here comes a sea will carry them by the board; hold on, hold on, mates, for your lives; that sea has fixed her—cut away the lashings of the boat on the booms—the next sea will carry it from the chocks to the quarter; bear a hand—bear a hand—here comes the sea. John, hold on by me—John, where are you—where—avast—I am alone—the sea blinds me—I am faint —I cannot swim a stroke—the water gurgles in my throat—it pours into my ears—down—down—down."

The last word died on his lips, his jaw fell, and all was over for ever with the kind-hearted steadfast seaman.

It would be a task of difficulty—one, the success of which might be doubtful—to portray the agony Paul felt when he was parted for ever from the only true heart which clung faithful to him in all weathers. It was a grief which made no display; his eye might have worn an expression more stern, and his face have been a little paler than common, but beyond that, no one could tell, by outward demonstration, the fire which burnt within. He gave his orders as usual; he confined not himself to his cabin, nor lacked his wonted energy in his direction of his vessel, or those who accompanied him; but if there was a possibility of displaying one act of respect more than another to a lifeless body on shipboard, that respect was paid to the inanimate corse of Gasket. No attention, no mark of affectionate attachment, of honour, of brotherly love, was omitted—nothing that could show how devoted he was to the true-hearted fellow, or how warmly he appreciated him, or proudly he took the opportunity of rendering every honour due to departed worth was left undone. All his crew saw that the death of Gasket was to Paul like parting with one of his heartstrings; yet they saw that he made not a parade of his grief; if he did "cover his face with his mantle," and bowed his head in bitter anguish, it was in the loneliness of his cabin, where no eye but God's could see him, and no lip mock him.

And when Gasket had lain in the deep sleep of death a day, he was sown up in his hammock. According to his wish, heavy shot were placed at his head and feet, that he might go steadily down to his deep sea grave, and remain there. His body was wrapped in a British flag, for Paul knew, though he never asked him the favour, that it was one most desired; it was the last act of friendship, of affection, he could show him, and he was glad to be able to do it, although the heart which would have leaped with joy to have known it was still and cold for ever. When evening came, the ceremonies observed at the burial of an officer at sea were performed. The whole of the surviving officers and the crew assembled to see the body lowered into the deep, and the respect withheld from him in life was now shown by all on board. True courage, true honour, and worth, will always eventually surmount prejudices, and such was the case with the crew and Gasket; now that he was gone never to return, they felt the loss they had sustained. The sea had gone down, and was as smooth as a lake; the evening was clear and calm, and its peaceful stillness added to the solemnity of the scene. The prayers for the repose of the dead at sea were read in an impressive manner. When the chaplain had concluded, the word was given, and the body descended swiftly into the sea. The waters closed over it, and shut it out from the eyes of friends or foes for ever.

CHAPTER XII.

"He paused—no sound
Broke from within! and all was night around.
He knocked and loudly—footstep nor reply
Announced that any heard or deemed him nigh;
He knocked—but faintly—for his trembling hand
Refused to aid his heavy heart's demand.
The portal opens—'tis a well-known face—
But not the form he panted to embrace.
Its lips are silent—

* * * *
* * * *

His steps the chamber gain—his eyes behold
All that his heart believed not—yet foretold!
* * * *
He asked no questions—all was answered now
By the first glance on that still marble brow;
It was enough—she died—what recked it, how?"

BYRON.

THE progress of the Serapis was very slow, the more especially as the wind had abated to a calm, and the canvass they were enabled to spread was of very limited extent. Ten days elapsed ere they succeeded in entering the Dutch harbour, named by his Christian Majesty Louis, for Paul to repair by the 1st of October. The States-General were neutral, or professed to be so, though they had a slight leaning towards France, and therefore, when Paul arrived with his vessels, and it was made known that he had achieved an important victory, there was not that rejoicing displayed which had greeted his arrival at Brest with the Drake, but that he had created a considerable sensation was pretty evident by the attention he received from the States-General. He was permitted to establish a hospital for his wounded seamen and prisoners, and received supplies of workmen and materials to repair all the damage which the Serapis had received in her action with the Le Bon Homme Richard. The English ambassador viewed these favours as anything but according to the proper conduct of a neutral state, and immediately demanded the restoration of the prizes Paul had made, which were in the Texel, and required of them likewise to deliver into his hands "Paul Jones, a subject of the king, who, according to treaties and the laws of war, could only be considered as a rebel and a pirate." No immediate answer was given to this, and when the ambassador resolutely urged the matter they declined to interfere. This would not satisfy the Englishman, and he persisted, until he had obtained from them an order for Paul to depart from the Texel, which was virtually delivering him up, for the Texel was blockaded by a fleet, and the most vigilant watch kept for his appearance.

The Dutch government had not given this order without warmly contesting their right to protect Paul Jones, but the English ambassador pressed upon them the argument that neither Paul Jones nor any of the officers of his squadron were furnished with regular commissions; for Holland was not in a position to be in a state of hostility with England, and therefore did not recognise the independence of the United States. But this point was speedily settled; for, as all the ships, save the Alliance frigate, commanded by Landais, which belonged to the Americans, were the property of the French King, he sent commissions to all the officers, commanded Paul to give up the ships and prisoners to the French ambassador, and as our hero refused to accept a commission from France, he took the command of the Alliance, from which Landais was with disgrace displaced. When this matter was all arranged, the Serapis, the Countess of Scarborough, and the remainder of the prizes which Paul had taken, sailed from the Texel, under the convoy of a Dutch fleet, to the mortification of the English ambassador, who hoped to heal this wound with the capture of Paul.

The Alliance was a new frigate, well found, and in the completest order. She was a very fast sailer, and Paul felt certain that, though the harbour was closely invested by British vessels of war, he should contrive to elude their vigilance. He waited for a fair wind; and when one sprung up he set his men to work in the night to alter the paint of his ship. He hoisted no flag, and gave his vessel as much the appearance of a large merchantman as possible, hoping, in the haze of the dawn, to run clear of "the sharks." It happened fortunately for him that the wind, which was fair for him, was fair for others also, and a great many vessels went out of the harbour at the same time as himself, and the attention of the cruisers were so distracted by the number of ships bound for different ports, and misled also by the alteration of the paint, that our hero contrived to get away, even unchallenged. He was not long in gaining a French port, and proceeded at once to Paris as swiftly as horses could bear him.

The loss of Gasket was every hour more evident; he missed him in so many ways that he never could have believed would have been affected by him. There was no one to whom he could unburthen his heart respecting Alice—to whom he could repeat his hopes, expectations, fears, and desires; there was no one to whom he could speak of the effect of his victory, and the honour it would obtain for him; there was—in fact, he had no friend at his side to whom he could lay open his soul, and bitterly he felt the want. He had a strange melancholy foreboding that now everything was smothed from his path, that the only real wish of his heart, the aim and end of his ambition, would not be gratified. He imagined that he should not, after all, wed Alice. He knew her strength of mind as well as her love for him; and he knew that if she had once formed the determination never to wed him if he raised his hand against England, her father would be as unable to induce her, as he had been when he wished her to shun him. Since that interview when they parted, as she had said, for ever, he had struck one of his most decisive, as well as strongest blows against his country; and it was hard, however agreeable, to his wishes, to fancy, that with the sound of that victory in her ears, she should hold out her hand and claim him, joyfully, for her husband. But then, again, sanguine hopes came to his aid; he knew that she loved him deeply—dearly, and he trusted that, when she found the opposition which so long she had struggled against was cleared away, and she was free to bestow her hand upon him, and when she knew he had perilled life and everything to gain fame and name for her sake, she would forego her determination and wed with him. Our wishes are weighty aids to arguments, and Paul found them so; he came to the conclusion, after all his sorrowful imaginings, that he should yet wed Alice, and yet be happy.

It was gratifying to him to see the joy and honour with which he was received everywhere. No sooner did he stop at any town to recruit, or give up his passport for examination, than it was made known that Commodore Paul Jones, who had defeated the English by hundreds, and taken an incalculable amount of prisoners and gold was there. Crowds surrounded him, and their acclamations rent the air. At every town it was the same, and in Paris the enthusiasm knew no bounds. He was visited immediately upon his arrival by crowds of nobility and high personages, and lauded to the skies. If any man's head could be turned by flattery, praise, and "the intoxication of success," then was there sufficient to have turned a stronger head than Paul's. He was, however, too anxious respecting Alice to be led away by these eulogiums, and the first place he visited was to the Hotel du Nord, Rue Richelieu, and made inquiries for Mr. Manners. He felt chilled when he heard that he had quitted the hotel, and neither the landlord nor waiters knew anything of his abode; they said they believed he was in France, and near Paris, but where, it was impossible for them to say; they promised, however, to make the most diligent inquiries, for Monsieur le "Commodore" was too powerful a man for them not to do all in their power to oblige. He retraced his steps with a heavy heart, and all his forebodings at once returned. Upon reaching home he found La Fayette waiting for him, and received from him the warmest congratulations as well as enthusiastic praise. In the midst of his fervent remarks, he checked himself, and exclaimed with something of a mile—

"But, my friend, all this, while you wear a dull face and a gloomy brow; you do not respond to my ejaculations of gratification at your success as though you relished them; have I mistaken the way to arrive at your heart, or has your honest friend and follower been reading you a lesson respecting the impropriety of raising your chastising hand against the "land of the free?"

"He, poor fellow, will never read me a lesson more," replied Paul, "would to heaven that he could! He was killed, marquis, by the bursting of a gun, and thus I lost one of the truest, kindest-hearted beings, in the shape of a friend, a man might be proud to claim."

"He turned away his head as he spoke, and the countenance of the marquis instantly became grave. He took Paul's hand, and wrung it earnestly, as he said—

"Peace to his memory! I could see that, though a blunt seaman, he was most worthy. He was a diamond in the rough; you knew his value, and prized him accordingly. May his long sleep be light and happy!"

"I thank you," replied Paul; "to have prized him as I did you must have known him, and received from him the same tokens of devotion as he shewed to me. I am unable to explain all his worth, but I can feel it deeply, and, as you kindly say, may his long sleep be light and happy! It is not, however, this bereavement alone which affects me; it is the inability to find one to whom I am attached, heart and soul."

"A maiden!" exclaimed the marquis, regarding our hero with a look of astonishment.

"Even so," returned Paul, speaking earnestly. "It is vain to deny that I love her, and most devotedly, for years. There existed no obstacleto our union, save her presence in Paris, when I quitted this city to take command of Le Bon Homme Richard. She was expected to arrive in a few days, and on my return I flew to the hotel where I expected to see her; judge my grief and astonishment when I learned they quitted the hotel some time since, and have left no clue to their present residence. I have made every inquiry to help me in discovering them, but in vain. It is this which makes me wear so sorrowful a face."

"If they are in Paris, or near it, I will discover them for you easily," said La Fayette. "I have the means and always the will to oblige you; but come, attire yourself in your gayest garb, his Majesty has sent me to present you to him, and the court will be a full one to witness the presentation. It will be a magnificent sight; come, chase away your sorrow, all will soon be well."

Paul thanked him, and hastily attired himself in a rich court suit. He accompanied the marquis to the palace, and was recived by the French King in the most flattering manner. There were the noblest and the highest in the land assembled—a galaxy of the richest and fairest, and his heart, indeed, beat high with honour, when Louis, in eulogising his bravery, and his services, presented him with a superb sword, on which was inscribed—

"VINDICATI MARIS.

LUDOVICUS XVI. REMUNERATOR

STRENUO VINDICI."

Nor did the honour rest there, for the cross of Military Merit was bestowed upon him also; and this was the greater honour, for upon none was this conferred but those who had served under the French Government. And where was Alice, that she witnessed not the proud honours he received? Where was she, that she should not feel her heart glow to behold him surrounded by the noblest, "the observed of all observers?" Where was she, that she should not see him raised to the height to which he had aspired in order that he might win *her?* Where?

Paul, through the aid of his friend, La Fayette, discovered that they resided in a house somewhere in the suburbs of Paris, but could not ascertain the precise place. He discovered, however, that a soldier who had been something of a servant to them, was acquainted with their address, but he was a sour, surly fellow, and resisted every overture made to him to disclose it. Paul resolved to obtain it by stratagem. He disguised himself as a common sailor, went to the spot where the fellow was on duty, and contrived to enter into conversation with him. He affected to be rough and jolly, and with a little tact contrived to get the desired information from him. As soon as he obtained it he scarcely exchanged a dozen more words with the soldier, but hurried to his home and changed his attire. There was a host of letters upon the table awaiting his perusal, but he opened not one; he hastened to the house which contained his Alice—his Alice? that was yet to be discovered. He reached the house, it was nearly dark, the window blinds were closed—his heart beat strangely—a weight like lead was on it, he felt low-spirited to a degree. He knocked again, still no reply; and his third knock was loud and startling. A girl answered the door—she was weeping. He felt a pang shoot through his heart with a violence almost sufficient to destroy him. He asked, hurriedly, for Alice; the girl repeated her name, but ere she could answer, Mr. Manners appeared before Paul. His face was pale, and his air constrained. He asked Paul into the house, and bade him prepare for sorrowful news. Paul felt his tongue cleave to the roof of his mouth, he could only articulate—"Alice, Alice."

"She has been dreadfully ill, but, thank heaven, her agony has ceased. I am right in saying so, for her sufferings were terrible."

"And now—she is well—she is well," gasped Paul.

The old man shook his head, and said, in a solemn voice—

"She is well, I trust—in heaven. Young man, she is dead.'

Paul uttered a wild cry, and fell insensible to the ground; for hours he could not be recovered, but when he was brought to his senses, and found that it was, alas, too true, he placed his hands to his head, and, crying in a tone of the bitterest anguish—

"For this—for this I fought against my native land!"

He rushed out of the house, and fled at the top of his speed; wildly, he knew not where.

www.ingramcontent.com/pod-product-compliance
Lightning Source LLC
LaVergne TN
LVHW061240100826
845148LV00008B/993
9781535808415